A BIRD FROM AFAR

Anshul Chaturvedi has been fascinated with the Second World War for most of his life – some of his earliest memories are of watching *Battle of the Bulge* in primary school and scattering toy soldiers of the British and German Armies across his room afterwards.

Another subject of interest, right from his teenage years, is Subhas Chandra Bose. Chaturvedi has written about Bose for some years now – his political legacy, his affinity for Vivekananda etc. It was perhaps inevitable that these two fascinations were to converge in the shape of this novel after decades of running parallel.

A journalist by profession, Chaturvedi is currently an Associate Editor at the *Times of India* in Delhi/Noida. You can follow him on Twitter at @AnshulChaturvdi and Instagram at @_anshulchaturvedi.

Advance Praise for *A Bird from Afar*

'Subhas Chandra Bose has always been both an admired and a controversial figure. Anshul Chaturvedi goes beyond the admiration and the controversy to chase down the mystique of the man Bose was and why even today, when almost all the heroes of our freedom struggle are but fading memories, Bose continues to mesmerize us as the political option India somehow missed out on. A compelling read'

– **Pritish Nandy**, author, journalist and filmmaker

'An intriguing "what if" of the Second World War is if Hitler's armies, instead of losing in Stalingrad and North Africa, were to win and arrive on the north-west frontier of India in the winter of 1942. With them is Subhas Bose and the Indian Legion – the army he formed in Germany from Indian prisoners of war. Chaturvedi blends what might have been with what did happen, Japan and the INA fighting on the eastern front of India, to narrate a taut, fictional tale of how Bose could have liberated India. He combines a sure grasp of history with an ability to convert little-known facts into a marvellous fictional page-turner, establishing himself as the Robert Harris of India'

– **Mihir Bose**, author of *The Lost Hero: The Biography of Subhas Bose*

A BIRD FROM AFAR

A Novel

ANSHUL CHATURVEDI

PAN

First published 2021 by Pan
an imprint of Pan Macmillan Publishing India Private Limited
707 Kailash Building
26 K. G. Marg, New Delhi 110 001
www.panmacmillan.co.in

Pan Macmillan, The Smithson, 6 Briset St, Farringdon,
London EC1M 5NR
Associated companies throughout the world
www.panmacmillan.com

ISBN 978-93-90742-32-5

1 3 5 7 9 8 6 4 2

Typeset in Fairfield LT Std by R. Ajith Kumar, New Delhi
Printed and bound in India by Replika Press Pvt. Ltd.

Cast of Major Characters

A. C. N. Nambiar: Subhas Chandra Bose's trusted confidant in Europe and his deputy at the Free India Centre in Berlin

Abid Hasan: Subhas's trusted associate and interpreter from his Berlin days

Adam von Trott: German lawyer, diplomat, covert anti-Nazi activist. Appointed as director of the *Sonderreferat Indien* – the Special Bureau for India – by Keppler to liaise with Subhas

Admiral Wilhelm Canaris: Chief of the *Abwehr*, the German military intelligence service. One among the senior-most German military officers engaged in clandestine opposition to the Nazi regime

Captain Gurbachan Mangat: Officer in the Indian Legion's First Battalion

Colonel Erwin Lahousen: Officer in the Abwehr, part of Admiral Canaris's staff

Colonel Schomberg: British consul in Pondicherry

Emilie Schenkl: Subhas's Austrian-born wife. Came from Vienna to Berlin when Subhas reached the latter in 1941

Faqir of Ipi: Aka Mirza Ali Khan, Pashtun tribal leader on the Afghan–India border, engaged in guerrilla warfare with the British forces for several years

Field Marshal Erwin Rommel: Field Marshal of the *Wehrmacht*. Amongst the most acclaimed military commanders of WWII. Commander of the Afrika Korps in 1942

Field Marshal Wilhelm Keitel: Chief of the *Oberkommando der Wehrmacht* (OKW), the German Armed Forces high command

General Franz Halder: Chief of Staff of the *Oberkommando des Heeres* (OKH), the German Army high command

General Wavell: Officer of the British Army. Commander-in-Chief, Middle East, 1940–41. Moved to the role of Commander-in-Chief, India, July 1941 onwards

Hauptmann Manfred Armbruster: *Luftwaffe* officer (German Air Force), appointed by Rommel as Liaison Officer to Subhas for the German forces on the Indian front

Heinrich Himmler: *Reichsführer* of the *Schutzstaffel* (SS) – the foremost security, surveillance and policing organization in the Nazi regime, and, therefore, one of the most powerful men in Hitler's Germany

Jam Saheb Digvijaysinhji: Ruler of the princely state of Nawanagar; successor of Jam Saheb Shri Sir Ranjitsinhji

Joachim von Ribbentrop: Foreign Minister of the Reich

Lieutenant General Hiroshi Oshima: Japanese ambassador to Berlin

Lieutenant General Shōjirō Iida: Commander of the Japanese Fifteenth Army based in Burma

Louis Alexis Étienne Bonvin: The governor of all French possessions in India – Pondicherry, Karaikal, Mahe, etc.

Major Fujiwara Iwaichi: Military Intelligence Officer of the Japanese Imperial Army, tasked with assisting independence movements in Southeast Asia during WWII

Major General Mario Balotta: General Office Commanding (GOC) of the Italian Army's 132nd elite Ariete Division

Major Gurdeep Dhillon: Subhas's right-hand man and a staff officer in the Indian Legion

Mian Akbar Shah Shahib of Nowshera: Organizer of the Forward Bloc in the North-West Frontier Province, key aide of Subhas

***Oberstleutnant* Kurt Krappe:** Commander of the Indian Infantry regiment 950, the first unit of the Indian Legion, and commandant of the Legion's training camp

Orlando Mazzotta: The alternative identity assigned on an Italian passport to Bose for his journey from Kabul to Berlin, and then for his initial period of stay there

***Reichsmarschall* Hermann Göring:** Chief of the Luftwaffe. Next only to Hitler in the formal German power structure

Wilhelm Keppler: Secretary of State at the German Foreign Office

The immediate objective of the Forward Bloc was an uncompromising struggle with British Imperialism for winning India's independence. To this end, *all possible means should be employed and the Indian people should not be hampered by any philosophical notions like Gandhi's non-violence, or any sentimentalism like Nehru's anti-Axis foreign policy*.

– Subhas Chandra Bose, *The Indian Struggle*

Today I regret that I have to return to India with the conviction that the new nationalism in Germany is not only narrow and selfish, but arrogant ... The new racial philosophy which has a very weak scientific foundation stands for the glorification of the white races in general, and the German race in particular.

– Subhas Chandra Bose, letter to Dr Thierfelder, March 1936

Prologue

THE YEAR 1942 WAS TOUGH FOR THE ALLIES IN THE COURSE OF the Second World War – perhaps the worst thus far.

In January, the Japanese overran Malaya and invaded Burma. General Rommel began a surprise offensive in the African theatre of war. In February, the Singapore garrison surrendered. Thirty-five thousand Japanese troops took 130,000 British, Australian and Indian prisoners. In March, Rangoon fell to the Japanese.

In May, the Japanese occupied the whole of Burma. The German Army inflicted 250,000 casualties on the Russians at Kharkov. Rommel launched an offensive against the Gazala line. In June, Tobruk surrendered to Rommel, and, later, his forces reached El Alamein. He seemed unstoppable. On the Russian front, Germany launched Operation Blue and a total of 118 Axis divisions marched in the direction of southern Russia and the oilfields of the Caucasus – with Stalingrad on the way.

In the midst of all this, an Indian leader camped in Germany since 1941 had been working furiously to build an army of Indians – an army that he hoped would march with him overland towards the Indian frontier. That hope, however, rested on how two Axis offensives developed at this point in time – one at Stalingrad, the other in North Africa.

If the Axis failed here, he would have to make other plans.

If they won, the road would be open for his men to spearhead a dash to Delhi.

PART I

1

Karna/Arjuna

'Is it possible for man to realize Absolute Truth? Everyone takes one relative truth to be the absolute in his life and then uses that as a yardstick to judge good and evil, happiness and sorrow of this life.'

– Subhas Bose, letter to Hemanta Sarkar as an eighteen-year-old, July 1915

Indo–Afghan border
15 November 1942
1 a.m.

SUBHAS SHIFTED UNEASILY. THE MAKESHIFT ACCOMMODATION, A few miles from the front line, was both cold and uncomfortable. But his mind barely registered the physical environment. He fumbled for the switch and, in the dim light of the bulb, reached out for the battered copy of the Gita on his bedside table.

'You'll need your sleep tonight; it's not going to be an easy day,' Emilie said gently as she sat up, watching him with a knowing look in her eyes. Once he started reading at such an hour, sleep rarely returned.

He nodded but said nothing, his face a reflection of multiple sentiments, many of them conflicting. Even if he were in the mood to converse, he probably would not have been able to decipher whether or not he was looking forward to the morning.

The morning? The H-Hour, the time of the attack, was just two hours away, at 3 a.m., he reminded himself.

'This is what you want, right? This is what you have spent so much of your life trying to put in place?' Emilie prodded him.

He stayed quiet for a while. And then sidestepped the question.

'You know what's strange, Emma? That we have to fight each other to win our freedom. Of all the men on this side, all the men on that side, perhaps a third or a quarter will be Europeans, whether the Germans and Italians here or the British there, maybe a few Americans as well. On the Burma front, it will be about a sixty–forty mix of Japanese and INA soldiers. Overall, more than half the men on *both* sides will be Indians, at war with each other. By the time it ends, many Indians will have killed other Indians in a battle that is, strangely, about letting Indians rule India. I can do nothing to change that unless I call it off at the eleventh hour.'

Emilie looked into his eyes but did not engage. She knew the futility of interrupting once he had started a conversation with himself.

Then Subhas laughed. 'Here I am sitting with the Gita, mulling it over!'

'But why does that make you laugh?'

'It's ironic, isn't it? If anyone ought to understand the dilemma, the hesitation of fighting your brothers on the battlefield, it should be an Indian soldier. It is that hesitation that gave the Gita to the world,' he softly chuckled. 'However unpleasant, some battles have to be waged.'

'Ah! So you are Arjuna today, philosophizing before the battle begins?' Emilie smiled.

'I dare say I am closer to Karna in this battle, Emma ...'

'Why would you say *that*?'

Her hand reached for his. The silence stretched for a few moments, disturbed only by the sounds of orders being issued in the camp, NCOs gathering their men, trucks revving up.

'I'm not pitying myself. I don't think I should have done anything differently – so don't worry about my state of mind. But I have seen enough to know that I will not be very popular, however this ends. Am I comfortable with what Hitler has done? Have I not heard stories of how the war has been waged in Poland and Russia? Fortunately, the men I deal with have largely been soldiers who fight by the rules, be it Field Marshal Rommel's armies or the Italians, but even if he keeps the Gita closer than I do, do I not understand the difference between Himmler and a professional soldier? I'm not naïve, Emma.'

'I don't think anyone is levying *that* charge against you, Subhas,' Emilie smiled.

'I am already being proclaimed a puppet of the Axis Powers. But if the Axis had not stood with me, despite all our differences, how would an Indian Army rise outside India? They did it because they are at war with Britain, true – but that does not negate the fact that they *did*. The Axis have been brutal in the way they wage war on many fronts, there is no denying that. I am, however, now too deep in this to disengage. Karna did not support all of Duryodhana's actions, but he was in his debt, wasn't he? He lived and died on that side of the battle. There is some dignity even in that, I feel ...'

The man, who had the charisma to defeat Mahatma Gandhi's nominee and be elected president of the Indian National Congress less than four years ago, went silent.

He was not a Mahatma, after all; he did not have a halo. There was never a shortage of people who were not particularly fond of him. It was a heavy burden to bear, even if he rarely let it show.

'But then, much as it pains me to accept it, the Soviet system that the British and the Americans fight by is no less brutal in waging war, be it against an enemy or against its own people. On the western front, the war in Europe was more civil for all sides, if any war can be called that; on the eastern, the result was barbaric. The shadow of that hovers over me as well. I am referred to as the "Indian Quisling", a lackey of Hitler's. Should I explain to them that if I *had* to be a lackey, I could well have begun with worshipping the Mahatma and saved myself so much trouble?'

'How much can you explain in the midst of a war? Let it be. There will be time, later.'

'There are days when all this troubles me. But I tell myself, once I have chosen the "less virtuous" side in this battle – a battle in which there are *no* hands which are not drenched in blood; it is just the volume of blood that varies – this is the side I have to stand with now, till either the battle ends or my life does.'

'Why are you analysing all this right now, Subhas?'

'Because it's amusing to think that I am facing Arjuna's dilemma while playing Karna's role in this version of the battle,' he smiled wistfully. 'Anyway, history will judge all this at its own pace. I do not care for it, beyond a point. I think I will spend some time with Swami Vivekananda as well, before the guns open up. Let people say what they will ... Is it a joke, building an army for a country that has been colonized for 200 years? "Do even evil, if you must, like a man," said Vivekananda. Even if some see fighting alongside Hitler and Mussolini's troops as evil, I must at least do it manfully!'

Emilie smiled. She had seen this often enough. When gripped by a dilemma, Subhas would grapple with it in his mind until he had convinced himself. Once it was over, he was at peace again. Often, the Gita or Vivekananda served to tip the balance when he was on the fence, as they seemed to have done now.

Pacing around the small room, he turned to her again and asked, 'Does any of this make me sound a little disoriented, Emma?'

'Does it matter? I wrote down all that you said for months as you put together your book, years back. Everyone only read what you put *into* the book – but I also know all that you wrote and then pulled out of it. I have heard your lucidity and I have also heard your ramblings. You don't have to explain things to me. I believe you will be vindicated once this battle is won, and India is free.'

'Free! I wish. But freedom is not just the absence of the British, is it?'

He was pacing around now, in the limited space the room offered.

'What have we brought ourselves to in India – a foreign power pushes one community against another, fans the hatred of one faith for another, and we play along! We are so fragmented, lost in our smaller and smaller circles of language, rituals, geography, caste ... We need someone like Bismarck to make a country out of us.'

'Germany may not be the ideal model right now, don't you think?'

'That's not what I meant. The lessons ... Have we not seen across Europe how the hatred for another's race or language can make beasts out of the best of men? Has not hating the Jews diminished Germany? Are you yourself not judged for marrying me, someone not from the "Master Race"? A Jew who fought for Germany in the Great War is made to walk with a Yellow Star of David on his sleeve in Berlin, today! What has been happening between the Serbs, Croats, Bosnians – I shudder to think of that, a hundred times over, unfolding in India if the country is not kept united.'

He walked to his small meditation corner, gazing at the figures kept there.

'You know, my worry is not as much about pushing the British out as it is about keeping India and Indians together. Else, Hindus and Muslims will start killing each other as soon as we are "free", and even fifty years from now, or even longer, their descendants will continue hating each other. The *military* challenge of dislodging the British empire is just the first step – there is a lot to be done beyond that!'

The chatter in the background grew louder.

'Churchill would be vindicated if a million Hindus and Muslims went about slashing each other's throats. He can then turn around and tell the world that we are narrow-minded savages, who were being kept in check by the white man.'

He placed the Gita back on his side table.

A soft knock was followed by his adjutant's voice: 'Time to get ready, sir.'

Subhas snapped out of his reverie.

'I'll get ready, Emma. You stay safe. I'll write to you as often as I can.'

'I know you will.'

2

To Battle

'Throughout my life it was my ambition to equip an army that will capture freedom from the enemy. Today I congratulate you because the honour of such an army belongs to you.'

– Subhas Bose, in an address to the Indian Legion, June 1942

15 November 1942

Order of the Day
Soldiers of the Afrika Korps

AS WE HEAD INTO ANOTHER ROUND OF BATTLE, PERHAPS THE concluding one for the Afrika Korps – for after this, there are no more hostile frontiers to the East – I expect you to do, as you have always done, your best for the fatherland.

As we march to India's borders, we march with our Indian and Italian comrades-in-arms. When we, as we surely will, deliver a final, decisive blow to the English empire, we look forward to meeting our Axis partners, the brave soldiers of Japan, who are launching a parallel offensive on India's eastern borders, even as these orders are being read out to you.

Our fellow soldiers who proudly wear the uniform of the Indian Legion, men who have proved their fighting skills as we advanced many hundreds of miles across Egypt, Syria, Iraq, Persia and finally through Afghanistan together, have sworn an oath of allegiance to both the Führer and to the Leader of the Indian Legion, Herr Subhas Chandra Bose. They will, therefore, be expected to look at both the military requirements of the situation, as advised by the German and Italian Armies, as well as the political requirements, as instructed by Herr Bose, and we must bear that in mind as the battle unfolds.

I have no need to remind you that you must observe the rules of war for which the Afrika Korps is known. Bear in mind that there will initially be many Indian troops in the British Army facing us, who may have been former comrades of the Indian Legion's soldiers alongside us. We do not look to enter Indian territory to spill the blood of Indian soldiers, even though they are fighting to preserve the British empire at present. We look to engage with them and in this, we will be led by our comrades of the Indian Legion. We do not want to inflict unnecessary casualties upon Indian soldiers fighting for the British side, even when in a militarily superior position. Further, we look to minimize any civilian casualties.

This is not a battle of ideology or annihilation, but one of necessity.

In a situation when combat with Indian soldiers of the British Army is unavoidable, the primary objective of German and Italian troops will be to seek surrender; to engage and disarm, and not to kill or injure. The Legion's soldiers have already been advised on this by their officers and Herr Bose. Indian soldiers and officers of the British Indian Army, wherever captured, shall immediately be placed in the charge of the nearest officer of the Indian Legion.

Erwin Rommel
Field Marshal

❖

The hills of the Hindukush and the land that is Afghanistan have never been strangers to the sounds of guns and war cries.

These hills, therefore, seemed not to be perturbed in the least as the sky was lit up much before dawn on 15 November 1942. At precisely 3 a.m., hundreds of artillery shells began the elliptical journey that had been minutely worked out by the laws of physics and by the range finders of the Wehrmacht and the Legion. A second later, if one could freeze frame at that instant, one would tire of counting them all floating mid-air, heading east in a coordinated sequence that would have been almost elegant, had it not been brutal. At 0300 hours and three seconds, the first shells launched after 1857 by Indians against the British Army in India landed with a thundering synchronized roar. The gunners simultaneously screamed at the top of their voices to equalize the pressure on their ears, adding to the intensity of the moment.

The battle that, to Subhas, was both hugely undesirable and completely unavoidable, was finally underway.

❖

A mile and a half from the starting line of the offensive – code-named 'Operation Tiger' in honour of the springing tiger that was on the shoulder emblem of every Legion soldier – Subhas Chandra Bose, former mayor of Calcutta, former president of the Indian National Congress and a former political prisoner, felt like a shell frozen mid-air: he was neither insulated from the battle, nor engaged in it.

The bitter November cold of the mountains did not stop the sweat dripping from his brow as he stooped over the map. The room was damp, the air stale. But you could hardly expect sunshine in a command centre, 15 feet below ground. His pulse was erratic. Today, as the Indian Legion's Axis-supported attack on the western borders of British India finally rolled out, was not a day he could have concealed his anxiety and his enthusiasm even if he wanted to.

General Mario Balotta, a battle-hardened veteran of the Italian Army's 132nd elite Ariete Division, stood at the table watching, surrounded by his staff officers, as the very first pins began to move on the map. Rommel's aide-de-camp, Captain Westphal, scribbled notes in his diary. Half a dozen officers of the Legion attended to their assigned tasks in the command post, wondering if they would, one day, speak of this day to their grandchildren.

Every other man of any authority in the room was a professional soldier. Subhas was the only man who had not come out of a military college, had not led men in actual battle – a fact of which he was acutely aware. Gazing at the map, observing the minute shifts made by the team of plotters, with the keyboards and printers clacking against the muted, distant background of shells exploding and rifles being fired incessantly; this was not an experience he was fully familiar with.

Yet, he could not afford to falter or freeze. Of all the decisive moments in his tumultuous life, in this one, he just could not.

He remained glued to the map, as if willing the pins depicting the Legion and Axis units to move east of their own accord. Then, shaking himself out of the stupor, he turned to the dependable Major Gurdeep Dhillon, a man who had been by his side from the day he had passed out after taking the oath of the Legion. Dhillon had been glued to the radio operator's side for the past hour.

'How is it going?'

'As we had anticipated, sir: slow, tough and bloody,' Dhillon answered.

'Give me the details.'

'Since we took the call to not opt for intensive artillery barrage, we kept to a short ten-minute burst. The Germans had advised at least a half-hour saturation salvo, so they weren't very happy about it all – according to them, such decisions will add to our infantry casualties. Our units aren't asking for air support either, at least not right now, not that we have too many planes to call up. It is mostly infantry-to-infantry exchange of fire, and the British units, as you would expect, are dug in well – they've been waiting for this. You won't see any rapid movement in those pins you are staring at so intently, sir.'

Subhas broke into a wry smile for the first time that day.

'There's something else that you need to note, sir: there seems to be a 50 per cent or more English component in the units that are facing us. Among the rest, the non-English front-line soldiers, the deployment right on the front line seems to be primarily constituted of Gurkhas.'

'That means they are thinking like we are,' Subhas said with great interest. 'We have hardly any Gurkhas in the Legion, so they will be least susceptible to appeals from former comrades in the Legion. The good thing is that this means they believe that other units *are* vulnerable and are keeping them away from direct contact with our men.'

'Quite possibly, sir. This also explains why there has been heavy sniper fire directed at the propaganda teams who are addressing Indian troops over megaphones – even more than that directed at officers. Three of them have been hit already. Two are critical while the third had his brains blown out.'

Subhas kept staring at the map, quietly.

The 'price in blood' he had often spoken to the Legion about? That price was being paid, starting today.

3

I am Back, India

Radio broadcast, 17 November 1942

My fellow countrymen

I SPEAK TO YOU TODAY WITH SADNESS AND WITH GREAT HOPE.

The sadness is because I regret that we were not in a position to reach out to you in August, when the Quit India Movement had shaken the grasp of the British over India in the strongest manner since 1857.

Our military situation was not conducive at that time; the German forces were still at the Nile and were also waging a bitter battle at Stalingrad. The Japanese Navy was waging a difficult combat with the American fleets in the Pacific. We did not know then how those battles would end, or how long it would take to bring them to a favourable conclusion, and it would have been unwise of me to have called for you to rise in anticipation of an Indian Army, your very own army, reaching your borders to give the British a response in the only language they appear to understand when it comes to India – the language of firepower.

The sadness is also because no matter what we do, some Indian blood will be shed on both sides of the war front before the Union Jack is taken down.

I consider all those wielding guns to defend the British Empire to be my brothers in arms, who have not yet realized either British intent or Indian sentiment. To that degree, the British policy of racial segregation and physical isolation of soldiers has served them well, up till now. The Indian Legion is not *a religious or a racial army, and it comes to liberate and help build an India that is not obsessed with religion and caste.. The same holds true for the Indian National Army.*

It is my hope that my country will overcome the fear of oppression that has been drilled into our very souls for years and years and rise to reclaim its space in the world. Such moments do not come often – and they have to be seized with both hands when they do.

Bapu, you and I have had our political differences, but, like all Indians, every word you say carries great weight for me. I understand what you feel when you said during the Quit India movement, 'Personally, I am so sick of slavery that I am even prepared to take the risk of anarchy'. Bapu, I have attempted, since the day I left India, to come back with the alternative that India needs – one that does not force it to choose between slavery and anarchy. Now I appeal to you, my countrymen, and to you, Bapu, to rise and embrace that; to finally throw away the sickening slavery that we have endured for a century. Even if you are unsure of what this brings, do not stand aside or encourage your followers to stand aside either. Instead, stand up to your own words and, this time, take the risk of anarchy!

In September, after the brutal crushing of the Quit India movement, while our forces were still a long distance from India's borders, Mr Churchill said something in a speech in the House of Commons that pained me both for its arrogance and for its closeness to reality. I would like to repeat it today. He said: 'It is fortunate, indeed, that the Congress party has no influence whatever with the martial races, on whom the defence of India apart from the British Forces largely depends. Many of these races are divided by unbridgeable religious gulfs from the Hindu Congress and would never consent to be ruled by them.'

This *is what Mr Churchill relies on, and this is where India has to prove him wrong. Mr Churchill says the martial races have no engagement with what is happening in the country. He says there is a 'Hindu' Congress and he needs that so-called Hindu Congress and the Muslim League to distrust each other.*

He needs us to be afraid of independence so we have to run back to him and then he can tell us how, when, and in how many parts we will get independence.

Therefore, I would like to inform Mr Churchill – and I would like to remind our brothers willing to fight to ensure that he continues to rule our motherland – that a great majority of the men who have fought, bled and died in the last one year as part of the Indian Legion, who fight and bleed today on the frontier, are from these very 'martial races'. Pathans and Balochs, Sikhs and Jats, Rajputs and Marathas – they all accompany me as we come to reclaim our motherland.

The martial valour of these races was not ingrained into them by the East India Company; it has been there for centuries. They have always fought for their honour. And – whether or not the Congress party has any influence with them – they now understand their honour lies not in upholding the Union Jack but in uprooting it.

Those who do not – well, we will, even if reluctantly, fight them, and we will defeat them, even if it is painful; after all, who understands the need for such a battle better than an Indian Army? Have not many of us learnt the lesson of fighting even our brothers if they be on the wrong side, from the time of the Mahabharata?

Give us your blessings, the elders of India. You were born into an enslaved nation but you should not die in one. Give us your support, the youth of India; rise with us, end the farce of a handful of men ruling millions of us because we cannot muster the sense or the courage to fight against them together.

I will speak to you again, soon. And when I do, it will be from Delhi.
Jai Hind!

Yours, in life and in death,
Subhas

4

The Making and Unmaking of an Army

'If one regiment mutinies, I should like to have the next so alien that it would be ready to fire into it.'

– Charles Wood, Secretary of State for India, 1861

'It is the aim of the Legion – through close cohabitation of the different religions, the comradeship of daily life, military discipline, discussion among comrades – to further mutual understanding and tolerance in order to bridge the century-old gap between the many different groups in India and thus to foster an Indian national consciousness.'

– Rudolf Hartog, *The Sign of the Tiger*, quote by Kritter

The Frankenberg Camp
Eastern Germany
21 March 1942

'SQUAD, LOAD!'

The six soldiers – all Indians in field-grey uniforms – cocked their Karabiner 98k bolt action rifles as the German *Hauptfeldwebel* (Sergeant Major) bellowed: 'Squad, aim!'

The two blindfolded men tied to the posts struggled. One had a turban and a flowing beard, while the other was reciting an indistinct prayer.

'Squad, FIRE!'

A volley of rounds rang out. After a pause of a few moments, at a sign from the sergeant major, the rifles were reloaded, and a second volley thudded into the already limp frames. Blood spurted out and gathered in a slowly expanding crimson pool at their feet.

Other uniformed men gathered around and watched, quietly. Some sullen, some detached.

'Did we *really* need to do this, sir?' Captain Gurbachan Mangat, of the Legion's First Battalion, asked the Legion's commander-in-chief, Subhas. They both stood at a vantage point, 50 metres away. 'Perhaps there could have been a lighter punishment, since it is a matter involving sentiments?'

'I know where you are coming from. But it is precisely *because* it is a matter involving sentiments that I agreed with the commanding officer's decision on the court martial and its verdict, Captain. If we allow this to spread today, how will we check sentiments overriding discipline and teamwork when our army is 50,000-strong?'

The captain did not aggressively counter Subhas, keeping to the discipline of the uniform, but his expression remained unconvinced. This dual execution would create unrest and the officers would have a tough time keeping it under control.

❖

The two men sentenced to death by the firing squad had both been part of a tragic case of religious animosity that had erupted at the training camp of the Legion.

It began with Ibrahim, a convert to Subhas's ideology, who actively campaigned for greater mixing of the Muslim recruits with the Hindu and Sikh soldiers and encouraged a non-conservative approach to religious practices and less fixation with community rules during wartime in a foreign land, thousands of miles from home. In 1939, he had been among the crowd that had cheered Subhas as he had stepped off the train at Peshawar. As a soldier in the Fourth Indian Infantry Division deployed in North Africa, he had been taken captive by the Afrika Korps in 1941. Shortly thereafter, his Prisoner of War (POW) camp had a surprise visitor – Subhas. What he had said in 1939 had made some sense to Ibrahim. What he was saying now made much more sense. This man was not speaking to Ibrahim as a Hindu speaking to a Muslim. He was closer to Khan Abdul Ghaffar Khan's spirit than Jinnah was. For some reason, Ibrahim believed in the genuineness of what he was saying, what he was asking of them.

For weeks, Ibrahim would speak to groups in the barracks, explaining why mixed-faith units were the future, questioning the nitpicking over religious practices during wartime, and asking his fellow soldiers to not become fixated on what the clerics said – to look at things beyond the Muslim–Sikh–Hindu trichotomy.

Not letting go of his campaign despite receiving threats from a group in the barracks, Ibrahim was cornered and stabbed a dozen times one night, by a group of ultra-orthodox men who considered his remarks blasphemous.

The furious inquiry by the commanding officer drew a blank at the outset, as few men were willing to give testimony as to what had occurred.

A day later, a subedar major, who was a Sikh man (the Legion still used British ranks, rather than German, for the sake of continuity), triggered an argument with some of the men who shared Ibrahim's barracks, while making his inquiries. After some offensive remarks about religion were reportedly made, the spat turned into a fistfight, and, before the military police could reach to restore order, the infuriated subedar major had pulled out his *kirpan* and ran it through two men. Both died before the day ended.

As per the Wehrmacht's wartime code, irrespective of the nature of the provocation, there was no other punishment except execution for this. The subedar major was sentenced to death by firing squad. The Legion's officers handpicked a firing squad of one Muslim, one Hindu, and two Sikhs to emphasize that orders had to be carried out irrespective of personal beliefs. When the order to fire was issued, three of the men carried it out, whereas, one of the Sikh soldiers deliberately and defiantly shot wide of the condemned prisoner.

Oberstleutnant Kurt Krappe, the commander of the Indian Infantry Regiment 950, and commandant of the training camp, had the defiant soldier imprisoned and discharged from the Legion with the consent of Subhas. But that, unfortunately, was not the end of the bloody tale. The other Sikh boy, who *had* carried out his orders without question, was found stabbed to death in his bed, the next morning.

Krappe led the investigation himself this time and, within a day, two men had been rounded up: the Muslim soldier who had led the group that killed Ibrahim, and the Sikh soldier who had killed the fellow soldier for playing his role in the firing squad as assigned.

These were the two who had just been executed. The firing squad – three Hindus, one Sikh, two Muslims – had been picked by drawing lots and informed in advance of summary dismissal and imprisonment for defiance. This time, there was none.

Subhas, as the supreme commander of the Legion, had the option to review their sentence.

He had declined.

That was what Captain Mangat was speaking to him about. He, along with several other officers, realized that the tensions in the barracks could have been reduced, had Subhas agreed to a less harsh punishment. But on this subject, Subhas was obstinate. So far, the camp had seen eight men executed and over a dozen imprisoned – Hindus, Muslims, Sikhs – for various shades of communal and ethnic animosity and violence.

❖

'I am sorry, but I do not fully understand these priorities, Your Excellency.'

Lieutenant Colonel Krappe had a bemused tone. It had now been two hours since they had stepped out for a camp inspection at 6 a.m. Krappe, eager to demonstrate the meticulous military training he was putting the Legion through, was by now chafing at the endless – and seemingly pointless – questions Subhas had about the barracks, the kitchen and the prayer areas of the men.

'*I*, on the other hand, fully understand where your question is coming from, Oberstleutnant,' Subhas appeared lost in thought, the firing squad executions and the chain of events that led to them still playing on his mind. 'You must be intrigued, and irked as well, at why I am discussing the accommodation, food and prayers of the men at length but have not asked a single thing about their combat training.'

'Only intrigued, Excellency,' Krappe smiled.

The Legion's political leader and the German officer appointed to command its first regiment and oversee the training camp had developed a working relationship over the past few months, one that allowed Krappe to crack the occasional joke at Subhas's expense without causing offence.

'These men fight for many things, Kurt, but the way they have been trained and kept by the British, they have never fought the basic battle that any soldier fights – in the defence of his country's sovereign interest. They are Indians who fight the Germans, the Italians, the Japanese, they fight in Iraq, in Egypt, they fight in Malaya and Burma – but they never fight for India!'

'And I assume this tour of the kitchens and barracks has something to do with changing that, Excellency?'

'Yes, actually, it does. The kitchen can be a great divider in India, Kurt. Don't treat it casually if you wish to lead this unit into war someday. In any case, why should I pretend to assess how efficiently they can fight, or how well you can train them, Oberstleutnant? That would be downright foolish on my part. The Indian soldier, when properly trained and equipped, has proved he can fight and die as bravely as any other in the First World War as well as in the ongoing one. And, as of today, the Wehrmacht is the most brutally efficient military training machinery in the world – a fact that is not questioned by either the Axis or the Allies. So neither do these men need me to tell them how to learn to fight better, nor do you need my advice on how to train them.'

'Excellency is in a generous mood. If only all those who say you are never satisfied could see you today!'

Subhas smiled at Kurt's comment, then continued.

'Militarily, these men just have to be sharpened, they already are trained soldiers, after all. Culturally, it is the reverse; they have to unlearn. And *this* is the tough part. They are used to speaking the same language, eating the same food, worshipping the same god as the men they live with. They are also habituated to eating separately, praying separately, keeping distance from men of other faiths and habits. This model has worked, militarily, for England, worked very well indeed – and this has kept this army as just a collection of regiments, Kurt, not as one army guided by a common goal.'

'Should we not just stay with that, perhaps, instead of trying to change things in the midst of a World War? Soldiers are slaves to habit.'

'No!' Subhas was emphatic. 'This is also what led to those men killing their fellow soldiers here. This Legion is *not* just another few thousand men flung into the churn of this great war. The Legion is the core of the future *national* army of India – the defender of an independent, undivided India that extends from Afghanistan to Burma.'

He paused, as if visualizing that on a map.

'Such an India will need to learn to coexist despite differences. Its army will have to be an army of the entire nation. Before that happens, *these* men must learn to live with each other, to eat at the same table as others, to have more than one form of prayer in their barracks, to respect each other's faiths and beliefs and eccentricities. The training that we undertake is not just about tactics and weapons. We have to break down the regimentation instilled by the British Army. A British official once wrote that they should be willing to kill each other, if ordered, without question. I need them to be willing to die for each other, without needing to be ordered.'

'To occupy a nation with a population many millions greater than that of the occupier – it is an intelligent strategy, no doubt. Perhaps this is what impresses the Führer about the English model of keeping India for so long.' Kurt smiled.

'True. But their political need has meant that they have poisoned the land, the minds of the people. That is where my obsession with making soldiers of different beliefs and different languages live and eat and fight together in the Legion – and in the INA – comes from.'

He went quiet for a while, again.

'Can you believe it, Kurt? India stays colonized through the military strength of Indian soldiers who can kill unarmed, helpless crowds, and can kill other soldiers as well, when ordered. And why is that? Because too many of us in India today live in our own little wells, we are obsessed with our kitchens, our customs ... And that, Oberstleutnant, is why *this* is so important. Making them share space, share food, share conversations ... Be slow in the beginning, though, else you'll have a mutiny on your hands every month.'

❖

The Hauptfeldwebel yelled out a command. The ground reverberated with boots stomping. Some 1,200 men stood to attention. The emblem of the springing tiger on their shoulder distinguished their uniforms from the default field grey of the Wehrmacht Non-Commissioned Officers (NCOs) and officers training them.

Krappe stepped up. A Legion NCO stood next to him to translate into Hindustani.

'Soldiers of the Indian Legion! In the presence of the Supreme Commander of the Legion, Subhas Chandra Bose, I have some announcements regarding how your training and allocation of units after training will be carried out here. Pay attention, for they are not negotiable.'

He paused as the NCO translated, then resumed.

'We will, at all times, bear in mind that the Legion is aligned to the political programme and priorities laid down by His Excellency Bose. Therefore, the methods of the British colonial army – of putting together regiments, companies and platoons according to caste or tribe – are *not* the methods the Legion will follow. We will mix Pathans and Sikhs, Dogras and Jats, Punjabi Muslims and Rajputs, Bengalis and Garhwalis, Marathas, Madrasis and Gurkhas, not just in regiments, but in companies, and even down to the section level. It is the aim of the Legion to help all soldiers develop understanding and tolerance, to create an Indian national consciousness, and this we will do – as we have already been doing – through men of different religions and regions working together in tight teams, through the comradeship of daily life, through our unforgiving military discipline, and through discussions. I expect that to be understood and obeyed.'

A murmur ran through the assembled soldiers as the translator finished. Subhas was tempted to step in, to add, but he did not want to preach to the men the rationality of his arrangements just yet – they had enough to handle at the moment. He would let it be absorbed at its own pace. His presence during the commandant's address would be enough to indicate that the move had his backing.

Leaving the troops to the Hauptfeldwebel, Krappe and Subhas walked half a kilometre to a secluded part of the camp, fenced in by barbed wires. Half a dozen men, three each of the Wehrmacht and the Legion, fingers resting on the triggers of their rifles, accompanied them inside the gate of the cordoned-off compound. The sentries snapped to attention as they entered.

'These, Excellency, are the Indian soldiers and officers who shall be sent ahead to the POW camps, since they have stated that they have no interest in joining the Legion or in fighting for the Axis.'

The hundred or more dishevelled, unshaven men looked sullenly at Subhas and Krappe. Subhas looked intently at the men, then asked for the senior officer.

'That would be me, Captain Amanullah,' a voice rang out from a corner. The captain got up disinterestedly. Stepping a few paces ahead, he folded his arms across his chest.

'In case you are going to ask us the same thing that they have wasted three days doing already, Mr Bose', let me save you the time and energy: We swore an oath to the Crown, and that is that. Unlike those men who now fight for a Nazi army, we do not break our oaths. We will happily serve our time in a POW camp, rather than betray our loyalty.'

A handful of officers stepped ahead and stood around him, emphasizing to the men that this was their collective position.

'I don't have an issue with you not wanting to fight the British, Captain. We do not coerce men to join the Legion. Even pragmatically, why would I want men who do not believe in our cause to be forced into joining? You would simply desert and rejoin the British forces at the first point of engagement. But I do have an issue with this theatre, this illusion of you here being the loyal soldiers, and those men, who, God willing, will one day march to India's borders, being the traitors.'

'I am not interested in what you believe, Mr Bose, but since you are here, and we have no choice but to stand and hear you out, you may as well as do it and get it over with.'

Amanullah's fellow officers smirked. The men inched forward, however, despite the disdain of their officers. Subhas was, after all, a curiosity – the Congress president from barely five years back; a name heard as often as that of Gandhi and Nehru at one point – who was now addressing them in Germany. Soldiers who were formerly their comrades, who may well have arrested him in India once, standing guard around him in grey uniforms.

It was quite a contrast to anything else any Indian leader had ever done, if nothing else.

Subhas's speeches and addresses had so far made first a dozen, then a few hundred, and then a few thousand captured soldiers believe in a new cause. He saw no reason, therefore, to curb that instinct just yet. The disdain and the contempt, the charge of being a Fascist stooge, the Legion being described as a collection of disloyal oath breakers – all this, he was familiar with.

'Remind me what you took an oath for, Captain – to fight for what, exactly? Preserving the Empire?'

'We are fighting for democracy, not for fascism, Mr Bose!' A diminutive lieutenant lent his sharp voice to Amanullah's.

Subhas laughed.

'Let's not be delusional. You have, essentially, taken an oath to keep your *own* land enslaved. And you fool yourselves by believing you are fighting to defend the honour and liberty of the motherland of others. You travel a thousand miles to kill and to be killed, supposedly to free people of nations that were conquered by the German or the Italian armies, a few months back, but you are fine with your country being ruled by the Crown of England since 1857? These men in grey who you think are traitors to India have *me* as their supreme commander. Who is your commander, Captain? The Viceroy? General Auchinleck? Wavell? Did you even have an Indian general to command you in the army you fight in?'

'We are a professional force, not a group of killers like the Nazis, so spare us the moralizing,' a third officer smirked. But the expressions on the faces of many of the soldiers suggested that, to at least some of them, the point had gone across.

'It is this detached "professionalism" that makes the British Indian Army the world's primary colonial armed force, gentlemen!'

Subhas was genuinely worked up now.

'It is this "professional" army that keeps India occupied. It very professionally helped the British keep Burma and Singapore occupied. It fights Afghans. It keeps the Union Jack flying high in Iran and Iraq, even though neither country wants to be under the British boot. The men of an enslaved country go out and help their masters make slaves of others as well. Yet, *they* are the "professionals". And *these* men,' he gestured to his Legion guards, 'who want to pick up a gun to finally fight for their *own* nation, *they* are the traitors? Bravo!'

No smart comment came back this time.

'Was it General Dyer who personally killed all those civilians at Jallianwala Bagh? Or was it the Ninth Gurkhas, Fifty-fourth Sikhs and Fifty-Ninth Scinde Rifles who fired those 1,600 rounds into an unarmed crowd because Dyer gave the order? And do you know what the brutal irony of that is, distinguished officers of a chivalrous army?'

A sullen silence was the only response he elicited from the group. Every soldier there was silent as well, hearing him now. This was an alien conversation. In their military careers, nobody in a military establishment had ever questioned the basics of what they did. Those who did not comprehend his clipped English looked to the few who did, for translation.

Subhas wasn't done with the officers just yet.

'Do you know, gentlemen, that just five years after 1857, the Secretary of State of India, a gentleman by the name of Charles Wood, explained clearly *why* he wanted the Indian Army to be both insulated and segregated, so that no mutiny may threaten the Empire again? He wrote that he wanted such a spirit – and I have never forgotten those words since I read them – "so that Sikh might fire into Hindu, Gorkha into either, without any scruple in case of need". *That* is the irony of Jallianwala Bagh – that Sikhs, Gurkhas and Hindus fired into a crowd of Sikhs, Hindus and Muslims. To do what? To demonstrate the might of the British Raj. They would fire and kill each other as well, the next day, if ordered to. Wood was so grandly vindicated. That all is "duty". But to think of firing at the *British* to liberate India? That, to you, gentlemen, would be disloyalty!'

Looking away from the sulking group of officers towards the men, Subhas switched to his Bengali-accented Hindustani.

'*Jawans* of the Indian Army! If you are asked to kill peacefully protesting countrymen of yours, will you not do it? Of course you will, if it is an order. After all, you are trained to obey orders. But even here, the angrez will play you because he always appeals to your narrowest identity. He will usually not bring in men of the same region to crush protests; no, no, he is too smart for that. He will push ahead the Sikhs if he needs to attack the Afghans. He will bring the Gurkhas to crush protests in Punjab. He may ask the Madras regiment to be sent if he needs protesters shot at in Bengal. So Indians keep killing Indians to defend the British, for a salary. It is time to change that, it is time to change some things ... Are you proud of being a part of the Great British Commonwealth, fighting shoulder to shoulder with Australians, Canadians and New Zealanders against Rommel? If you are, good! It is good to be able to fight without distinction with fellow soldiers. We all bleed the same. But while at home, some of you cannot even bear to have food with another caste in the regimental *langar*! What is the point of having crossed the seas and seen the world, then?'

The atmosphere was tense now. The Legion's soldiers exchanged glances. They had experienced the unsettling effect of his speeches to POWs firsthand. The expressions on the faces of the prisoners ranged from introspective to furious.

Subhas was not to be held back by any of that, though; he had been through similar situations many a time by now.

'Do you not understand that this manner of thinking keeps us enslaved? You are defending the rights of other nations – or at least you think so. Do you never feel the need to hold that rifle for defending your *own* land? Do you just fight for your salary and your rations? If you can find glory in that, I wish you well. You joined the army and became part of the Crown's forces. I could also have been part of the system that rules India for the Crown. I had been selected for the ICS – I would have been a "Collector sahib" many, many years ago. But I could not convince myself. I left that. I was the president of the Congress party. I could not compromise on some things; I left that, too. Have you heard of that?'

'Gandhiji and you had differences and then you resigned,' a jawan's voice came from the gathering.

'Yes. I wanted to fight! For what is more important than ending this slavery, this division? Your officers talk of oaths. You have an obligation to that oath but not to Hindustan? Is *Namak* greater than *izzat*? My goal is to go and seek death or glory on the borders of our nation with these soldiers. You can stay in camps and have your Red Cross rations and live a safe life till the war ends. Maybe you will even get a pension from the King. I will not force you to join our war. I assure you, in the presence of the camp commandant, *nobody* will force you. We fight for our convictions. If you do not share those, it is better that we go our separate ways, my friends. Jai Hind!'

He turned briskly and strode out of the enclosure.

That evening, he received a note from Krappe: 54 of the 126 soldiers had volunteered to join the Legion.

❖

'So what do you think of our efforts here, Herr Ribbentrop?'

The Foreign Minister of the Reich sat at the head of the table in the compact conference room. He had been engaged in a quiet conversation with Lt Gen. Hiroshi Oshima, the Japanese ambassador to Germany. Subhas and Krappe were the only others present.

Ribbentrop's security detail stood guard outside. If Subhas was intrigued at the necessity of additional guards within the training camp, he did not express it. He had by now understood that every leader in the Reich carried his own retinue and did not trust men who may have loyalties to another. Ribbentrop may not have been living in as much grandeur as Reichsmarschall Göring or Himmler, but he was still not an inconsequential man.

'This is promising, Excellency. My compliments to you and to the Oberstleutnant. I am sure we will have to expand this to other locations in the next month or so if the numbers hold. However, the Oberkommando des Heeres (OKH) has some reservations about these men operating on an actual front within the next few months.'

'And these would be—?'

'Numbers, essentially. No matter how impactful your recruitment efforts are, no matter that we have three camps, the total numbers of this Legion will be, at best, in the range of 45–60,000 men. The Axis resources allocated for Operation Tiger are minimal, frankly, and given the overall situation, the Wehrmacht may not be able to spare more than two divisions. The Italians may, depending on how much influence you have with the Duce, provide some support. But the overall numbers to attack British India from the western frontier do not add up to 100,000 men, if I am gauging things correctly. That is ridiculous. When we invaded Russia last year, we went in with—'

'Three million troops, I know. About thirty times this number.'

'And yet you ask me what reservations the OKH has,' the minister smiled. 'Is it not prudent to wait till we have a reserve of at least eight to ten infantry divisions for there to be a reasonable chance of success, at such a great distance from our supply chains?'

'Are we discussing prudence now? What numbers did Rommel have when he dashed to the French coast? What numbers did General Yamashita have when he took Malaya and Singapore last month, General Oshima? A total of 35,000 Japanese soldiers took 120,000 prisoners in that campaign, did they not?'

'They did, indeed!' Oshima beamed. 'The resonance of the fall of Singapore still echoes around the world.'

'We *cannot* wait. The Japanese have the momentum, they are already in Burma. Churchill had not imagined that Singapore could fall. He, therefore, has no strategy to handle an attack from the East. If we give him time, he will devise one in due course. The momentum will be lost. The Indian National Army has 40,000 new volunteers from the men who surrendered in Malaya and in Singapore. We can raise a combined Japanese–INA force of about 100,000 on the eastern border, and if we can strike simultaneously on the western border with a similar number – let us say 60,000 of the Legion and 40,000 of combined German and Italian forces – India will rise like it never has. We must do it together – and we must do it *while* we have the upper hand!'

'May I, sir?' Krappe looked to the three, all of whom outranked him in the hierarchy.

'Yes, Oberstleutnant?' Subas nodded. 'Please do speak. If these men go into battle, you will probably be among those leading them.'

'On paper, the infantry available to defend India will be far too much to overcome with these numbers. Unless we plan to compensate with air attacks and heavy artillery.'

'No, there will be no random bombing and shelling of cities. This is not a conquering army, but an army of liberation. You cannot send in bombers to subdue enemy resistance there as you did in Warsaw or Coventry or Belgrade. You cannot kill Indian civilians to win a battle against British soldiers. I absolutely forbid that. This will be a battle fought only on the front lines.'

'Which means it will rely almost entirely on the infantry.'

'Yes. Which is why you are primarily training infantrymen for the Legion, as is Major Fujiwara for the INA.'

'And how do we overcome a numerical superiority when we are denied the "blitzkreig" model, Excellency?'

'That superiority is the creation of an image, Oberstleutnant. This is not a military but a psychological operation. The mood in the country is no longer of fasting and burning foreign cloth. If there is any outbreak of public sentiment, I expect more buildings to be burnt than cloth. The Indian civilian is angry and fed up. It is only the Indian *soldier* who is still on the fence – if he sees that the fellow Indians facing him at the front and his family at home both want a free nation, he may realize that he has been fighting for the wrong side all along. But then there *was* no right side to fight for, until now. He will turn, I assure you. And without the Indian soldier's blind, unquestioning loyalty, what is British power in India, Krappe? A mirage. How will they fight? I will not let trains run to supply British forces, I will have telephone lines snapped, power cut off, food supplies stopped. The British cannot fight on in India if India's population rises and the military's loyalty shakes.'

When the war commenced, the army in India comprised a little over 200,000 men, of which some 44,000 were British. After 1941, it was hiring over 50,000 soldiers each month. At the end of 1941, it stood at about a million.

But India's *own* defence had never been a priority for this force, since a land attack on India, let alone on two fronts, had long been seen as improbable, if not impossible. It was taken for granted that Fortress Singapore and the Royal Navy would never let a battle reach India's eastern borders. The best-equipped and best-trained Indian divisions were, almost by default, sent out west – they fought in Egypt and Eritrea, to keep the oilfields safe for the Allies in Iraq and Iran.

A large number of the trained troops still available to India were rushed to Malaya and Singapore to stop the Japanese – and promptly lost as POWs. And so, as 1942 began, India had nothing worth the name in terms of tanks, armoured cars, bombers or fighter planes. An estimated 500 anti-aircraft guns were seen as the bare minimum required for India's defence, and there were barely thirty available.

Part of the reason for the low quality of military resources present in India was Churchill's distrust of modernization of the force. Folklore had it that when General Auchinleck asked the War Cabinet for tanks to prepare one armoured division in the Indian Army, Churchill pointedly asked him: 'But, General, how do you know they won't turn and fire the wrong way?'

Subhas was banking on this to be true – for the soldier to turn and fire his rifle 'the wrong way'.

'The British like to spread the impression that they have a million men in India. That is a lie. My information network in India is infinitely superior to that of the Axis. My numbers take into account the divisions lost in North Africa, the ones that cannot be pulled out from Iraq and Iran because of Rommel's threat; the massive surrenders in Malaya, Singapore and Burma. So far, the total resources available to Commander-in-Chief Wavell are about 300,000 Indians and 60,000 British. These numbers will not be able to stop us unless all 300,000 are willing to kill and die for Wavell – and *that*, I assure you, will not happen. They will delay us, yes, if they bring *all* the forces to the frontier and keep none for internal security, but even then, they will not be able to stop us. And I expect the Legion to be stronger by the time it gets from here to the Indian frontier in the west, not weaker.'

'And why would that be?' Ribbentrop's tone was curious, but his expression suggested that he was being converted to Subhas's point.

'You will recall the very first meeting we had last year, in Berlin. I had proposed that if the Afrika Korps can reach Basra, Iraq, the Indian Legion troops can join them there for a drive to the east. It may have seemed a daydream then, but I have thought it through more since. The great majority of the Allied forces in that region are Indian soldiers. The Legion will lead the Axis movement eastward in the area, not the Germans. That will put the "British Indian" soldier against another Indian soldier for the first time. Many of our men who were taken POWs in North Africa are from the divisions currently in the Middle East. Will the Indians fighting for England fight to the death against my men? They may not all join us, but many will step aside. We are already in touch with men in many of these units and have inputs on their morale and mindset. I anticipate that at least 5–10,000 of those men may be willing to join us, though I am not sure whether I would want them to without having been trained in the ways of the Legion, both in military and cultural terms.'

'But this movement east will need at least eight divisions. Assuming that such forces are available, and this is the plan that unfolds, why would there be such a small Axis component in the final force for the attack on India on the western front?' Oshima queried.

'This, again, is something we have been discussing for a year. The minister is right when he says he is factoring in barely two German divisions finally being available to join a possible attack in India, since it is the Legion that will advance from there, while the Afrika Korps will consolidate through the region. Some of Rommel's divisions will have to pause in Iraq for protecting the oil installations. Some will have to do the same in Iran. Others will need to be deployed in Afghanistan along the Russian border. Across all three theatres, a secure route will have to be held steady for supplies and transport. A small core force, perhaps led by Rommel himself, can be with the Legion at the final frontier. But we have to get there before the momentum of the Japanese move into Burma subsides; before the British can consolidate either front.'

Ribbentrop laughed.

'As you can see, General, Oberstleutnant, the Legion's Supreme Commander has made his plans all the way to the start of battle! Of course, much will depend on how General Paulus fares in Russia and Rommel in Africa, in the next few months, but he has a point. And you have to gamble in war. Let us work to get the Legion battle ready here in Germany – and our Japanese friends can simultaneously work on the Indian National Army. Who knows, Excellency Bose may actually get the battle he so keenly seeks, within 1942!'

5

Go East to India

> 'As the next step we are going to advance south of the Caucasus and then help the rebels in Iran and Iraq against the English. Another thrust will be directed along the Caspian Sea toward Afghanistan and India. Then the English will run out of oil. In two years we'll be on the borders of India.'
>
> – Adolf Hitler, quoted in Albert Speer's diaries

> 'Above all we must have anxious regard for the continuing soundness of the Indian Army which alone stands between the Japanese and their ultimate objective which must be a union, military and economic, with the German Army on the Persian Gulf.'
>
> – Viceroy Linlithgow to Winston Churchill, February 1942

BETWEEN THE NORTH AFRICAN BATTLEGROUND AND AN AS YET peaceful India, lay the Middle East.

How events unfolded there through the second half of 1942 would depend on how Field Marshal Rommel fared in Egypt, and General Paulus at Stalingrad.

If Germany lost these two battles, the British could take a deep breath, for the danger would have passed. If Germany did not lose, however, the Axis would be positioned to threaten

Iran and Iraq, more so if neutral Turkey, believing that the Allies could no longer win the war, allowed them passage. Syria was administered by Vichy France, now an Axis ally for all purposes.

Iraq and Iran had been, not inaccurately, described as countries over which Britain had a 'semi-colonial' hold when the war had begun. That hold began to get tighter and more unpleasant as the war progressed; they were too vital to Britain's strategic and economic interests to be allowed to exercise real independence.

The limited independence they had did not last very long.

Iraq's army unsuccessfully resisted a British occupation of the country in April 1941. The British were provoked by an attempted crackdown on their military presence in Iraq by the pro-Axis Prime Minister Rashid Ali.

The German assistance Iraq had hoped for once the British–Iraqi confrontation broke out had not reached, German forces being engaged in Greece and preparing for the Russian offensive at that point in time. A sullen force of some 40,000 Iraqi soldiers were, for the time being, submitting to the British military control of their country.

Iran had been jointly invaded by the Soviet Union and Britain in August 1941, for that was the only way to have guaranteed access to Iranian oil for the Allies.

The country had been Axis-friendly for some years now. In 1935, Persia had changed its name to 'Iran' (land of the Aryans) – a suggestion that reportedly came from the Persian ambassador to Germany, heavily influenced by the Nazis. A largely anti-Soviet and anti-British sentiment prevailed among the populace. Again, a bitter, defeated local army – 130,000-strong – had stood watching, hoping for a blow from the Axis that would help them rise against their conquerors.

Apart from the northern part of Iran adjoining Azerbaijan, which was Soviet-occupied, the bulk of the Allied control of Iran and Iraq was British. Technically British, that is; most of the soldiers who raced to seize installations and cities in both countries were – this being the key part here – Indians.

The sixth, eighth and tenth Indian Divisions had been key to the Allied occupation of both countries. Some units had been boarding at Karachi to go to Singapore, when they were diverted to Iraq, instead, on Churchill's orders. Now, in 1942, Marathas, Gurkhas, Balochs and Sikhs kept the oil flowing for His Majesty's requirements through the Arab pipelines.

This was a diminishing presence, however. The 60,000 Indian soldiers initially deployed in Iran and Iraq in early 1942 had reduced to 25,000 by August, as forces were rushed further west to stop Rommel's advance in North Africa.

India had already deployed its best troops to Iran and Iraq in 1941. The war was, after all, never expected to come to the Indian borders; the Axis were to be held off far to the west. The best of those troops then rushed further to stop Rommel.

If they could *not* hold him, however, the situation meant that Iraq and Iran both, in 1942, had a combination of three factors that could influence how any military conflict there unfolded: an anti-British population, a defeated army that resented the occupation, and the bulk of the (diminished) Allied strength in the hands of soldiers of the British *Indian* Army.

If Iraq and Iran were to come under Axis control – or in control of a local Axis-friendly regime – through this combination of factors, an Axis force advancing through that route would be able to drive east and reach India's western borders without having to look over its shoulders, with a friendly local population and an abundant supply of fuel.

It was a combination that gladdened Subhas Bose, the

eternally curious student of international relations and dynamics.

❖

Command Centre, Peshawar
18 November 1942

'May I ask you a question, sir?' Major Dhillon was hesitant as he addressed Subhas.

Dhillon, presently one of the four men acting as staff officers to the Legion's supremo, was seated next to the flickering fireplace. Subhas, General Balotta and Captain Westphal were sipping what passed for coffee. The slow and bloody battle had been raging for three days now.

Subhas nodded.

'More of an observation, sir. I, for one, didn't think you would agree to be confined in the command centre when this was underway.'

'I know, I didn't think so, either!' Subhas laughed, surprising him. 'I know that it makes for grand photographs to be present on the front line. Don't I understand positioning, motivation? I've given speeches and won elections before I began to build an army.'

'Yes, of course – sorry, I didn't mean to make a comment.'

'No, nothing to apologize for, Major. I'm not taking offence. I've preferred to stay here since the objective today is not theatrics or gathering applause. This is a fight, and a strange one, where most of the "enemy" are fellow Indians, fighting by habit, by reflex, and because they do not see what else to fight for – at least not yet. I went back to seek comfort in the Gita, the night before the offensive, and it was surreal to be reminded that the core dilemma of Arjuna was fighting against his kin, his own people ...'

'Won't the Germans claim all the glory of victory if this succeeds, sir, if you are nowhere to be seen?' Dhillon's voice dipped a few decibels.

Subhas, surprising him again, broke into a smile, and exchanged glances with Balotta and Westphal.

'You don't have to lower your voice, Major; we are not in a Gestapo cell, are we? And to answer your question: I am not so vain as to jeopardize a battle as key as this for personal glory. I am vain, I cannot pretend I am not, but not to that degree. You know as well as I do that Field Marshal Rommel's understanding of a changing battle situation is far superior to that of most generals on either side, let alone mine. My patriotism hasn't warped into mere jingoistic self-obsession. Even though some two-thirds of the men in this operation are from the Legion, I would prefer to not try to teach military experts their job and leave the operational command and control to Rommel.'

'Maybe a joint command, sir? Like the oath of the Legion is to both Adolf Hitler and to you?'

'That oath – I have my views on it, but I prefer not to express them right now. And, as for joint command, attempting dual control of an active battle is outrageous. I have spent enough time in Germany to understand what happens when amateurs impose their views on a battlefront. Delegation of ground initiative is, in fact, critical to how the Wehrmacht functions and why it so often wins tight battles despite a lack of numerical superiority. If you get the time, do read up on the military philosophy of *Auftragstaktik*. Top leaders, too, often make the mistake of micromanaging. It's an absolute miracle that Berlin's micromanagement did not lead to debacles at both Stalingrad and Alamein, or else we would be seeing a very different end to 1942.'

Westphal maintained an impassive expression even as General Balotta broke into a guffaw.

'I will pretend I have absolutely no idea who or what you may be referring to, Bose, by this micromanager, but I am beginning to understand why the Duce gets along so well with you,' he laughed while landing a friendly slap on Subhas's shoulder, who winced. Never comfortable with gestures of uninvited familiarity, he stayed quiet.

The Italian then brought up a question that had clearly been on his mind for some time.

'But if it is really about leaving it to the experts, how do you explain the pressure you put on the OKH and on Ribbentrop about the deployment of German units with your Indian Legion? I hear that Field Marshal Paulus has been furious at the Sixth Army being used merely as a holding force for this operation, despite his famous victory at Stalingrad, despite breaking through right till the Soviet–Iranian border. He had expected to be asked to regroup, refit and march into Iran and Afghanistan. Now he is simply being asked to hold his line as the Afrika Korps moves into India at the end of the Egypt–Syria–Iraq–Iran sweep. Everyone knows that you argued vehemently for Rommel and against Paulus, when Operation Tiger was being finalized. I also hear that Ribbentrop and Canaris supported you, and that that tipped the scales.'

'I will not deny that, General,' Subhas seemed glad for the distraction of the conversation at this point in time, and continued without needing to be prodded.

'I had two grounds to make those requests. One was purely operational as the men of the Legion had joined the spearhead of the Afrika Korps in Iraq and in Iran, and were familiar with those German units by now, having fought alongside them. The Germans, too, had understood the dynamics of letting the

Legion engage with the Indian soldiers on the British side by now – propaganda and megaphones, rather than just opening up a barrage of fire at each point of contact with the enemy. Why throw all that away and start building up coordination afresh?'

'Valid. And the second ground?'

'The second ... That was more complex, I could not really write a memo on that, so it had to be handled in a more roundabout manner. Of course, you know some of what is happening in Russia – Italian units were at the right flank, holding the line against possible counterattacks when Paulus's army finally entered Stalingrad in the second week of October. In the journey till that point, they cannot have not seen how the war had been waged.'

'Our men deal with the army, not the SS – but, yes, of course they have seen.'

'Have you heard about what the units that come behind the advancing armies are doing? Did Stalingrad have to be so indiscriminately bombed with no concern for civilian casualties? Hasn't Leningrad been starved deliberately? Prisoners are kept in open camps without a roof over their heads, which, in the Russian winter, is simply a death sentence deferred by forty-eight hours, General. The German armies fighting on the Russian front have acquired ruthless reflexes. But that is not how they fought in France and that is *definitely* not how Rommel fought in North Africa.'

'But isn't all warfare ruthless, Herr Bose? Would the Russians be any different if it was the other way round?' Westphal, caught between welcoming the respect for Rommel and defending the Germans' actions in Russia, spoke up.

'Can this battle be fought the same way as the German–Russian one, Captain? Is it to be fought as a racial fight to the death between the Aryan and the Slav? In a battle such as the one we are fighting, with *this* army on the other side – an army that has thousands of fellow Indians with whom we need to engage – I cannot have a rampaging, bloodthirsty force that is looking to kill, rather than subdue. That is why I insisted – lobbied, call it what you will – with the OKH, with Canaris and with Ribbentrop, that the Axis Army that marches to India can only be supported by Rommel's Africa Korps and the Italians. *Not* by the Sixth Army, definitely not with the SS units embedded within it.'

'How did you conclude that Rommel is the "right" man for the India campaign, Herr Bose, even if Paulus isn't?' Balotta's expression was quizzical.

The Italian–German coordination in North Africa had hardly been the warmest. Rommel was seen by many as too publicity-driven and willing to ignore the Italians when it suited him. Further, the terms of the Rome–Berlin Axis obliged Berlin to refrain from taking unilateral leads in Arab affairs, which were accepted as falling primarily within the Italian sphere of influence. Berlin, of course, did not respect that.

'There are many things; maybe I will write about them, once this is all over,' Subhas chuckled.

❖

Subhas had managed to get one point across to Ribbentrop, and then to Mussolini, over time: the value of the Indian Legion was not just about the numbers added to the anti-British front. The propaganda value for the Axis to have Indians fighting against British Indian Armies would be immense, more so when they were facing Indians fighting for the Crown. If the

British could not blindly trust the Indian soldier, and hesitated to deploy him in sensitive situations, their effective military strength in India would be hugely reduced without a single bullet having been fired.

There was much fear in India as well, of the brutal, marauding Germans. The Indian soldier deployed by the British had also heard much about it. He would, therefore, hesitate to surrender, fearing what they might do to him and to his family back home, if they ever reached India.

The men who made up the initial core of the Legion were those taken prisoners by the German and Italian armies led by Rommel in North Africa. These men had fought the Axis; they were the prisoners of the Afrika Korps and the Italians, before they were brought to Germany, met Subhas and agreed to join the Legion.

They were the best witnesses or ambassadors to convince the Indian soldier on the other side – their fellow soldier till a while ago – that the approaching forces did not necessarily pose a risk to either India's safety or his life.

❖

Camp office of the C-I-C
Persia and Gulf Command
Kerman, Iran
2 October 1942

Lt Col. William Hardinge, Chief of Staff of the British Tenth Army, walked into the foreboding, dimly lit office of the Commander-in-Chief, Persia and Gulf Command, and saluted smartly. His heels clicking together on the marble floor echoed across the room.

Gen. Henry Maitland Wilson, reading the report brought in earlier in the day by Hardinge on behalf of his boss,

Lt Gen. Edward Quinan, Commander of the Tenth Army – the primary British force in the Middle East – looked up absent-mindedly and gestured for the junior officer to take a seat. He seemed lost in thought.

'This report – it isn't very encouraging, Colonel.'

A wry smile crossed Hardinge's face. Irrespective of the situation, the British knack for understatement remained firmly in place.

'No, sir. Neither is the situation on the ground.'

'Why have things come to this stage, Colonel?'

'Well, sir, it all comes from our failure to stop Rommel before the Nile and the Russians not being able to push back the Germans at Stalingrad – not that you need me to state that. Once that happened, things were bound to get complicated, sooner or later. We had to face a two-front challenge with severely limited resources: the German Sixth Army at the Russia–Iran border and the Afrika Korps at the Syria–Iraq border. We just don't – didn't – have enough resources to hold both fronts.'

'But the Sixth Army has not advanced into your areas of responsibility, has it?'

'No, sir, it has not. The primary aggressive manoeuvre in the region has been by the Afrika Korps, crossing Egypt and then initiating hostilities commencing from the Syria–Iraq border. They were given unhindered access to Syria by the Vichy French. Nevertheless, the very presence of the Sixth Army at the other frontier has necessitated the deployment of substantial forces in a blocking role, thereby, reducing the resources available to halt Rommel.'

The General squinted at a small-scale map on his table for a few moments. He then looked up at Hardinge.

'I know the Tenth Army is a professional force, but the speed at which you have buckled under this advance is inexplicable, given the total numbers that I can see were available to you.'

'Those numbers aren't real indicators of our combat capacity anymore, General. That's a point we have made multiple times but, I am sorry to say, Headquarters tends to discount that as mere exaggerated excuses for our failures to hold our defensive line.'

'That point – I assume you are referring to the subversive Indian influence on your infantry?'

'Indeed, General.'

'You know, Colonel, I fought in the first war, as you are well aware. Indian infantry fought for us in Turkey, in France, everywhere. In this war, too, it bore the brunt of much of the fighting in SE Asia and North Africa. What has changed now, that you are unable to push the enemy back with Indian infantry on this front?'

'Well, sir, we have made the point in more than one report – what has changed things is the presence of the formation led by the rebel leader, Bose.'

'And what exactly does he manage to do, this Bose?'

'He has an Axis-equipped formation made up entirely of Indian soldiers. The Germans call them the "Legion Freies Indien" – the Free India Legion. We estimate the strength of the Indians to be no more than 30,000. Almost all of these are POWs taken in North Africa, who later agreed to join his force. The Legion is always used on the front line of the advance, and it is as focused on propaganda as on fighting to influence our Indian soldiers.'

'And are they influenced?'

'I wish I could say they are not, sir, but this man is a dangerous influence and a skilled communicator. He sends out daily radio broadcasts. Very few soldiers have radio sets, and we have banned listening to him, but still, word spreads. The Legion also plays out his messages to our soldiers over megaphones all night. Pamphlets and letters, ostensibly addressed by him to them, are dropped by low-flying aircrafts over areas where Indian units have been deployed. He incessantly attempts to portray the Axis forces as an "army of liberation" fighting to get to India's borders. He has also referred to the Congress' Quit India campaign and instigated the soldiers to support the activists in India by joining the Legion. The propaganda is clearly devious but is, regrettably, not entirely ineffective.'

'A combination of military and propaganda offensive, clearly.'

'Yes, sir.'

'But you don't seem to have lost too many men to desertions. Why is your fighting capacity so reduced, then?'

'It's not just about straightforward desertions, sir. The majority still fights as professionals. A few cross over each night under cover of darkness, but those numbers are not massive. The greater issue with discipline has been the unwillingness of men to fight to the end against the Legion's forces; there is a tendency to give up their positions and arms rapidly when faced with a severe assault.'

'Are these new units?'

'Surprisingly, no, General. This is true even of troops that have displayed great fighting power against German-only units in the past. The rumour is that some of these "surrenders" are staged or pre-decided by men on either side of the battle line – men who have earlier served together. So these troops can be "captured" in active battle, rather than be seen as deserters, which is against the "izzat" or the prestige of the infantryman.'

Wilson fiddled with a pencil as he evaluated the implications of what he was hearing.

'This brings deployment issues. What is lost is lost, but this will impact how we allocate resources tomorrow as well.'

'Yes, General. The officers are on edge. The impact of the desertions and surrenders can be seen in the reluctance of many officers to use predominantly Indian units on the front line when they are up against the Indian Legion.'

'And Indian units make up what percentage of our total infantry in your command area?'

'About three-fourths of our total strength, sir.'

The General did not respond.

After a minute of awkward silence, Hardinge decided to continue.

'What is not in the report, sir, and what General Quinan wanted me to state to you in person, is that, frankly, we can no longer function as an effective fighting force in this region. The loyalty of a significant proportion of the Indian forces is suspect in the present circumstances. We think it would be advisable to have them board a ship and sail back to Karachi, rather than to keep them on the front line and possibly lose them to the enemy, along with arms and equipment. The British resources in the region are simply too few and cannot put up a credible front without the Indian units.'

'But where do we fall back to? What is the holding line? The Iran–Afghan border?'

'Falling back is also proving difficult as rebel forces in both Iran and Iraq have been extremely active, General. Communication and transport have been badly hit. Afghanistan may be no better. Intel strongly suggests that the Afghan regime is looking to do what Turkey did and is unlikely to offer military resistance to Axis forces if they reach the Afghan border and head towards India. German intelligence and diplomatic efforts have been extremely active. There is some rumour of Germany guaranteeing the Afghans protection against any Russian or British military aggression for a thirty-year period as a quid pro quo for passage via their territory. If our units retreat east towards the Afghan border and look to put up a stand there, we may well be surrounded and disarmed, and end up losing all existing forces.'

'The Russians aren't willing to take the pressure off us? Even briefly?'

The Colonel smirked.

'The Russians don't want to fight the Germans on this front right now, unless the Germans go on the offensive. They are much weakened. I understand they are conserving and rebuilding forces for a possible offensive to retake Stalingrad in the spring. To open a new front just to help us in the defence of India is not really a military priority for Stalin.'

'What is General Quinan proposing, then?'

'Under the circumstances, General, with your approval, we intend to withdraw as many units as possible to the port of Bandar Abbas, while we still hold it, and thereafter have them proceed via sea to Karachi for refitting and subsequent deployment in the defence of the Indo–Afghan border, where this battle will finally be fought – and, hopefully, this campaign will be held and pushed back. We request you to organize naval support.'

The commander-in-chief of the Persia and Gulf Command looked at the map on his desk wistfully.

Ever since this offensive had started, British forces had moved east and then just kept moving east while this German–Indian force had pushed ahead – Egypt, Syria, Iraq, Iran. If he agreed to these proposals and evacuated the remaining troops standing between India and the Axis, defending what little territory they held to the west of Afghanistan, there would, effectively, be no Persia and Gulf Command left for him to oversee.

But once you could not absolutely, blindly rely on the Indian soldier's willingness to fight for the Crown, did you really even have an army anymore in this region?

He nodded his consent to Hardinge.

❖

Command Centre, Peshawar
18 November 1942

'But that phase, General,' Subhas continued as Balotta listened. 'It was an all-out propaganda war. A war we won. To convince my countrymen not to die for safekeeping England's oil in Iraq, but to instead march to India and set it free, *if* that choice was even available – was not that difficult. They barely had any English officers to stop or threaten them. Over 10,000 men deserted and joined the Legion. We did not immediately throw them back into action, of course, and sent them to a small retraining camp at the Iran–Afghan border instead. The local population either stayed neutral or supported the Axis – they were quite angry with the British, generally. The Iraqi and Iranian Armies, happy to see anyone beating the British, willingly helped the Axis search for fleeing Allied units and safeguarded our supply routes. As a result, Rommel, with the Legion, practically had a free pass from Egypt to India, compared to the tough fighting in Libya and Egypt. So when I hold a view as to which units should be deployed if the Indian Legion's cooperation is needed, I cannot be entirely ignored today.'

Did he sound smug? He had reason to be.

'There is more psychology to be understood here. Even where the English troops deployed for the defence of India are concerned, Rommel's record against the British in North

Africa and through the Middle East now makes him appear as this unstoppable force heading east,' Subhas continued. 'The British soldier has come to see him as unbeatable – and the psychological value of that itself is worth five extra divisions. When it is Rommel, the likelihood of the British soldier surrendering rather than fighting to the death is higher, since in his mind, there is no disgrace in losing to such an acclaimed General, and you are not mistreated once in captivity.'

'It is a matter of pride to hear of him being spoken of in this way, Herr Bose,' Westphal beamed.

'I am hardly the only one who speaks of him this way!' Bose broke into a smile. 'Pompous Churchill himself referred to him as a "great General" in the House of Commons! Think of that – it takes a lot to get *that* man to talk respectfully of anyone, let alone a German officer!'

'What Churchill says of *you* is not as elegant, sir!' Dhillon quipped, the atmosphere almost cheerful. Was it absurd to have small talk even as bullets were flying at India's borders? If it was, Bose did not let it unsettle him. His ability to switch off everything and retreat into his mind had stayed with him since his teen years.

'That's all right. Compliments or insults, there is still one thing common to British assessment of both the Field Marshal and me – standing orders to the SOE to kill us, wherever and whenever they can.'

'Ah, that shared distinction is a matter of prestige indeed!' the general laughed aloud.

'Pardon me for having gone on and on about Rommel, General, but that does not mean this is about the Wehrmacht's glory alone. I have not been locked indoors at Streissand Avenue for the whole of 1942, have I? I know what is happening. The Italians have treated Indian prisoners of war with no malice whatsoever in North Africa. That was an important factor in convincing them to fight alongside the Axis. I must give you credit for this; once the fighting is over, the Italians don't usually carry forward individual hatred or collective prejudice. That's something we all could learn from them.'

Balotta beamed.

'Oh, and did you know, General, there are some 90,000 Italian prisoners in camps across India? I have some thoughts on that which I have sent to the Duce. If I get a positive revert to my note, I will discuss this in greater detail with you, shortly.'

'Ninety thousand? That many?' Balotta was surprised.

'Yes, a very large number of the POWs of the Tenth Army from the 1941 campaign were shipped off here, supposedly "away from the action". I don't think the Allies expected to have the war come to India's borders. But here we are!' Subhas smiled again.

Getting up, he turned to Dhillon.

'And to come back to your original question, my friend. My primary task was not to pick up a gun and guide men in battle. I am not physically the fittest man in the country and I am not a soldier, though I can fire a decent shot with my Beretta by now, after all the time at the shooting range. What I have played so far is essentially and primarily a political role – but that is worth many guns. That is my role today as well. I will wait till the time comes for me to do more.'

❖

The Guardian's India correspondent
19 November
New Delhi

The Viceroy, Lord Linlithgow, today issued an appeal to the British Indian Army to not be influenced by the false and misleading reports being broadcast on the so-called 'Azad Hind Radio' and by the pamphlets being dropped by the Fascist forces over battle zones.

'The enemy, having realized that he cannot win a military victory in the face of our determined resistance, is resorting to a misleading, mischievous, and devious campaign of misinformation aimed at demoralising the brave Indian soldiers who have steadfastly stayed loyal to the Crown and held back the forces of evil threatening their motherland,' he said in a statement addressed to all combat troops.

This came in the backdrop of recurrent radio broadcasts in Hindi, Urdu and several Indian languages appealing to native soldiers to lay down their arms or to defect to the so-called 'Indian Legion' led by discredited former Congress leader, Subhas Bose. The Viceroy expressed satisfaction that these had only a limited impact and the great majority of Indian soldiers were unaffected by such appeals aimed at subverting the oath of loyalty to the Crown sworn by them.

'What else can we expect from the lackeys of Hitler, who have, under the tutelage of Goebbels, mastered the art of misinformation?' Lord Linlithgow asked, expressing his belief that such efforts to breed disaffection in the Crown's troops would inevitably fail, and that the native soldiers would continue to be the sheet anchor of the British regime as they have been for decades.

Ends

6

Berlin Blues, Part I: The Restless Mazzotta

'The Indian world has already been so disturbed by the presence of the Japanese on its frontiers, and by the fall of Singapore, that the man of compromise, Nehru, has been eclipsed by Bose.'

– Adolf Hitler, March 1942

'The collapse of Russia will have a weakening of England in its wake. We would be a threat to India then. If necessary, we form with Mr Bose an Indian self-government, which we have avoided so far as we did not want to prevent England making a conciliatory move.'

– Ernst von Weizsäcker, note dated 31 September 1941

Ten Months Earlier

Zentrale Freis Indien (Free India Centre)
Berlin
1 January 1942

THE STREETS STILL BORE TELL-TALE SIGNS OF A NIGHT OF REVELRY, even if subdued. Berlin had stayed up late to welcome 1942, unfazed by the bitter cold. There were, of course, those who did not look forward to the year, to one more year of war, but they had prudently kept it to themselves. Even after Germany turned east to attack Russia in 1941, most Berliners, insulated by distance and filtered communication, had expected the war to be over by Christmas. But 1941 had ended, and it was clear that reports of Russia's imminent collapse, much like reports of Mark Twain's death, had been somewhat exaggerated.

Those who briskly walked past the austere exteriors of 2A, Lichtenstein Allee, on the first morning of 1942, had no reason to give it a second look. There was nothing to distinguish the building from a dozen similar ones along the street. There were two Wehrmacht guards at the gate, but then every other building in the city seemed to have sentries. The guards themselves seemed relaxed, their Schmeisser MP 40s casually thrown over their shoulders as they exchanged notes with the drivers of the two official-looking Mercedes wagons parked inside the gate, their polished hoods glistening under the sun when it occasionally broke through the grey sky. The occupant of 2A had visitors. Given that they were here at 9.30 on the morning of the first of January, it was probable that they were not the sort who would have stayed up late to celebrate the previous night.

Few knew whose office 2A was. Fewer still knew the nature of his business, though a small board would have answered a curious passer-by's query by declaring that it was the Free India Centre. The board had come up quietly in November, as if wanting to acknowledge the existence of the Zentrale Freis Indien, but uncertain whether it wanted it to be widely known.

To the guards, the primary occupant was a bespectacled Oriental gentleman by the rather un-Oriental name of Signor Orlando Mazzotta. If they wondered what an Italian-sounding gentleman was doing serving as the boss man of an Indian centre, they did not bother to ask it. Stranger things had happened in wartime Berlin.

But Orlando Mazzotta of the Free India Centre was an anachronism, since neither existed. Orlando was a fiction of the past, while Free India was a vision for the future.

All this philosophy was very far from the minds of the Berliners traversing Lichtenstein Allee. And India was very far from Germany, as 1942 began – even relative to Germany's easternmost advances in Soviet Russia and North Africa.

Few Germans had ever seen India. The most frequent reference to it for them probably was when the Führer spoke of Russia as 'Germany's India' – a comparison that had often infuriated the Indians at the Centre. But since they could not attempt to battle the English without Germany's support, they had kept quiet. Even if Max Müller wrote with reverence about Ramakrishna Paramhansa, even if the original Swastika was inherently Indian, it meant little to the German citizens outside the dark wooden gates.

Inside those gates, a small group of men were discussing issues that affected the fate of distant India, this morning.

If people could see within, they would have seen the mysterious Mazzotta in a room with four men, two of whom were in uniform. One of the uniforms was familiar, that of a Wehrmacht *Hauptmann* – a captain. The other liveried individual was not German. With distinctively Oriental features, it was that man who, at this moment, was being addressed by Mazzotta.

'I am so glad you could make it here, Major Fujiwara. I need to take a decision on whether I should stay on in Germany or move my headquarters to Southeast Asia. If Germany is unwilling to take a clear position, I cannot sit here and wait any longer.'

Subhas Chandra Bose – the man still carrying the passport issued in the name of Orlando Mazzotta, which had been handed to him by the Italian ambassador to Kabul in March

1941 – turned around and gazed out of the large French window at the gloomy Berlin sky. Those who worked closely with him were used to these moments when he seemed to forget about the presence of others around him. Hands clasped behind his back, he paused for a moment to look at the smartly turned-out sentries, their brilliantly polished boots catching his eye, even from a distance.

The allocation of the Centre, which was described as a 'diplomatic accommodation' in the paperwork of the Foreign Ministry, had caused much heartburn. What sort of a diplomat was Bose, and what nation did he represent? Also, what was his relationship with Emilie Schenkl, who had an office of her own within the Centre? These questions were asked by many, but not loudly. Despite being a foreign national supposedly looking for the host nation's support, Subhas was known to not take snubs lightly.

Major Fujiwara Iwaichi of the Japanese Imperial Army, a man who had invested much time and energy in building contacts with the Indian community in Southeast Asia over the past few months, had made a lengthy and dangerous journey to Berlin upon Bose's request.

As the chief of intelligence of the Japanese Fifteenth Army, and as the man running the 'Fujiwara Kikan', the military intelligence operation set up by the Imperial General Headquarters to liaise with the Indians, Chinese and Malays in Southeast Asia, it was his responsibility to understand how the independence movements in Asia were unfolding – and, more importantly, the relationships Japan could look forward to forming with them.

Right now, as 1942 was commencing, it was anything but clear. There were many claimants to Indian leadership, not just in Asia but in Europe as well. Fujiwara himself had been talking to Pritam Singh and Mohan Singh in Malaya, and had built a good rapport with former Indian POWs. The Italians had been setting up small units made up of converted Indian POWs with Iqbal Shedai's advice in Rome; however, by the end of 1941, Bose was building a full-fledged Indian Legion that was presently undergoing training in Annaburg – that seemed to be the one project which could fall into place the quickest.

Even so, the efforts in Europe and in Asia were rarely coordinated.

For all the talk of the Axis being a 'pact of steel', the communication between Germans and the Japanese was horribly fickle. Bizarre as it was, Germany had given Japan no information about invading Russia and, in turn, had been given no information about Japan's attack on Pearl Harbour, barely three weeks back. Both were potentially world-changing events. But then, that was the tradition of the Axis: Italy had launched its Greek misadventure without informing either Germany or Japan.

Reconciled to the absence of coordination or even communication, Fujiwara – a man who had invested a huge amount of energy and time in understanding India's issues and sensitivities – had, therefore, pragmatically accepted Bose's invite to Berlin. So here he was, at the end of a long and taxing journey.

'You are too hard on us Germans, Herr Mazzotta!' chuckled von Trott, sipping his black coffee.

Trott, director of the Sonderreferat Indien – the Special Bureau for India – reported to Keppler, the Secretary of State at the Foreign Office. Keppler, in turn, reported to Ribbentrop.

Ribbentrop was the sole Nazi to have displayed enthusiasm for Bose's suggestions from the day he had landed in Germany – a combination of political propaganda and trained, armed, uniformed Indians marching into India, supported by the Axis, to bring down the Union Jack.

'Am I?' Subhas smiled.

'Yes. There are people who have not yet forgotten what you said after your visit in 1936. I do not think many people in Germany still get state accommodation in Berlin after expressing such views in public. Some do get accommodation, of course, but the host is more often the Gestapo!' he laughed bitterly.

'It is *because* I write things "like that", why, you can say things "like that" in my office, Herr Trott, is it not?' Subhas smiled, equally dryly.

The unsaid was not lost on Trott.

If Subhas knew of Trott's sympathies for the anti-Nazi officers in the Wehrmacht, or of the convenient cover that his role as 'principal coordinator' with Subhas gave him to travel to locations that would have otherwise raised the Gestapo's eyebrows, he kept it to himself. But then, Bose kept so much to himself that only a simpleton would assume that if he did not speak of an issue, it meant that he did not know of it.

'What *has* he been saying?' Fujiwara turned to Trott.

Subhas himself was fluent in German by now, but for Fujiwara's sake, everyone was speaking in English. If anyone in the room was struck by the irony of the language of the common enemy being the only one they all shared, they did not bring it up.

'Just some – what should I say – unflattering things, Major. Some views that I hope you do not share. About the "new nationalism" of Germany being "narrow and arrogant", and things like that, which I am sure Mazzotta's friend Herr Ribbentrop will not take too kindly to him repeating.' Trott was in a jocular mood.

'Ribbentrop is my friend?'

'You *should* count him as your friend, Mazzotta! You don't

have too many. And that is because you are a hard man to please. You are not happy with what Gandhi does in India. You are not happy with what the Führer says in Germany. You are not satisfied with what Churchill offers to your country. You are not satisfied with the pace of how quickly Japan advances to India's east. You are not happy with the speed at which work is proceeding on the Legion, nor with the numbers. You are always dissatisfied!'

The room collectively broke into a soft laugh. Subhas did not mind. It was essentially true.

'That's all right. It has been nine months since I reached Berlin, and all I have done is have the world change while I watch as a bystander. Now 1942 has started and all that I see in the name of communication from the German establishment is a handful of "Happy New Year" greetings. I did not come here for accommodation and meals. I need a concrete plan of action. I think I have good reason to be dissatisfied.'

Dr Alexander Werth, Trott's colleague, and one of the few Germans in Berlin to be openly sympathetic towards Subhas, joined in.

'The Italian ambassador in Kabul has described you as the "only pragmatist amongst India's leadership". But sometimes, you run out of that pragmatism and also patience. The party here has no love lost for you. The Foreign Office is the *only* entity in Germany that actually believes in you. The OKH is ambivalent. It has gone along with the Foreign Office so far, but it will support you in the long run only if it feels there is a military consequence of all your talk. And, militarily, German forces are very far from India as of today. So are the Japanese, for that matter.'

Trott took Werth's cue as Subhas played around with the cap of his antique fountain pen, an indulgence from his last visit to Rome.

Rome! Rome would have been better than Berlin, perhaps. The Duce was an easier man to work with than the elusive Führer. If only he had the troops to match! And if only his officials were not wasting their time competing with the Germans on the 'Muslim Indians' project of Jinnah-supporter Iqbal Shedai, stealing away Indian POWs who should have been sent to Germany. POWs who could have been part of the Indian Legion.

'Werth has a point, my friend. Has nothing been done? It is Ribbentrop who has got us over a million Reichsmarks to set up the daily broadcasts to India. It was just two months back, in November, that the Zentrale Freis Indien started, and you already have the status of a diplomatic mission. The Sonderreferat Indien has been working for most of 1941. We, with the support of Herr Keppler and Herr Ribbentrop, of course, have not been sitting idle either. The year 1942 may bring you disenchantment as it arrives, but you are being overly cynical if you assert that nothing has happened since March 1941 when you first landed in Berlin, Signor Mazotta!'

Subhas turned to him and threw up his arms, exasperated.

'No more "Mazzotta", please? Everyone who matters in Berlin seems to know who I am. If we are to broadcast over the radio to India, I can hardly announce myself to my countrymen as Mazzotta. I will have to tell them, and you will have to tell the world, that I am in Berlin. The British know I am here, unless you missed the *Daily Mail*'s "India's Quisling No. 1 flees to Hitler" headline. The Italians have always known I am here. The Russians know too, that much is obvious – I came via Moscow, when you had not yet gone to war with them. So who are you keeping my presence a secret from? The cloak-and-dagger business is irritating. I itch for action. Instead, all I seem to do is write notes and hold meetings.'

'Come with me to Malaya, there is action there. We are

marching to Singapore!' laughed Fujiwara. 'And now that we are at war with the Americans as well, there will be no shortage of action there for the rest of the year, I assure you.'

'I may well take you up on that offer, Major,' Subhas replied warmly, 'since nothing is happening in Berlin that brings me any hope. Herr Hitler met the Japanese ambassador, General Oshima, last week. I am informed that it was General Oshima who asked for the meeting – to urgently request Germany for proactive action and understand if Germany plans to do anything at all regarding India. It is possible that Japanese soldiers will be in control of all of Malaya by the end of this month. Who knows, they may even reach Burma after that! Japan has asked Herr Hitler what Germany would do if the Japanese overrun Singapore. But I understand that Hitler – as so often in these matters – has not committed to anything.'

'The Führer thinks over military options deeply before taking a final decision. He has planned some of the most spectacular military victories in the past two years,' Werth intervened, lest he be accused of agreeing with an anti-Führer remark.

'Is that the real reason here?'

'What reason are you suggesting?'

'Well, there are days I feel he hopes that the European will not be whipped by the "Oriental" – no offence, Major. General Oshima has been told that any German advance beyond the Caucasus, into Iraq and Persia, is something the Führer will consider later, depending on how the war against Russia proceeds. We can't predict how Germany's war against Russia will go, but the Japanese are certainly moving ahead in Asia quicker than the Germans in Russia. So one has to wonder where India's opportunity lies.'

Subhas was in Congress President mode now. Had an audience been present, he could have probably given an impromptu speech on the necessity of seizing decisive moments in history.

'None taken. The "Oriental" is indeed surprising many across the world right now. Send Mr Bose back with me, Mr von Trott, I will take him to his Bengal once Burma is in Japanese hands. Soon!' Fujiwara clapped Trott's back and chuckled.

If Fujiwara had thought this would appeal to Subhas, he was proven wrong immediately.

'Why is everyone so keen on sending me to Bengal from the Burma border? Is it based on my local popularity in Bengal? Am I fighting here for a free Bengal or for a free India? Do you think only the Bengalis will rise up for me?' Subhas fumed, his notorious temper briefly on display, without the filters of diplomatic protocol. 'Have I spent years trying to make sense of India's place in this war only to have to appeal to such sentiments? The fixation with language and religion and caste loyalties have done too much damage to my country already. Indians have listened to me here, and I trust they will listen to me in Peshawar, Quetta, Amritsar, Delhi, Bombay, Madras, equally. Not just in Calcutta. I cannot enter India branded just as a Bengali leader! No. Ideally, it is from the west that I should go to India.'

An awkward silence ensued.

Captain Walter Harbich, so far a silent observer, cleared his throat.

Assigned by the OKH to liaise with Bose, Harbich was now familiar with his charge being almost permanently on simmer mode for some months. An unusually silent man, perhaps more suited for the clandestine world of the Abwehr, the German military intelligence service, than for the jackboots of the Wehrmacht, his expression was that of a bemused, indulgent parent watching his children spar with toy swords.

He stepped up to the massive map on the study's wall.

'To reiterate what has been the considered view of both the OKH and the Foreign Ministry, from what I know, definite plans for India can only be drawn up on this map when – and if – German troops have crossed the Caucasus and taken the Suez. As of today, that depends on many things that are not in your, or my, control, Herr Bose. If we do seize control of the Caucasus and the Suez in a few months' time, your troops will come into play. I suggest you use that time to sharpen your sword, work with the men. You don't want to have that opportunity and then see your men defect back to the British Army at the first point of contact.'

Despite Subhas's raised eyebrows at the last remark, Harbich remained unfazed, his manicured hands moving generally in the stretch between the Suez and the Indus.

'However unpleasant it may sound, if the Wehrmacht does advance in that direction, the first priority for Germany may be the oil of the Caucasus and of Iraq and Persia; oil that will sustain the forces of the Reich for the next few years, more so if we have to move further east. If we have these territories, building and protecting oil infrastructure will be the priority. The forces will probably look to pause for a while, consolidating gains, since battles in that region will not be very easy. India will come in as a priority only after that, when your proposed Legion may enter serious combat.'

Harbich was not entirely accurate, though. Much before the invasion of Russia, even before Subhas had reached Berlin in 1941, Hitler had been plotting what his troops would do after defeating the Soviets. He had instructed the operations staff of the OKH to present a plan for an invasion of India. General Franz Halder, the Chief of Staff, had done as instructed and come back with a report that a total of seventeen divisions – armoured, motorized, infantry and mountain – would be required to reach and attack Afghanistan as a preliminary to an Indian offensive. But this was not something the secretive OKH was comfortable discussing with Mazzotta/Bose. And the Russian campaign was chewing up divisions at an unexpected rate.

'But I do not ask that Germany spill her blood to liberate my people! All I ask is that Germany help me seize the moment. It is romanticism of the most bizarre kind for anyone in India or elsewhere to expect that the English will walk out of their prized possession because we go on fasts or decline to wear English suits. *Indian* blood will have to be spilled and *Indian* loyalties to the Crown will have to be challenged, for, finally, they rule us through us,' his voice rose a level. 'Villagers not paying tax on salt will not bring down Churchill if Herr Hitler's bombers rampaging over the London sky have not yet managed to do so. No, we will have to engage with the British soldier's guns and the Indian soldier's conscience when we step on Indian soil. And for that, the Legion will have to bleed.'

He paused – to gather his thoughts or to emphasize his point, who knew?

'There is no easy way to do this. I do not ask that the Wehrmacht deliver Delhi to me, neither do I have the patience to wait years for the situation to stabilize in the Middle East. I will be more than happy to take the Legion beyond the springboard that I am given in Persia, Captain. A total of 50,000, perhaps 60,000 Indian men, with nominal German or Italian support, I believe, will be enough to break through the fort's gates,' he glared through his spectacles, as if challenging Harbich to counter him.

Stepping up to the map, Subhas continued. 'Have you not studied the composition of the Allied forces in the region? Egypt, Iraq, Persia – the majority of Allied soldiers everywhere in that region are Indians. They may fight to the death against Germans – but what if the vanguard of the army advancing from the west is also Indian? What if *that* army shows to them that other realities exist, gives them a greater reason to fight a better war, makes them question their loyalty to British paymasters? From Persia, if I have the ammunition and the oil, I do not need too many of your men – maybe 15–20,000 specialists in logistics, artillery and armour, and special operations. And basic air support. The Wehrmacht understands the art of war better than anyone else today – I cannot question or underrate that. But the great majority of the infantry on the ground, shedding its blood to move ahead, will be Indian.'

'This route,' his fingers jabbed at the Khyber, 'has, for centuries, been a nightmare for India. An army marching down the Khyber has meant destruction for Delhi. For once, there will be an army that will march down from the Khyber to *liberate* Delhi, not to obliterate it.' His fingers wistfully traced a route down the map that ended at the capital of British India.

Harbich did not rise to the bait and nodded slowly as he evaluated the rationality of Subhas's argument. 'Let me organize a meeting with Herr Ribbentrop and General Halder. You can make this point yourself.'

❖

In the complex and conflicting power structure that Hitler had built, different wings of the system working at cross-purposes were more often the rule than the exception. For Subhas, though, it had worked so far. Though the Nazi Party remained coolly indifferent to his presence or plans, Ribbentrop's Foreign Office was an enthusiastic supporter of his vision. It was, therefore, the primary official support system for all his activities. The army High Command – the OKH – had gradually warmed up to his ideas as they acquired the shape of an armed, trained body of soldiers willing to fight against the British.

Even though the OKH did not endorse Subhas Bose's plans to the degree that Ribbentrop did, both wings distrusted each other enough to try to ensure that the other did not become the sole custodian of the maverick Indian leader and his upcoming Legion. Having done the groundwork to get Bose to Berlin and then setting up his radio broadcasts, then establishing the Sonderreferat Indien as well as the Zentrale Freis Indien, Ribbentrop did not want to see the OKH steal credit by presenting a military plan for India in conjunction with Bose.

That competitive collaboration was also how things worked between the Germans and the Japanese. And between the Germans and the Italians. Subhas was working simultaneously with the Germans, the Italians, and the Japanese.

It was, he often thought, worse than handling the theatre in the Congress after winning the Tripuri election.

7

Revenge and Restraint

20 November 1942

MAJOR DHILLON'S EXPRESSION CONVEYED WHAT HE WANTED TO say well before he said it.

'This is bad news, sir.'

Subhas looked up at him quizzically, tearing his eyes away from the day's military summary. Preambles always irked him and he was not in his mellowest state of mind currently.

'So give it.'

'The bodies of some Indian Legion soldiers who had been ambushed have been recovered from a building the British have withdrawn from, sir.'

'I regret that, Major, but surely we have entered battle being mentally prepared for casualties?'

'They were not casualties of combat, sir. They were executed.'

Subhas stood up, abruptly, heading for the door. 'Walk with me. Give me the details!'

'A badly injured British soldier was left behind when the rest evacuated the building. In another part of it, we found our men lined up from one wall to another, all shot identically. The prisoner we took was afraid he'd be killed in retaliation, so he was quick to speak. Apparently, these prisoners had been ambushed and kept there under guard. They were to be taken to a POW holding area. But the unit's English CO happened to come by and, upon seeing who the prisoners were, went hopping mad. He screamed that the captured Indian Legion soldiers, no matter what uniforms they wear, were to be treated not as Wehrmacht POWs but as deserters of the British Indian Army and, therefore, were to be given the punishment due for desertion during war. Despite protests from the Indian NCOs there, he had them assembled in a line and shot by a firing squad, sir!'

'How many men?' Subhas's face tightened into a grimace.

'At least fourteen bodies in that building itself.'

'Is this a one-off officer gone mad in the heat of battle, or are there more such instances?'

'This is the first time we have received information of someone actually carrying this out, sir, but our intelligence suggests that many British officers share that point of view. I fear this may encourage others to do the same.'

'Right.'

Stepping out of the complex, Subhas asked for his vehicle and escorts to assemble. As he waited, he indicated to the major to take notes on what he was going to say next.

'First, we must send a message over the wireless, in the clear, to the commanding British General of that jurisdiction. Make it clear that we consider this as a war crime and we will place the concerned officer, when he is in our custody – assuming he survives the battle until then – on trial. If found guilty, he will be sentenced by a Military Tribunal appropriately.

'Two, we must instruct all our units *not* to retaliate in kind. Any prisoners – British or Indian – must be treated as per the rules of warfare. Even if the men who carried out this execution, or the officer who ordered it, are taken captive, they must be kept in custody, not subjected to jungle law or mob justice.'

Dhillon paused for a moment, measuring his words, before responding.

'I am not sure how well that will be received by the troops, sir ... They kill our men in captivity, and we treat them as per the Geneva Convention? Imagine if this had happened on the Russian front – we know the Germans would have taken no prisoners for a fortnight!'

'I am not interested in military leadership by populism, Major. I may not have graduated from a military academy but I do have some sense of military structure. We have not come here to participate in competitive barbarism.'

'But, sir—'

'I'm sorry, Major,' Subhas raised a hand to stop him. 'I am as furious as you are. But the entire country is watching how this battle unfolds, every Indian soldier fighting for the Union Jack is watching, and everyone is trying to get a sense of what this Indian–German–Italian–Japanese force is about. Enough has already happened at the hands of the Germans in Russia and the Japanese in China. This is the Legion, not the SS. And this is an army that will have to carry out my instructions simply because it is predominantly Indian – except when I voluntarily abdicate intervention. You will, therefore, ensure my orders are carried out, and inform our allies that I have issued them, and that they are applicable to *everyone* in the Indian Legion.'

There was the slightest hint of cynicism in Dhillon's expression. It lasted but a moment, but it didn't go away quickly enough for Bose's bespectacled eyes to miss it. The Legion's commander paused for a moment, weighing something in his mind, and then added a line to his list of instructions.

'Also, Major, if these instructions are breached, I will *then* do as the Germans do – I will have the first man to disobey a direct order from me in wartime, be it soldier or officer, shot by firing squad. Dismissed.'

This time, Major Dhillon's expression did not betray what he was thinking. A salute snapped, heels clicked, and he was gone.

❖

To: Keitel, Field Marshal, Chief of Staff
From: Rommel, Field Marshal
22 November 1942

Subject: Developments in the Progress of Operation Tiger

I am glad to report to the OKH and the Führer that the situation on the ground has been developing satisfactorily, considering the circumstances and restrictions under which operations are being handled.

The Fifty-first, Sixth, Fifth and Twenty-second Regiments of the Indian Legion, the 516th Artillery Division of the Afrika Korps and the Italian 185th Parachute Division Folgore and 132nd Division Ariete have been the primary spearheads of the offensive across the Jalalabad, Khost and Chaman sectors.

The political decision to not use massed air power on the enemy since the units are composed of a mixture of Indian and British troops, as well as the terrain that is in many areas hostile to the use of tanks, has necessitated that infantry action with close artillery support stays the primary military option available to us, at least till such time we break through to the plains of Punjab.

The concentration of infantry deployed by the enemy is presently a mixture of units with a high percentage of English soldiers and of native Indian regiments that are classified as 'martial', particularly the Gorkha, Baloch and Sikh regiments. They have displayed resilient defensive abilities so far and forward progress is in the range of 200–500 metres a day; a push for quicker advances would make it necessary to accept higher troop casualties. The model of the ground battle has been similar to campaigns in the hills of Yugoslavia and Greece, but the limited use of heavy air support has meant that the advance has not been as swift or decisive as the Balkans campaign.

The summary of casualties so far, after one week of a battle of steady attrition, is as follows:

- *Wehrmacht: killed 72, injured 110, missing 13.*
- *Italian parachute division: killed 64, injured 118, missing 36.*
- *Indian Legion: killed 442, injured 1,643, missing 148.*

The casualties on the enemy's side are estimated to be 1,200 killed and 2,000 injured. So far there have been 367 POWs taken into Axis custody, of whom eighty-six are British. There have also been defections on both sides. However, that is not a cause of concern for the Indian Legion yet, as 103 Indian men from the enemy's side have crossed over to join Bose's troops, while only twelve men from the Legion are believed to have crossed over to the enemy.

The local population has so far largely stayed at a distance and has neither actively assisted nor hampered the Axis war effort. We have suffered some casualties on account of explosives planted along troop convoys, which we believe to be the work of local agents of the SAS. Investigations are underway. However, no reprisals on the civilian population have been ordered in any instance. Local commanders attempting to initiate action against civilians as a retaliatory measure have been disciplined.

Troop morale is high, especially in the Indian Legion. The Legion frequently uses Indian music in the camps as an integral part of keeping up morale and motivation levels and it is also played over loudspeakers to the Indian units on the British side. Herr Bose has expressed his desire to address enemy troops to urge them to cross over, but he has so far been kept at some distance since Abwehr reports indicate the presence of British snipers and SAS agents on the front line assigned to take him out.

8

Berlin Blues, Part 2: Uneasy Allies

'If Singapore is lost, India becomes the centre of the war, one might say, the centre of the world.'

– Orwell, 'Talking to India', BBC India Service, February 1942

'The British are fully aware of the great danger that is threatening them in Egypt. They fear that the German–Italian forces may establish contact with the Japanese.'

– Hitler–Raeder Naval Conference, February 1942

Abwehr Headquarters
Tirpitzufer, Berlin
27 January 1942

THE BUILDING AT TIRPITZUFER HAD THAT CURIOUS MIXTURE OF anonymity that intelligence organizations seek and the fear that they generate. A faceless, dull grey structure, it was clearly not one of the flamboyant projects that Albert Speer was creating in Berlin. But then the Abwehr, the Reich's Military Intelligence wing, wasn't a Nazi-created entity and had so far escaped, much to the relief of its chief, Admiral Wilhelf Franz Canaris, the detailed attention of the most powerful.

By 1942, however, there was enough to differentiate the Abwehr from organizations such as the SD (the political police) and the Gestapo. Canaris, the Abwehr's boss since 1935, had quietly become the last umbrella that still had the ability to shelter a professional military or intelligence man who did not want to sign up for the party's peculiar worldview. If you weren't a committed Nazi but didn't want to be sidelined, at best, or land up in one of the camps in Poland they furtively spoke about, at worst, you tried to find sanctuary in Uncle Will's camp. He knew too much about too many people for even the most feared and powerful names in the regime such as Heinrich Himmler or Reinhard Heydrich to dislodge him, despite their barely hidden discomfort with his autonomous empire.

At least not yet. Not while the war was still on.

Colonel Erwin Lahousen, a man who had found sanctuary in Canaris' empire and was grateful for it, looked at his watch and waited for his guests to turn up at his austere but expansive office. Portraits of Hitler and Canaris stared at him from the wall behind his desk. There were days when he felt as if they were assessing how effectively he walked the tightrope between them.

The door opened. Lt Gen. Hiroshi Oshima, the Japanese ambassador to Germany, strode in purposefully, followed by Colonel Yamamoto Bin and Major Fujiwara. Salutes were exchanged. A moment later, Subhas Bose entered, accompanied by A. C. N. Nambiar, his trusted confidant and deputy at the Free India Centre. Werth, von Trott and Harbich were already present and waiting in the dimly lit conference room, along with other officers Subhas was not familiar with. It was cold.

Despite his packed schedule, Ribbentrop had met Subhas in the earlier week. The foreign minister did not want to lose this wildcard to the Japanese, who were advancing every fortnight now, slicing through East Asia as if they faced no opposition.

Meanwhile, Subhas was increasingly growing impatient. He wanted all available Indian POWs to be made accessible to him – which meant stopping the dual training being done by the Germans and Italians, thereby, splitting the men willing to join the cause. He could wait no further and was insisting that training start immediately in Germany, for all those who were willing to join this Legion to march to India. And, in characteristic Subhas reflex, he wanted all Axis powers to acknowledge that his word would be the final one in their deployment and command.

For the first, Ribbentrop had to speak to the Italians, since many POWs from the North Africa were in their custody. Nominally, at least, Italy was the senior partner on that front, even though Rommel, the German general dispatched there, did not seem to register that fact. For the second, he had to get the OKH on board. This was why the meeting had representatives from both the Axis formations operating in North Africa, Brigadier Ricci from the Italian 132nd Ariete Division and Colonel Prittwitz from the Twenty-first Panzer Division.

Japan had been at war for less than two months and it was already making the blitzkreig on France and Belgium look like a plodding effort, as Japanese troops ran through massive chunks of Asia – much like the Wehrmacht had through much of Europe, except that here there was no European master race. The Japanese were tossing aside the colonial armies that had ruled Asia for over a century on the hitherto unquestioned supremacy of the white man's military might.

Oshima's stature in Berlin had grown twofold since December. Subhas, who had been a welcome guest at the embassy on many occasions since October, could barely conceal his glee as Japan competed with Germany – perhaps set to pass it as a power that could knock out the British from their hold over the Indian subcontinent. The German dithering throughout 1941 would have to change, or he would have to tell them Berlin wasn't the only option for him to plan a strategy for India.

Lahousen had convened the meeting at the prodding of the OKH and Ribbentrop, both worried that the increasing Subhas–Japanese bonhomie and the British collapse in Southeast Asia could lead to a situation in which the Reich would no longer be a key player in decisions involving India.

'I believe there was quite a celebration last night at Hotel Kaiserhof?' Lahousen asked Nambiar, breaking the ice.

The Indians in Berlin had observed 26 January 1942 as Independence Day. The date had been observed by the Congress as Independence Day for some years. Four hundred guests had attended, including a cross-section of Berlin high society and German, Italian, French and Japanese diplomats.

'Yes, indeed. It was very well-attended. A day when the Indian flag was flying on the Kaiserhof!' Nambiar exclaimed. 'And truth be told, I could not hold back tears when the German orchestra played "Jana Gana Mana". It felt surreal to see hundreds of Europeans standing to attention for the Indian anthem – even if it is just the anthem that the Free India Centre has adopted.' Nambiar was wistful. 'It was a memorable day. Just that Subhas wasn't present there.'

'Bear with us for a few days more. A formal announcement of his presence in Berlin is imminent, and then we can put "Orlando Mazzotta" to rest, and Subhas can step out publicly,' Lahousen smiled. 'Now, to business: we can start with Herr Bose first, if that is all right with you, Excellency?' Lahousen asked Oshima, who nodded his consent.

Subhas cleared his throat. The German winter was very

different from Kolkata in January. His health was no longer what it used to be after years of imprisonment in squalid conditions. But this was not a day he could have spent resting.

'Your Excellency, I must congratulate the Japanese Imperial Army for what it has accomplished since the first week of December. And I must request the German authorities to recognize the change of mood throughout Asia as news of the Japanese victories spread across the region. As the Japanese advance in the direction of Burma, we should have a specific plan of action to increase the spread of propaganda, especially by radio. To my Japanese friends, I make the submission that, in the meantime, they treat all Indians in the areas they gain control of with respect, and segregate the Indian soldiers captured as British forces surrender, so that Major Fujiwara can assess their willingness to fight for Indian independence.'

He then addressed the Abwehr colonel.

'You, Colonel, I strongly urge to take action on the discussions we have had earlier on Indian and German operatives being dropped by parachute into the tribal territories of the North-West Frontier Province. The myth of British invincibility is disintegrating. You will find greater receptivity today even from those who were earlier wary of engaging with us.'

Nambiar was taking meticulous notes.

Lahousen got up and exchanged glances with Harbich and Trott. He was going to speak for all of them.

'It is easy to speak of planning an advance to India's borders this year, but even if the military situation were to develop in a manner favourable to the Axis, there are three other aspects we must all pay attention to:

'Firstly, as of now, in January 1942, there is no certainty of how long the Russian campaign will extend. The original expectation was that it would conclude in 1941 itself.

'Secondly, the role of the primary point of mobilizing Indian POWs in Europe, is not one that is, or could be taken for granted to be as naturally yours. It could very possibly have gone to Iqbal Shedai. He has been in Europe longer and has enjoyed the trust of the Italians for many years. In view of the influence the Grand Mufti has in Berlin, in view of the importance of Islam in the Near and Middle East, a policy in support of pan-Islamic movements could be an obvious possibility for the Axis – which would make Shedai a far more attractive choice than you. That possibility must not be overlooked by the Axis.

'Thirdly, you are now an expelled leader of the Indian National Congress, and the political organization loyal to you, the Forward Bloc, has limited reach. In a sense, you are playing this game with no cards at all, Herr Bose. Given that, it has not gone too badly so far, has it? So if you ask me, even the December agreement was not inevitable. And I hope you will not mind me saying this, but you would have saved all sides much effort if you tried to find a way to work with Shedai. Perhaps you could try that even now?'

The December agreement that Lahousen was speaking about was the culmination of months of tussle over the Indian prisoners of war in Axis hands, mostly from North Africa.

The Italians and the Germans had met in December 1941 to discuss issues so as to have a more coordinated approach to 'the Indian question'. The Italians finally agreed that the formation of an Indian Legion had to be exclusively in the hands of the German armed forces. Both Axis powers also agreed to not encourage the Muslim League/pro-Jinnah lines politically; the Hindu–Muslim divide was seen as an element that suited the British narrative of a disunited India held together by them.

This had been a major victory for Subhas, since the Italians so far had been relying exclusively on Iqbal Shedai for all matters pertaining to India. The strongly pro-Pakistan Shedai, a former member of the Ghadar party, had been living in Italy since the 1930s. He had, over time, earned the confidence of the Italian Foreign Ministry.

The Italians, at this point in time, were looking to set up a *Battaliogne Azad Hindoustan* with Shedai's assistance – essentially, a duplication of the German–Bose effort to the set up the Legion Freies Indien.

Both looked at the same pool of manpower – Indian POWs – but with very different political ends in sight. The December agreement had finally placed the entire weight of the Axis behind a Bose-led legion to be trained by the Germans.

The decision led to much bitterness, not that it had not existed already. Shedai, a Punjabi, had earlier commented on the questionable military capabilities of the Bengali Bose and had suggested that he was best employed by the Axis to write articles for radio broadcasts. Subhas, on his part, made no secret of the fact that he thought Shedai and his associates had fooled the Italians into believing they were men of importance in the Indian nationalist movement while they were inconsequential, and had not anticipated anyone of stature – that is, Subhas – to actually reach Europe from India to call their bluff.

Shedai and Subhas, therefore, did not part as friends.

Subhas, slightly irked, now turned to Brigadier Ricci.

'Working with the Italian project with Shedai is not an option, and it *will* not be an option,' he said in a tone of finality. 'It is not about cooperation. It is about the basics of the country which has to be built after the British are gone. Shedai's agenda is nothing other than building an army of Indian Muslims. He is *not* supporting the Axis or Indian independence; he is supporting the division of India, the same agenda as Britain. He is living Jinnah's dream in Rome, looking forward to a partitioned, splintered India. His broadcasts are thoroughly communal. I will oppose the idea of partitioning India along the lines of religion till the day I die, and so, Herr Trott, General Ricci, I will also oppose every individual who thinks like Mr Shedai, be a Hindu, Muslim or Sikh, till I have a voice. That is non-negotiable.'

'But is the Muslim League's view not a reality, Herr Bose? Is the Hindu–Muslim issue in India just a creation of the British? Why not accept it and work along with the likes of Shedai? Hindu and Muslim troops can be trained separately, kept in separate units. You then already have two separate armies ready in case India does choose to partition in the future. Aren't soldiers in any case already organized along the lines of their religion and region, or something like that, in the British Indian Army?' Ricci joined in on Lahousen's side.

Subhas took a deep breath that was audible to all.

'Am I qualified to advise you on the organization of Italian troops? I think not.'

He paused for a moment to let what he had left unsaid settle in everyone's mind, then resumed.

'Yes, gentlemen, the communal divide is not just a creation of the British, but it has certainly been fanned by them for decades. When you see the Muslim soldier and the Hindu soldier and the Sikh soldier in the Indian Legion today, you mostly see comradeship. But it is not always spontaneous; I have to work for that. I have seen enough of racial and ethnic prejudice in Europe to know where it leads. Shall we "liberate" an India where Hindus and Muslims have the same relationship as the Serbs and Croats in Europe? I am gathering neither mercenaries nor fanatics. I have to build the core of a new army that will liberate India – and perhaps even *run* India till we are in a position to embrace a more mature model of governance. And the way that army thinks and works has to reflect how we want India to be tomorrow. Please understand: the Legion is not just a military tool. It is a political statement. It has to reflect today what India will be tomorrow!'

Harbich looked quite unconvinced.

'You disagree with Mr Jinnah, but you also disagree with Mr Gandhi. The Congress has expelled you. Yet, you are assuming cheering crowds and waving flags will greet you as your Indian Legion crosses into Indian territory. How do I rule out the possibility that the Congress calls for a campaign of no support to your "Fascist-supported" venture. Where would that leave the campaign, if it ever falls in place, that is?'

Subhas gave him a dismissive look.

'The people of India will, without question, rise to support any group of men who are willing to shed their blood to bring them independence. I do not believe, I *know*. As to the Congress, I will cross that bridge when I get to it. I have already burnt and crossed many bridges there. You must not think that respect for the Mahatma's personality is the same thing as acceptance of all his political views, even within the Congress. The Congress resolution at Bardoli, barely a couple of days back, concluded with a very engaging wordplay: it spoke of "arrogant imperialism" being indistinguishable from "fascist authoritarianism". Nehru's position generally is that the British are morally superior to the evil Germans, but this resolution is not quite taking that line.'

He paused for a moment, then smiled, wickedly.

'Now, don't interpret that to imply anything that it is not – I am not saying that what you have here in Germany is fascist authoritarianism. The Congress is.'

Trott laughed. The Japanese suppressed a smile. Lahousen stayed impassive.

'Get me to the Indian frontier – then you all can leave

it to me. My biggest political fear is of the British coming to a political settlement with the conservatives within the Congress while we spend all our time in memos and meetings. The Congress would then begin to mobilize India's people to actively fight against an approaching Axis army. The more time we waste, the more likely it is for that to happen.'

Trott disagreed.

'As an observer of Indian political affairs, I would want to caution everyone here that these military decisions should not be influenced excessively by the not-so-congenial relationship you have with the leadership of the Congress. If we rush in with a campaign in 1942 itself, we risk heavy losses. Why can't we wait to plan this for 1943?'

'*1943*?' Subhas threw his hands up in a gesture of surprise. 'I'll tell you why we cannot wait. Firstly, you will not be able to get fifty miles into India, from either the east or the west, even with the Indian Legion spearheading the charge, if the Indian soldier in the British Army is loyal to Britain. Not fifty miles! That should be the *one* military fact both the Wehrmacht and the Imperial Japanese Army do not lose sight of. That soldier has stayed loyal to the Crown despite everything the Congress has done in the last twenty years. He is the backbone of British control. If the Congress also asks Indians to support the Allied cause, it will be that much harder for us.

'Secondly, let me remind you what my friend Jawahar said in 1940, not long after the Swastika was hoisted in Paris. "Launching a civil disobedience campaign at a time when Britain is engaged in a life and death struggle would be an act derogatory to India's honour." Defeating Britain would be derogatory to India's honour! And the Mahatma has clearly stated that "we do not seek our independence out of Britain's ruin". He doesn't – but I do.'

He paused for effect.

'I must convey a cause of concern to you. Colonel Lahousen, Captain Habrich, Herr Trott, I request you to communicate this concern to your respective superiors, since our military strategy cannot be worked out if our political thought is not clear. On the one hand, I see some within the Congress getting emotional, even apologetic, about dislodging Britain from India if it seems to cause Britain any distress. When Britain is weak, the Congress is hesitant. When Britain is no longer weak, it will pay no attention to the Congress and will, even if it withdraws, almost certainly split the country.'

'On the other hand, the Führer seems as emotionally upset as the Congress on some days, hearing of British losses in December and January at the hands of an Asian army. The possibility of a German–British détente always hangs in the air. Am I the *only* man who is interested in a comprehensive British defeat on the subcontinent? Is this how war is waged? Let us decide if we are looking at war – or merely at posturing. If it is the latter, I have no use for it, and should then gladly head to the east where our Japanese colleagues do not seem to be as sentimentally affected by seeing the Union Jack's dignity take a blow.'

'Germany's commitment to Britain's defeat is no less than Japan's, I am sure,' Oshima attempted to diplomatically steer Subhas away. But he continued.

'Japan is uncompromisingly anti-Britain, General Oshima. It is, however, not that simple in the German context. The unflattering views about Indians that the Führer holds – views that are still there in every copy of *Mein Kampf* in millions of homes in Germany – don't help. And then there is his barely concealed desire to make peace with England. The possibility of the British actually signing a peace treaty with Germany, leaving the German war machine free to focus on the eastern front, is something I often hear about, even if in whispers.

What if that happens? Would I not be then packed off by the Gestapo and handed back to the English as the first gesture of goodwill of the rediscovered friendship?'

Oshima's wrinkled hand reached out to calm Bose down, a rare gesture from the veteran soldier, as he attempted to deflect the embarrassment Bose was causing his German hosts.

'Let us not forget that they have taken up the fight against Britain in 1939 while Japan has only been at war with them for two months. Surely, our German colleagues will convey your concerns ahead.'

The German colleagues' faces stayed expressionless amidst this unfamiliar questioning of the Führer's objectives.

'What do you expect – in specific military terms?' Habrich asked after a quiet moment.

'I would expect the immediate despatch of at least 200 commandos, of whom the majority should be from the Indian Legion and a few from the Abwehr or the Wehrmacht, to the North-West Frontier Province. These men will work to create support bases, locate sites for airstrips where small planes can land, and establish stores where ammunition and weapons can be stored. Forward Bloc activists in the region are waiting to support them. The Fakir of Ipi will be critical if we are to one day fight in that region. If we start now, he will also realize that we mean business. On the east, I would recommend radio stations to be set up along the Indo–Burmese border as soon as the Japanese enter Burma. And we start the recruitment and retraining of a few thousand Indian POWs, the ones willing to fight alongside us.'

Oshima smiled benignly, like a teacher watching a favourite pupil put on an impressive debating performance. If the Germans were irked at the Abwehr-hosted meeting becoming increasingly Japan-centric, they did not show it.

Nambiar stepped up and handed Subhas a sheet of notings for reference.

Subhas glanced through them, then continued.

'I can envision a situation six months from now, when German forces, having made progress across the Soviet Union and across the Middle East, reach Afghanistan and prepare it as a launching point for a possible land offensive into India – an offensive to be led by the Indian Legion. When that happens, Japanese forces simultaneously launch a two-pronged attack: on land, across the Burmese frontier, as well as by sea, landing in strength at Chittagong, Calcutta, Bombay and Karachi. Both the German and Japanese advances would ideally be led by Indian soldiers. A simultaneous east and west, land and sea action, supported by the Indian population, fighting to create a free, undivided India. *That* is my objective. If that will not lead to a collapse of the British military and administrative structure, nothing will.'

Lahousen looked up.

'Six months is ambitious ... Irrespective of how the war in Russia goes this time, your legion simply does not have the numbers to effectively take on the British Indian Army.'

Subhas was expecting that to come up. He had had extended discussions on this with Ribbentrop as well.

'I understand that concern. I have done my homework on the actual forces deployed in India. My informants update me regularly on troop deployment and movements. If the British strength there is so immense, surely some of these men would have been sent east to push back the Japanese and reinforce the retreating troops in Malaya? They haven't been – because they don't exist.'

Oshima nodded.

'As I have summarized earlier, the British government in India has a maximum of 70,000 British troops that will be unquestionably loyal to the regime, plus about 300,000 Indians who are, as of now, loyal to the Crown. They cannot withdraw any forces back to India's western borders from the Middle East because of Rommel, nor from the east because of the Japanese, so I expect these numbers to stay static. The battle with the 70,000 British soldiers will be military. With the Indian soldiers, however, it will be political and emotional. We do not look to defeat the Indian soldier as much as to win him over.'

'And you don't want to wait to build up an invading force of equal or greater strength?'

'No, I don't want to wait. I believe a force of 50,000 to 60,000 Axis-supported Free India soldiers on each front will be adequate to fragment the British force. Or even less. Because the country will rise internally, disrupting railways and communication. We will airdrop agents and weapons across the country. I know we do not have the numbers yet, but I am hoping that as Japan moves ahead, the large numbers of Indian soldiers presently deployed in Singapore and in Burma will have many men who can be persuaded to fight for their country.'

'Right. The minutes of this meeting will reach Field Marshal Kietel's desk tomorrow, and we will await his views,' Lahousen said. 'I do think, however, that planning a 1942 action factoring in yet-to-be-captured Indian soldiers captured in Singapore and Burma is taking too simplistic a view of the war situation. Singapore is extremely well-defended and is a symbol of British prestige in the region. The forces deployed there are over 125,000 in number. The Japanese forces in the region are less than 50,000. Our assessments indicate heavy fighting to defend Singapore. If they have to fight on only one front, the British still have enough loyal infantry to make advances very costly.'

In response, Fujiwara got up and walked up to the map on the conference room wall.

'Though I believe we will take Singapore, Colonel, I too have a question for Mr Bose. General Wavell, Commander-in-Chief in India, is certain that Germany's principal aim in 1942 will be directed towards the sources of oil in the Caucasus and Middle East. Our intercepts indicate that he has been asking for additional troops. He is going to work very hard to prevent the joining of the German and Japanese forces. To think that an untested force like the Indian Legion will simply walk into British India from the western frontier may be – how do I put it – very optimistic? I still believe, therefore, that Indian troops will be better placed if they work primarily with the Japanese Imperial Army, to India's east.'

'But you don't have that many Indian POWs anyway, Major, do you? General Rommel and the Italians already have several thousand Indian POWs from the campaigns across North Africa. You have far fewer such prisoners.' Harbich asked.

'As of today, yes. But that is changing. We are in Malaya, and we already have more than 35,000 Indian POWs. Many of them are ready to fight against the British if properly led. As Mr Bose is aware, a former British Indian Army officer, Mohan Singh, is already building a structure. If our plans hold, we will have Singapore, and who knows, Burma as well, within the next few months. Given the composition of the British Indian Army in those parts, I expect that more than half of any Allied prisoners we take will be Indians.'

'If that happens – even if that is a big "if" – it will give us enough volunteers to have a strong deployment of free Indian soldiers on both India's west and east before this year ends,' Subhas concluded.

❖

As the cars carrying the officers and diplomats roared out of the driveway, Subhas and Fujiwara sat across the table. The German butler, part of the staff deputed by the Foreign Office, placed tea before the Japanese, coffee before the Indian, and exited the room without a sound. Subhas was sure he would be just outside for the duration of the meeting, with his ear to the door. Unless, of course, the room was bugged as well. The phones were all tapped, of that he was sure.

'I assume you have read through all reports on the Indian POWs?' Fujiwara asked. Subhas nodded.

The Indian soldiers fighting to keep Britain in the war evoked mixed responses: mercenaries enabling a colonial power to rule their own country? Brave men loyal to their salt and regiment? Confused men of indeterminate loyalties simply looking to earn a living?

One's view of who these soldiers were depended on where you looked at them from.

'December and January have been good for Japan. The British are on the backfoot everywhere. I am personally ensuring Indians captured during battle are treated well. I have put most of the Indian POWs captured in Malaya under the charge of Mohan Singh and Pritam Singh. Mohan Singh and Indian POWs from the 1st Battalion of the 14th Punjab Regiment have been restoring law and order in Alor Star, and so far, we seem to understand each other,' the major summed up.

'How many men do you think will be open to picking up arms to fight the British Army, Major?'

'If I ask them to, a few hundred at least. If someone like Mohan Singh can gain their confidence, a few thousand. If *you* ask them to – who knows?' Fujiwara let that hang in the air for a moment.

'That is easier said than done. I don't know how this will unfold. Given the choice, I would want all Indians to be trained afresh together. But there is a huge distance to cover between North Africa and Malaya. Men can be brought from Africa to Germany with little trouble – there is hardly any Allied opposition worth its name. But can we bring men from Asia?' Bose mulled as he sipped on his coffee.

Fujiwara laughed. 'Even if you ignore the logistical challenge of moving thousands of men from Asia to Germany in wartime, you are assuming, Mr Bose, that the Imperial Army will simply pick up and gift these men, who are willing to fight the British, to our German friends. Why would we not want them fighting the British on the frontiers *we* are fighting on?'

Subhas looked up and did not respond. Instead, he put his cup down.

'Shall we step out into the lawn for a moment? The sun will do me some good.'

Fujiwara smiled.

A minute later, the two resumed their conversation, out of the range of any listening devices.

'I'm not assuming anything,' Subhas explained, his calm tone a contrast to his temper, a short while back. 'But I can hope and plan. I cannot be on two frontiers at once. I would really want to see an Indian Legion at India's western frontier and be there myself when it happens. But you know a lot depends on how the war in southern Russia and Africa goes for the Germans. If it goes badly, I will accept that it is not to be, and will gladly accept your hospitality in the east.'

'It will be my pleasure to have you there. It would greatly strengthen the army we are presently trying to build.'

'Thank you. But till the day there is any chance of the first plan working out, I will attempt to build the core of a new Indian Army where I am,' Subhas continued. 'And Germany is where I am right now. I know you will look at the interest of your nation, as I do for mine. If I can bring this journey to a conclusion, and if the British are defending their western frontier against an Indo–German force, it will work to your advantage as they will not be able to spare much strength to stop you in the east. I will try to support you and the army being raised there as best as I can from Europe.'

'I am sure.'

'If the logistics prove manageable, I will want you to send the leaders of these efforts to mobilize Indians, the names you spoke of earlier – Rash Behari Bose, A. M. Nair, Mohan Singh – to meet me in Berlin. Despite the shared name, I have never had the pleasure of meeting Mr Rash Behari. He sounds like someone who could handle this operation in the east for us.'

'This is not easy. But I will try to arrange that.'

'Oh, and before we head back, one more thing, Major.'

'Yes?'

'I am aware of what you have done almost single-handedly. I have heard of a few other Japanese officers being appreciated for the manner in which they are dealing with the Indians – both the POWs and civilians. But your army does not have a very good track record in China and elsewhere. And I am sure there will be others who may not display the sensitivity you have. In case you find it difficult to stop any misbehaviour on their part, being part of the hierarchy, please have word sent to me – I will raise it to Tokyo via General Oshima.'

Fujiwara nodded quietly, then took his leave. The handshake of the Orientals in the Aryan heartland was firm, almost warm, at least to the degree that you could use the word for anything associated with the reticent Subhas.

❖

The journey from the Free India Centre, Lichenstein Allee to Subhas's residence in Sophienstrasse was short and uneventful. After spending many months living at the Hotel Esplanade and then the Kaiserhof Hotel, he had been allocated the spacious Sophienstrasse residence, previously the home of the American Military attaché.

If it was not three degrees above freezing as dusk settled in Berlin, Subhas would have liked to lower the top of the Mercedes convertible on the way, though it was a request that the chauffeur always asked him to reconsider. The Abwehr had relayed recently to Berlin the standing order of the British Special Operations Executive to assassinate Subhas whenever the opportunity arose. Orders that were issued in early 1941, soon after it was believed by the British – mistakenly – that he was in hiding either in Kabul or Istanbul. He was in neither, of course, but the orders had been sustained, and also reconfirmed after that, twice.

The standing assassination list as of June 1941, which the Germans knew courtesy of a SOE war diary captured in Egypt, had seven names: four German officials, an Italian colonel, the Grand Mufti of Jerusalem, and Subhas Chandra Bose.

Subhas had laughed heartily when informed of the list. 'They declare me to be a fascist day in and day out on radio, but the advisory for my assassination describes me as an "Indian communist" – and that at a time when fascists and communists are fighting to the death! So it's not just the Congress that's confused about my political affiliations.'

The sombre officers answerable for his security had not appreciated the irony. They had instead put a two-ringed security cordon in place. For the British to put a bullet in Subhas's brain in Berlin would have been an embarrassment of massive proportions. Sentries guarded the Lichenstein Alle office and the Sophienstrasse residence. An armed driver and gunman accompanied Subhas wherever he travelled.

Beyond the visible, uniformed layer of security, Subhas was certain there were plainclothes men present at both locations as well as at all the venues he travelled to. There were moments he tried to figure out whether they were from Canaris' Abwehr, Heydrich's SD, or Himmler's Gestapo. Were they in the field to protect him, or to watch and report his movements?

Who could tell in the Germany of 1942?

Subhas decided not to dwell on this further as the Mercedes swept into 6/7 Sophienstrasse. He looked out to see Emilie standing at the balcony, waiting for him.

9

Berlin Blues, Part 3: First Love

> 'I am like a wandering bird that comes from afar, remains for a while, and then flies away to its distant home. For such a person why should you cherish so much love?'
>
> – Subhash, letter to Emilie Schenkl, March 1936

HE HAD BARELY STEPPED INTO THE LIVING AREA WHEN HE HEARD something he wasn't expecting.

'I am half hoping these meetings don't lead anywhere.'

'*What*?'

He paused, taken by surprise.

'Why would you say that, Emilie?'

'Because you have reached here at great risk, and all that you talk of is to go back, to keep fighting—'

Emilie broke off mid-sentence as her voice choked.

'Have you not done enough, Subhas? Is India yours alone to defend? It has over 300 million people, but I don't see anyone else planning to rush headlong into this war for it. Who gave you this exclusive, individual responsibility?'

A sombre Subhas pulled up a chair next to her but did not interrupt.

'In 1936, when you sent me a letter as you went back to India, you wrote things that made my heart sink. I have read that letter so often that I can recite it from memory now. Amidst all that you wrote about your love for me, *those* lines tore into me. Not a day passed for year after year when I hoped they would not come true ...'

She paused for a moment, then the words rolled off her tongue like a well-memorized narration.

'"I do not know what the future has in store for me. Maybe I shall spend my life in prison, maybe I shall be shot or hanged." Amidst all else, Subhas, every day after that, I was torn between the strength that letter gave to my soul and the dread it brought to my heart. Till that day, last year, until I heard – incredibly, from you – that you were in Berlin and were calling me to meet you. And now you are doing all that you can do to recreate that – to go back into the fire, to again write me a note saying maybe you will be shot, maybe captured ... Can we *never* look forward to a life together without a sword hanging above your head?'

It was not the tone of a rant or a complaint, but of a straightforward question. The genuineness of it unnerved Subhas for a moment.

Was there a clear answer?

'I think it is I who tends to go and stand under the proverbial hanging sword, Emma,' Subhas started, laughing, and then paused as he realized that Emilie looked hurt, rather than distracted or amused.

Self-consciously, he wrapped an arm around her and mumbled an apology.

'I know you are right from where you see it, Emma.'

'And how different is it from where you see it?'

'The state of my country burns me from within like a terminal illness. There is no peace to be had by looking away or saying that this is not my business. I have carried that pain for decades. And how do I put it, Emma, but I have ... I have—'

'"I have already sold myself to my first love, my country; I have very little left to give anyone" – you put it very well, Subhas, many years back. In writing.' Emilie smiled. 'But rest assured, I do not hold that against you; indeed, perhaps one part of me respects you all the more for that. But *you* are my first love, Subhas. Not Germany, not Austria. You. This is an unequal love that we have to balance.'

Emilie's smile was gentle, but her eyes were anxious. There was so little shared time in the past, and there seemed very little of it in the future as well. Only the most optimistic writer of tales could begin to write a story about them and end it with a 'happily ever after'.

But what was to be done about it?

'I am sorry, Emma.'

She squeezed his hand, took a deep breath, composed herself, and drew herself up to her full stature.

'Tell me something, Subhas.'

He looked at her, expectantly, hesitantly.

'I may not be as politically active or aware as you are, but for the past many years, I have been witness to this great, increasingly uncomfortable belief in power all around me. The power of mobs and sticks, then the power of soldiers, of guns, of bombs. Power, strength, force – Heil! That is the only language I hear.

'When I first met you, I was an Austrian. Today, there is no Austria. Forgive me for saying this, but the columns of soldiers that marched into my country to "unite" it with Germany – how do I put it? The cheers were loud, but the fears we kept close to our chests. You couldn't talk about them. The Nazis in Austria gloated endlessly at the great unification but people like me, my family ... we are not so sure it is a good thing. I already hear of how Jews, Communists and many others have been having a hard time after the *Anschluss*.'

Emilie had rarely spoken on this subject. Subhas listened closely.

'Everywhere Hitler turns, he sends guns and people have to die for the good of Germany. Why do you, Subhas, also want to argue your case through the language of guns? Why do you also want to march with battalions of Hitler's soldiers? For years, I have heard, read, or typed out myself, your political thought. You have been angry, even contemptuous of the Nazis all through the 1930s. Why are you allying with them so actively today? Are you beginning to think like them?'

Had this come from Nehru on the stage of a Congress meeting, Subhas would have responded instantaneously and unapologetically. But this was closer to home, quite literally.

He took his time.

'No, Emma. I have not gone from being a critic to a fan of Nazism. Nor am I fascinated by waging war. It does not give me a high.'

'Then why are you so keen to head into conflict, that too alongside Hitler's soldiers?'

'Let us step out for a minute?'

They stepped out into the balcony and then onto the lawn.

The night was chilly, but clear. The moon lit up Berlin softly. The blackouts at night made the sky look sharper, the stars more vivid. For a moment, Subhas was lost in his thoughts. But a conversation was on hold. Gathering his thoughts, he made his case softly, to the individual he cared for the most.

'The use of armed force is *not* my first instinct, Emma, as you well know. You have seen my political writings for years now. Neither is seeking German assistance – more so with the regime in power today. I have led an active political life for many years now. I have tried *every* possible way to forge a political path that would lead to India's independence – within the Congress, outside the Congress. Unlike *Mein Kampf*, surely, in my political thoughts over the years, you will not find the undercurrent of applauding violence, of searching for greatness at the cost of others. Right?'

A slight nod followed in response.

'But I have realized that the British will not – indeed, they cannot – walk out of India driven by a sense of morality, or respect for liberty, or the whole talk of how they are fighting to defend liberty against tyranny. No, none of that for India. Not even the USA thinks the Atlantic Charter applies to India! At home, by now, even my opponents in the Congress realize it, even if they dare not say it publicly: armed insurrection, not spinning khadi, is what we need now. We can protest peacefully for decades, to no end. It puts them morally on the defensive, yes; but they will never, ever leave India on that ground.'

It was chilly. He tucked his hands in his pockets.

'They rule India based on their military strength – which is also a combination of a few of their own troops and many, many more Indians willing to serve to defend them. The strength of their own military machine and the loyalty of the Indian soldier – these two things keep their flag flying. Unfortunately, I have to attack both. I wish there was another way, but there isn't. They entered on the strength of bayonets and that is the way they will be goaded out. Only when they can no longer hold India militarily, will they give up.'

They walked together a while. It was getting colder.

Emilie gave no indication if she agreed with him or not.

'Which, of course, brings me to the second part. Where, Emma, do I find those bayonets, and the men to wield them? Men, money, materials – how do I conjure them up in numbers enough to challenge the empire on which the sun supposedly never sets? And I have to do that *now* – while the balance of power is not decisively on Britain's side. See my predicament?

'Even if the men I am gathering are Indians, they are Prisoners of War, with nothing more than the clothes they wear as possessions. Why will the Germans or the Italians just gift them to me, train them, arm and equip them, unless I have a plan – a plan that in some ways, if not entirely, aligns with their military and political goals?'

'Do they really need you marching physically to meet their goals?'

'Maybe, maybe not. But *I* need that. I do not want foreign soldiers to liberate India, Emma, understand that – it would then be just one European power dislodging another, and India would still be dependent, if not subordinate. It is an *Indian* army I seek to build, desperately, urgently. You do not understand what that means for India. We have forgotten, after 1857, what it is to see an army that fights for India, not for India's rulers.

'And so, Emma, if there is no option but the military one, and if the Axis is the foremost military opponent of the British empire today, what do I do? If the men I need – trained Indian soldiers – are, almost without exception, POWs in Axis hands, tell me, where do I go? Shall I go to neutral Switzerland which has no evil dictator? But it cannot offer me anything beyond an invigorating hill vacation. Shall I go to the land of the free, America, which has soldiers being unloaded at India's ports every month to assist the British war effort? Shall I go to Soviet Russia? I may well have considered that, truth be told, but the genius of Adolf Hitler's strategies has made Russia an ally of Britain as well.'

He took a deep breath and they turned to walk back towards the balcony. As he exhaled, a white cloud floated briefly. The temperature had dipped quickly. He had come to like winters. They gave him more scope to think, for some reason.

'The decisions I am taking are imperfect ones, Emma. I

know that. But not taking those decisions is a far worse option. Shall I, after all, just keep myself safe and die of old age while still making radio broadcasts to India?'

'That would be a sight!'

A smile crossed his lips.

'I will live with the consequences, Emma. And I am nobody's Quisling, nor can I ever be – you know me well enough for that. If anyone here thinks they will, at the end of this story, make me a figurehead if and when we actually get to India – well, good luck to them!'

For the first time in the day, he burst into hearty laughter.

Emilie smiled.

'True. Good luck to anyone trying to make you do something you don't believe in.'

She stepped onto the balcony, then paused, turned, and looked back at Subhas, still on the lawn, looking at the stars.

'But there is one condition you will have to accept.'

A quizzical expression on his face served as the question.

'I will not have you flying off on your eastward journey yet again, a bird from afar, while I sit here, waiting endlessly, petrified by every telegram. I will come with you, whenever you go on that journey, wherever it takes you.'

As he looked at the unwavering gaze of that gentle face, the man who stared down wielders of great political power almost by habit, knew that he had no option but to yield.

❖

Berlin
29 January 1942

Dear Sarat,

I am in a peculiar situation, and since no good will come of weeping about it, I have opted to have a good laugh instead.

I cannot seem to be able to find people who want to take on the British empire.

For years, I have attempted to goad the Mahatma and the Congress into an all-out declaration of war against the British rule but have been frustrated by the half-hearted measures that the Congress is so fond of.

Imagine my surprise and dismay at realizing that even when I come to the capital of the nation engaged in actual war, I still find the same reluctance and half-heartedness.

While in Dalhousie, I had written about Britain and Germany in an article for the Modern Review *in 1937. In 1942, I am both validated and disappointed that my understanding of the situation was quite accurate.*

At that point, I had reiterated that in 1914, Germany did not believe that Britain would take up arms on behalf of Belgium and France, and that historians admitted in the 1930s that had Britain made her intentions clear to Germany beforehand, it is quite likely that Germany would have kept away from the Austro–Serbian conflict and thereby stayed out of the World War altogether.

I had theorized that Germany wants to expand to the East but avoid a war with Britain.

I wrote in 1937 that Germany will not repeat the errors of 1914 and will not go into a second war if it knows that Britain will be against it. However, it might get trapped into one just as it had been in 1914, thinking that Britain would keep out of it.

That seems to be just what has happened.

My readings of Germany's reflexes before the war began were entirely accurate. Germany is obsessed with looking East, and just as it had been in the last war, it was genuinely surprised when Britain and France actually declared war when German troops marched into Poland.

Hitler finally attacked in the West only because he wanted a free hand to reshape the map of Central and Eastern Europe. If he could have got it peacefully, he would have gladly taken it. Once that choice was taken from him, he decided to act, and the Wehrmacht, perhaps the finest military machine on the continent at the moment with its very fine Generals, delivered.

But we – those like me – who seek to ally with Germany in our battle with Britain, need to understand that had Britain and France not joined the war on behalf of Poland, there is absolute certainty that Germany would never have declared war on Britain. Hitler did not start out looking to go to war with Britain. And even when he has, his heart is not quite in it.

And then there is the racial mindset of the Nazi party. Not all Germans are Nazis but almost all committed Nazis are racist – that is my takeaway from numerous conversations over the past months and years. And the committed Nazi thinks very differently, in racial terms, of the people who live to the east and west of Germany.

My understanding is that even at this stage, not only does Hitler harbour the thoughts of making peace with Britain, but also that he is deeply uncomfortable with the events in East Asia overturning his understanding of the hierarchy of race.

The easy Japanese victories over the British, the Dutch and the French are militarily good news for the Germans, but they are not easy to accept for those Germans that believe in race being the primary defining factor of military prowess (I sometimes sense that even in the training of the Indian Legion by a few German instructors who look at the colour of the soldier rather than his fighting ability, but I am not one to accept such things quietly, as you know, I raise hell).

The political doctrine of the Nazi party can be summed up with 'Drang Nach Osten' *– Drive to the East – that was first spelled out by Muller van de Bruck in* Das Dritte Reich

(The Third Empire). *His ideas have, of course, been amplified by Hitler in* Mein Kampf. *The core thought behind the Drang Nach Osten is that Germany should give up its idea of becoming a naval or colonial power, and its expansion should instead move towards the East. This theory states that it was Germany's blunder to come into conflict with Great Britain in the past. It is safe to assume that Hitler, if he has absorbed other elements of this theory, would believe in this part, too.*

It is reasonably certain to my mind that Hitler did not expect Neville Chamberlain's government to declare war on Britain. And so, yet again, as in the previous war, Germany finds itself in a situation where it is at war with Britain while it would rather focus its efforts entirely on the East.

One part of the German leadership, therefore, is always looking to not humiliate Britain beyond a point. Or keeping back channels open. I wonder if the bizarre flight to Scotland that Rudolf Hess went on last year, had something to do with all that.

Anyway. So, dear Sarat, what is the takeaway?

Whether it be Tripuri or Berlin, in a large group of people supposedly at daggers drawn with Britain, I seem to be the one most strongly opposed to the policies of His Majesty's regime, with generally lukewarm support for my extreme views.

I know we will get some military support, since everyone understands that the loss of India would deliver a massive blow to Britain's prestige, resources and manpower, but Germany will not send hundreds of thousands of its best – it looks to subdue, not vanquish Britain. A handful of German divisions, at best, maybe even just one or two, will be available if and when the situation is conducive. I will therefore have to raise large numbers for the Indian Legion before that stage. I can sense that it is Indian blood that will have to flow freely before India is free. Nobody is going to gift that freedom to us.

Which is a good thing, I think, for then we shall be in no one's irreparable debt once we do seize that freedom

Subhas

P.S. This may take a while to reach you. Earlier, I only had to have a letter evade the British CID for it to get to you, now I have to keep it away from the Gestapo as well!

10

The Wolf's Lair

> 'After the speech of Herr Hitler, I issued a very strong statement to the Indian press ... I am still prepared to work for an understanding between Germany and India. This understanding must be consistent with our national self-respect. When we are fighting the greatest Empire in the world for our freedom and for our rights and when we are confident of our ultimate success, we cannot brook any insult from any other nation or any attack on our race or culture.'
>
> – Subhas Bose, Letter to Dr Thierfelder, March 1936

East Prussia
27 April 1942

THE PROLONGED SILENCE MARKED BY THE DRONE OF THE propellers in the background was broken as Subhas finally disengaged from the window – he was fascinated by the scenery – and turned towards his fellow passenger.

'You know what the irony is, here?'

Von Trott turned to him, a bemused expression on his face. He could find no humour in the day at all.

'I have had many sessions with the world's foremost advocate of non-violence. Now I have to engage with the world's foremost advocate of violence. Has anyone endured such divergent shades of greatness, from the Mahatma to the Führer? I don't see Himmler having a chat with the Mahatma anytime, or Jawahar with Herr Hitler, so I suppose that just leaves me in a one-member club.'

Von Trott smiled but stayed silent. He wasn't going to comment on the Führer while heading towards his abode. It was possible to get away with impudence as Bose, but as a mid-level German official, he could land up in a concentration camp if he was heard cracking a joke about The Leader.

Subhas knew of von Trott's intensely anti-Nazi political affiliations. He had often pretended not to notice when von Trott used Subhas and the Free India Centre as a cover for travel that he could not have otherwise explained.

'I just hope I don't come back disappointed again, though. Great people, having achieved greatness, usually don't like listening to views that don't align with theirs. Even the Mahatma.'

Von Trott stayed quiet.

'Isn't it odd?' Nambiar's voice came from the seat behind Subhas.

'What do you mean?'

'The fact that this is going to be your first meeting with Hitler. You have met Mussolini so often and yet never Hitler – why would that be?'

'Well, you'll have to ask Herr Hitler that, I'm afraid,' Subhas laughed. 'But yes, the Duce has not been as inaccessible.'

'Did you really need to meet him if we have managed so far without it?'

Subhas smiled. Nambiar's discomfort at dealing with the hardcore Nazis was something he had never made a secret of.

'I know where you are coming from – but it is rather late in the day for us to reconsider this, my friend,' he said, his tone jocular.

'Is the Duce easy to deal with?' Von Trott interrupted this line of conversation, finally finding a non-threatening topic he could engage with.

'I don't know – but *I* found him easy to deal with. We've met some five or six times since 1934. Italy was by far the first European state to understand and appreciate the importance of India'.

'Hasn't Germany backed India more firmly?'

'I don't know ... When I travelled within Europe in the 1930s, I found Germany displaying increasing signs of racism, while the Italians were largely free of this virus. However, towards the end of the 1930s, Germany, as we all well know, overtook Italy in military muscle and ambition and now Mussolini finds himself overshadowed by Hitler. But Italy remains the country that first took the Indian cause seriously, and at the same time did not classify Indians – and most of the world – as somewhere lower in the race 'purity' hierarchy, and that's not something I can forget just because I am currently in Berlin.'

'But, Subhas, Germany is your base; it is training your future army. And yet you're never fully sure of how it stands?'

'Well, no. I don't think Germany would have engaged with my plans to this degree if it had not realized that Rome would readily host me if Berlin didn't. Japan is equally keen to build ties with an emerging Indian leadership, since it sees India as falling within its zone of influence. Italy sees the Mediterranean, and by extension, the Middle East, as its zone. But Ribbentrop isn't going to be happy to see Italy and Japan invest as the primary stakeholders in a Free India project, cutting Germany out, so he has pushed through so much, despite a lot of opposition. If this call was being taken primarily by Hitler and the party – not by the Foreign Ministry – I would probably have had to shift to Rome by now.'

The flaps opened on the wings with much squealing as the plane began its descent on the Rastenburg airstrip in East Prussia.

❖

The Wolf's Lair was about 8 kilometres from Rastenburg. As they had flown in, Subhas had occasionally looked out for a glimpse, but had seen nothing. Nothing was what any pilot flying overhead usually saw, for the time and energy invested in camouflaging the complex was massive. The bushes and grass, artificial trees and nettings ensured that the complex appeared as unbroken woodland when seen from above. Hidden below, Hitler lived in a bunker built with steel-reinforced concrete walls, 2 metres thick.

Security Zone 1, the core of the Wolf's Lair, was where Hitler's own bunker was located. The men of the SS-Begleitkommando des Führers (FBK) watched carefully as the group of visitors were searched and sent ahead. The FBK were the only armed guards allowed near Hitler.

The Führer Bunker was not what Subhas expected the abode of the world's most powerful man to be. The atmosphere felt oppressive, the air dank, the lighting dim, the corridors low and the rooms cramped.

They were escorted to Hitler's meeting room where Ribbentrop was already present and waiting. He seemed to be in a more conciliatory and receptive mood than usual and began by apologizing for not having reverted to Subhas's letters demanding an Axis Declaration on India. Was it genuine regret, or now that Subhas would finally be face to face with Hitler, did the Foreign Minister not want to be portrayed in an unflattering light? It did not matter much either way for Subhas.

Ribbentrop was still the strongest advocate of active German engagement with arming and building an Indian armed force. So was Admiral Canaris, actually, but Subhas did not know how much Ribbentrop knew of what Canaris thought on the matter. The Admiral survived by knowing as much about others as was possible, but letting others know next to nothing about himself.

They chatted for half an hour. The frostiness in Subhas's tone calmed soon. After all, if Hitler was unwilling to sign a declaration, there was precious little Ribbentrop could do. Von Trott and Ribbentrop's aides exchanged notes towards the end of the room, keeping their distance.

The incessant humming of fans to keep the air circulating was fatiguing after a point, more so after the flight. How did those staying here all the time not develop a sense of claustrophobia, Subhas wondered. He did not feel particularly comfortable in such locations. This one felt like the hideout of a cult.

Which, when he thought about it, wasn't all that far from the truth.

❖

The snapping of the guards to attention all along the corridor brought advance intimation of the entry of the man who still ruled Europe today, even if he wasn't conquering any more territory.

And in walked Adolf Hitler.

❖

'What was that all about?' Nambiar asked, perplexed, as they headed to their cars, an hour later.

Subhas looked irked, though he had kept an impassive expression during the entire meeting.

'That, my dear, was about a man who likes to speak but can't bear to listen.'

11

A Day on the Front

Front line
26 November 1942

GREY PUFFS OF SMOKE ROSE LAZILY IN THE ICY MORNING AIR. A Legion battery had just collectively fired a barrage towards the British line. Flashes of machine gun fire were visible even from this distance – about a kilometre or more away.

The rat-a-tat of the MG-42 took a few seconds to reach Subhas. His Zeiss binoculars stayed glued to his bloodshot, sleep-deprived eyes. He could see what he had been seeing each day for the past week: men crouched as low as they could, men seeking cover behind rocks, men letting loose bursts of fire from dug-in locations. Nobody, whether he had sworn an oath to the King Emperor or to the Führer and Subhas Bose, was foolhardy enough to stand up and dash around in this hilly terrain, silhouetted and easy prey for an enemy sniper or a spray of gunfire. German-made MG-42s took down the defenders, British Bren guns searched for Indian Legion and Axis targets. Bullets ricocheted off rocks and zinged past ducking soldiers.

On this terrain, when a man fell, he often literally fell – down the steep gradients, into the valleys, onto an escarpment below, if he was lucky. If the bullet didn't kill, the fall would. But the advancing armies were digging fewer graves in the icy, hard earth than the defenders. And gathering lesser wood for pyres.

Gradually, mile by mile, hill by hill, the Axis were moving forward, one day at a time. The pace, however, kept the Germans uneasy. They had always done better with sharp, swift attacks – and Stalingrad had been a horrifying reminder that in a slow war of attrition, the Heer was not the best army in the world. But then, blitzkrieg was not an option here. Not yet, not while it was still largely an Indian versus Indian test of infantry skills and grit. Not while the bulk of the Axis forces – almost two-thirds – were the Legion's. And definitely not while Subhas was thinking of post-war consolidation and reconciliation just as keenly as he was awaiting victory.

The Zeiss lenses also picked up the dispatch rider half a kilometre away, making good speed in the hilly terrain on his rugged BMW R12. He must have been in sight of a British rifle on that stretch of unprotected road, and he must have been aware of that, too. But a good sniper would not give away his position for just bringing down a DR. There is a certain safety in being too junior to be singled out, as all those who work in hierarchies know.

Subhas put the binoculars down and walked across to the camouflaged tent, a few metres away. He picked up the freshly brewed cup of tea that awaited him and exchanged notes with Hauptmann Manfred Armbruster of the Luftwaffe.

An anti-aircraft specialist, Manfred had been designated by Rommel as the liaison officer of the German forces to Subhas. Not because he expected to bring down planes here, but on account of his sense of military initiative. He was among the pioneers of using the 88 mm Flak anti-aircraft gun in anti-tank operations, something that Rommel had used to great effect while fighting in the desert. The fact that Manfred had politely declined to join the Nazi Party had done his case no harm in the Field Marshal's books.

A minute later, the noisy BMW, waved through by the guards, roared into the camp. The rider got off and threw a crisp salute at Subhas and Manfred.

'I have been asked to rush to you, sir, with a message from Oberstleutnant Krappe,' the DR said in that robotic military tone that all uniformed messengers seemed to acquire. Subhas took the envelope from his outstretched hand and read through it. Stiffening, he folded it a couple of times and paused, weighing his options. The rider looked on expectantly.

All conversation in the compound died down to a murmur.

Manfred observed all this with a growing sense of unease.

The Field Marshal had asked him to ensure that the Legion's supremo did nothing foolhardy in his absence. His expression, however, gave Manfred the distinct impression that whatever Bose was thinking of doing was not very prudent.

'Let's go,' the bespectacled leader of the Indian Legion snapped at his escort unit, even as he began striding towards the Volkswagen Kübelwagen parked in the compound. Caught off-guard, the half a dozen men assigned to his personal security within the compound scampered to the Opel Blitz truck and to the Kübelwagen. Alarms clanging in his head, Manfred instinctively dashed and stood between Subhas and the Volkswagen.

'Herr Bose, may I remind you that the Field Marshal has expressly directed us to ensure that you stay *away* from the active zone of the front line?'

'I am sure you have your orders, Captain, but I cannot afford to stay here and do nothing right now. And what needs to be done can be done only by me, not by the Field Marshal – so excuse me!'

With a gentle shove, Subhas put Manfred out of his way, hustled into the vehicle and glared at his driver, who promptly fired up the engine.

'Then at least wait! Let me gather an escort,' Manfred almost beseeched.

'*I* can't wait – but you can gather some more men and follow us if that makes you feel better. We're moving. Now!'

The Kübelwagen roared out noisily and the Blitz rattled and followed close behind. Two Legion men sat in the rear seat while Subhas sat in the front, next to the driver, his face reddening with fury. The other four rode in the truck; three at the rear, one with the driver.

Manfred leapt for the field telephone and yelled out orders as soon as it was picked. Once he kept it down, a kilometre away, men of a Luftwaffe 88 mm air defence unit rushed to their *Bunkerknacker* – the half-track that served as a platform for a mounted 88 mm gun. He then turned to the bemused despatch rider, who was still rooted to the spot next to his motorcycle.

'Will you tell me what that was about, before Herr Bose lands up in British captivity, perhaps?'

❖

If Manfred was having a panic attack at the realization that Subhas Chandra Bose, the Supreme Commander of the Indian Legion and the Indian National Army, had just driven off towards an active front line with nothing more than a Beretta M1934 in his holster and six Indian Legion soldiers armed with MP35 submachine guns, he did not show it.

Commanders dashing off like that was not unheard of; indeed, Rommel himself was known for his impetuous actions. But the Desert Fox was a professional and highly skilled soldier, usually had detailed information about the battle situation, and the (many) men around him were battle-hardened veterans. The handful of men with Bose were loyal to him, and experienced, but they were not yet comparable to the elite of the Afrika Korps, they had little information about the present situation on the front; Bose, for all the time spent with his Beretta at the firing range, was no veteran of the war front.

In another situation, two vehicles travelling on the exposed road, even in sight of enemy fire, would not stress the Luftwaffe veteran. It would be too insignificant a target to draw attention. But Bose's personal transport, much to Rommel's annoyance, had a personalized flag of the Indian Legion's commander-in-chief: a springing tiger fluttered briskly on the flag as he sped along. That, Rommel had stated, was as good as waving a red flag in front of one's own face in a bullfight, just in case the bull wasn't seeing things clearly enough.

Rommel had objected when he first saw that flag, but Subhas had stubbornly held his ground. 'I understand your concern for my safety, but my men must know that there is an *Indian* commander on the ground, Field Marshal; German and Italian staff cars cannot be the only things they see and salute' – he had held Rommel off with that. Or so he thought. 'If I am shot,' an exasperated Rommel had said, coldly and slowly, 'the OKH will send another General from Berlin, or from Rome. If *you* are shot, whom do we contact to send your replacement, Supreme Commander? Or have you made a will that lists out the next commander of the Legion?'

Even Subhas could not refute that line of questioning. As he had often done in such situations, he had conceded that Rommel made a valid point, and then had proceeded to do exactly what he wanted anyway.

And, therefore, now, as his Kübelwagen drove at breakneck speed over the half-kilometre stretch exposed to British troops on the facing hills, not only were his own men deployed along the route startled to see him approaching the front line, but anyone on the British side with a good pair of binoculars – or, more likely, telescopic sights on a rifle – could hardly miss identifying him.

❖

The first shot drilled a neat, circular hole at the left edge of the front windshield, missing Subhas by six inches or so. The driver swerved as the next shot ricocheted off the sturdy steel bonnet with a metallic ping. The men in the rear seat crouched low and looked to fire back, but there was no tell-tale flash visible.

Even if there had been, it would have been futile; the MP35s they were carrying were close combat weapons with an effective range of 150–200 metres. They were still about 600–700 metres from the front. The sniper who had marked out the car from that distance was clearly wielding a weapon with a range of over 600 metres; in all probability, the Short Magazine Lee Enfield Sniper with telescopic sights that could kill at 750 metres in the right hands. The bolt action, however, meant that there would be a gap between any two shots, in which the driver could veer off to either side and thereby force the sniper to adjust afresh each time.

Subhas crouched as low as he could while the driver floored the accelerator. Another 200 metres to go and they would be protected by a derelict, abandoned school building by the roadside that would hopefully deny direct visibility to the sniper.

But the sniper wasn't the only one who had noticed that the Legion's leader was on the move. A three-inch mortar exploded between the car and the escort truck, causing the latter to brake sharply. The front left tyre skidded off the road. The Kübelwagen continued at speed even as the truck braked – and so a gap developed.

Manfred's nightmare was coming true. Subhas's vehicle was now a standalone visual target, but moving fast, while the truck was a stationary one. The sniper, instinctively tempted by a static, helpless target, turned his attention to it for just a couple of rounds, and in that five-second period, the truck served to save Subhas by giving his driver just enough time to reach the cover of the building and screech to a halt, even as the echo of two shots bounced off the hilly terrain.

Subhas jumped out and turned to look back at his men. The truck was still standing where it was. It was going to stay there for a while, as the blood gushing out from the driver's throat was already making its way to the road. The Lee Enfield bullets rarely left a human frame without causing irreparable damage. A second bullet had hit the soldier in the front seat on the right shoulder, shattering it; scowling in pain, he crouched as low as he could, as did the three in the rear.

But they were safe for the moment, for the sniper, having shot off two rounds in that five-second window, was now training his scope back to the flag car. And then, though they could not hear it, he was swearing heavily as he realized that, so long as it stayed in that 20-metre patch that offered cover behind the building, he could not land a direct shot on the Kübelwagen. Subash was no longer in the line of sight of the sniper's position.

They both needed to wait it out.

❖

Oberstleutnant Krappe, commanding the Legion unit in the thick of action, cursed loudly, viciously, as he understood what was happening. He should not have informed Bose about the confrontation between the Legion's soldiers and the captured men of the British Army's Baloch Regiment. These issues often provoked unanticipated responses from him.

A group of sixty-odd Balochs on an isolated hilltop had been cut off and forced to surrender earlier that morning by a company of Krappe's regiment. While being herded back, words had been exchanged about loyalties and treason, which then escalated quickly to slurs on religion. Most of the Legion's men in this action were from an erstwhile Sikh unit. A few had lost their cool and stepped in, daggers drawn – literally – to prove a point to the Balochs insulting their affiliation, mothers and faith. Other Hindu soldiers had rushed to join them. Krappe had to fire in the air to restore order, but the restrained men were still straining at the leash; it just needed the officers to be away for a while, for more than a few captive Balochs to feel cold steel.

Attempting to understand why this particular POW lot was causing so much stress, Krappe had been briefed by the NCOs, among other things, about the 1897 Battle of Saragarhi that had left a distinct absence of affection between generations of Sikh and Pashtun soldiers. The technicality that Krappe pointed out, that most of the captured soldiers were Balochs, not Pashtuns, and that in the 1897 battle, the Sikhs had been fighting *for* the British and the Pashtuns against them – did not apparently make much of a difference as far as the anger triggered on the battlefield went.

Krappe had thought it important to keep Subhas informed of this, since right from the point of the Legion's training in Germany, he had been hugely obsessive about not letting divisive ethnic and religious issues gain momentum. He had, however, not anticipated the Supreme Commander driving off towards the front line, along a road exposed to enemy fire, flag flying, with what seemed to be non-existent protection.

Now Subhas was trapped at a point that afforded temporary reprieve from the sniper. Snipers, probably, he corrected himself, by now. Skilled veterans who would have zeroed in on the possibility of rendering the infamous Legion headless with a single Enfield round. Any man who took off the head of the 'Indian Quisling' would be awarded the Military Cross by the Viceroy himself, at the very least. The SAS had been trying without luck for over a year to score a hit on this thorn in the Empire's side and Downing Street had long waited for some good news about bidding adieu to S. C. Bose. Was today the day the welcome news would finally come over the wires?

The distant humming of engines alerted Krappe to the possibility that the snipers may not be the only cause for concern. That sound ... Familiar yet highly unpleasant. He was confused for a moment. Could they *really* be ... ?

'Spitfires, sir!' his adjutant exclaimed.

That was a surprise. The British had barely half a dozen of those to spare in this part of the front. They must have been scrambled from the Peshawar base, he guessed, barely five minutes flying distance from the front line, upon hearing that Subhas Bose was in the open and a possible target. The British communication lines had clearly not been disabled, for all the efforts by the men of the Faqir of Ipi and the Forward Bloc's sympathizers in this part of Hindustan.

'We need to get him out of there!' Krappe bellowed. It wasn't going to be as simple as just dashing for him, however; the front had now opened up and fire was coming in from all positions in enemy hands, aimed at tying down men where they were. Deputing a couple of officers to keep control of the POW situation, he began to figure out how to travel the distance to where Subhas's vehicles were stranded, even as he was deafened by the two Spitfires which roared overhead, flying extremely low, scouting for their target's location.

❖

Half a kilometre away, before the exposed stretch of road began, Manfred's blood froze as he saw what was happening. A pair of British fighters buzzing around, strafing, searching for Subhas's car, probably being guided over radio by spotters on the ground, was the stuff of nightmares.

Attempting to follow Subhas, Manfred had paused his slow-moving 88mm-bearing Bunkerknacker a fair distance from where the damaged truck was, given the intensity of small-arms fire raining down around the road. That pause had, unexpectedly, given him the perfect vantage point for this moment: a barely noticed stationary 88 mm that could aim at these planes from almost point-blank range in flak terms. He screamed instructions and the crew began to line up the feared fighters in their sights.

❖

The first Spitfire veered away from the sporadic rifle fire from the ground and commenced a dive towards the stranded truck. Subhas watched, distraught, as it came down to barely 200 metres, lined up its 20 mm cannons, and opened up. By the time the men assessed what was riskier – staying in the truck or being on the road – and decided to jump for it, it was too late. As the shells smashed into it and the fuel tank went up in a blast, the Opel's frame flew up in the air, seemed to hang there for one long moment, and crashed back onto the ground. The bodies of the men were flung around. Some blackened, smouldering, and still moving; others shattered and lifeless.

The Spitfire then gained height in order to provide covering fire as the second pilot, having by now spotted the only flag-bearing vehicle in the stretch, began to line up its run. Machine gun fire strafed the road a hundred metres ahead of the car. Subhas and the men with him scrambled and crouched along what little cover the adjacent walls and pillars offered. A couple of seconds later, the Kübelwagen was ripped apart by bullets that passed within a couple of meters of the crouching group. Metal fragments flew all around and blood gushed from Bose's forehead. The pilot zoomed past and began to come back for a second run, even as his partner fired short bursts to dissuade MG-42 fire from the ground.

The pilot focusing on Subhas had now changed his trajectory; he was coming perpendicular to how the smashed Kübelwagen stood, his guns aimed at the walls along which the group had sought shelter. Krappe watched with his heart in his mouth as the Spitfire came low, unchallenged, and opened up. The first burst smashed into the ground and dozens of ricochets hit the walls. The pilot corrected his sights, paused for a moment, and put his hand on the trigger again. The next moment, the fuel tank of the Spitfire exploded. The plane went into an abrupt dive, overshot the school's structure by barely 20 metres, and smashed into the ground a couple of seconds later, the propeller churning out the frontier's earth in great scoops before reluctantly accepting defeat. His neck snapped, the pilot slumped lifelessly on the controls.

'Good shooting, boys!' Manfred exulted to his crew.

The pilot circling overhead searched keenly for the anti-aircraft battery that had brought down his partner. Manfred's crew was looking to score a hit before he located them. They fired a burst, but the flak passed by the wings of the plane curling into a turn. The flash of the muzzle gave the Spitfire his target. The pilot slowed for a moment before sweeping down towards the road. As he descended and came within range, all machine gun posts in the area joined the 88 mm to send a stream of fire towards the sky, even as the Spitfire returned the compliment with bursts from the .303 machine guns aimed at Manfred's crew.

As this played out, Krappe dashed downhill towards the point he had last seen Subhas, tyres screeching on the hilly road, hoping to take advantage of the period in which the Spitfire was occupied elsewhere.

Ten seconds of the intense fusillade proved too much for the Spitfire's frame to absorb. Even as he held his line, the pilot lost control of his riddled-with-holes machine. Trailing smoke, it continued to glide down, heading right towards Manfred's Bunkerknacker in the manner reminiscent of what Japanese pilots sometimes were believed to do if they ran out of ammunition – a kamikaze attack. Manfred and his crew leapt from the truck. A few seconds later, the plane and the flak gun both went up in a massive ball of flame, a thunderclap echoing over the mountains. The explosions tossed Manfred a dozen metres away. The last thing he remembered before passing out was his head smashing into the hard terrain of the Hindukush.

❖

'What happened?' Manfred asked groggily.

Subhas and Krappe looked at him with concern while the Wehrmacht doctor observed him with clinical detachment. Manfred's head throbbed horribly, but the surroundings seemed reassuringly familiar. He was clearly in the camp headquarters. So he hadn't been killed or captured. He had survived. Unless, of course, Rommel was planning to have him court-martialled and shot when he was back for allowing that situation to arise.

'You're all right, Manfred? Thank you. If it wasn't for your 88mm, I would probably have been dead today,' Bose reached out, patting his arm gently. 'Many others are dead, though, including one of the men of your crew. To keep me alive. I'm truly sorry. I'm not sure that was a price worth paying.'

'This is war,' Krappe said softly. 'We all step out prepared for this, each day. And if a bullet has someone's name on it, it will find that man; you or I cannot do much about it. That splinter could have taken your eye as well, if not worse,' he pointed to the bandage visible from beneath Subhas's cap. 'The British have very few Spitfires in this area, perhaps five or six, which they rarely expose. You unintentionally served as bait for two of them to be brought down today. Those pilots wouldn't have expected to fly into action today, let alone get shot down here. That's how it goes.'

'May I ask, sir, why did you have to make that mad dash? What had happened?' Manfred asked, clutching his head.

Krappe stepped in and summarized the backdrop for Manfred.

'You risked your life to stop some *prisoners* from being beaten – or at worst killed – by your men? Is it *that* big a deal? Where have you been since 1939?'

'It is, to me, Manfred. It *is* a big deal. I cannot allow men to provoke each other, to kill each other, in the name of their faiths. I have worked very hard to make the men who fight for the Legion think along the lines of a country, not their language, their rituals, their religion. India is a country of many religions, and, sometimes, we are quick to fight each other. The British Army deliberately organizes most units along ethnic lines, the British government deliberately fans political differences between different faiths. I cannot allow decisions based on communal sentiments to gain legitimacy within my army – even if the price for it is being paid by the enemy.'

'But why does it matter, what those men think? They are in any case fighting against you!'

'Oh, it matters! Those men will also have to believe in us if we are to build a united India tomorrow. If Sikhs and Balochs hate each other, if Pathans and Rajputs hate each other, India will be at war with itself as soon as it is free. I had to – *have* to – speak to those men. Men on both sides. *My* men must know that they cannot lose their cool when provoked about faith. Then they are no better than a rampaging mob. *Those* men must hear from me, personally, that their lives are guaranteed by me once they surrender to the Legion, whatever their ethnicity, *whatever* their religion, whether they choose to fight with us tomorrow or not. They have to trust me, they have to trust my word.'

'You'll need a day or two to recover, Manfred. Leave his safety to me for a while. I'll take him to them in the morning,' Krappe said.

'Thanks, Kurt. And the flag must stay on my new staff car. That is not negotiable,' Bose said softly.

Manfred attempted to shrug his shoulders but winced. Krappe sighed.

❖

The men stood silent as the bodies of Second Lieutenant Sandhu, Sepoy Raghav Pandey and Havaldar Ali Mohammad, all of the Indian Legion, Captain Balck of the Afrika Korps, and *Feldwebel* (Sergeant) Gunther of the Luftwaffe were laid adjacent to each other.

The men assigned with handling subsequent ceremonies quietly did the mental maths: two men were to be cremated, three buried – one with Islamic rites, two with Christian rituals. All the priests would be engaged today. Men of four religions had died. They lay together, oblivious to the divergence of what language they spoke and what prayers they recited while life still flowed. Now, it was all in the past.

The bodies of the two Spitfire pilots had, earlier in the day, been returned to the British lines by a truck bearing a white flag, on Subhas's orders. He had thought about them, too. They had been sent to take his life, and were instead heading for a burial, thousands of miles from their home. Telegrams would go out to more than one home in the English countryside, as well. How many hundreds of thousands of such telegrams would have gone to homes across all these warring nations?

The statistics during wartime deadened one's ability to feel empathy for individuals.

But today, he wept quietly, bitterly, wiping his eyes recurrently with one hand while holding his glasses in the other.

War was war, his officers had said, and many, many thousands had fallen in this war so far. But this was not part of the larger toll of war, was it? If he hadn't opted to dash out to the front, perhaps these men would have lived another day. Perhaps they would have one day told their grandchildren tales of the battles in the mountains.

But now, these mountains would tell their tales, be their final resting place.

All his reading about religion, rebirth, karma, the Gita and Vivekananda now failed to stop the tears of the Legion's supremo, a man with many followers but few friends. Soldiers who had never seen Subhas shed a tear kept their distance, unsure of whether approaching him would comfort or infuriate him. And so, Subhas Chandra Bose, the embodiment of stoicism, sobbed silently next to the bodies of three Indians and two Germans even as a hundred or so men, Indians and Germans both, stayed quiet and gave him space.

❖

Field Marshal's Camp Office, North-West Frontier Province
1 December 1942

Dear Lucie,

You must forgive me, for I have been irregular in writing to you, the past weeks. This war goes on and on and there are phases when one loses a sense of time.

I remember writing to you in 1939, when the war started. I can recollect the very words: 'I think the whole war will peter out once Poland is done for'. I wonder if you sometimes laugh when you read such things I wrote at that point.

I am today some distance within the territory of British India, the region that the atlas will show you as the Hindukush. The soldiers of the armies in Russia would often allude to Napoleon's drive to Moscow throughout last year, and till very recently – it has after all barely been a few months since Stalingrad finally, finally fell. But even Napoleon would not have aimed to march to Kabul and beyond, to Peshawar, and to even dream of Delhi. Land forces do not manage such distances. The English, the French, the Portugese, the Dutch – they all came here, but they came in small numbers, over the sea. I do not know if any European soldiers have travelled so much over land to knock at these frontiers since the troops of Alexander the Great.

The one thing that scares me is harping too much on history, tradition and grandeur as some sort of infallible index of greatness. Julius Caesar. Alexander the Great. Cleopatra. So much that one has read about. And what have I done in this war? Rushed to Africa to save the armies of Rome from destruction. Seen the Wehrmacht smash the Greek forces in less than a month. Driven through Egypt fighting the British, with the people of that land as bystanders to our gladiatorial contests. Living in the glory of the past is a risky thing, Lucie. I hope we do not fall into that trap.

But to come back to India. Our Axis partners, the Japanese and the Indian National Army, are facing a tough fight on the Eastern front. Did you know, the distance between Peshawar and Kohima, essentially, is 2,400 km? The distance from Warsaw to Moscow was 1,250; from Warsaw to Stalingrad, 2,200! I am not sure people in Berlin or Tokyo have a sense of the immensity of this land that stretches from the Afghanistan border to the Burmese.

So many of the veterans of the Russian campaign have spoken to me of the endlessness of that land, that goes on and on and on, drives you down – you advance a hundred miles and another 300 await you. On some days, it scares me that India has similar distances and many times the people of Soviet Russia. The British Armies, we will handle, but if the local population were to stand with them and enlist in their army in large numbers, we would probably sink in the combination of distance and numbers. We simply cannot bring men enough to overrun an India that does not want us there.

This campaign therefore depends so much on the way the people of India – and the Indian soldiers on both sides – see the war.

And then there is this maverick of a man, who is partly the reason I *am here and not Paulus or Dietrich or any other General from the Russian front. A maverick who once was about to join the British Civil Service here; who was once the president of the Congress party, the biggest political force in this land so far. He is the key. On how this man convinces the Indian soldiers with the Axis to stay loyal, the Indian soldiers with the British to change their loyalties, and to the masses of this land to at least stay neutral, if not in our support – on that will depend whether our divisions and guns will lead us to a swift, decisive march and peace, or to a slow, grinding, endless battle of attrition against a never-ending mass of men and territory. The Führer once said of Heydrich – not that I liked the man – that he was worth two divisions. Here, as we commence our descent into India, Subhas Chandra Bose is worth an entire army to me.*

I hope he delivers, for his sake as well as ours.

This adventurous, impatient, uncontrollable man nearly went and got himself killed yesterday! My heart was in my mouth when I thought about how this operation would proceed without him – there is simply nobody else who can step up and do this. Thank goodness that he got back in one piece. Much of the credit goes to a Captain Manfred, the namesake of our boy. The young officer rushed to where our hero was and kept him alive amidst the chaos.

I hardly get the time to write but you and Manfred are always in my thoughts. He wrote to me saying he was looking to join the Waffen-SS. I have specifically forbidden it. He should stay with the Luftwaffe – that way he will also stay stationed within Germany itself. But Himmler's SS is out of the question. Do ensure that my decision is not flouted in my absence.

Yours, as ever,
Erwin

12

Update from the East

'... the British defence (against advancing Japanese) will not have sufficiently enthusiastic response from the people of India themselves.'

– Roosevelt's message to the US ambassador to Britain, John G. Winant

To: Gen Mohan Singh
Officer Commanding, Burma Frontier, INA
From: Subhas Chandra Bose
Supreme Commander,
Indian Legion & Indian National Army

Date: 30th November 1942

Ref. your note dated 27/11

Dear General Singh,

Please accept my heartiest congratulations at the efforts made by your troops and my condolences at the loss of so many of our brave freedom fighters.

When the history of India is finally written, they will be remembered with as much, if not more, respect than the names we today think of as our freedom fighters. Many of us have paid

with our liberty to bring freedom, but they have paid with their lives, willingly – we will forever be in their debt.

I wish I could be there with you at this moment. But I realize that I can entrust that front to you and your fellow officers, to Mr Rash Behari Bose – the military and political fronts are then in responsible and competent hands. You also have officials like Major Fujiwara who appear to be genuinely interested in strengthening an independent India that has friendly but equal relations with Japan.

On this front, however, if I leave, there is nobody quite there to lead the Legion or to deal with the leadership of Germany and Italy – Germany is a complicated and multi-layered association that challenges me substantially and I fear my absence will mean that the Legion will lose focus and resources. We will meet soon, however, of that I am sure, as our forces converge from both fronts – either I will call you to Delhi or I will travel to Calcutta!

I have read through your concerns carefully and I would like to assure you that I will not accept any compromise with the treatment and deployment of our men on the part of the Japanese officers.

I have cabled Lt Gen. Iida, since – as the commander of the entire Japanese 15th Army – he is answerable for the conduct of his officials on the ground. I have also marked copies to Lt Gen. Oshima, the Japanese ambassador in Berlin, who is a strong supporter of our initiatives and has assured me that he will convey his viewpoints to the General Staff of the IJA in Tokyo. I am not going to stand by and watch our troops be sidelined. I shall insist that the INA lead the assault on all strategic Indian targets – of course, that will mean our men will probably sustain more casualties, but such is the price to be paid for the ownership of our freedom.

I have also asked that all Indians taken as POWs be kept only in INA custody. That has been agreed to and a formal notification from Lt Gen. Iida shall reach you within a day or two. British POWs can be kept in custody of either side, based on the situation on the ground.

I understand that you have, of course, been associated with the INA since it was conceptualized in 1941, and most current officers are those who joined during that phase, but there are many capable officers who have joined the ranks of the INA from the forces that surrendered after the fall of Singapore in February, earlier this year. Do reach out to their ranks and I am sure we will have an even stronger leadership pool. Our struggles will not end the day we drive away the British and the challenges will be manifold for some time to come.
Jai Hind!

P.S. I would like a detailed note on the special detachment of women volunteers who are presently undergoing military training by the INA. This is probably the first-ever such military unit in Asia and the day it steps into action will be a landmark moment for the women of our motherland. I cannot emphasize enough the significance of this unit's formation.

13

The Italian Job

Jalahalli POW Camp, Bangalore,
8 December 1942
11.50 p.m.

THE DECEMBER NIGHT WAS DARK, BUT NOT COLD.

The sound of propellers first caught the attention of the guard on Tower B, but it did not alarm him. It was probably a training exercise of the Royal Indian Air Force at the nearby base, he told himself.

But the sounds grew louder. An experienced aviator would have, by now, identified the sound as that of a Japanese Shōwa L2D3-Ia transporter, not that of the RIAF's favourite Dakota. An experienced aviator would also have estimated that it was a group of at least a dozen planes flying low and coming in from the east. But there was no such experienced man on guard duty.

Not that the 400 or so men who guarded the camp would have paid great attention to their mannerisms anyway; the guard unit comprised mostly men who were not fit or young enough for active military duty, or else they would have been either at the Burma border or the Afghan one. The tower guards had medium machine guns (MMG), but the bulk of the men on perimeter patrol, accustomed to a peaceful coexistence with their captives, had the old dependable Lee Enfield 0.303 slung over their shoulders.

The 18,000 Italians lodged at the camp were among the 38,000 captured in December 1940 when Mussolini's ill-judged North African adventure was confronted at Sidi Barrani by English, Australian and New Zealander troops, before Rommel was despatched to pull him out of trouble. The Axis never lost the advantage that Rommel's Afrika Korps took later that year, but these POWs had been shipped off to India long before the Axis forces recaptured lost territory.

Italian prisoners were scattered all over India, out of sight and out of mind for all intent, with the single largest contingent at the Jalahalli camp on Bangalore's outskirts. No one here had seriously anticipated that interior India would ever be vulnerable to the Axis – and even now, as war raged on both frontiers, no one anticipated that Bangalore would have anything to do with it for a long, long time to come.

As the noise became louder, the guards in all towers anxiously craned their necks upwards, towards the clear, moonless sky. Perhaps they should have been looking downwards, for at that very instant, flames erupted from the central barracks and leapt skywards from a gap in the thatched roof – a gap that had not proved to be very difficult to create for the men of the Italian Ariete division. It was barely thirty seconds to midnight. It did not need a military genius to connect the two developments and realize that the fires were acting as flares for the planes above.

Almost at the stroke of midnight, the propellers seemed to pause right above the camp and the transporters opened their bellies.

First came crates, dozens of them, silken parachutes billowing, dropping silently in the windless night towards the camp. In less than a minute, the first ones crashed into the barracks, onto the parade grounds, near the perimeter, outside the perimeter. One even knocked the guard in Tower D off his perch. The prisoners rushed to the containers that landed in their proximity and began to try to pry them open with an assorted variety of improvised tools, though a few had cracked upon landing and already discharged their cargo.

Packed within these containers were hundreds of units of the Italian Army's favourite service rifle, the Carcano M91/41, a scattering of the Beretta Modello 1934 handguns and the Breda Mod 5G light machine guns, which had by now landed all over the camp, even as the sirens blared incessantly, whistles blew, and the guards rushed to deny their captives access to the weapons that would change the balance of power in that confined conflict zone within a few moments. Shots rang out. The guard on Tower C opened up with his MMG and sprayed a round on the prisoners running for the dropped crates. Somewhere around the twenty-second mark, a bullet from a Carcano went through his throat and he slumped immediately. The Lee Enfields cracked and Carcanos began to retaliate. The guards could not have known that 800 rifles had been dropped just on this camp. Even if half of those made their way to the POWs, the odds were fairly even.

Amidst the cacophony of the bullets and the propellers, most guards missed the second round of parachutes descending outside the perimeter.

What they were dropping did not look like crates. They, in fact, looked suspiciously like men in uniform. If the night had not been pitch dark, they could have been identified from their uniforms as paratroopers from the Eightieth Infantry Division La Spezia of the Italian Army – elite paratroopers, many of whose comrades were at the camp. A handful of them wore a different uniform, one that nobody in Bangalore had seen earlier, with the logo of a springing tiger on the shoulder. The group formed up quickly and began to approach the camp perimeter.

Sixty men cannot stay undetected for long, however, even on a dark night, and a few guards turned their rifles around and let off a dozen rounds in their direction. The paratroopers hugged the ground, set up half a dozen MMGs on tripods, and emptied their magazines in the direction of the fire. Having subdued the barrage of bullets directed their way, they then moved quickly, entering the camp's premises, sidestepping the bodies of POWs and guards that lay scattered, even as shots incessantly rang out from both sides.

Instructions in Urdu, Punjabi and Kannada echoed over megaphones, warning the Indian guard unit to lay down their weapons, assuring them that they would be unharmed if they followed. Over the crackle of gunfire, the loud instructions then switched to Italian, the paratroopers asking their countrymen to immediately assemble near the gates, to bring the captured guards to a holding area, and to leave it to the paratroopers to wrap up the isolated gun battles still raging in the compound.

Simultaneously, similar scenes were unfolding at multiple locations in and around the city. Twenty-two thousand Italian POWs lodged over eight camps in Jalahalli, Jakkur and Hebbal, and 200 or so local INA/Legion supporters had been preparing for this for the past two weeks. So far, the plan was working out.

If a light plane were to have been flying over the area by now, it would have noticed unexpectedly high vehicular movement. If the plane were to have come down to treetop level, it would realize that trucks, buses and an assorted variety of people-carriers were being driven rapidly across the roads of Bangalore. They were being met with few questions or police checks, since the local administration and the limited military personnel currently deployed were still deciphering whether this was a one-off raid or a larger military exercise.

The initial instinct of the locally deployed forces to rush

men to the POW camps was reversed when they received news of where the largest deployment of La Seiza men had been floating downwards to the ground – the Jalahalli air base.

The base had shortly before been strafed by a squadron of Zeros of the Imperial Japanese Navy Air Service – Zeros that had flown in with the transporters bringing in the paratroopers. Failed by their advance warning systems, that had no reason to expect a breach of air space by low-flying aircraft coming in from the east coast even as war raged on the borders, the handful of combat aircraft deployed at the base were destroyed in the first few minutes – a painfully recurrent pattern during the war for the Allies.

The staff at the air base had barely sent out messages reporting the loss of their aerial firepower when the next batch of transporters dropped 300 or so commandos in and around the base – and then, instead of turning back, to the stunned surprise of the detachment guarding the base, the planes began to assemble overhead in landing formation.

'Are you drunk, Corporal?' the officer commanding bellowed over the phone, his voice furious though still sleepy. 'Have you lost your mind? Why would Japanese planes be *landing* in Bangalore?'

'But they are, sir!' the Corporal's tone was incredulous. 'The first one just touched down. And we are surrounded, sir. I have forty men, and there are many more, at least 300 men, shooting at us – though they don't look Japanese. These are Europeans – Italians, possibly? These uniforms are similar to the ones the POWs in this region had been wearing when they first came in.'

'Get a grip, man! You're telling me that Italian paratroopers have been dropped by Japanese planes which are then landing at the airbase? That makes no sense! Find—'

The phone went dead as the Legion's sappers, atop telephone poles by now, snapped the lines.

What *was* happening?

❖

The Indian Legion sympathizers among the camp guards had had a busy fortnight, for the lives of both the inmates and the men being paradropped would not have been worth much if the timing or the drops had gone awry. But it had, so far, gone off with German precision, even though this was an entirely Indian–Italian–Japanese operation. This composition was on account of many military factors, but also influenced by Subhas's desire to reciprocate Mussolini's enthusiastic support for the Legion and the operation.

Unlike the Führer, who had to be prodded by Ribbentrop, Canaris and Rommel for anything supporting Indians against the British, the Duce had hit it off with Bose from their very first meeting.

Mussolini's support for the Legion had been both personal and generous and Subhas rarely had to face the frustration of battling the Italian bureaucracy for resources and decisions. And it was Subhas who had thought of this operation: opening up a new front by freeing and arming the over 20,000 Italians held captive around Bangalore under light security. It would not only create panic in Delhi, but also give the Duce a political victory at home. Italy was becoming an increasingly smaller player in the larger game as compared to the Reich, and a triumphant rescue of Italian prisoners so far from home would help Mussolini's image. Subhas had taken responsibility for the groundwork at the camps and for deputing a hundred Legion men, including a dozen Kannada-speaking ones, who were to act as local guides for what was to follow.

The challenge of coordinating between the precise, clinical men of the Japanese military machine and the flamboyant, swashbuckling Italians was a maddening exercise that had tested all of Subhas's composure. But this was his first *military* plan, as opposed to the political role of organizing and motivating troops, and he brought all his intellectual skills and patience to pull it off.

But it is not as if the Germans had had no role to play.

For several months, even as the Wehrmacht planners pored over maps of the Afghan–Indian border and the Japanese military analysed the Burma–India frontier, Subhas, looking for a military and psychological move beyond the ones the British would be expecting, had been reaching out via Canaris's Abwehr, to a man nobody was looking at.

❖

Louis Alexis Étienne Bonvin, the governor of French possessions in India, residing in tranquil Pondicherry, had been visibly unsettled for the past few days. He had not spoken much about it to anyone. However, had Hercule Poirot been engaged to inquire into the reasons that had left the governor in a state of acute unease, he may well have been able to track down its origins to a note delivered recently to the thereafter-distressed gentleman.

Bonvin did not like to be distressed.

Having served in the colonial service through his career, starting off in Africa, he had developed a taste for avoiding confrontation where cordial conversation delivered a solution satisfactory to both sides. Appointed as the governor of Pondicherry in 1938, he was, therefore, a surprisingly affable and popular administrator. Military grandstanding was not something that he relished. He lauded dying for one's nation, but personally preferred living to serve it instead.

Like many others posted far from their motherland, these were complex times for Bonvin. When Britain and France went to war with Germany, he was the governor of a French territory in a British-administered land. That, however, changed when France surrendered, and Marshal Pétain's Vichy France allied with the German side. His political loyalties and regard for Pétain meant that he had to act on instinct rather than reason. The day after the signing of the Armistice of 22 June 1940, he immediately recognized the government of Pétain, which technically made him a commander of troops and territories loyal to the Axis within India.

It was a move that was exhilarating, flamboyant, brave and militarily foolish.

The last part was brought to his attention in twenty-four hours by Colonel Schomberg, the British consul in Pondicherry; a man with a German-sounding name but a very British stiff upper lip. The Colonel had a very uncomplicated proposal: pledge loyalty to General de Gaulle instead of Pétain or prepare for an invasion of Pondicherry by Anglo–Indian troops.

This was June 1940. Hitler and Stalin were allies. No one had seen a Japanese ship or plane in the vicinity of Southeast Asia and no one expected to, either. Pétain was very, very far away. Colonel Schomberg was in his study, giving him deathly stares. Under the given circumstances, Bonvin made the right decision.

He buckled.

On 27 June 1940, Bonvin announced that the French establishments in India would 'remain on the British side until the final victory'.

Any remaining assumptions that the British would have been respectful or civil to the French forces that they thought could be of help to the Axis ended on 3 July, at the Battle of Mers-el-Kébir, on the coast of French Algeria, many miles from Pondicherry. Churchill had ordered the British Navy to sink the French flotilla anchored there, when they refused to surrender their ships, rather than take the risk of their falling into German hands. British naval and air forces sank a battleship and damaged five other ships, killing 1,297 French servicemen in the process. Anglo–(Vichy) French relations hit a new low.

Soon after, Bonvin had gone a step ahead and pledged the formal adherence of French India to de Gaulle's 'Free French'. De Gaulle then confirmed Bonvin afresh as the governor, thereby, moving him from the Axis to the Allied camp.

Whatever his heart may have wanted, whatever the internal tussles within it may have been, the Vichy government had promptly denounced Bonvin for treason.

In January 1942, the Permanent Military Tribunal of Saigon in French Indochina found the Governor guilty of 'delivery to a foreign power of territory belonging to France' and immediately sentenced him to death. As an add-on, it had also sentenced his wife to penal servitude for life.

Bonvin had since made peace with how things were, confident that the Axis would never get anywhere near him and continued to reign over peaceful Pondicherry.

Until now. Until the note arrived, that is. Delivered to him in the dead of the night by a French agent who had worked with him in Africa, bearing a message from an unusual trinity – Rommel, Subhas and Marshal Pétain. A note that suggested strongly that Pondicherry's famed tranquillity was set to be temporarily disturbed.

Essentially, Bonvin had to make a choice between current loyalties and the odds of survival in the long run. The note stated clearly that, post the imminent defeat of the British Indian government, the Axis forces were committed to capturing and turning him and his wife, Marcelle, over to the nearest Vichy territory to carry out the Tribunal's sentence against them. And that all members of the French military in his jurisdiction would be treated as deserters by Pétain – and would face the penalty for desertion in wartime. Unless ...

As a friendly reminder to take the note seriously, a single squadron of Japanese planes from aboard the aircraft carrier *Nippon*, that was anchored at Port Blair, had flown in at night and dropped a sortie of bombs around – but not *on* – the governor's residence. The antiquated air defence systems had proved utterly ineffective.

Bonvin then sat in his study, drinking fine French wine and thinking about life's dilemmas, tragedies, and how the more things changed, the more they remained the same.

And then he did the right thing, again.

❖

9 December 1942
1.50 a.m.

The Jalahalli air base was a maddening sight.

Hundreds of vehicles were driving at breakneck speed towards the base from all over. A vast majority of them came from the direction of the Italian POW camps scattered over the area. Commandos with fingers on the triggers of their carbines hung on to the rears of trucks or to the roofs of buses. Occasionally, they fired a burst to discourage the local police check-posts from putting their lives at risk. Some of them took a bullet in the gut and toppled over. The vehicle rarely stopped for that. Indian Legion drivers familiar with the area drove recklessly, given that they were driving to save their lives, literally.

As each improvised troop-carrier reached, men rushed out to board the transporters that had their engines running. Scattered shots still rang out from the few airbase guards who had not been captured, or by the fifty or so Indian Army men who had rushed to the base from the cantonment and were engaged in a firefight with the Italians. The balance of firepower was, however, at the moment, against them since each truck that came in brought more men, even as others kept on boarding the transporters.

Half a dozen fighter planes, Zeros, hovered overhead, their pilots more worried about the dipping needles on their fuel gauges than the likelihood of RIAF reinforcements reaching there before finishing the operation successfully.

The Zeros had taken off from the aircraft carrier *Nippon* that was, tonight, barely 60 kilometres off the coast of Pondicherry. They were flying in shifts. Unlike most carrier-based fighters, Zero pilots did not stress much about the risk of running out of fuel before getting back to the carrier; the Zero had an operating range of 1,800 kilometres, by far the best for any comparative plane in the world at this point in time. The Shōwa L2D3-Ia transporters that were flying in and out in an endless chain, protected by the Zeros over land, had a range of approximately 3,000 kilometres. They had flown in from Port Blair, which was 1,650 kilometres from Bangalore as the crow flies, and so they would have been extremely hard-pressed if they had to fly back there without refuelling, more so since all engines were kept running on the tarmac.

But they were *not* flying back to Port Blair.

They were taking off from Jalahalli and landing, barely a couple of hours later, at Pondicherry, where Bonvin – who had intimated the Viceroy at midnight of his decision to disassociate with de Gaulle and restore his allegiance to Marshal Pétain and the Axis – was watching a small army of 20,000 Italian POWs and 4,000 Italian and Indian Legion soldiers take shape, one planeload at a time.

It was a small army by the standards of WWII, but there was no other army in marching distance to combat it. As the Legion and Abwehr's intelligence had indicated, the British did not have more than 5–6,000 troops in this region, mostly barracked in cantonments. They could not pull out men from either active frontier to bolster those numbers immediately. They would probably try to starve or surround Pondicherry, but now, after the Bangalore–Pondicherry airlift, they could not just march in and occupy it – unless they raised a force of 40,000 or thereabouts.

Many of the transporters dropped men on the tarmac at Pondicherry and turned back, to take off yet again to ferry another round from Jalahalli. Zeros from the aircraft carrier *Kyoto*, watching the situation off the coast of Pondicherry, kept the skies clear of the few RIAF aircraft deployed for reconnaissance and patrol duties in this area. A dozen Zeros hovered above Pondicherry airfield while thirty others patrolled the carrier–Pondicherry–Bangalore corridor, keeping away the RIAF and strafing the anti-aircraft batteries that sporadically opened up.

After two rounds of ferrying, the transporters refuelled at Pondicherry and flew back to Port Blair, under Zero cover, till 60 kilometres off the coast. After that, it was a 1,400-kilometre flight where they would have to depend on their own armament against any RIAF attacks, but when flying in large formations, the collective firepower dissuaded the odd British fighter from engaging too closely. Other cargo-carrier planes had already landed at Pondicherry from Port Blair, dropped enough light weapons, uniforms and ammunition to equip 20,000 infantrymen from scratch, and turned back even as the first planes were descending over Bangalore.

❖

As the sun rose over the Pondicherry coast, both Bangalore and Pondicherry had come to terms with what had happened overnight.

The Viceroy's office and the Axis headquarters evaluated reports and attempted to make sense of them.

An unshaven, sleepless, bleary-eyed Subhas assessed the gains and losses from the operation.

To get the Italians and Indians by sea to Port Blair, which had been in Japanese/INA hands since early 1942, had taken a month, and it had taken Mussolini himself to get the Italian Navy to agree to do it; no Italian ships had ever sailed this far east in wartime. German U-Boats had been pressed into service to accompany them till Ceylon. To get enough planes from the Japanese to support the Italian operation, given that there had not been a single joint Japanese–German or Japanese–Italian action in the war yet, had taken all of Subhas's standing at Tokyo, including reaching out to Tojo himself.

Leaning on Bonvin had needed Canaris and Rommel both, who themselves had subsequently advised using Italian – and not German – troops for the operation. The French and the Italians had been on the same side in WWI. The likelihood of bad blood between locally barracked Italian troops and Bonvin's 6,000 French soldiers was less likely than if the troops were German, given how the Nazis had made a point of rubbing French noses in the ground during and after the armistice. The French would hopefully tolerate the Italians but would very likely hate Germans barracked alongside them.

That, of course, was just the political aspect. On the military side, Subhas went over the details again. Over 300 Italian POWs had been killed in the escape attempt, shot by guards in the camps, or by local police and army, on the way to the airfield, or in the shooting at the airfield itself. Two transporters had been lost when one that was landing crashed into one that was taking off – sixty or so men had died. Three transporters and seven Zeros had been taken down by anti-aircraft fire through the night along the route. Forty-six Italian paratroopers and twenty-two men of the Legion had fallen, either at the camps or in the shooting at the airfield. The total casualties, therefore, added up to over 400 men lost, but of whom only about a hundred were combatants sent into action.

Was 400 men a high price to pay? Most of whom were not men who had sworn an oath to free India, and may well have lived out the duration of the war peacefully, alive, irrespective of which side won? This was not an easy question to answer.

What was a fact, however, was that in one night, as a military strategist, his plan had added an element to the war for which the Allies had not been prepared. He could not have landed 20,000 new men that far south, but he had added that many to the Axis cause overnight. Pondicherry was now an Axis-controlled territory. Unlike the Andamans, it was not hundreds of kilometres away but right on the Indian mainland. Like the Andamans, it could not be recaptured easily, given how the Allies were placed militarily. The 30,000 men could be made into 50,000 in a month's time, resources permitting. A beachhead, but a very large one. More importantly, it would electrify the popular mood and irrevocably shatter the psychological insulation of the country's interior from the approach of the Legion and the Axis.

British India now had to reckon with Axis forces that could not be easily pushed back, to the west, to the east, and to the south. Troops could not be taken away from the south to reinforce the western and eastern borders without weighing consequences of what the force in Pondicherry could do. Naval access to the Indian mainland was now a work in progress for the Axis.

A third front had been created.

14

War of Words

'THE CONGRESS WORKING COMMITTEE HAS ISSUED A RESOLUTION that may interest you, Subhas.'

Nambiar walked in, holding copies of two newspapers.

Subhas looked up from his breakfast, a curious expression on his face.

'But the CWC is detained at Aurangabad, is it not? How would they pass a resolution and have it circulated while being held captive? I've spent enough time under arrest to know how that goes.'

'Well, let us say in this case, the British would have no reason to deny them the opportunity to send this out,' Nambiar smiled.

'And that would be because—?'

In response, Nambiar began to read out excerpts from the paper he was holding.

'The Congress, having taken due cognizance of the events proceeding from the combined Axis offensive which commenced in November, places on record its deep concern at the escalating nature of the conflict on Indian territory and appeals to both the Axis and Allied forces to desist from actions that adversely the safety and well-being of India's people, who have been dragged into this global conflict between Imperialism and Fascism against their will.'

'I can't disagree with that.'

'Yes, but it gets better. I'll leave out the jargon and give you the crux, which is: "The Congress also expresses its apprehension at the Imperialist war that Britain engaged India in, against her will, which is now at a point where Fascist forces have stepped onto the soil of this great nation without any popular mandate to represent Indian interests against Imperial Britain. The Congress emphatically reiterates its equidistance from the forces of both Imperialism and Fascism, and asserts that neither have a role to play in India's affairs."'

'Actually, I don't disagree with that either. Stop trying to get me worked up.'

Nambiar smiled mischievously and raised his hand, asking Subhas to pause, then proceeded to read out one last para in a slow, theatrical tone.

'As to the conflicting appeals made to the Indian soldier, the Congress believes that neither the Indians fighting as part of the Allied forces, nor the scattered elements that have reportedly crossed over to fight along the Axis, should be serving foreign powers in a battle for Indian territory. Since neither warring side has any legitimacy to enlist the local population, the Congress discourages the people from taking up arms for either regime and advocates a peaceful non-cooperative disengagement from the entire war effort. Neither warring power has any moral authority to be present on Indian soil. We call upon both parties to the conflict to step back and let Indians exercise their right to self-determination. Only an independent India can decide what part, if any, it wishes to play in this global scenario.'

Subhas was never known to have uttered an expletive in public. Did he do that now? Only Nambiar was standing close enough to know.

❖

Peshawar Base Camp
11 December 1942

Dear Jawahar,

I read the note issued by the Congress Working Committee. Given that

- *it could not find a word to say in appreciation of the man who has built a militarized force to fight and overthrow the British imperialist occupation of India, nor a word of gratitude to the men of that force, hundreds of whom have shed their blood*
- *it could not decide whether to praise or criticise the Viceroy's miserable handling of affairs and therefore opted to ignore it altogether*
- *it inexplicably equated the British, who have brought and kept armed forces onto our soil without our consent for two centuries, with the Axis, who have a handful of soldiers here today accompanying the men of the Indian Legion and the INA*
- *it gave no clear message to the men in arms as to whether the Congress expects them to die defending the Viceroy or encourages them to join the Indian Legion and fight to free India and instead preached, as often, majestic inaction that amounts to no real threat to the Empire.*

I must confess it hugely disappointed me, for was it not as recently as August when the Congress seemed to have come out of its stupor and passive affection for the Allies, and for once, without ifs and buts, stated that the British must 'Quit India'? Or was it just Gandhi, for once, pushing the party beyond its comfort level?

Language is your strength, my dear friend, but the point of it should be clarity, not obfuscation. All that I was able to deduce from the resolution was that there is a degree of disappointment at what is unfolding, and a corresponding degree of discomfort at being able to do little to influence the course of events either way.

I have left behind the bitterness of Tripuri, dear Jawahar, but the facts are still fresh in my mind. When a prominent section of the leadership of the Congress – you being additionally prominent among them – opted to practice obstructionism and non-cooperation towards me, when they made it clear that they would not support my presidentship and the journey would be one of strife and, dare I say it, sabotage, I did not engage in conflict. I stepped down.

Stepping down or backing out is not an option for me today. Much has changed over these three years. In 1939, I wrote to you, you may recall, and I quote, since Emilie has kept a meticulous record of my correspondence: 'Foreign policy is a realistic affair to be determined largely from the point of view of a nation's self-interest ... Frothy sentiments and pious platitudes do not make foreign policy.'

I know you had, and continue to have, a view that is very divergent from mine when it comes to the forces of Adolf Hitler and Benito Mussolini. I, equally, have not had reason to change my position significantly from what I had written to you then: 'It is no use condemning countries like Germany and Italy on the one hand and on the other, giving a certificate of good conduct to British and French Imperialism.'

These certificates, in any case, are not of great consequence any longer. Neither does Herr Hitler need my endorsement nor will anyone's goodwill change the direction in which the British hegemony over Asia has been headed from the day Singapore surrendered.

We are all, militarily at least, marginal players with grand statements, and we need to understand that if we are to make a force of consequence of ourselves and of our nation.

As the Axis armies head steadily closer to the heartland and to Delhi, as the question of the military result of the current situation becomes increasingly about when, and not if, the British forces will either flee or be taken prisoner, it is inevitable that we shall meet at Delhi again – or at Aurangabad – my dear Jawahar, perhaps sooner than you would have wished.

I bear the highest regard for the Mahatma, for Sardar, for you, for Maulana Azad, and for my erstwhile brothers in arms from the phase where the Congress was still actively an anti-Imperialist organization and not so concerned about putting Britain in trouble during the war. I also respect, or at least understand, many of the concerns that Mr Jinnah has. However, as the commander of the Indian Legion, and as the leader of the Azad Hind government in exile recognized by the Axis nations, I will have to undertake certain responsibilities as the military situation stabilises.

To that end, I will seek your cooperation with all humility. However, were it not to be offered, I will proceed with what is necessary despite either the indifference or the opposition of the Congress – or, for that matter, the Muslim League, or any other political formation.

Forgive me if I have been excessively harsh, but these are trying times and I have no patience for social protocols, any further. I wish the divergence of our ideological positions did not have the degree of impact it has had on our personal association. I hope in the time to come, we can emphasize on what we share rather than what we differ on. India will need all its able minds to work together, dear Jawahar, if it is to emerge united and organized, once the storm of war is past. If we all retreat into our ideological corners, we will not be doing justice to the hour for which our motherland has waited this long.

Subhas

P.S. This letter will make its way to you at Aurangabad via trusted associates. If you wish to respond, the same person will arrange the letter's journey back – however, since I am changing base every third day at the moment, the chances of a note reaching me amidst the flux of the front are slim.

15

The Children and the Spymaster

22 December 1942

THE STURDY JUNKERS JU 52 TRANSPORT RUMBLED THROUGH THE night sky. It was chilly and the seating was primitive, at best. Subhas peered out of the window and could just about make out the Messerschmitt Bf 110 escort flying half a mile out. A second one would be on the other side, he guessed, even though the Luftwaffe did not expect to meet the RAF over this part of the war zone – not with the nearest RAF fighters now being based out of Lahore, several hundred kilometres away.

Now that the fighting had shifted to the plains, the mobility and speed of the Axis was proving tougher to handle for the British Indian Army – more so because the British and Indian parts of it were not always on the same wavelength. The British were better at dogged, defensive fighting, which they demonstrated through November in the hills, making the Axis bleed for every hill taken. But now, in mid-December, with some Indian units defecting en masse, some not interested in fighting to the finish against the Indian Legion's combination of firepower and emotional propaganda, and only a few staying insulated, the fighting on the plains of the Punjab was less equal than it had been on the hills.

The Multan air base had been handed over by the Indian detachment guarding it against the Legion's hundred paratroopers without a shot being fired, following which, transport planes had landed another 800 men within a couple of hours. Across the western plains, airports, bridges and radio installations were falling to the Axis without bloodshed. Subhas was on the radio each day, appealing to the Indian soldier on the other side to not risk his life to keep the British flag flying in Delhi, and to instead help him unfurl the Azad Hind banner there. Pamphlets were distributed by the thousands over the front line by air.

Loyalties were being tested regiment by regiment, company by company, platoon by platoon. Subhas was recurrently invoking Mangal Pandey to remind soldiers that loyalty to their motherland was above the duty to their foreign paymaster – that '*namak*' was not above nation.

But right now, Subhas was flying away from the scene of battle, along with Rommel's trusted aide Westphal, for a meeting that could not be made public.

Nazi Germany had layers within layers, wheels within wheels, empires within empires, and if you wanted to check one empire, you had to reach out to another. Just the way that if you wanted to check the British, you had to reach out to the Axis.

❖

The Ju 52 landed with a bone-rattling thud. Clearly, nobody was taking care of the airstrip at Gwadar. Rudely awakened by the jolt, Subhas looked at his watch. The slow but sturdy plane had taken its time to get to the port city from Quetta, where they had stopped to refuel after taking off from Peshawar. It was not yet dawn. The small squad assigned to be with him, just a dozen men from the Legion and from Rommel's personal bodyguards, handpicked for loyalty and the ability to stay silent as much as for combat skills, got him from the plane to the waiting truck in a matter of minutes. The Bf 110s circled overhead for a while before coming to land. The planes would refuel and prepare for the return flight. He did not intend to stay for very long.

At about the same time as Bose was landing, the placid surface of the Arabian Sea was disturbed as the U-123, a submarine with an elite crew lent by the Kreigsmarine to its very important passenger, broke through it to emerge silently, a kilometre from shore. Though there was no significant Royal Navy presence in the region, the passenger who had travelled this far to meet Bose – instead of in Berlin – out of the range of Himmler and Heydrich's omnipresent agents was too precious for unnecessary risks to be taken. The crew kept engines running at full readiness to dive, if needed, while messages were exchanged by flashlight with operatives on shore. The U-boat's skipper had enforced absolute radio silence through the long journey and he was not going to breach it now.

A few minutes later, two small boats came and picked up the passengers for whom the submarine had come all the way from the French coast. The submarine's crew, too, were on standby. They expected to commence their return journey in three hours' time.

❖

Subhas, Westphal and Dhillon sat quietly in the sparsely furnished cabin on the boat anchored off an isolated stretch of beach. Guards stood on the boat's deck and patrolled the shore adjacent. The sound of a small motor approached, there was an exchange of words in German. Then the boat rocked slightly as a smaller craft pulled up adjacent and feet clambered aboard. A few moments later, the diminutive figure of Admiral Wilhelm Canaris, the chief of the Abwehr, stepped into the cabin, followed by Colonel Lahousen.

A frail, deceptively timid-looking man, Canaris had been described by a friend as 'the most unmilitary of persons'. Few at the time understood that he was running a parallel military establishment that was either indifferent or actively hostile towards most Nazi goals.

In September 1939, upon realizing what the SS had done with civilians and Jews in Poland, Canaris had travelled to Hitler's train – inexplicably named 'Amerika' – to register his protest but had been held off by the chief of the Armed Forces High Command, General Keitel. Legend had it that the Abwehr chief told the army chief, in the presence of his staff, that 'the world will one day hold the Wehrmacht responsible for these methods'. The fact that he got away with it reflected his indispensability to the regime and his iron grip on the Abwehr, which he had run since 1935.

His efforts to stop the work of the Jew-hunting *Einsatzgruppen* killer squads in Russia, had, however, earned him the lifelong enmity of Reinhard Heydrich and the SS–SD establishment. Rumour had it that on one occasion, he personally brought Jews off a concentration camp train by identifying them as Abwehr agents. Fact had it that he intervened to stop the execution of captured French officers in Tunisia. His deputy, Hans Oster, had gathered enemies of the regime within the military structure and brought them into the Abwehr, where they could function as military professionals without needing to prove their personal loyalty to Nazi methods or to anti-Semitism.

Canaris, against all odds, ran a wartime military machine that sheltered those being hunted by the SS or the SD.

For Canaris to meet Subhas one-to-one publicly in Germany, or indeed anywhere the SS or the Gestapo would have ears on the ground, would be awkward, if not dangerous, for both of them. More so when Bose had rankled the SS.

Lahousen was now to stay on in India to assist Canaris's plan for the nation. The Abwehr had an extensive network in Afghanistan and the adjoining regions of the semi-autonomous tribal territories. A discussion about the plan had brought Canaris here. But before that could be taken up, there was something Subhas had written to him about.

'I have gone through the note you sent, Mr Bose. Please elaborate on it.'

Canaris' tone was soft, his eyes absorbing, scanning, yet giving nothing away. His English was fluent; no translator needed be present. Subhas did not know if the man could be completely trusted. But there was nobody else of that stature – more importantly, that degree of power – in Germany, whom he could say these things to, with the possible exception of Rommel. And he needed to stop what was coming. It was a risk he would have to take.

'I will apprise you of the basic facts of the case, Admiral, though from what I have heard of you, there is very little of such matters that you are not aware of.'

'My job is to stay informed.'

Subhas smiled at the understatement.

'Admiral, I am extremely concerned at a development regarding a large group of Polish children – about a thousand – many of whom are believed to be Jewish. I understand that these children are from Eastern Poland and many of their parents are either no more or in Russian custody. They have travelled overland from Ashkabad in Turkmenistan, and from Krasnovodsk, via Persia, before the German forces came through. Upon reaching the Persian Gulf, they travelled by ship to Bombay.'

'But they are not in Bombay now.'

'No, for they could not deboard there. For all its condemnation of Germany's approach towards the Jews, for all its declaring war in Poland's support, the British government in India initially declined to let them get off at Mumbai. At which point, the ruler of this princely state, Nawanagar, Jam Saheb Digvijaysinhji – who had apparently heard of their plight from the head of the Polish government in exile, Padrewski – stepped forward to host them. So they were allowed to enter Bombay, and after three months there, they were shifted to this location called Balachadi in his territory. Which is where they are today, and have been for some months now.'

'I have heard about some of this, yes. What role do I have here?'

Subhas realized that Canaris knew both the information he was sharing and the questions he would thereafter put. He continued, nevertheless.

'At our present rate of advance, I expect that Axis ground troops will cross through Nawanagar within a week or so. No princely state has so far offered armed resistance when we have sought the right of passage, and I do not think it will either.'

'Your concern is not local, then.'

'My concern is a note from the office of Reich Security Main Office of the SS, Department IV, to the Chief of Staff, Afrika Korps, asking that the Polish children be gathered once that area is under Axis control. These children are then to "be made accessible to officers of Department IV" who will "ascertain as to how many of them are Jewish," and then will "advise on further course of action" or some such phrase. This is the first time that any such request – instruction, whatever it is – about racial profiling has come up in our theatre of war.'

Westphal put forward a document in front of the spymaster. Canaris read through, his face devoid of expression, as always. He then turned to Subhas.

'You are being asked – or rather the Afrika Korps detachment with your Legion is being asked, just so we have the protocol correct – to hand over these Polish children so the SS can identify the Jews among them. That worries you, I surmise. But does that surprise you, Herr Bose? Unless my homework fails me, did you not object to a resolution to offer Jewish refugees space in India in 1938? Why are these handful of Polish children a cause of concern for you today?'

Dhillon and Westphal winced. Even Lahousen, a silent observer to this discussion, was surprised. Few men spoke that bluntly to Subhas, at least they did not anymore.

Subhas took it on the chin and did not flinch. 'I do not see things the same way I did in 1942 as I did in 1938, Admiral. Just as in 1938, I saw some things differently from how I saw them in 1932. And I am not embarrassed to admit that. In 1938, when Jawahar spoke of the Jews in Germany, I thought this was an internal matter concerning Germany, that it was political posturing which would settle down. I was wrong.'

At the end of 1938, Subhas, the then Congress president, had blocked, along with the CWC, the passage of a resolution by Jawaharlal Nehru to welcome Jewish refugees to India. The innocuously worded resolution had stated: 'The Committee sees no objection to the employment in India of such Jewish refugees as are experts and specialists and who can fit in with the new order in India and accept Indian standards'.

Subhas's opposition to the proposal had been based on his stated view that 'foreign policy is a realistic affair to be determined largely from the point of view of a nation's self-interest' – ergo, he did not see that as being in India's self-interest. Nehru was of the opinion that Subhas 'did not approve of any step being taken by the Congress which was anti-German or anti-Italian'.

'A rather large error of judgement for someone as politically perceptive as you, is it not, Mr Bose?'

'Perhaps. In 1938, I did not fully comprehend the degree of hostility the Reich fostered towards Jews. That is probably a bad reading of the situation. But is that unique? In 1938, Chamberlain declared that he had obtained "peace for our times", Admiral. In 1939, Stalin thought he had a few years of peace with your country after the Ribbentrop–Molotov pact made Hitler and Stalin allies. People far better placed than I seem to have reason to rethink what they took at face value in 1938 and 1939 – or am I the only one?'

A wry smile crept over the spymaster's face.

'Your silence on the state of Jews has been somewhat conspicuous, as contrasted with your compatriot, Mr Nehru, is it not? I mean no offence – I just want a sense of where you stand on this.'

Subhas got up, put his hands on the small table, and looked into Canaris' eyes.

'I cannot control, change or influence what *any* of the powers do – be it Britain, be it Russia, be it Italy, be it Germany. What power do I have? I do not believe fasting, lecturing and writing letters shape the policies of international powers. Mahatma Gandhi had a view on world peace. He wrote a letter to Hitler. And what does that amount to?'

'You do not believe in sentimental statements, I understand – a practical politician, right?'

'I believe in taking up issues when I can *do* something about them. I have an army of a few divisions, adding up to less than 100,000 men, split over two fronts, trained, fed and armed by the Axis. Every bullet the Legion fires puts me in greater debt to the Axis – a financial debt that I am committed to pay with free India's revenues. What was the force Operation Barbarossa was launched with, Admiral? 3,000,000 soldiers? Did your Field Marshals commanding those 3,000,000 troops tell the Führer or Heinrich Himmler to fight a fair war, to stop the ghettoization, or worse, of the Jews? Did you, *Admiral*, physically step in to rescue anyone by putting a gun to Himmler's head? No? *You*, a lifelong Naval officer, the head of the Abwehr, speak of these things secretively, lest there be a piano wire around your neck tomorrow in some basement in Berlin, do you not?'

Canaris stayed impassive. The officers in the room cringed.

'But *I*, standing on India's borders to undo the 200 years of British colonization of my motherland, with a force that began with 600 POWs, should have opposed the mechanisms of the Nazis in Europe. How? By sitting on a fast, maybe with a banner, on the steps outside Himmler's office? That moral posturing means nothing! If India is worth something tomorrow, an Indian leader's voice will be taken seriously. *Then* my word will have value. I am fighting for an Indian leader's word to be militarily, politically, worth something before we lecture other nations!'

'I am not questioning your personal ideology, Herr Bose. It was merely something that intrigued me.'

Subhas took a moment to check his temper.

'Admiral, I do not harbour the delusion that the Führer or the Reichsführer-SS will develop a different perspective towards anyone – the Jews, the Slavs, the political dissenters – on the basis of my opinions. And so I keep those opinions to myself. But I will not have all that enter my country with their loyalists. I cannot let the SS, or for that matter you, or Rommel, do something like what that note suggests, with my cooperation. If any German forces attempt to seize Jewish children in India, I will order the Legion's men to stop them – by force, if necessary. You tell me how it goes from there.'

Canaris exhaled slowly. He then turned to Westphal, Lahousen and Dhillon.

'Officers, if you please, I would like to speak to the Indian Legion's Supreme Commander in private.'

PART II

16

Frontier Mail

'I am inclined, however, to think that in proportion to their numbers, and considering India as a whole, the Muslims have never ceased to play an important role in the public life of the country, whether before or under the British rule – and that the distinction between Hindu and Muslim of which we hear so much nowadays is largely an artificial creation, a kind of Catholic–Protestant controversy in Ireland, in which our present-day rulers have had a hand.'

– Subhas Bose, *An Indian Pilgrim*, 1937

'British propaganda has tried to create the impression that the Muslim League is almost as influential a body as Congress, and that it represents the majority of India's Muslims. This, however, is far from the truth. In reality there are several influential and important Muslim organizations which are thoroughly nationalist.'

– Subhas Bose, radio broadcast, March 1942

Indo–Afghan Border
27 December 1942

'THIS IS NOT A GOOD IDEA, SIR.'

Hauptmann Manfred Armbruster's face was drawn into a permanently etched frown and his eyes reflected an unflattering combination of stress and sleeplessness.

'This could be a trap, sir,' he repeated.

'I know, I know,' Subhas benignly muttered as the heavy Kübelwagen heaved and rolled on the dirt tracks that maps kindly referred to as roads.

The mountain wind was chilly and bitter this January morning as dawn broke. The convoy of eight vehicles – Subhas's car, two truck-mounted 88 mm guns, and five trucks packed with Legion troops – had been on the road since 3 a.m., driving largely guided by the moon and parking lights. The RIAF was not a factor in this part of the world, but it was still an ideal ambush territory.

Their destination was Gurwek, on the Indo–Afghan border. Peshawar to Miran Shah was about 250 kilometres and Gurwek was another 50-odd kilometres from there. The 300-kilometre journey had to be covered in two days, mostly travelling in the dark. Another hour or so of the rattling ride was left.

Subhas mused at the stark, desolate beauty of the terrain. No wonder the British forces had struggled for several years to dislodge the man he was headed to meet. This region of freezing winds and hot blood was not one you could hold down at gunpoint. The Mughals had experienced it, the British were discovering it over and over, and who knew how many other armies would grind themselves down in the future in the same futile exercise?

The German military advice was to saturate and dominate the area with force, but he had reminded them of both the failed British efforts and of the German experiences in such terrain in Yugoslavia. This terrain and its men did not lend themselves well to 'control'; far better to converse and collaborate than have a test of firepower.

The Afrika Korps did not have either the manpower or the single-mindedness of dominance at gunpoint, and so the point was not pushed. India was too remote for the elite SS to be present in any numbers of consequence, but Subhas was under no illusion that they would have amicably agreed to anything where collaboration came before coercion.

It was, however, the Indian Legion that was the dominant military element of the Axis advance into India, and it was advancing surely, if sometimes slowly. And so, in complete defiance of the Axis advice, the Legion's leader was making the last part of this journey by himself, with only 120 of his soldiers. The Italian and German officers in Peshawar were already placing bets on the likelihood of him being held hostage at the end of his overly adventurous stunt.

Subhas knew that, but his mind was not engaged in such possibilities.

He conceded superior military strategy to the Axis, but he did not think as highly of their approach in dealing with people in most of the lands they stepped onto. If the Germans had been less of an occupying force and more of a liberating force, many of those who were glad to be free of Moscow's iron grip in 1941 would have willingly become part of the Axis effort on the eastern front, he felt; but the racial undercurrent to military strategy meant that Germany inevitably created enemies, where, with a more chivalrous code of war and more respect for the local people, it may well have had the opportunity to build allies. The Japanese had frequently been mirroring that reflex in the east.

Any foreign power that thought force was the way to deal with the mountainous people of *this* region was going to engage in an endless battle of attrition.

Subhas had to form his own strategy: he was here to build a nation, not to conquer territory.

❖

The convoy slowed as it approached a narrow bridge. Two trucks parked across were blocking the track. Twenty or so turbaned men stood at some distance, guns slung across their shoulders. Subhas quietly nodded at an officer sitting next to the driver. The officer, a captain, spoke on the radio set in his hand and all the vehicles in the convoy braked softly and stopped. Manfred noticed that the rumble of engines did not, however, die down; none of the drivers had switched off the ignition.

The captain, Abdul Ghaffar of the Indian Legion's Sixth Regiment, stepped out and marched towards the informal checkpoint, even as half a dozen men leapt out of the last trucks and stood on either side, fingers on the triggers of their MP35s. He spoke briefly in a dialect neither Subhas nor Manfred understood – they assumed it was Balochi – nodded and walked back. By the time he had stepped back into the vehicle, the men of the local militia had climbed into their trucks – that looked very much like captured British Army transports – and the first one was already beginning to drive over the culvert.

The captain had been taken POW when the 4/10 Baloch was overrun by the Axis in North Africa in June, that year, and had agreed to join the Legion, the next month. He had grown to be a trusted resource for Subhas for some time. Initially, he was among the key officers to deal with the Legion's Baloch troops, and then to convince Pathan and Baloch soldiers captured in battle to fight along the Legion. This region they were driving through was familiar territory for him. Subhas was depending on him today to send a message, just by his presence, to his hosts.

He now spoke briefly to Subhas. At word from him, the engine revved, the Kübelwagen kicked into first gear and pulled away sharply. The men keeping an eye on the road clambered back in, as the other drivers followed. The second truck of the local militia waited till the last Legion truck – carrying one of the 88 mm guns – had crossed, then joined the convoy as the rear-guard. With one 'host' truck at either end of the convoy, the Legion and its commander continued the journey into uncharted territory.

❖

At Gurwek, Mirza Ali Khan – better known to his followers and the British as the Fakir of Ipi – was informed of the imminent arrival of Subhas Chandra Bose.

It was said that the Fakir had miraculous religious powers that protected his followers from bullets. Subhas took that claim with a pinch of salt, but he admired the clearly miraculous leadership and political skills that a man needed to bring the warring tribes of Waziristan together so effectively.

Refusing to accept British suzerainty, positioning himself as the leader of a movement to carve out an independent Pashtunistan, the Fakir had made life miserable for the British for years. Brigade-strength British forces supported by bombers had failed to capture or even weaken him.

As a gesture of support for his anti-British operations, a small detachment of Indian and German soldiers had been despatched to his headquarters during Operation Bajadere, in which a hundred or so men were para-dropped by the Abwehr in January 1942 at various points across Afghanistan, the Persio–Afghan border and the Indo–Afghan border. These men worked to plan and execute sabotage operations and gather information in preparation for a future land assault from the west – the assault that was finally underway.

❖

The wind was still chilly, and the sky overcast as the convoy roared into the secluded camp and came to a halt. Dozens of armed men stood around the camp perimeter, atop vantage points, and at the gate of what probably was the cottage that housed the Fakir. The two trucks carrying the dual-use 88 mm guns positioned themselves to face any surprise visitor from the air or any artillery from the mountains nearby.

At a command from Captain Ghaffar, the 120 men accompanying Subhas segregated into groups of thirty each. Three groups took up positions at vantage points at some distance from each other. The fourth acted as a bodyguard unit for Subhas. The Fakir's men – and the host himself, keenly watching from a window – kept an eye on them. But the features, the physique, and the name tags – that Subhas had insisted for each man – made it abundantly clear that this was home for the visitors just as much it was for the hosts.

It was no coincidence.

The only Germans in this convoy, apart from Manfred, were those manning the 88 mm units. About fifty of the men were from the original 4/10 Baloch, including most of the officers. The rest were originally from the Fifth Battalion (Pathans) of the Fourteenth Punjab regiment and had joined the INA after Singapore's surrender.

Subhas had been determined to go to this meeting with a contingent entirely made up of Baloch and Pathan soldiers, as a political message. The Pathans had, therefore, been moved by sea, two weeks earlier, been reissued with Legion kits upon landing at an Iranian port, and had then travelled up from there to an assembly point, just a couple of days back.

If the men guarding Subhas at Gurwek, in the heart of the Pashtun uprising, were all Pathans and Balochs, if he could put his safety entirely in their hands in *this* place, then nothing needed to be said – it was understood that he could not be given lessons in how either the Fakir or anyone else were the sole custodians of Pathans, or of the region – or, indeed, of all Muslims.

The only non-military person accompanying him was Mian Akbar Shah Shahib of Nowshera – an enterprising man he had met in 1939 and appointed as the organizer of the Forward Bloc in NWFP. Akbar Shah had put up with some pressure and flak for joining the black sheep of the Congress in 1939, when the Congress was by far the major force in the NWFP, primarily on account of the personal stature of the Khan brothers. But Subhas's stature had grown in his absence, more so once the news emerged that he had escaped to Kabul via Peshawar disguised as a Pathan in 1941.

❖

Subhas was aware that the Muslim League and the Viceroy were in a comfortable equation: The Quit India movement could have been a far greater problem for the regime if the League had not decided to keep its distance. To talk of India as two nations had served Britain very well – it played the role of adjudicator, arbiter, protector and umpire, as the country's largest communities seemed to be unable to agree on most things; or at least their political leadership couldn't.

Churchill had defended keeping India colonized despite American reservations and had kept it out of the purview of the Atlantic Charter by arguing that India would lapse into civil war the moment British control slackened, that the religious divide was too deep for India to be left to the Indians. An India that splintered apart as soon as British control was lifted would not only legitimize the past century of colonization, it would also be, militarily and politically, a far better option for Britain.

A single, integrated India – with a huge pool of manpower – emerging as an independent state in the middle of the war, an Axis-friendly state at that, would mean British influence being wiped out in South-East Asia for decades. From the Suez to Singapore, there would be no state sympathetic to, or controlled by, the Allies.

The most bitterly, uncompromisingly anti-British leader in the country becoming the controlling figure in a militarily and politically integrated India that extended from Afghanistan to Burma, more so at this point of time, was a very, *very* bad projection in meetings in London at the moment.

An independent but split India? Not as bad.

❖

Subhas had come here to start gathering support for his political initiative since he trusted that the Fakir would keep his word if he made a promise. As would the other man, a man of a different political philosophy, who was also present here at his request, and who now stepped out along with the Fakir, physically towering above him.

Subhas stepped forward and respectfully hugged him, taking care not to cause him pain – the icon was still nursing some injuries.

'Look at you, in a uniform and all!' Khan Abdul Ghaffar Khan softly laughed as he stepped back and looked at Subhas. 'Our Fakir here gets sad if he does not fire his gun for a few days, but he has always been like this, he is *that* sort of Pathan. But you? I had heard of this but I could not believe it. Our Subhas Babu, our Congress president from Calcutta, is now coming to meet us in uniform and with soldiers! *Mashallah*!' He chuckled again.

He then switched from Hindustani to Pashto and turned to

his host. 'Forgive me, Mirza, we are both old Congresswallahs. In 1938, Subhas was the Congress president, and in 1939, too, before he got angry, left the presidency and then the country as well. And now, look, Churchill is after his life as he has come to India with Hitler and Mussolini's armies. He is a big player on the world scene, this Mr Bose!'

As Akbar Shah gave a quick translation of what had been conveyed, Subhas reached out to hold the Frontier Gandhi's hands. 'You are my senior in political experience and in stature, Khan Sahib. Do I not know that you could have been Congress president in 1931 itself but declined it? And when I came to Peshawar in 1939, after resigning, to spread word about the Forward Bloc, did I not hear of the iron grip of the Khan brothers on the NWFP?' He laughed. 'I was convinced that without the blessing of Khan Sahib, I would have a meaningless tour. But the people of the region, and Peshawar in particular, were very kind. I can never forget that.'

'Yes, of course, I remember that visit. I had to keep my distance – you know that it was the decision of the party at that time to have nothing to do with you, and I have been a loyal soldier, always. But you did not really need my support in Peshawar, like you did not need the League to talk to Muslims in Bengal – I have to admit, Subhas Babu, even in Muslim majority areas, you have managed to connect to people directly, without needing mediators. What minor differences we may have had, they are all in the past ...' the *Khudai Khidmatgar* smiled.

In 1939, when the Congress offered conditional support to the British war effort, Khan, a man of peace, was unhappy with the decision. He resigned from the Congress. It was not until the Quit India movement took off, three years later, that he was agreeable to work with them again. In October, his participation in the movement earned him two broken ribs and a prison cell. Which is where he was, until a few days back, when a unit of the advancing Legion, sent by Subhas, unlocked his cell and escorted him back home.

'We all have to now come together, no matter what differences we may have had, Khan Sahib'. Subhas then turned to Mirza Ali. 'I am grateful to the renowned Fakir of Ipi, whose fame has travelled from here to not just Kabul and Delhi, but to Berlin and Moscow. I am thankful to you that you agreed to host and arrange this meeting. To make it abundantly clear that I come as a friend of the Baloch and Pashtun people, and not as head of a hostile army, you will see that I have entered this far into your territory with no German or Italian forces, just these hundred or so men – for most of whom these hills are home. I place my safety in their hands. And we collectively, today, have put ours in your hands.'

Akbar Shah continued to play interpreter for Subhas.

'There is no fear here, Mr Bose. You are the guest of a Pathan and have nothing to fear. I am surprised but also proud to see the men who are wearing your army's uniform. All my life, I have seen men in uniform fight us. To think of them as *not* our enemies – that is new!' Mirza Ali laughed and gestured them inside the hut.

'When I got off the Frontier Mail at Peshawar station, last year, dressed as a Pashtun, of course I could not speak the language, but otherwise I think I carried out my role very well – you can count me as an honorary Pashtun!'

Both Khan Abdul Ghaffar Khan and the Fakir broke into a laugh as they stepped inside, followed by Subhas and Akbar Shah. Outside, the tension in the air dropped a few degrees. Sporadic conversations in Pashto between the militia and the soldiers began to chip away at the frosty wariness in the camp.

❖

'You know I have never been in favour of breaking India up, Subhas. In my entire career, I have never been comfortable with violence, with political blackmail, with going on the road and bullying others to prove a point. I am still just a Khudai Khidmatgar. All I want is respect and development for my people, and for the whole country, of course. I am afraid that we will be torn away from India if Pakistan becomes a real project ... But you know all that. Tell me, what do you want from me?'

'Your support. Your word means a lot in this part of the world.'

'I agree with most of your views, Subhas, but that doesn't mean I am a fan of Hitler and Mussolini. I will work with you for Hindustan, not for anything else. There is much I have learnt from Gandhi's philosophy and methods. I know you do not agree with him on many things, politically. But don't ask me to fight him.'

'I am not asking you to fight Mahatma Gandhi, Khan Sahib. I am trying to build a country in which you and Gandhi can both practise the politics you believe in. All I ask of you and the Fakir of Ipi is to believe in and support the proposals that I have sent across to you. The older British India is disintegrating, fifty or more miles each day, and we must build our new India quickly, else there will be anarchy in the interim.'

Subhas then turned to Mirza Ali.

'You have your own space here, where the British don't interfere anymore. But the British will not be in India much longer, and they are already irrelevant for you – every soldier they have is deployed to fight the Legion and the Germans. They have fallen as far back as Lahore already. Your jihad against them is over. What is the future? There is a new reality emerging. Today, even though this region is in the middle of a war, there are no other armies entering your area of influence to replace the British – and that is because I have drawn lines on the maps that the advancing Axis is not crossing, out of respect for you.'

The tormentor of the British nodded slowly as Akbar Shah translated.

Subhas continued.

'But things are changing. Where do you want to be when it settles down? Where do you want the Pashtuns to be? Is it necessary to fight, always? You have lost two sons to the fighting already. I have seen Europe at close quarters, recently. Trust me, fighting, at best, can be a brief *means* to an end. If we fall too much in love with it, it becomes the end. People and nations are getting lost in their own worlds, that *their* own people are the only right ones, *they* are the only brave ones, true ones. Nazis versus Communists. Serbs versus Croats. Aryans versus Slavs. Shias versus Sunnis. Protestants versus Catholics. Hindus versus Muslims ... Will we stay in the same trap, after seeing all of it? Do we not need to move ahead, to grow together, to not always have to keep a finger on the trigger?'

Badshah Khan appeared lost in thought for a couple of minutes, even as Akbar Shah conveyed the point to the Fakir.

'I know you and Khan Sahib do not think like the Muslim League, neither do your people. Just six years back, Mr Jinnah's Muslim League got *zero* seats in the NWFP in the 1937 elections! And let us be realistic: in this part of the world, do you really want to create an independent Pashtun nation with rifles for defence and do you really think it will work? How long before some larger army walks in? You are a brave people, but how many battles will you fight? You are our brothers. Why do you need to build walls between us, like you needed with the British?'

This time, Akbar Shah did not translate, but looked at Gaffar Khan, who nodded and turned to the martial leader, and began to speak, slowly and deliberately. It became a conversation, then heated up into a more engaged discussion. Akbar Shah joined in to make an occasional point.

Subhas spread a map before him and quietly waited for them to disengage and fill him in. On a couple of occasions, Akbar Shah returned to Hindustani to convey the crux of something to him.

Subhas stepped out of the cottage and walked up to where one of his units was waiting. He chatted with the men, spoke to them about the vibes of the men of the Fakir. They briefed him on the gossip they had picked up in the camp – including the bounty the British had offered for any sniper who picked him off.

After half an hour of this chatter, the Frontier Gandhi stepped out of the cottage and called out to him.

'We have some proposals – and some questions,' he said, once they were back inside. 'These are sensitive times, and we feel we should speak in the same voice, at least for the NWFP.'

'Of course. I am not looking to do any standalone deals, either – why would I meet you both together, otherwise?'

'But before we get there, I have a personal question. Many leaders say that if the Muslim League kept up the pressure, the British would have agreed to a partition of India into a Hindu-majority and a Muslim-majority part in some time. Some say that the hopes for a Pakistan have been raised among the Muslims, that Jinnah is already planning what areas will be included in it, and that blood will flow and riots will happen if the British leave without a Pakistan being created. I am a man of non-violence. I do not want to see that happen.'

'Khan Sahib, you're right. I have also been told that if we

don't assure the Muslims of India of a separate country before we finally take over, thousands will die in riots and in "direct action" by the League's leaders. The Viceroy is sending the message that the only hope for the Muslims is that the British continue to control India, because that will soon give them a Pakistan, whereas, the Axis and Legion's armies, once in control of Delhi, will never let a Pakistan come into being.'

'Is that propaganda?'

'Actually, no. He is right: I will never let India be broken if I have a say. Yes, I realize that the Muslim League and some others have the ability to cause a lot of disturbance in that situation. I also expect, given the experience of past years, that there are enough people of both faiths who are willing to riot and kill if a situation gets ugly. Both sides have people who will guide mobs to kill – some out of genuine religious hatred, some to acquire political clout. So, yes, the threat of rioting is very much there.'

'And should we accept that threat, risk the lives of innocents?'

'No, Khan Sahib. If we say a firm no to partition, perhaps thousands will die. But if we have a partition, I *assure* you, *lakhs*, perhaps tens of lakhs, will die. It will rip the country from both ends. There will be deaths either way, now that mutual suspicion has been planted and has taken root. But if we are firm, only a few will die, and then the issue will die, too. If we are weak, many will die, and will keep dying for years and years. Partition will create a neighbourhood of enemies, do you not see that? I will not let it happen till I am alive. I don't care if the British had assured it, or even if Bapu had. To break a country because we are afraid of two months of riots – this is very short-term thinking. Once we break it, we won't be able to undo the damage for fifty, seventy, maybe even a hundred years!'

The sound of Subhas's fist thumping the table echoed through the small room. A guard peeped in through the window, unsure if the Fakir needed help.

'Have you seen how the division of people along ethnic lines has been going in Europe? The resulting hatred will simmer for decades. Let 10,000 die now if that is the price. Our soldiers will suppress violence wherever there are riots, without considering which community is rioting – our bullets will not discriminate. I have tried to build an army that fights *together*. I will, Inshallah, do the same with the country! Will you help me with that, Khudai Khidmatgar?'

A bemused Mirza and a surprised Akbar Shah watched as the tall Khan wordlessly stood up and embraced his guest.

❖

Gurwek Base Camp
6 January 1943

Mr M. A. Jinnah
South Court
Mumbai

Dear Mr Jinnah,
I had intended to meet you personally, but the speed of the advance of the Indian Legion and the Axis forces requires my presence at other locations at the moment. However, the nature of the topic is such that I cannot wait till the fighting has ceased to bring it up with you. I am, therefore, sending this despatch to you in strictest confidence. I expect it will be kept that way.

I am attaching with this letter copies of the letters of support issued to me, endorsing the replacing of British Indian administration by an integrated, unified Indian Union, with the specifics of administration to be worked out later through administrative structures that may be put in place by the Government of Azad Hind.

The letters also endorse that all issues relating to the specific concerns and issues of the Muslim community would be addressed shortly after the formation of such a government, and that all issues – except a partition of India along communal lines – *will be open to mutual discussion.*

The signatories in these letters are:

1. *Khan Abdul Ghaffar Khan*
2. *Mirza Ali Khan, The Fakir of Ipi*
3. *Abdul Samad Khan Achakzai*
4. *Sayyid Husain Ahmad Madani*
5. *Allah Baksh Soomro, representing the Sindh People's Party and the Azad Muslim Conference*
6. *Maulana Hussain Ahmed Madani, representing the Jamait-Ulema-e-Islam*
7. *Allama Mashriqui of the Khaksar movement*

I am informed that the Viceroy has been engaged in communication with the Muslim League for some time and has indicated a willingness to consider a future partition of India, along lines that are yet to be finalised. I write this to affirm that the Viceroy will not be in a position to control India militarily, shortly, and that the provisional Government of Azad Hind, while respecting your views on the political issues facing the country and seeking your support in securing peace and harmony, will discard the possibility of a partition in its entirety.

The Muslim League secured 6.7 per cent of the votes in the 1937 elections. For a nation with a Muslim composition of about 22 per cent as per the 1931 census – that ratio being 24.7 per cent in British India, where the voting took place – these numbers do not indicate why the League should be considered as the sole voice of the Muslims of India.

I have been advised that you have envisioned the western parts of British India as the starting point for a future Pakistan. I have gone back to study the 1937 results, and I do not see how the existing population of those areas is inclined to support the League's policies:

- *In the NWFP, the League did not have a single seat in the sixty-member assembly.*
- *In Sind, it did not have a single seat in the sixty-member assembly.*
- *In Punjab, it had one seat in a 175-member assembly.*

Going purely by the geographical expanse of these three states, where your leadership secured a total of one seat out of 295, for you to suggest how their political future should be shaped and for the Government of the day to give you the stature and legitimacy to even discuss separating them from mainstream India, appears incredulous to me.

I am, of course, well aware of the fact that the communal divide in the country has regrettably sharpened post 1937, which has given the Muslim League greater political stature today. I have also not forgotten the Sind Assembly's resolution of 1938, or the fact that leaders not belonging to the Muslim League, such as Sir Sikandar Hayat Khan and Fazal-ul-Haque, have in the past expressed a degree of support for many of your current ideas, and for the Lahore Resolution of 1940.

However, I believe strongly that some unfortunate positions taken in the post-1937 period, both by the League and the Congress, have served to create this atmosphere, and that I will be able to explain my position to them and convince them to change their standpoint. We cannot allow five years of mutual suspicion and political misunderstanding to divide people who have coexisted for several hundred years.

I had written to you in 1938, as the then Congress President, if you may recall, that 'Is it not enough that the Congress is not only willing but eager to establish the friendliest relations with the League and to come to an honourable understanding over the vexed Hindu–Muslim question?'

Of course, I no longer speak in that capacity, but the sentiment is still mine. I am not only willing but eager to establish the friendliest relations with the League, and I still desire an honourable understanding. I would expect no less from you.

You must accept that you cannot accuse me, even if it were to be politically convenient, of being anti-Muslim, or even of being anti-Muslim League.

It was just three years back, in 1940, that I had supported the Calcutta Corporation Alliance with the Muslim League, despite being viciously attacked for it. I did not then pay heed to those I described as 'communally minded Hindus' who wanted the League to be an untouchable. I will, today, also not pay heed to the League if it were to be similarly and exclusively communal-minded in its approach.

I have followed the writings of Swami Vivekananda for some years. In 1898, many years before we began to riot on the streets on communal grounds, he wrote: 'For our own motherland, a junction of the two great systems, Hinduism and Islam – Vedanta brain and Islam body – is the only hope.' I am deeply in love with my motherland, as no doubt you are, too. It will be my endeavour to bring into being an India that is as close to that description as I can.

I hope that can happen with your collaboration and I assure you of all possible respect for yourself and for the League in that situation. I will, however, make all effort towards it, even if it were to be in the face of your opposition.

I hope to discuss this with you in person, shortly, given how the military situation is unfolding. In the meantime, I would advise you to lend your support, if you wish, to our efforts. You can, of course, opt to wait till you have made up your mind.

The one thing I would request you not to do is to provoke any disruption of public peace as a political show of strength. I am already branded – Nazi, Fascist, collaborator, and more – and I am no mahatma or apostle of non-violence. I have built a battle-hardened army with the support of German and Italian troops. Mobs running around with sticks and stones will not scare my men. Neither will I go on a fast. In the areas that are being liberated from the British forces at increasing pace, the soldiers of the Indian Legion and the Indian National Army – who belong to all faiths – will put down any public disorder or rioting, whether instigated by Muslims or directed against them, with all the force available at their disposal.

Subhas C. Bose

17

A Death on the Train

AS 1943 BEGAN, THE WAR, THAT HAD BEEN ON FOR OVER THREE and a half years, showed no sign of ending anytime soon.

The Axis victory at Stalingrad had been close. Despite the final victory that came at an extremely high cost – and may well have never come if the underrated and underequipped Romanians had not stood firm against hurried Soviet counterattacks to the south of the Stalingrad front – the battle had raised many questions about the infallibility of the ever-extending German armed forces. The Russians had held on to the city for agonising months amidst horrific fighting and almost succeeded in their counterpunch.

The world had watched the battle of brutal attrition, fixated, and realized that the days of the Wehrmacht sweeping through city after city, were coming to a gradual end. Even within the German armed forces, which suffered massive casualties, almost as bad as the Russians, resentment at how the Führer obsessively micromanaged the entire battle for a target that did not have significant military value was brewing. Keitel could no longer think of repeating his 1940 description of the Führer as 'the greatest warlord of all time' without much sniggering by the General Staff itself.

Even if Germany still seemed supreme on land, the U-boat terror in the Atlantic was a thing of the past. Allied bombing raids continued to get through to German territory on a daily basis. Hitler ought to have long back sacked Luftwaffe's head, Reichsmarschall Göring – he could not stop the Dunkirk evacuations, he could not win the Battle of Britain, his supply support to the Sixth Army when the Russians put acute pressure on supply lines was 5 per cent of what Paulus needed – but Hitler continued to place personal loyalties ahead of professional competence. Göring invested more energy in garish costumes and adding to his art collection, than to the equipment the Luftwaffe needed to sustain the war, and yet, flourished.

Italy as an ally did not add significant military muscle, though Mussolini now looked like a reasonable man, once the world had got to know Hitler. The Romanians and Hungarians were in a bitter spat over the allocation of resources on the Russian front, having suffered huge casualties while buffering the flanks of the German advance. The Japanese Navy had not yet bounced back from the defeat at Midway in 1942. Japan, prudently, was still *not* at war with the USSR, despite the Axis pact, while Germany had jumped to what most Generals saw as a foolhardy call to declare war on the US immediately after Pearl Harbour.

It was obvious to the Wehrmacht that it was not going to be possible to simultaneously and recurrently win on land, on sea and in the air – at some point, a ceasefire, a compromise had to be reached, so that Germany could consolidate its gains before it burnt itself out. And before the Prussian military prestige became irretrievably subservient to the Jew-hunting, camp-managing SS and SD. From Bismarck to Hitler, Göring and Himmler, it had been a long journey.

But there would be no talk of peace till Hitler lived. If he had got to Stalingrad, he would not rest till Moscow and the

Caucasus. If he got Moscow, would he not probably ask his Generals to advance into Siberia?

He was long past rational advice.

❖

Befehlswagen (command car) aboard the Führer's special train

Unmarked Location on the German–Polish Border
9 February 1943, 11 a.m.

The SS sentry's boots were so shiny that Lieutenant Fabian von Schlabrendorff could have adjusted his cap in the reflection. But then to guard the most powerful man in the world was not a duty to be taken lightly, and like much of Nazi Germany, efficiency and symbolism were tightly intertwined here as well.

Von Schlabrendorff was a familiar face for the train's staff, as a frequent emissary from the office of Major General Henning von Tresckow, Chief Operations Officer of Army Group Central. As the adjutant to Tresckow, he was entrusted with bringing despatches from the front when they were deemed to merit the Führer's attention. After a perfunctory check through the outer layers, he now stood before the door to the armour-plated coach that functioned as the command and conference centre when Hitler was on the move, on this one-of-a-kind train.

The train itself, though equipped with two coaches that carried a variety of anti-aircraft weaponry, stood inside a tunnel, today, as was the preferred practice when it was not on the move. Over two dozen guards were scattered around and atop it.

'An extra bag, today, eh?' The SS *Sturmbannführer* (Major) on duty asked.

'Just a couple of bottles of Cointreau,' von Schlabrendorff laughed. 'I was made to run to arrange for them on the way here when the general heard that Reichsmarschall Göring was with the Führer today. I believe he is quite fond of the liqueur. Do try not to disturb the packing too much, please, the Reichsmarschall frowns at clumsy handling of gifts.'

Keeping the bag aside for inspection, he took out his Walther P38 from the holster and deposited it with the Sturmbannführer.

After a detailed pat-down at the hands of the sentries and the depositing of his sidearm, he waited patiently as they examined the bottles. The sniffer dog paused for a moment as the bag and bottles passed by, but did not bark. There was something here, but this wasn't what it had been trained to raise an alarm for.

The door of the coach opened. Göring stood there, scowling.

'Ah, there you are! Have you brought what I have been waiting for or do I have you sent to the Russian front, Lieutenant?' His voice boomed in the confined space.

'I'm here, Reichsmarschall. I shall be there in a minute, once the checking is done.'

The big man scowled.

'Get here on the double!'

Thirty seconds later, having snatched his package back, carrying a set of files in one hand and the gift from General Tresckow in the other, von Schlabrendorff stepped inside the Befehlswagen.

❖

Lahore Camp Office of the Axis Command
9 February 1943, 8 p.m.

The door burst open with a bang as the Wehrmacht Adjutant ran into the situation room without knocking, breathless and ashen-faced.

Rommel threw up his head angrily. Subhas was bemused. It was rather unlike the Germans to breach protocol, especially with a Field Marshal. The other officers in the room, curious, turned to see what was unfolding.

The adjutant approached Rommel wordlessly, clicked his heels, saluted, and stretched his hand out to present the message held in his trembling fingers. He could hardly be drunk, Subhas thought, so what was so dramatic that he could not keep his hands from shaking?

Rommel stiffened visibly as if he had placed his hand on a live electric wire.

'Are you sure? Who has sent this out?!'

'It has come from the Chief of Staff, *Generaloberst* Kurt Zeitzler himself, Herr Field Marshal. A second message confirming the same has also come from the office of Admiral Canaris. He has requested you to contact him at the earliest.'

'Leave us.'

The adjutant saluted, turned and left the room – this time, silently.

Subhas, General Balotta, Rommel's own staff officers and Subhas's adjutant, all stared at Rommel, who seemed overwhelmed. Nobody broke the silence for a minute.

With a deep sigh, Rommel looked up, as if wondering whether to share the information he had with the room's occupants. He paused for a moment before speaking. It wasn't as if something of this magnitude would not be burning the wires across the world in the next couple of hours, anyway.

When he did speak, it made the adjutant's dash and quivering look like the most underwhelming response ever by a German soldier.

'The Führer has been assassinated.'

18

An Alternate Threat

BERLIN WAS HUDDLED IN A PANIC.

Everyone was left guessing. The Generals called each other on secure lines. The Luftwaffe was headless. The party was stunned. The SS was ready to kill on the least suspicion. The Abwehr probably knew everything and said nothing. Men like Speer, Goebbels and Ribbentrop, who did not directly command uniformed forces, did not know whether the men guarding them would play protectors, prison wardens or executors, if it came to that choice.

Perhaps they all should have been better prepared for such a day. Political opponents had attempted to get to Hitler for long, well before he had set out to invade half the world.

Communists and Jewish groups and an assorted group of anti-Nazi elements would have dearly loved to see him dead, and they did try many a time. But Adolf recurrently had had the luck of the devil.

After 1938, an alternate threat had emerged – the German armed forces themselves.

However, the initial aim of plots by senior officers was only to dethrone the former Corporal who seemed bent on humiliating and firing Generals and subjugating the army even as he dragged it into an endless war. As the war stretched on, the aim – with some help from British intelligence – moved up to eliminate him altogether. However, Hitler had fortune firmly on his side on more than one occasion. Despite multiple failures and an increasing desperation, conspirators within the Wehrmacht itself continued to make plans to strike again.

For once, a plan had not failed.

The explosion aboard Hitler's command car, as he was holding a discussion with Göring, had torn apart his legs and guts even as Göring was flung aside, severely injured. The closed space of the cabin, the reinforced walls of his special armoured train, and the fact that it was standing within a narrow tunnel had all served to magnify the impact of the explosion. Three of his staff officers had also been killed instantaneously. Everyone inside the coach had ruptured eardrums.

Amidst the fog of chaos, it was rumoured that a Lieutenant from Army Group Central had left a bag inside the cabin that Göring had perhaps dismissively accepted without taking a closer look at. Facts were, however, difficult to ascertain, since Himmler had ordered the entire unit detailed to protect the train to be arrested and taken to an unknown location.

A few officials in Berlin, however, did not need to read the interrogation reports to know what had happened. They knew that the bomb that had made its way into the command car had been adapted from a British plastic explosive seized by the Abwehr from an SOE agent. The mechanism differed from conventional explosives – it used a pencil detonator that consisted of a thin copper tube with copper chloride. The acid took about ten minutes to go through the wire holding the spring-loaded firing pin. A silent, inconspicuous time delay was, therefore, possible without a smouldering fuse or the tick-tock of a clockwork mechanism – the things that the security detail and the sniffer dogs were trained to look for.

Now that it *had* happened, in the conspiratorial and

regimented world that the regime had built with such care for years, this was the perfect trigger for a free-for-all.

❖

'You should be there in a day, Field Marshal.'

Rommel's stressed face looked up at Subhas.

'Yes, you should. You know the system better than anyone. I have not appreciated your advice on Indian politics, and so it is legitimate for you to dismiss my advice on Germany's politics. However, I will still offer it.'

Subhas looked genuinely concerned about Rommel.

'Since Hitler is no longer there and Göring, who otherwise would have been the successor in all likelihood, is incapacitated, you are likely to have all three wings competing to take control of the state structure – the Nazi party, that is Bormann, the SS, that is Himmler, and the Wehrmacht, which has many powerful men, but none as popular with the German masses as you are. Also, if I may add, none is as acceptable to the global community. Imagine a Germany looking to finally establish workable peace by the middle of 1943 – who do you think will inspire greater trust among Stalin, FDR and Churchill? Field Marshall Rommel or Heinrich Himmler? I detest Churchill, but he is still a factor to figure in – and he has commended you, of all the places, in the British Parliament.'

'It is good I do not have my colleagues present here, else I would be up for a treason charge just for hearing you out, Herr Bose!'

'True, but I am not a citizen of the Reich, and I have not sworn an oath of loyalty to it, have I? I have the right to speak my mind, and there is no reason for you to have to report me to the SD for that. It is not as if you have never heard other officers express their views on the larger direction the Nazi regime has been heading in, have you?'

Rommel did not respond to that.

'Surely, it is not possible that no entity has already moved to seize power, even if quietly? Whoever had Hitler assassinated, would have a plan in place. Surely, it is not possible that you have no information of what is happening in Berlin right now?'

Rommel paused for a moment, then nodded.

'It is rumoured that General Olbricht, the head of the Replacement army, has issued orders to his commanders to seize control of key points in Berlin, and in Munich, possibly also in Vienna. But not all his commanders have obeyed. Some have reached out to the OKW, some have informed Himmler. I believe shots have been exchanged at multiple locations. The larger picture seems to be of a Wehrmacht versus SS jostling to occupy key headquarters.'

'I would suggest you land in Berlin as soon as possible, Field Marshal, perhaps engaging a Fw Condor currently deputed to long-range patrolling in the Arabian Sea from a base in Iran. It should be able to get you there with only one stop for refuelling. The Abwehr and Admiral Canaris will prefer to push yours and the Wehrmacht's case to hold power in Germany right now, over either the Party or the SS machinery – and would back you ahead of a more Nazified General.'

'Me?! And what will happen if and when the Reichsmarschall recovers and orders me shot for treason for having even *discussed* this with the Admiral, if I were to do so?'

'You are a great strategist on the battlefield, but not so much in the battles of the court, Field Marshal. If Himmler's men were the first to reach the spot and seize the train as well as the men posted with it, as we have all heard, it stands to reason that the injured would have been taken by them as well. Now, surely, someone as senior as Göring cannot be simply dropped on a hospital bed, can he? He must surely be in the care of the best medical team possible – Himmler's personal physician, in all likelihood. The same thing that happened when Heydrich was injured in the Prague attack last year. And you do recollect how that treatment went, don't you?'

'Yes, of course, I do. Heydrich appeared to have been recovering after the initial surgery, but then suddenly collapsed and went into a coma from which he never woke up. Sepsis, perhaps, is what I was told.'

'Curiously undiagnosed earlier, even though he underwent surgery and his recovery was a matter of the Führer's direct concern. But I rest my case. If a competitor for power is in the care of the medical staff handpicked by Himmler, I would not place my bets on his recovery. No, I don't think we will be seeing the Reichsmarschall again. Cruel as it is to say this, perhaps the Luftwaffe will, therefore, be saved from self-destruction. The Battle of Britain, Dunkirk and then Stalingrad have both been monumental failures for it, even if Germany was occasionally victorious on paper.'

'You take a great interest in how Germany is working – exceptionally so, for someone caught up in a battle of a great magnitude himself.'

'Well, I have been writing on Germany and the situation in Europe since the 1930s. I also take a great interest in Italy, in Britain, and in Soviet Russia. Most leaders in India take no interest in world affairs, more so in the military and political dynamics – perhaps I have to compensate,' Subhas laughed. 'But do you disagree with my viewpoint, Herr Rommel?'

Rommel smiled, and in the first gesture of that sort between the two men, placed his hand on the Indian's shoulder. He then made a slow, careful point.

'I will issue a note on the situation and on the delegation of military duties, since I don't think I will be back very soon.

We are halfway through the campaign, though, and frankly I don't see the British pushing us back. The only worry could be a military deadlock if it becomes a city-by-city fight; urban fighting is slow, messy, and involves many casualties and civilian loss as well. That apart, the General Staff of the Afrika Korps, the Italian senior staff and the Legion's own officers, I am sure, will be up to the military challenges that unfold. I will leave the coordination with the Eastern Front and the Japanese to you, since your association with them has been, frankly, better than ours.'

'I agree. And if you could specify just one more thing in that order, Field Marshal?'

'And that would be?'

'The oath that all men of the Indian Legion took, in Germany, and then at the locations on the way when POWs opted to join the Legion and fight for us?'

'Yes ...?' A look of understanding entered Rommel's eyes.

'The men had to swear to obey Adolf Hitler, and to accept me as the leader in the fight for the freedom of India. They are now free of the first part, you realize, so as of today, they have to abide by an oath of loyalty to only one leader.'

The Field Marshal nodded and stepped out, silently.

❖

Lahore
16 February 1943

Captain Ghaffar stepped in with a ragged-looking man, shuffling along, smelling as if he hadn't taken a bath in a while. In Subhas's office, he would have been out of place, but then, this was not his office. They were inside a dingy Lahore storehouse about a kilometre and a half away from his camp office; Subhas was himself dressed as any local resident would be, with a muffler concealing his face. Four of his men, all in mufti, guarded the entry points.

Once the door was shut, the demeanour of the vagabond changed rapidly.

He stepped up to Subhas, took out a note from deep within his smelly clothing and handed it over. Once Subhas was done reading, he gestured towards the Captain. 'I need to speak to you in person, sahib,' he requested feebly in Urdu.

'It's all right, Ghaffar. I can take care of myself. Of course, keep your ears open if it sounds like we're having a scuffle here.' The Captain's unsure expression did not mirror Subhas's smile, but he reluctantly made his way out and shut the door behind him.

The agent, known to Subhas only as Silver, then switched to impeccable, unaccented English.

'Admiral Canaris has requested that you destroy that note after having read it – in my presence.'

He offered a lighter.

Subhas paused for a moment before accepting it and setting the lower corner of the note aflame.

They both watched it roll and curl up before he dropped it to the floor, still smouldering.

'The admiral has requested me to reiterate that there is an extremely heightened threat perception so far as you are concerned.'

Subhas shrugged. His expression said, 'What's new?'

'I suggest not taking it as a routine warning. British intelligence is of the view that with a combination of three developments within a short period – Hitler's death, Rommel's absence from this front and, hopefully, your assassination – the Axis-Legion offensive will be decapitated and they may, even now, be able to achieve a stalemate, even if it means holding on to less than half the country. Their learning is that as Stalin has shown in Russia, it is possible to build a counter-fight or a stable defence even after losing half of your original territory, once an enemy offensive slows to a halt. Your death would make the political objective of this offensive unclear and the momentum would most certainly die out.'

There was no shrug this time.

'The battle of attrition is, in any case, proving to be slow, more so on the eastern front, where the progress from Burma has been worn down by the advance through hilly terrain. The admiral thinks a decisive psychological step is needed in the east – what it should be is something you are best placed to decide.'

'Do convey to the admiral that I will pay attention to both things – trying to stay alive and finding a breakthrough for the eastern deadlock. Has he also reverted on the query I had put?'

'Yes. In the given situation, he says that even if you were to do as you have proposed, there is unlikely to be any immediate countermeasure, more so given the situation in Berlin right now, since bigger issues will engage Herr Himmler. However, if Herr Himmler were to be subsequently in a position of greater authority, it is likely that he would remember any gesture of defiance and seek some degree of retaliation.'

'That is all right. Neither Herr Himmler nor I know how the war will unfold and if either of us will be alive for him to extract vengeance for my acts that displease him. We will take it as it comes. You should go now. Hopefully, we will meet again.'

❖

As Silver disappeared into Lahore's bylanes, Subhas, Captain Ghaffar and the four men, all in civil clothes that would not draw attention on a Lahore street, walked the kilometre and a half back towards what currently served as his camp office – the erstwhile Deputy Commissioner's Office in Data Gunj Buksh Town. Walking on the streets clad in a Pathan suit took Subhas back in time to the Calcutta–Kabul journey and, for a few moments, he wondered whether all that had been happening was for real.

As per the British administration's plans, he was to have spent the past two years in prison, or at the very least, under house arrest. Instead, he had been on an endless journey, one lonelier than anyone around him could understand.

He had barely seen Emma after the battlefront had opened up; as per his own instructions, she was still at the base camp where they had been when the offensive started. He had managed to get a few letters sent to her, and one smuggled back home to Calcutta, but that was about it. He could not rely on receiving Sarat's reasoned advice anymore and he was having to trust or mistrust people placed in key positions based on his personal reflex and nothing more. Rommel had been a measured, seasoned mind, especially in military matters, but he was unlikely to be back in India for many months now.

Lost in thought, turning onto the track that led to the rear exit of the compound that they had left from, he did not notice the debris flying towards him till almost the last moment. His hand rose up instinctively and a piece of concrete bounced off his forearm. The thunderous echo reached his ears a split second later. It took a couple of seconds for him to comprehend that the building that had been his office for the past fortnight had just been blown to pieces. The men with him had all been hit by flying debris, but as they were still a good hundred metres or so from the structure, they had had time to evade any potentially fatal blow.

The guards at the office had not had the opportunity to evade anything. As whistles blew and the Legion's soldiers and medics came running, he could make out the lifeless frames of at least three uniformed men on the lawn.

'There could be more bombs. We have to get you out of here!' Dhillon ran up to him. 'Are you all right?'

The forearm throbbed with pain, and he had a sense that it would be blue in a while, but Subhas had no desire to have that attended to just then. 'I am fine. Take care of everyone who has been injured, first. Then update me on the casualties.'

❖

'How often has the commander left this compound in the last ten days like he did today?' Major Dhillon asked.

'Never. We have stepped out three or four times, but it has always been in the flag car and with at least two escort vehicles,' Captain Ghaffar responded.

'Exactly. When the flag car is parked inside the compound, the assumption is that he is in his room. Around this time at noon is when he typically holds the daily review.'

'So the bomb was timed to go off on the assumption that he is still in the building, and would be in the midst of a discussion with other officers at noon? Which means that the undetected visit to meet that agent is what saved him – and us?'

Dhillon nodded.

'I would think so, yes ... The target was Subhas Bose, but since he stepped out quite unrecognizable and almost nobody knew that he *wasn't* in the building, whoever placed the explosives would have had no reason to change the plan that had already been set in motion. It isn't a very large building and the explosive force would be enough to kill most people within. He was just plain lucky today.'

'It did kill all the three men inside, and three guards outside. What an unfair way to die! At least on the front line, you have a fair chance.' Ghaffar was despondent.

'You are young, officer. After a couple of years of fighting, you will realize that there is no fair way to die,' the more experienced Major responded.

He then dragged himself out of his melancholy mood.

'Let's keep the philosophy for when we have won. There will be more dead men before that day. As of now, we shift the office to a new complex that can be guarded more effectively, and probe into how a bomb could have been planted in his office. Who all have had access to the building?'

'The list is going to be long. The man – or men – who kept it could be from the upkeep staff, though I doubt that. The usage was the handiwork of a professional. I would think either a British Army agent, someone from the SOE, or, most likely, a Legion soldier who is working for either of the two – someone who was basically asked to join the Legion after being captured, probably deliberately, and work for them. A Trojan horse.'

Dhillon stayed quiet for a while as he processed this. This would have to be shared with Krappe and a few others. He then turned to leave the room, paused briefly at the door and looked back at Ghaffar.

'Let's find him.'

❖

'Why are you surprised? Isn't it the most obvious thing? Why should they *not* try to kill me? And in a legion that is made entirely of soldiers who had first joined to serve British officers, among some 100,000 men – the strength expands a bit each month now – even if 2 per cent are still loyal to the British, will there not be, what, 2,000 soldiers who may not actually be loyal to our cause? Are you aware that some 20 per cent of the Axis forces in Stalingrad were Russian volunteers? Why are you getting agitated over this?'

'This is disloyalty!' Nambiar was furious.

'Of course, but loyalty is oversimplified. If you had a brother also in the army, and he was, let us say, killed in action against the Germans or Italians. Would you not perhaps hate them, and by extension, hate the Legion's commander for allying with them? Are the Russians who can't stand Stalin disloyal? Are the Germans who can't tolerate the Nazis – and God knows I know far too many of them – disloyal? Let it be. This is a risk we have to run. We can filter the men who come into close access, yes, but at the end of the day, you and I cannot start doubting our men because one or two of them probably work for the enemy—'

'*Certainly*, not probably.'

'All right, certainly work for the enemy. There will be many, many more such men as we take on the administration. The British have ruled India for 200 years almost entirely on the strength of the Indians who were loyal to them. There *will* be many who will stay that way. Let's just try and ensure that they don't manage to kill us. The rest, que sera sera.'

'What are you doing here, Subhas? Retire and write philosophy!'

Subhas looked at Nambiar for a moment, then sighed.

'Trust me, if I could, I would do it today.'

19

Oh, Calcutta!

Approximately Seventy Kilometres Off India's Eastern Coast
25 February 1943

THE TWO DORNIER DO-217NS COASTED OVER THE MOONLESS night sky.

The Bay of Bengal stretched endlessly below, a pitch-dark emptiness as far as one could see.

It felt surreal. 'Is this how people would feel if man went into outer space one day?' Subhas mused.

Both planes were observing strict radio silence to avoid alerting the British air defence systems; the Dornier was a decent fighting machine, but not an exceptional one, and the crew had little desire to engage in aerial combat unless absolutely necessary. If the propellers stopped turning on account of any mechanical failure, there would be nobody to even register that fact for hundreds of miles.

It was a sobering thought.

The Germans did not have any of the night-fighter versions of these long-distance reconnaissance planes in this part of the world, but the Italians did, and, on Subhas's request, these two had made their way to India earlier in the week. Then, in two days' time, the planes had taken Subhas from Lahore over a circuitous route, bypassing all zones where Allied air presence was still a potential threat, till he had landed in the INA/Japanese-held Andamans.

After resting, refuelling, and adding final touches to his outrageous plan, in consultation with Forward Bloc leaders and the INA officers, and exchanging messages with Rash Behari Bose, they were on their way.

The aerial distance from Port Blair to Calcutta is about 1,300 kilometres. The Do-217N had a range of 2,100 kilometres and a top speed of about 560 kmph, so the flight would take about two and a half hours, since, for the most period, they would stay to the ceiling of about 31,000 feet. The few Hurricanes available to the British in this region could fly well above that, though, so it did not mean they were out of harm's way.

Having taken off at 7 p.m., they had been flying for over an hour and a half now. The pilots expected to reach Calcutta at approximately 9.30 p.m. In case either of the planes crashed or came under attack, the brief for the other was to break radio silence and veer east to find a landing spot in Japanese-held Burma. If no radio message went out, the teams on the ground were to assume that the plan was in place.

Subhas looked at his Rolex – Emma's most indulgent gift to him. At just about now, 8.30 p.m., three other planes would have taken off – the ever-dependable Japanese Shōwa L2D3-Ia transporters – in Kohima. At the same time, some 500 Forward Bloc cadres, armed with an assortment of seized and smuggled weapons, were stepping out in Calcutta, as per a pre-decided plan of action.

The last week had seen the Intelligence Bureau (IB) sending out advisories that there had been 'increased reports of subversive activity' but no specifics had been cracked as yet.

Calcutta was about to get an interesting closure to the day.

❖

It was a regular evening at the Maidan. Geriatrics strolled and engaged in political discussion, children ran around and made a general nuisance of themselves, families just sauntered around and stood together gobbling *phuchka*s at the odd stall. It was not yet hot enough for 8.30 p.m. to be uncomfortable.

The Maidan was vast. It was also the one place for the city to assemble, if it needed to. It had seen enough political drama over the past decade or so, but today was going to be different. On any given evening, you could find half a dozen policemen, usually in groups of two, keeping an eye on the general proceedings and ensuring that His Majesty's peace was not disturbed. It was usually an uneventful duty.

And so, when six men leapt out of the shadows and encircled the two policemen standing near the main gate, it was unexpected. Even more unexpected was the presence of the two pistols pointed at them. At different points in the Maidan, two other groups were engaged in a similar exercise. Soon after, six khaki-clad men, hands tied, found themselves assembled together in a corner of the Maidan. Two of the aggressors, pistols in hand, stayed there to keep guard over them, while the rest quickly ran around, asking families, children and the elderly to leave the area.

Even as they left, perplexed, others were entering the Maidan in groups of twenty or thirty and assembling around the perimeter. The massive space of the Maidan and the dimly lit, moonless ambience swallowed up the building volume of men – and women – who had all, apparently, decided to spend some time here, late in the evening.

The city no longer had a military presence of consequence since every fighting man who could be spared was on the Japanese front, but the Calcutta Police was still efficiently functional. As of now, however, there was no reason for the nearest chowki to notice anything out of the ordinary. The men on duty would not be thought to be 'missing' for another couple of hours – unless something else occurred to draw the attention of the police before that.

❖

A subdued throbbing sounded from the skies above.

❖

The sound of propellers was not a very familiar sound in Calcutta, even though a war was ongoing. No attacking aircraft had flown over the city for almost three months. The Japanese had launched a couple of half-hearted bombing raids, primarily targeting the Howrah Bridge, in December 1942, but that had not recurred after a furious Subhas had cabled the entire hierarchy, including Premier Tojo. Indian civilian casualties at the hands of Axis air attacks or artillery had been a complete no-go zone for him, which had, of course, slowed the pace of advance on both fronts. Carpet bombing and artillery barrages were both deliberately excluded as a battle strategy in the fight for India. To hear that the Axis had dropped bombs that may have killed Indian civilians – with no reference to him – sent him into an almighty rage.

Japanese field commanders strongly disagreed with this sanitized model of warfare, but political considerations prevailed, and Subhas had his way. The price of it, as Silver had conveyed in Lahore, was the risk of a slowdown in the Axis offensive. The Germans and Japanese both were masters of lightning-quick offensives and had smashed cities without second thought, through artillery or air attack. This cautious model irked their Generals endlessly. Subhas's counterpoint was that the Legion and the INA were bleeding more than the Axis; popular support for the advancing armies was vital in India – there were many who, not without reason, saw the Axis as having a track record of brutal occupation – and, therefore, *his* word would be final in choosing what model to follow.

So far, it had held. But if things stalled militarily, would that continue?

❖

Even as air raid sirens went off through the city and the handful of anti-aircraft gunners raced to their positions, at many locations, shots rang out to dissuade them. Skeletally guarded, they retreated, called for armed assistance – and waited for it to arrive. But in most cases, it wouldn't.

❖

The Maidan's entry points were by now manned by 'sentries' with armbands and pistols. After access had been controlled, thirty men ran to form two parallel lines along a pre-decided stretch of the ground. A minute later, they had lighted a combination of torches and flares.

Even at night, no pilot could miss the Maidan in Calcutta. The men lined up on the ground now indicated a makeshift runway track that was visible from a kilometre above.

The local police and military staff in the city braced to understand what part of the city would reverberate with explosions, even as an SOS went out for the Hurricanes at the Barrackpore air base to take off and intercept. But no bombs fell. Instead, one after the other, guided by the flares, three planes lumbered down onto the extended length of the Maidan, bouncing badly off the uneven surface, parachutes slowing their landing as soon as the wheels touched down –

a model similar to what fighters were using to land on the shortened runway aboard aircraft carriers.

And so, at just about 9 p.m., over a hundred uniformed men of the Indian National Army, most of them equipped with Arisaka Type 44 rifles, had rushed out of the three transporters and formed a perimeter guard around the Calcutta Maidan.

The local Forward Bloc espionage network had indicated the presence of a maximum of twelve Hurricanes for the air defence of Calcutta. Twenty Japanese Zeros now patrolled the city skies, even as the first British pilots took off and flashes of gunfire became visible to those on the ground. The dogfights, however, prevented the few anti-aircraft batteries, where the crew had safely managed to take up positions from opening fire for fear of bringing their own planes down.

Two Zeros had disengaged and headed out towards the sea even as the formation was about to reach Calcutta. They now served as escort for the two Dorniers that approached the city.

If the passengers in the Dorniers could have looked down and had a clear view, they would have seen crowds emerging from multiple parts and heading towards the Maidan. The city's gossip quotient was at fever pitch. Word had found its way to the local IB – which promptly flagged it to Delhi – and to the state government, headed by Prime Minister Fazlul Huq. His office called Home Minister Khwaja Nizamuddin. The secretaries of both men thought someone was drunk and was wasting their time.

'The grapevine says Subhas Chandra Bose will address a rally at the Maidan today?'

Nizamuddin needed a handkerchief to wipe his tears, so hard did he laugh.

❖

REPORTS OF S C BOSE PRESENCE IN CITY ON YOUR PART NOT SUBSTANTIATED/CORROBORATED BY ANY OTHER INPUTS. ADVICE AGAINST CREATING PANIC OR UNREST IN CITY. CONFIRM FIRST-HAND VISUAL SIGHTING REPEAT CONFIRM FIRST-HAND VISUAL SIGHTING BEFORE FURTHER COURSE OF ACTION RECOMMENDATION

The Deputy Superintendent of Police in the IB's Calcutta office read the message again in disbelief. He then wordlessly handed it over to his colleague at the adjacent table.

'This is not the time to exchange messages! Don't they understand that the city will be a madhouse if this is true? Our only chance is in seizing control of the Maidan. Crowds are already blocking all access routes. I hear there are armed soldiers escorting Bose. Both the police stations near the Maidan are besieged by crowds, and shots were fired back when the police fired in the air. Twelve, maybe fifteen, thousand men are on the roads and that number is going up. I need armed constabulary – first to disperse the crowd, then to seize Bose! And they send me teleprinter messages!'

The older colleague scratched his head and nodded in sympathy.

'I don't know why they shifted the capital from Calcutta to Delhi. That city is full of pompous idiots who know nothing but think they know everything. Take it easy.'

'*Take it easy*? Why should we, when we have a chance to seize Bose?'

The colleague gave him a sympathetic look.

'Well, first, you *don't* have a chance to seize Bose unless you deploy a very, very large armed unit. Which means you will have to manage a visual confirmation. For that, you could go with uniformed men – which will mean the crowds will stop you, you will maybe end up firing, and then the crowd will overwhelm you. Unless you have, let us say, 200 men, and you are planning an operation like that by General Dyer in Amritsar.'

The DSP threw up his hands and stared at his cynical colleague. That did not put off the latter.

'Even then, since you say Bose has armed men with him, and there are Japanese planes in the sky even as we speak, I don't think a one-sided slaughter of the crowd, like at Jallianwala, will happen again, will it? Or you could go by yourself, in mufti, walking across, if you feel brave enough not to be spotted and identified?'

'But what if he *is* here and we let him disappear from the Maidan? There will be hell to pay!'

'You do realize, my friend, that the bosses at Delhi may not even have control of Delhi in some time? They don't have control of Karachi, of Peshawar, of Lahore, of Pondicherry, of the Andamans, of Kohima ... Unless you can change the course of the war today itself, to try to shoot locals in Calcutta in an attempt to arrest Subhas Chandra Bose may not be the best move you ever make – for your career, or for your safety. Think about it.'

❖

Guarded by a small detachment of INA soldiers, the Shōwa transporters were parked on one side, but now their massive lights lit up the Maidan and provided greater visibility for the Dorniers. Their descent was, therefore, easier on the pilots and the passengers. Gunfire continued to erupt in the sky but the Zeros had, so far, kept the Hurricanes away from the landing areas. They could stay in combat for an hour, at the most, before the fuel gauge would force them to head back. The clock was ticking.

Subhas had done the maths and the military planning for Bangalore, but, this time, he was part of the exercise. He thought of Nambiar's parting remark and laughed to himself: 'If you *don't* make it back from there, Subhas, after this hare-brained scheme of yours, if the British don't kill you, I swear the Germans will!'

The planes slowed to a halt. The Maidan by now had some 8–10,000 people inside, most having come in the past half hour as Forward Bloc leaders spread the word and invited loyalists and party cadres. Among the men who had hurried in curious disbelief to the Maidan was Sarat Chandra Bose, resident of Elgin Road, the elder brother of the relentless thorn in the Raj's flesh. Subhas's loyalists had been getting messages across to him, but no mention had been made of this bizarre activity that he was hearing of. Could it really be true?

❖

Surrounded by a dozen INA men as soon as he stepped out of the Dornier, Subhas Bose grandiosely set foot on the soil of Calcutta for the first time since having fled in anonymity in 1941.

❖

The crowd fell silent for a moment as the people gathered closest to the plane, strained their eyes to recognize him. After all, the last image the city had of Subhas *babu* was of the moustachioed man recovering in bed after a prison stint that had done him little good. This uniformed, boot-clad, clean-shaven man, his very strides reflecting the immense arrogance of landing in British-controlled Bengal in this manner – was he the same man Calcutta had always loved, across divides of religion and caste?

And then a frenzied wave spread out like a ripple right to the last rows, pressed against the Maidan walls, even as the INA men kept a nervous watch on anyone likely to pull out a pistol and shoot Subhas. They need not have worried, though; the crowd was so packed and charged up by now that any such would-be-assassin would have barely had the time to point a gun before the people around him took him down.

With the help of a ladder, Subhas climbed atop the wing of his plane, looked around, and waved.

The crowd's roar was louder than anything the planes' engines had generated.

❖

'I have only limited time in hand, so please hear me carefully.'

Subhas's voice echoed across the Maidan, megaphone in hand, even as a mile away, a plane – impossible to identify in the darkness – plunged to the ground and exploded in a fireball. He spoke, of course, in Bangla.

'From today, all of Bengal is to stop working as a support system for the army fighting our brothers in the INA. Whatever part of the government is helping the British war effort is to be stopped. No trains should reach with ammunition or fuel or more soldiers. No trucks should be able to pass through roads leading to the frontier. No ships with military supplies should be able to unload at any port. Not a single bullet, a single shell, a single litre of fuel should pass through Bengal to the army defending the British Raj. If you do that, in twenty, if not fifteen days, we will pull off the Union Jack from Calcutta. Can you do it?'

The roar of acceptance reverberated through the ground

like a world cup-winning goal had been scored in a football stadium. The DSP, now perched in mufti on the outskirts of the Maidan with two constables, did not need any visual confirmation to know that Subhas Bose was very much there.

'But remember, *obstruct*, do not destroy. Do *not* set fire to railway stations, do *not* destroy tracks or roads. We will be using them a month from now to bring our men ahead! Lay siege to police stations, but do not attack them. Do not fire except in self-defence. They, too, are our brothers. The men who work for the government today will also maintain order in the streets for the Azad Hind Government tomorrow – the police stations, the hospitals, the railway stations. Do not attack, do not destroy, do not become a mob. However, if they threaten you with machine guns ...'

He paused for a moment as the crowd almost leaned forward for a clue.

'... tell them Subhas will return and avenge all wrongs, so beware!'

The roar this time was even louder, even as it blended with cheers and whistles.

'You will hear of more detailed information and instructions soon on a daily basis. Start tonight. Paralyse the war machine. Declare Bengal free of the British! But remember one thing, and remember it very carefully.'

He paused again, and then stayed quiet. After a few moments, a silence descended on the ground, interrupted only by the staccato sounds of machine gun fire above the clouds.

'Our fight is against the British. It is *only* against the British. Our fight is against no Indian. People will instigate you, and sometimes you will react. But I will have nothing to do with those who hate and kill for religion. So hear me carefully, and spread the word.'

'My Muslim brothers, let me tell you that I have met with Khan Abdul Ghaffar Khan, I will shortly meet with Mr Jinnah, and I believe that we will meet and speak again after we have driven out the angrez. Do not allow yourself to be fooled that you need protection after the British. Do not stand aside from our struggle and look to the Viceroy. The British will go, but we have to live together, this is *our* land! Look around you at the men who are safeguarding me today in uniform, look around you at the leaders of the Forward Bloc who brought you here today. There are Hindus, there are Muslims, there are Sikhs, there are Communists, die-hard atheists. We do not choose or differentiate on the basis of how you pray, or if you pray at all.

'My Hindu brothers, every time someone teaches you that Hinduism has to be defended by picking a sword against others, do not look very far – go to Dakshineshwar, think of Ramakrishna Paramhansa. Read what he taught and ask those who teach you Hinduism if *they* know our religion better than Ramakrishna and Vivekananda! Bengal is blessed to have had them, and Bengal will, therefore, have to repay that debt by showing the rest of India how to live as they taught.'

The hurrahs had died down by now. His words were being absorbed quietly. Bengal had lost many lives to communal violence in the recent past.

'And, before I go, from this distance, Sarat, my *real* brother – I am told you are here – I will come home soon. If the police trouble you because of today, tell them my men are watching, and while you are in their custody today, *they* may be in our custody tomorrow – so let them be careful! Tell Ma that she will have to wait a bit longer to see me – I have Mother India's debt to repay first.'

And, for a moment, the politically charged atmosphere was broken by some emotion and some laughter across the gathering. A visibly awkward Sarat, still very far from Subhas, was lifted on the shoulders of the crowd. Applause broke out.

'I have to leave. Join the battle from today. Repeat after me: Jai Hind! Jai Bangla!'

Hoarse throats yelled at the top of their voice even as Subhas clambered back into the Dornier and its engines started rolling.

Police jeeps and trucks had by now approached the Maidan from multiple sides but the number of policemen available at each point – six somewhere, twenty elsewhere – could neither push the crowd aside, nor threaten to shoot without risking their own lives. The news of the captured policemen at the Maidan serving as a sort of informal collateral had also been conveyed to the local police and perhaps influenced their call. Perhaps Subhas was too popular for some policemen to even want to make the effort to intervene. Perhaps the local administration was unsure which government would rule in the coming months and did not want to be in prison if a new one came earlier than expected.

Whatever be the driving force, the gathering was left undisturbed by the police as it stood watching the Dorniers take off from the dusty Maidan, engines revving madly on account of the shortened runway space available.

Four Zeros circled overhead to protect against a Hurricane attack on the Dorniers when they were at their most vulnerable, and then to serve as overland escort. Other fighters stood by to provide short-distance cover to the transporters which rushed to take off as the INA men clambered back in. A Hurricane swept in despite the Zeros and riddled the tail of the last plane, bullets smashing into half a dozen men inside it, but the plane itself did not suffer mortal damage. The Zeros, now running low on fuel, did not give chase.

The Dorniers, the Zeros and the Shōwas headed eastward

towards Imphal, as sporadic anti-aircraft fire tracked the route of their journey.

❖

> CONFIRMING REPORTS OF S C BOSE PRESENCE IN THE CITY BASED ON FIRST-HAND VISUAL SIGHTING REPEAT FIRST-HAND VISUAL SIGHTING. ALSO CONFIRMING DEPARTURE OF S C BOSE BASED ON FIRST-HAND VISUAL SIGHTING. CURRENT LOCATION OF S C BOSE: ALTITUDE APPROX 15,000 FEET NORTH-EAST OF CALCUTTA MAIDAN AND INCREASING. REQUEST ADVICE ON FURTHER COURSE OF ACTION.

The DSP's response to Delhi would have done any writer of satire proud.

❖

Secret/Most Urgent

From: Governor of Bengal
To: Viceroy

26 February, 1930 hours

Reference the activities that occurred in the Calcutta Maidan yesterday, concerning which your office is already in receipt of IB and RIAF briefings:

Suffice to state that the situation as of today in the province of Bengal is comparable to the worst period of civilian unrest during August–September, with the added disadvantage that the availability of armed personnel to restore order is less than a third of what had been deployed during that period of time, owing to the deployment on the Indo–Burmese front post the commencement of hostilities in November.

The situation at the front does not permit the withdrawal of forces for internal security roles. However, unless the internal situation were to subside of its own accord, it would severely impact our ability to sustain the front that is already under considerable duress. A well thought-out and structured effort to hamper the war effort has been on display over the past twenty-four hours.

Telecommunication lines, roads, railway signalling equipment, postal communication, loading and unloading of all forms of transport military have been severely damaged or restricted. Cantonment vehicles have faced a civil boycott to the extent that they have not been able to procure foodstuff at the local vegetable market for the daily kitchen. Police stations immediately outside Calcutta city have been surrounded, made ineffective and locked in for all practical purposes. Power supply lines leading to the cantonment, the air base, the railway yards and police stations have been repeatedly damaged.

It may also be mentioned here that while three Japanese Zero aircrafts were brought down by our valiant pilots during combat, of which two pilots have been captured after landing via parachute while the third was killed upon crashing, the efficacy of the air base has been adversely impacted on account of four Hurricanes being shot down and another three being severely damaged. This development reduces available combat aircraft at Barrackpore from twelve to five, which, as you would concur, is a most undesirable state of affairs, more so if there were to be subsequent aerial engagement over the city.

The appeals of the duly elected Government of Bengal have so far failed to counter the upsurge of the insurrectionist sentiment.

It is evident that the psychological and propagandist impact of the presence of S C Bose has been substantive and the fact that the administration was either unaware of the development, or did not lend credence to reports suggesting the same, are highly regrettable and need to be brought to the attention of the Director IB through your offices.

It is requested that additional armed troops be despatched to Bengal as rapidly as may be practicable from other provinces in order to enable the functioning of logistics and supply lines, and in the meantime additional transport aircraft be deputed to the Barrackpore base to enable supplies to be dropped by air where needed critically.

❖

Secret/Most Urgent

From: Viceroy
To: Governor of Bengal

27 February

Reference your note dated yesterday:

Appropriate note is taken of the situation in Bengal. However, let me speak plainly. Given the advance along the western front, where the enemy has crossed Lahore, Ferozepur and Ludhiana and is approaching Ambala – which is less than 200 kilometres from Delhi – the criticality of defending the national capital does not allow for any forces to be redeployed. The reserve units in the relatively less-affected Deccan peninsula have had to be deployed to garrison Pondicherry on account of the Italian units there that are receiving supplies and equipment by sea without significant impediment by our naval forces. Weakening that land perimeter may allow the Axis to enter the south unopposed and have unforeseen implications for us. I have therefore no reserves in India to divert to you immediately without creating equivalent disorder in another area.

The Prime Minister himself is furious at the episode and accountability is being demanded at all levels of the intelligence hierarchy.

I will endeavour to arrange any resources that appear feasible in the course of the coming days. For now, however, you only have my sympathy and best wishes. I would additionally caution you to observe with care the discipline and loyalties of the troops deployed in Calcutta as well as the police; Bose has proved to be a particularly corrupting influence on uniformed men and the adulation of deserters ostensibly belonging to his 'INA' in Calcutta cannot but be a cause of concern for us.

20

Two Nations?

'If India is to be free, it cannot be a land specially of Hinduism or of Islam – it must be one united land of different religious communities inspired by the ideal of nationalism. [And for that] Indians must accept wholeheartedly the gospel of harmony of religions which is the gospel of Ramakrishna-Vivekananda.'

– Subhas Bose

'The growth of sectarian movements among both Hindus and Moslems accentuated intercommunal tension. The opportunity was availed of by interested third parties who wanted to see the two communities fight, so that the Nationalist forces could be weakened.'

– Subhas Bose, *Indian Struggle*, 1935

'Religion should not be allowed to come into politics ... religion is merely a matter between man and God.'

– M. A. Jinnah, speaking in the Central Legislative Assembly, 7 February 1935

Lahore
28 February 1943

THE ADJUTANT KNOCKED SOFTLY ON THE DOOR BEFORE OPENING IT.

'Mr Jinnah is here, sir.'

'Thank you. Would you please leave the two of us alone and ensure we are not interrupted till we are done?'

The Adjutant nodded and swiftly stepped aside, even as the clip-clop of leather soles on the marble floor announced the arrival of his guest.

The leader of the Muslim League, sharply dressed as always, strode in, escorted by two Legion soldiers.

Subhas got up from his desk and extended his hand. The two men, both once loyal Congressmen, both now at some ideological distance from the parent organization, shook hands and settled down across Subhas's makeshift study.

Once upon a time, any meeting between them would have naturally happened in the presence of the Mahatma, and he would play the role of adjudicator and counsellor. Today, they had both drifted so far from him that even the thought of it would not occur to either.

The guards shut the door and took position outside it.

'I hope the boat to Karachi and the flight from there were not very uncomfortable. But having you travel over land would have been risky, even though your Packard, I hear, is a very comfortable car.'

'I may have preferred the La Salle, the weather is good for a long drive in a convertible. But then one does not just drive through a country at war, not in such times.'

'You would have been safe in British-controlled India, though, wouldn't you? What remains of Linlithgow's regime is unlikely to pick and put *you* into prison.'

'And should I be apologizing for that?' Jinnah snapped at the half-concealed barb. 'Mr Bose, may I remind you that I have agreed to undertake this journey and entered Axis-controlled territory at my risk in the hope that we are looking to find common ground. If this is about smart remarks, I have wasted my time.'

'No, of course not, you don't have to be apologetic about that. If I am not apologetic about being on good terms with Mussolini, I am not going to judge you for being on good terms with Linlithgow. But it's a fact that the Viceroy would have been far weaker had you not been on his side – Quit India would have come very close to crippling the functioning of the government last year, if you had supported the Congress' call.'

'And why should I have done that? Did the Congress pay any attention when we had a difference about a movement the last time? Am I answerable to either Gandhi or to you? The tone of your letter was hardly conciliatory, Mr Bose. I have not put up with bullying by either the British or Mr Gandhi, and I will not be bullied by the Germans or by you.'

'You have hardly been bullied by the British, Jinnah Sahib,' Subhas chuckled. 'You have been quite comfortable in your home in Mumbai while all the Congress leadership was in custody. Linlithgow has had you as his strongest ally outside of London for the past two years. You have practically offered the British the support of the Muslim League in exchange for the postponement of the federation. So let us not bluff each other. I am not saying you have no reason to have a grudge against the Congress, but please don't tell me that you are fighting both the Congress and the British, because you are not.'

Jinnah let that pass without rebuttal.

Subhas checked the confrontational reflex he was getting pulled into.

'Putting all that aside, let me make my position clear. I understand how put off you were by what Jawahar said in 1937 – the line about there being "only two parties in the country, the Congress and the British". That was, I agree, excessively arrogant of the party. As was the refusal of the Congress to induct even two Muslim League members in the UP government. I know what bad blood that caused.'

'The bad blood goes way beyond that – and I assume you don't need me to tell you that.'

'Yes, of course. Your view of the Congress has changed during Mahatma Gandhi's reign – and I can't say it is without reason. Your counter positions, however, have only served to sharpen the divide till it is close to unbridgeable. We have exchanged our share of letters through my tenure as Congress president and there is no point in reiterating those things.'

'What *is* the point of our meeting, then?'

'We would hardly request you to travel all this way if there was no point. There is much that we need to speak about in today's situation. Firstly, let us be realistic about what has changed for you in the past six months.'

'Enlighten me.'

There was little attempt to conceal the sarcasm. Subhas smiled and reminded himself to not add to the tension in the room.

'You have been looking at one Indian political organization – Gandhi and Nehru's Congress – and at one European power to adjudicate issues between it and you: the British. Now, though the Congress is, of course, still the most relevant political force in India, the situation has changed in many ways. At the moment, at least, you do not have to negotiate with Jawahar or the Mahatma, but with me – someone expelled by the Congress not so long back. Someone who was in an alliance with the Muslim League in Calcutta right till the time he left India. You can hardly pitch me, either to your own party or to Muslims in general, as some rabid anti-Muslim. Around 40 per cent of the Indian Legion comprises Muslim soldiers, as does over 30 per cent of the INA fighting on the eastern front.

Many Muslim leaders, starting with the Frontier Gandhi, are willing to back my judgment at this moment, as I wrote to you.'

'You think you can undermine my connect to the Muslims of India?'

'I am not undermining anyone. All I am saying is that I do not need to speak to the Muslims of India *via you*, necessarily. And let us look beyond Hindus and Muslims for a moment: the global powers that will have some role here are Germany and Italy, apart from Japan, and you have zero association or bargaining power with any of them. The Grand Mufti, incidentally, has been an ardent fan of German policy, so I don't see the Germans needing *your* endorsement to send a message to the orthodox. They have a stronger card if that is the game we are playing.'

Though he kept a poker face, Jinnah had not seen that coming.

'But I would rather not play that game – and I know that, as an individual, you are as uncomfortable as I am with letting the priesthood enter politics. Your strongest ally on the Axis side remains Iqbal Shedai, but he is a weakened force today. The Italians have not really had a key role for him after the German–Italian agreement of December 1941.'

'Is that all?'

'Humility may not be my defining trait, but neither is it yours!' Subhas laughed, breaking the tension in the room momentarily. 'Jinnah sahib, it is my view – and I may well be wrong – that if Sir Sikandar Hayat Khan had not passed away in December, he would well have been placed to challenge you for the leadership of the Muslim community, and that, too, as a man with great influence among the Hindus and Sikhs of the Punjab. He supported your position on many things, but I think I would have convinced him to see reason and not agree to a Pakistan. His Unionist Party, by its very name, was not the same as the Muslim League. Lest we forget, Sir Khan had more than once referred to the proposal as one for "Jinnistan"!'

The acclaimed barrister's expression grew increasingly irked.

'Having said all that – and you know all of that is true – I do not wish to speak to you as an opponent.'

'So you are playing both good cop and bad cop by yourself, Mr Bose? We are both too old for this. Why not bring Mr Nehru along to play at least one part?'

Subhas laughed.

'I am not doing that, Jinnah sahib – pardon me, but you are. I have seen how your positions have changed and hardened over the past few years. You are the man who, Jawahar's father literally said, was "leading the way to Hindu–Muslim unity". You were the man who, through the 1930s, fought for the rights of Muslims *within* India, and for that, you have the community's justified respect. *That* is the Jinnah I would want to discuss India's future with.'

'I don't need a refresher on who I "have been", Mr Bose. There is nothing to be done about the past. You have been part of "Gandhi–Nehru–Bose" not so long back yourself. Are *you* still there? The Congress that "Mahatma" Gandhi built in these past years had many strengths – but it did not have the space to accommodate either my views, or yours. So let us not be naïve.'

This was not a point Subhas could counter.

'Why should I not keep away from Gandhi's movements?' Jinnah continued. 'Have I – have we – been treated as equals? What does the Mahatma want to make of India – do you even understand that? The Ali brothers were fanatics, they were calling for a jihad – and Mr Gandhi was accepting *that* as a political movement! Even Kemal Ataturk did not think that the Caliphate had a place in a modern nation and abolished it in Turkey barely five years later. But here, in India, we fanned those instincts through the Khilafat. And, in 1943, you are talking to *me* about politics driven by religion, as if Gandhi's politics have kept away from playing up religious identities!'

What Jinnah was saying was unpleasant – but Subhas could not say it was inaccurate.

'When the Muslim League started in 1906, where was I? Cheering loudly, with a green flag in hand? No, I was at the Calcutta session of the Congress, helping draft the address of Dadabhoy Naoroji, when your Mahatma was virtually an unknown entity in India. And today *I* have to explain why I prefer to speak to the Viceroy rather than to Gandhi's Congress, a Congress that has no space for me?'

Subhas pushed his chair back and walked to the other side of the desk.

'I have gone from being a disciple of the Mahatma to being somewhat disillusioned, so, yes, I understand most of that. And I have followed your disengagement closely. My notings for my next book, in fact, have a record of what you said at the Muslim League session in December 1938—' Subhas put on his spectacles, opened a bookmarked page from his diary, and read out:

'I have no hesitation in saying that it is Mr Gandhi who is destroying the ideal with which the Congress was started. He is the one man responsible for turning the Congress into an instrument for the revival of Hinduism. His ideal is to revive the Hindu religion and establish Hindu Raj in this country, and he is utilising the Congress to further this object.'

Jinnah nodded.

'Yes, I said that in 1938, and I will say it again in 1943. I was a Congressman before Gandhi was! I joined the Muslim League in 1913, only after making it clear that my loyalty to the League and the Muslim interest would not be at the expense of the larger national cause – I set out the condition *in writing*! You spoke of Motilal Nehru, but do you recall what Gokhale said about me in 1915? "It is freedom from all sectarian prejudice which will make Jinnah the best ambassador of Hindu–Muslim unity".'

'I recall that. I cannot say that your issues with Mr Gandhi are without justification.'

Jinnah was, for a moment, in flashback mode.

'I spoke at the Gujarat Sabha's event to welcome Mohandas Karamchand Gandhi, "the hero of South Africa", when he landed in 1915. And what did he say that day? That he was glad to "find a Mohammedan not only belonging to the sabha of his region but chairing it" – as if my core identity there was not that I was the chairman of that society, but that I was a Muslim. Patronizing from day one, literally. At the Nagpur Congress, five years later, when I stood up to speak about why I disagreed with Mr Gandhi, the crowd shouted me down, insisting I address him as "Mahatma", while he watched, not saying a word to them. Of the seventy-eight who he selected to march to Dandi, do you know how many were Muslim? Two. And I am supposed to be the one opposed to unity, and he is the saint who is taking everyone along. Indeed!'

Jinnah may well have been making an impassioned point in a court of law. His voice echoed through the sparsely furnished study.

Subhas stayed quiet for a few moments.

He glanced at a portrait of Swami Vivekananda that hung behind his desk, paused for a moment, and turned back to the primary advocate for Pakistan.

'There is nothing damaging to any faith if the Hindu *religion* is revived, so long as we keep religion and politics apart. Ramakrishna has tried to do that, Vivekananda has tried to do that, and how threatening has that been to anyone? I have followed Vivekananda as much as I could have, I have fought for my right to Durga Puja in prison till I had it – and how much of a threat to Muslim safety have I been? Just a thought I want to leave you with.

'Secondly, when you say that the Mahatma looks to establish "Hindu Raj" – I do not think that is how *he* looks at it. However, I have not spoken to him for almost two years. If there is a sense that he does, you will find me fighting him on this, as tenaciously as I have fought him on a hundred other things. I have not watched my legion's men die in thousands in the journey so far – Hindus and Muslims and Sikhs, supported by men from another continent who are of none of these faiths – to come all this way to build a single-faith Raj in the end. Equally, Mr Jinnah, I will fight you with all that I can command if you set up a single-faith Raj as a counter. I *know* that you are a man personally free from sectarian prejudice, even though you have now chosen to wear the hat of a communal cause as part of your politics. You have to trust me that I am a man free of sectarian prejudice as well.'

'There are deeper issues at play here, but I am not questioning your personal sense of secularism – else I would not have bothered to meet with you.' A lit cigar having made its way to his hand, leaning back in his chair, the leader of the League seemed to be evaluating the conversation so far.

'Neither am I questioning yours,' Subhas responded, 'which is why I request you to not be a hardliner politically, when you aren't one personally. If my being a Bengali and you a Gujarati does not make us distrust each other, why are we playing identity politics when it comes to religion? This is not the time for it. You don't have to cheer me on – but don't make getting this country together a bloodier task than it already is! Let us give India a chance. I and the Forward Bloc have as many grudges against the Congress of Gandhi and Nehru as you and the League have, and you *know* that. But I will *still* try to work with them as soon as the British are out. Can you not, at least, work with me?'

'Why is this such a touchy issue for you, Mr Bose? You can still have a lot of power in the given situation. The Axis is with you. Why are you complicating it by trying to have the idea behind the Lahore Resolution rolled back? Why not go along with the plans the League has for the communities to just part ways amicably – and then be the leader of the Hindu part?'

Subhas laughed out loud.

'Part ways amicably?'

'And why would you find this amusing? Are you also of the belief that there can only be animosity between Muslims and Hindus?'

'Not in the least, my friend. But I am of the firm belief, after observing closely what has unfolded across Eurasia, that a parting of ways will *not* be amicable – it will, in fact, sustain violence and strife in this region for decades. Surely, you have also seen contemporary historians already explaining that the roots of this war lay in the boundaries drawn in Europe after the Great War in 1919? Surely, you have seen what has been unfolding, for instance, in erstwhile Yugoslavia?'

'I do not see the point that you are making.'

'The point I am making, Jinnah sahib, is that there will be no "amicable" division.'

Subhas paused for a minute, waiting for Jinnah to disagree. But there was only silence.

'Not *while* it happens, not *after* it happens. There will be a massive bloodbath and migrations of unprecedented proportions. We will create two nations which will both nurse horrendous memories and hatred of what the other did to them for years to come. Fifty years from now, maybe even longer, we will have left a legacy that ensures that the next generations will still be obsessed with Hindustan versus Pakistan and Hindu versus Muslim. Sage minds will look back and ask, but why did the men handling things back then allow this to happen? Could they not see ahead? Were there no statesmen, only politicians? We must decide which of these we wish to be. There is no Viceroy to adjudicate between us, Mr Jinnah, and no Mahatma to advise. If we decide, today, in this room, that India will not be split – then India will not be split.'

'I was told you have by now become a total fanatic, a follower of Hitler. Oddly enough, you seem to have mellowed instead.'

'Have I? I doubt that the Mahatma will agree when I meet him. And people who know the least about me tend to talk the most about me, so do not take them too seriously,' Subhas smiled. He then went across to open a drawer in his desk and pulled out a sheet of paper.

'I wrote this down a couple of days back. I thought it was another good reason to argue against a partition. A very non-political reason.'

'And that is?'

Subhas handed over the sheet.

It had a list of names, nothing else.

He read through them: 'Dhyan Chand, Iqtidar Ali Shah Dara, Richard James Allen, Md Hussain, Ahmed Sher Khan, Carlyle Carrol Tapsell, Baboo Narsoo Nimal, Ernest John Goodsir-Cullen, Syed Md. Jaffar, Ashan Md Khan, Joseph Gallibardy, Roop Singh, Gurcharan Singh Grewal, Lionel C. Emmet, Mirza Nasir-ud-Din Masud, Paul Peter Fernandes, Joseph Phillip, Shabban Shaahab-ud-Din.'

Despite himself, Jinnah could not help smiling as he realized what Subhas had handed him.

'While we have been squabbling through the 1930s about

whether Hindus and Muslims can live together, Hindus, Muslims, Sikhs and Christians were training together, working so well as a team that they won the Olympic hockey Gold, smashing Hitler's Master Race in Berlin itself. Just seven years ago, in 1936. You want to deny Dhyan Chand to Muslims and to deny me the right to applaud Dara? I am not even getting into cricket here, given how the English hammer us still, but surely you do not want an opening bowling pair like Amar Singh and Nissar to be split up and to bowl against each other? You want the men in the Indian Legion to yet again choose sides and make enemies out of the men they have fought alongside?'

'Well, you are at least making a better effort than Mr Gandhi and Mr Nehru to hard sell me the idea of a united India, I will grant you that!'

'I want to read out to the words of a prominent Indian leader that, I hope, you will acknowledge argues that idea even better than I do. These are from 1924, from the annual session of the Muslim League ...'

'A Muslim League leader's views which are identical to your own?'

'Indeed!'

He opened his diary and read out: '... we must not forget that one essential requisite condition to achieve Swaraj is political unity between the Hindus and the Mohammedans; for the advent of foreign rule, and its continuance in India, is primarily due to the fact that the people of India, particularly the Hindus and Mohammedans are not united and do not sufficiently trust each other ... I am almost inclined to say that India will get Dominion Responsible Government the day the Hindus and Mohammedans are united. Swaraj is an almost interchangeable term with Hindu–Muslim unity.'

Subhas put down the diary and his spectacles.

'That is the core – we do *not* sufficiently trust each other. The day we are united, we will be a force to reckon with – and who cares for Dominion status now? Freedom is literally days away!'

'Can we have some tea if we are to discuss this issue further?' the Muslim League's supremo asked, his face impassive.

It had been almost twenty years now since a younger, less bitter M. A. Jinnah had made that speech at Lahore.

21

Reminders from Rajputana

THE BREAKTHROUGH POINT FOR THE AXIS/LEGION HAD COME, as geography dictated, once they came out of the hills onto the plains of western India. As the primary forces worked their way towards Delhi, through the Punjab, a smaller, secondary wing moved in a more southerly direction, looking to control the major cities through which any significant road movement would happen for either side.

As plans developed to now bring additional Legion troops finishing training in Germany by sea, and have them disembark at a port – perhaps Karachi – to take the fight into western India, the forces already in India began drawing up plans to establish a secure land corridor by which troops and tanks landing in or around Karachi could either head towards Mumbai or in the direction of Delhi.

From Ludhiana, therefore, regiments wheeled away in a southerly direction. The open, flat terrain left little scope for the British to dig in and ambush advancing columns. Strong defensive positions, where built, could simply be bypassed and starved into surrender without engaging in battle. The local martial traditions of Rajputana were appealed to feverishly, and Subhas was unapologetic about appealing to the local youth and soldiers from the region to revolt against the British.

Radio broadcasts were made, appealing to locals and to employees of the petroleum companies to seize petrol pumps and installations and prevent the British from destroying them.

Despite that, when the units faced a fuel crisis, transport planes took off from Lahore, landed on the endless straight stretches of road without great difficulty, unloaded thousands of jerrycans, and took off, dodging machine gun fire from the British ground forces. Two Luftwaffe pilots met a fiery end, while being watched by helpless Legion troops, incinerated within seconds when their petrol-packed planes caught fire, strafed while descending; the fireballs were visible for miles.

❖

Subhas's policy towards the numerous princely states was uncomplicated: in wartime, his advancing troops would not travel in loops around the territory of each individual state. He had, by means of a radio broadcast as well as a note sent to as many key rulers as could be identified, conveyed his message. The crux of his note was that the Axis/Legion would respect the sovereignty of individual states at this point of time and not engage in conflict with the troops of any princely state, except in self-defence. Equally, however, the right of passage could not be denied to advancing troops, and if it was, they would claim it by force of arms if need be.

There was a footnote as well: beyond the right of passage, the Axis/Legion would not engage in any hostile activity towards any princely state, with the sole exception of a state providing shelter to British forces. Any state that offered such shelter would be assumed to be in alliance with the British forces and deemed to be in a state of war with the Axis/Legion forces.

❖

After ten days of feverish action, the line of advance of the front was roughly along a line that connected Ludhiana–

Bikaner–Jaipur–Ajmer–Udaipur. Upon approaching the last city, on the specific instructions of Subhas, and much to the surprise of the British colonel defending the sector, the Legion's forces veered to the fort of Kumbhalgarh.

The few patrolling units in the region were utterly unprepared for 300 German trucks roaring down the road to Kumbhalgarh from Ajmer, while British defensive positions awaited them on the Bhilwara–Udaipur road. The fort was, among other things, the birthplace of Maharana Pratap. Subhas – micro-managing the events there via radio, much to the surprise and irritation of his command headquarters – had half a dozen Rajput soldiers lead an assorted group of Pathan, Sikh and Baloch men to the fort's top and unfurl the Free India banner.

A photographer documented all of this for the Legion's newspaper, the *Bhaiband*.

And then, in the midst of a war, Subhas sat down to write.

❖

Bhaiband – *The Legion & INA Newspaper*
Edition dated 3 March 1943

A Reminder of the Day When Rajputs and Afghans Fought – Together!

Subhas Chandra Bose

Courageous soldiers of the Indian Legion!

There is a moment from our war, earlier this week, that I wish to share with you personally. It is to my deep regret that the conduct of war did not enable me to be present there physically, but I was engaged with our fellow soldiers very closely and I am still overcome by that sentiment. The photographs accompanying this article will give you a sense of what I describe.

On the morning of March 7, as the British waited at roadblocks along the highway towards Ajmer, our men headed, instead, towards the historic fort of Kumbhalgarh. The majestic fort represents the grand military traditions of India, especially standing for what you believe in, no matter how powerful an adversary be. Our men entered the fort, paid homage at the temple where, it is said, Maharana Pratap himself used to pray before heading into battle, and hoisted the flag of Free India on the ramparts. The unit that was entrusted with this task was a mixture of Rajputs, Sikhs and Pathans/Afghans. And I will explain why this is important.

After hoisting the flag, these men and a few others, drove from the fort to a small place nearby. And there occurred a scene that has perhaps not been seen in a few hundred years.

It was a scene that reflected not only the military defeat of the British armies in India, but even more significantly, the defeat of their philosophy, their ideology of keeping our soldiers divided along religion and region.

Four trucks, two each of Rajput and Afghan/Pathan soldiers, drove from the fort to a nearby location, a shrine. Comrades, you may not be aware that in the famous of battle of Haldighati, while Maharana Pratap survived to fight another day, his commander laid down his life – he was beheaded by the Mughal army. Our soldiers, Rajputs and Pathans, went to the shrine offered a chadar *at the* mazaar *of that General, the valiant fighter Hakim Khan Sur. They then went to Haldighati and paid their respects to* all *those who fought bravely for what they believed in – including the Rajput soldiers who fought for the Mughals and the Afghan soldiers who fought for the Maharana.*

They took a pledge to respect valour and courage on all sides, even that of the enemy, and irrespective of caste and creed.

Soldiers of the Legion! The Rajput warrior is brave, and the Afghan warrior is brave. That is true when they fight against each other, that is even more true when they fight alongside each other. Courage is not the family property of any race or religion. After the battle ended, the blood of neither the Hindu nor the Muslim – and both fought on both sides – that was soaked up by the soil could be differentiated.

History reminds us that while we – Hindus and Muslims, Rajputs and Afghans – have fought each other, we have also fought alongside each other.

It is now time for us to let go of the first part and remember the second.

And even when we fight, we must not hate. Some of our brothers still fight for the British. Even if we aim to defeat them, or to capture them, we must not lose our sense of balance in the heat of battle. It is all right; such fights, as you can see, have happened earlier. Situations may make brother fight brother on a given day – but they are still brothers. After the battle is over, it is not necessary that anger and hatred are carried forward for generations.

When we are told, by the British or by others in our motherland, that we cannot fight together if we are of different faiths, regions or language, that we are enemies to each other – then also, remember: if Maharana Pratap trusted Hakim Khan Sur to command his army, shall we not trust our brothers who pray differently? Are we greater patriots than him? If Sur trusted the Maharana and lost his life in battle for him, is the Afghan, the Pashtun, even more loyal to his land than that general was? Will he not fight today to liberate Rajputana?

If our history teaches us that we are enemies, what does Haldighati teach us? Hindus fought Muslims sometimes, yes. And Rajputs fought Rajputs sometimes. And Muslims fought Muslims sometimes. Today, we Indians are fighting other Indians because we believe in different things. Are we, therefore, enemies for life?

Let us trust in each other, fight together as brothers. Not just till the guns are firing, but after they fall silent as well. Let not your language, your religion, your caste divide you from your fellow soldier. You are the builders of new India, my men. March together! March to victory!
Jai Hind!

22

Friendly Fire

'I shall never tolerate any interference in the internal policy of the Free Indian State... no one should make the mistake of concluding that external collaboration with the Tripartite Powers means acceptance of their domination or even of their ideology in our internal affairs.'

– Subhas Bose, broadcast, 17 June 1942

Unclear Power Structure in Post-Hitler Germany, New Chancellor Doenitz Widely Seen As Compromise Candidate

Reuters
New York, 1 March 1943

Three weeks after the episode, as the world continues to come to grips with the shocking – and to the free world, very welcome – assassination of German Führer Adolf Hitler, the ramifications of that power shift within Germany continue to remain hidden beneath the impenetrable layers of secrecy that the Nazi state has so meticulously built up.

Political observers have had no clear sense of the battle to claim Hitler's power – even though his position was officially filled up, forty-eight hours later, by the long-serving chief of the German Navy, Grand Admiral Doenitz, who was sworn in as the president and chancellor.

It is widely known that the structure – or the absence of it – in the Nazi administrative apparatus has multiple competing elements: the Nazi party itself, helmed by Martin Bormann; the men who were individually powerful primarily on account of access to Hitler, Ribbentrop and Albert Speer; the powerful SS/SD structure reporting to Heinrich Himmler that is a state within a state with both police powers and military divisions in the form of the Waffen-SS; and the Armed Forces, the Wehrmacht, elements of which have been recently on the backfoot despite massive military expansion and Germany effectively turning into a military state.

Within them, Luftwaffe chief Hermann Göring, seen as Hitler's chosen successor and with the rank of Reichsmarschall that technically means he outranks everyone else in uniform, has, for all practical purposes, run an immensely powerful autonomous empire, including ground troops in the form of Luftwaffe Divisions. The fact that he could not, despite that, step into the Führer's role suggests strong opposition from SS Supremo Himmler, with whom he has a deep personal rivalry, as well as from the Wehrmacht Generals, who have long questioned his military capabilities and administrative acumen. Göring reportedly continues to be in a hospital and has not been seen after the day of the explosion that killed Hitler and left him badly injured.

Doenitz, therefore, a man who directly only commands the Navy, with no ground troops loyal to him, is seen as the least controversial choice for the moment, while the tussle for actual power in the backdrop plays out between the hard-line Nazis and Himmler's empire on the one hand, and the Wehrmacht's Generals on the other, many with Prussian pedigrees.

While Doenitz has called for a thorough investigation into the assassination of Hitler, and over a dozen senior officials are already in custody, there is the tacit acknowledgment that it could not have been planned without the active assistance – or at least the passive support – of elements of the Wehrmacht who have long been at odds with the direction in which Germany's military strategy has been headed.

It is understood that these Generals, acutely worried about overreaching beyond their military capabilities, have been pressing for a political solution on the Eastern Front so as to stabilize and consolidate the grasp that Germany has on the entire European continent. The Nazis, however, have been opposed to that on ideological grounds, seeing, as they have brutally demonstrated, that they see the war in the East as a fight to the finish, influenced heavily by their hostility towards both Communism and the Slavs as a race.

The dissenting Generals have also pointed out the relative pragmatism of the Japanese, who, throughout 1942, despite recurrent pressure from Germany, have refused to declare war on Soviet Russia, thereby enabling Russia to concentrate all her forces on the German front. It is also understood that Mussolini's Italy, though a Fascist state for longer than Germany, has been dragging its feet on aligning with the Nazi line on Europe's Jews.

What implications these developments have on the state of the war remains to be seen. The post-assassination statement issued collectively by the Allied powers spoke of the 'irony of intrigue and violence, so intrinsic to the Nazi state, consuming its founder as well' but indicated no change in the political or military stand towards Germany.

Internationally, the primary differentiator of the new regime appears to be that of the persona of the new Chancellor: the German Navy is seen as the least politicised or Nazified of the three services, since it is neither headed by a political loyalist (as in the case of the Luftwaffe) nor seen to be either actively engaged in, or at least complicit, in war crimes, the entirety of which is yet to be understood (as in the case of the Wehrmacht, more so when fighting alongside the Waffen-SS).

In the meantime, reports have not suggested any significant slowdown in military hostilities from existing theatres of war, from the Atlantic U-boat attacks to the Russian front to the continuing Axis advance into British India, where a small contingent of German and Italian forces are supporting the so-called 'Indian Legion' led by former Indian National Congress president turned Fascist supporter, S. C. Bose, a man whom British Prime Minister Churchill has more than once referred to as 'India's Quisling'.

Despite the limited Axis troop commitment to the region, the potential loss of India would be a massive logistical and manpower blow to the British, after the unexpectedly rapid Axis advance through Egypt, Iran and Iraq on the West and the Japanese occupation of SE Asia and Burma in the East. Battle has raged since November, but the British forces still hold on to about half of India, as well as almost the entire coastline with the exception of the Vichy France territory of Pondicherry.

❖

4 MARCH 1943
LONDON TO NY
URGENT/IMMEDIATE
GERMAN POST-HITLER POWER SHIFT STOP DOENITZ SACKS KEITEL STOP APPOINTS ROMMEL NEW CHIEF OF OKH STOP SPECULATION RIFE OTHER CHANGES IMMINENT STOP SS-WEHRMACHT FIREFIGHTS REPORTED STOP UPDATES TO FOLLOW

❖

Rajputana/Gujarat
11 March 1943

The European British troops had fallen back towards urban strongholds towards the interior, while many of the Indian soldiers with them had deserted and melted into the surrounding villages, aware that the Legion did not yet have the manpower to spare to go hunting them from village to village. As the Legion and accompanying German troops gained control of Udaipur, after two days of fighting and forty-odd casualties, the units paused to stock up on fuel, service their vehicles and tend to the wounded.

Not all the men, however, were interested in pausing and resting.

A small German detachment of fifty-odd men, who had flown in from Warsaw a week ago, had joined the Wehrmacht detachment heading for this sector at the last minute, much to the surprise of the major overseeing the company. He had initially demurred but the paperwork authorizing them bore a signature that he did not dare to disobey, even in post-Hitler Germany.

Now that Rommel had been called away to handle greater issues in Germany itself, the Afrika Korps was currently rudderless as Rommel's designated replacement, General Hans-Jürgen von Arnim, looked to first stabilize his existing sectors in Egypt and North Africa before heading out to India. Armin had been deputed to handle the sectors Rommel vacated as he moved west towards India in end-1942. It was now, notionally, a peaceful sector, but Axis intelligence reports strongly suggested that American forces were planning a major landing in North Africa from that period itself – the 'second front' – and Armin was loathe to be accused later of not having a defensive strategy in place if that did happen sometime soon. The Indian front was progressing reasonably well by Subhas's own model that combined emotional appeals with military action. No reason, therefore, existed for detailed German engagement with the front at a senior level at the moment, more so when the lines of power within Germany were fuzzy and the wires were buzzing all day.

These newly arrived troops kept to themselves, awaited instructions, and the day after Udaipur was in Axis hands, drove out south after sunset in four trucks commandeered by the Wehrmacht.

'Four? They need just two!' The quartermaster's point was valid, more so when every truck mattered since infantry without mobility was useless in an offensive role in the plains. And to venture out without a local liaison team from the Legion was also a breach of standard German operating practice in the Indian theatre of war. But the major's query to his commanding officer, presently still stationed at Lahore, resulted in another 'let them' response – these were, after all, reflexes born of many years of accepting the unwritten hierarchy of power in Nazi Germany.

India was not a front where German soldiers got into too much trouble. The policy of 'Legion first' in all forward movement had meant that German casualties through the campaign were nominal, almost miniscule, when compared to the Russian front. Why stick your neck out in a relatively peaceful zone – more so if it may get you into the bad books of Heinrich Himmler?

❖

Balachadi was about twelve hours away from Udaipur. The front was peaceful and hardly vital to the war effort; British forces could not be wasted patrolling interior Kathiawad with hundreds of kilometres of active war front. The four Wehrmacht trucks, loaded with jerrycans of petrol to not have to stop along the way in unfamiliar territory, two men with MG-42s keeping watch atop, drove at speeds that would be not considered prudent, more so for night-time driving. The exercise itself would not be considered prudent. Barely half a dozen men in the unit spoke passable Hindustani, and that on account of having done a stint as instructors at the training camp of the Indian Legion in Annaburg.

Why were fifty or so black-clad men of the SS, the elite of the German war machine, driving out by themselves in Wehrmacht trucks across interior India with hardly a soul in sight at night?

It would make little sense to an outside observer, but the war had, by now, blurred the lines between normal and bizarre.

❖

It was 7.15 a.m. by the elegant Swiss watch on the Sturmbannführer's wrist when he first caught sight of the rectangular red flag of Nawanagar fluttering from the check-post. He signalled to the driver, who slowed down. Messages were exchanged from one truck to another. If the maps he had been handed were accurate, it should be about half an hour's drive from this state border check-post to the assigned location at Balachadi.

The plan was to execute the assigned task and drive back before any questions could be asked. At a pre-decided location on the road back to Udaipur, on a stretch that was wide enough, the trucks would cordon off a kilometre-long portion, a transporter plane would land and collect the cargo, and the men would drive back, join the Wehrmacht contingent, and work on the next assignment.

They had undertaken such assignments many times in the past – the primary difference being that the 'cargo' was usually despatched by train, while this time precious aviation fuel would be spent flying it to a Polish location. Did that make military sense? Not their job to question. In some things – in many things, perhaps? – parts of the Reich still placed ideology over rationality.

The trucks approached the checkpost. The two men who spoke passable Hindustani got down.

The perplexed guards may or may not have noticed that the two MG-42s atop SS trucks were trained at them. It would be safe to assume that they had not been briefed about what to do if German military trucks rolled up to their gate, early one morning.

They had not fired a shot outside of a firing range in years. No shot had been fired at them in decades. Nawanagar had faced no military threat in a long, long time. It had also had a very peaceful association with the Crown. The most noticeable offensive action that anyone in the state had taken against the British had been a subtle one: the leg glance of Jam Saheb Shri Sir Ranjitsinhji that frustrated bowlers on cricket pitches in both India and England. But the SS would not know of that, nor of the Ranji Trophy that had started in 1934 after his death; the Germans did not play cricket.

Ranjitsinhji, who passed away in 1933, had been succeeded by his nephew, Jam Saheb Shri Sir Digvijaysinhji, the present ruler. It was his decision to reach out in 1942 to help over 600 Polish women and children aboard a ship, seeking and being denied refuge in India, that had brought this unexpected visit to his territory's gates.

The leg glance was all about deft timing and elegance; what the SS unit was now doing was, however, more in the nature of a flat-batted shot. Conversational skills were not part of the rigorous training for the *Schutzstaffel*; they preferred more direct action.

In the space of about one minute, a dozen men had surrounded the post, the phone lines had been sliced through, the guards had been disarmed of their antiquated muskets, and, with perhaps a bruise or two as a free add-on, they were trussed up and tossed aside. Another minute later, all the trucks were roaring full-throttle on the road to Balachadi. If the guardians of the Polish children there had any sense of what was approaching, they would not have been smiling as they served breakfast to their wards. Very few of those 'picked' by the SS for being Jewish had been seen playing anywhere subsequently.

❖

The rush of wind as the trucks drove at 80 kmph did not make it easy to hear anything else, but the Unterscharführer manning the MG-42 atop the second truck had the nagging feeling that he had heard a horn honking. He half-turned to look back, and paused. Three trucks, identical to the ones the SS unit was in, were racing behind them, headlights flashing. They were still about 2–300 metres away, too far to see clearly, but these could only be Afrika Korps or Indian Legion. The Unterscharführer tapped sharply on the roof of the driver's cabin, then ducked down below to yell a word of caution at his comrades.

The SS column gradually slowed to a halt – an edgy, uncomfortable slowing. Engines kept running. The sentiment seemed to be reciprocated by the team following. Two of the trucks halted almost 250 metres away; one then stayed parked in the middle of the road, blocking it, while the other went off the road and parked alongside dense roadside foliage.

The third approached the SS trucks and stopped about 50 metres away.

Captain Randhir Singh Jamwal of the Indian Legion got down and walked towards the German unit.

The young officer had been sleeping in his bunk at Porbandar when he had been woken at 3.30 a.m. and issued with a task he would never have expected in this part of the world. It had taken him an hour to arrange the minimum number of men that would be necessary for the assignment and to roll out towards Balachadi. He could have waited for greater numbers, but then he risked reaching too late to have stopped what he was supposed to stop. He preferred the risk of being outnumbered to the risk of not reaching in time – and then explaining that to the man who had assigned him the duty. It was not every day that Subhas Bose verbally instructed you to carry out a military task.

The Sturmbannführer stepped ahead. The captain saluted first as the German outranked him. The SS officer saluted back, sharply, and asked, in passable English: 'What can we do for you, Captain?'

'I have orders to ask you not to proceed further inside the territory of Nawanagar, Major.'

The SS officer smiled. The Reich's allies would need some understanding of the hierarchy. The Italian, Hungarian, Romanian armed forces had been through the same adjustment issues in the beginning. It was understandable.

'I take my orders directly from SS *Gruppenführer* Heinrich Müller. I have been assigned to collect and deport any European Jews who have escaped from areas that are part of the Greater Reich. This is as per the policy laid down by Reichsführer-SS Himmler himself.'

'Sir, whatever be your internal instructions, surely you should be communicating about that with the Afrika Korps units here, instead of heading out on independent operations?'

'This is none of your concern, Captain – but I will still inform you. A note was issued last month from the Reich Security Main Office of the SS, Department IV, to the Chief of Staff, Afrika Korps, asking that the Polish elements reportedly present at this location be gathered once that area is in Axis control, and be made accessible for suitable authorities to ascertain as to how many of them are of Jewish descent. However, there has been a regrettable disinterest on the part of the Afrika Korps, which has recurrently written that they have not been able to deploy any troops for this action – apparently on account of the Indian Legion providing no infrastructure, logistical or translator support. I have, therefore, been instructed to handle it directly.'

'Still, sir, that is no reason to—'

'You do realize that as an officer of the SS, I cannot revert and report failure to comply with directions on the grounds that a captain of the Indian Legion advised me otherwise?'

'Sir, I understand that you are following instructions. However, there is no legality or applicability of your rulebook on this territory. And that has been conveyed to me directly by the Supreme Commander of the Legion, early today morning. Additionally, you have informed neither the Legion nor the Nawanagar administration and, needless to say, the manner of your entry into the state's territory has not been civil. Irrespective of your hierarchy of command, I am, therefore, under orders to ensure that not a single Polish refugee on Indian territory is taken away, by any forces, of whatever nationality. I have to ask you to stop right here. I would request you to turn back and let us escort you back to Udaipur.'

'Or else?'

'Sir, no matter what your reputation or record be, you are leading fifty or so men, hundreds of kilometres into Indian territory. All I need to do is flatten the tyres of your trucks and your adventure is over. I can call for reinforcements, you cannot. Let us not make this into a confrontational situation.'

The Sturmbannführer issued a command in German. The clickety-clack of assorted weapons being cocked resonated for a moment.

'Yes, I have fifty men, but you don't seem to have more than twenty, twenty-five, right, Captain? I agree; don't make this into a test of power. The Jews are ours. Poland is now German territory, and they are Polish citizens, not Indians. Why are you putting the lives of your men on the line for them?'

'We put our lives on the line for whatever we are ordered to, Major. They came here seeking refuge, it was granted, and today it falls upon me to ensure that they are protected. You may not get it; you are putting the lives of your men on the line not to take out a key military target, but a group of children. Is that a worthwhile exercise for men acknowledged to be among the most feared fighters in the world? Why not help us fight the British instead?'

'You are delaying my schedule, Captain, I do not have the liberty to engage in political debates at the moment. I will proceed.'

'I will then stop you by force.' The Captain unholstered his pistol.

The Legion's men heard the crack of the MG-42 a second after he was hurled off his feet, the 7.92 mm bullets having smashed into his shoulder. The overeager SS Unterscharführer atop the truck had not waited for his officer's command. It would have been better for him if he had, though; he was standing upright, clearly silhouetted, away from cover, and if there was some irony in the fact that the bullets that thudded into him the next moment were all manufactured in Germany, he did not have much time to reflect on that.

❖

The Jam Sahib of Nawanagar had maintained a regiment of Lancers for decades, consisting of two squadrons and a company of infantry. By the time the transports carrying sixty or so men from that company approached the venue of the SS-Legion standoff, the crackle of bullets had been echoing for forty minutes.

The SS truck parked in the centre of the road, the one from which the first bullet had been fired, had attempted to speed off as the exchange of fire started, but both sides had MG-42s and rounds from the other side had gone past the thin metal, into the driver's cabin; at barely 250 metres, it meant nothing to a heavy calibre bullet. The truck had smashed into a tree, many men had been flung out, and at the end of the first two minutes, with about 500 rounds poured into it, almost all men aboard that one vehicle were out of action – unconscious, wounded, or dead.

But the SS had fought in far worse situations and not flinched. Twenty or so men put out of action still left thirty others – thirty who fanned out across the area, took cover behind the foliage and their vehicles, climbed the nearest trees to have better vantage points, tossed grenades towards the Legion's trucks, and riddled the six men in the front cabins of the two trucks on the main road before they could jump off or move the trucks to cover. Most of the Legion's men had been in the truck that had parked off the road, sheltered by tree trunks from a straight line of fire, else it would have been all over by now. The still-outnumbered Legion unit realized that it could not overwhelm the black-clad without taking heavy casualties. It kept to a defensive, holding operation, staying behind cover, blowing the tyres off all the other SS trucks, and sending a messenger back to the checkpost on foot. Three kilometres could be managed in ten to twelve minutes, lesser if he was running for his comrades' life.

So when the Lancers spread out and marched along what was now the rear of the SS unit's position, it was a deadlock between twenty-seven SS men and sixteen Legion soldiers. It wasn't clear if Captain Jamwal was still breathing, but nobody had been able to get anywhere near him since he lay bleeding right in the middle of the road.

The Lancers had not seen active fighting in a long time – and absolutely none against men as highly trained as those of the SS – but even then, sixty rifles trained at your back can make a difference, even if half of them miss the target. Four Germans sustained severe injuries from .303 rifle bullets before the SS shifted attention to the rear as well – but that left fewer guns facing the Legion. Six or seven Lancers fell quickly, after which they, too, went on the defensive, taking cover, but blocking off the entire stretch on the other side as well.

With the balance of numbers now shifting, the next senior-most officer in the Legion, a lieutenant, asked his men to pause firing and called out to the Germans, hoping that there were still men or officers alive who understood English.

'Men of the Schutzstaffel! You are not going to reach your destination. You have no transport. The road is cut off on both sides. You do not speak the local language. You are not going to receive any reinforcements. But we are. Make your choice. We can wait till evening, till more of our men arrive and your ammunition runs out. Or you can surrender now!'

❖

'Herr Himmler is *furious*! Absolutely furious! He demands an immediate apology and repatriation of the Schutzstaffel soldiers in your custody, Herr Bose!'

'There is no question of an apology. I will take a decision on the repatriation in a week's time. In the interim, please convey to the Reichsführer-SS that I considered having the entire squad shot, but did not go ahead with that only on account of the otherwise excellent relations that we have had with German armed forces, and the message that I received from Field Marshal Rommel. These men were not on a military assignment, they were there to forcibly take away children. How do you think Herr Himmler would react if I sent a hundred men from the Legion's training centre at Annaburg into Germany's interior to kidnap people whom I thought were politically or racially not acceptable to me?'

'We are allies, Herr Bose. This is not acceptable!'

'We are allies in the conduct of war. India is not Austria, my friend; we haven't merged into Germany. No battle was being fought in the state of Nawanagar. You were not chasing escaping British troops. I cannot intervene in the internal policies of your state, no matter what I think of them. And you cannot intervene in the internal matters of India – more so, with no reference to me! Don't sell me the absurd argument that those children don't "belong" to India. Everyone on Indian soil freed of the British is now my responsibility and my forces will protect them whenever and however needed. And if you have an issue, raise it with the Afrika Korps – better still, raise it with Field Marshal Rommel. The SS has no formal liaison with the Legion – please communicate via the Wehrmacht structure. And rest assured, if there is another misadventure, I will not hesitate to repeat this. Dismissed.'

The Sturmbannführer glared at Subhas, then turned, and walked towards the door.

'Sturmbannführer!'

The man turned back. Would the defiant Legion commander finally offer an apology he could convey to Himmler?

'You forgot to salute before leaving.'

❖

'How is the pain?'

Dhillon and Ghaffar gathered around as Subhas stood by the bed of Captain Randhir.

'It hurts when I breathe, sir, and I take care not to laugh, but apart from that, the painkillers help me manage.'

'I should not have put you in that situation. You had little time and were outnumbered, from what I have read in the reports, yet the original instruction was followed – nobody was allowed to reach the Polish centre.'

'That's our job, sir – to ensure orders are carried out.'

The young officer winced as he spoke. His right shoulder, smashed by multiple bullets, had been operated upon and was throbbing despite the painkillers pumped into him.

Subhas took a chair next to his bed and spoke about what was troubling his mind.

'Some of my officers asked me, Captain, if it was the right call to take – to have eight of our men killed, another five injured, and to have a royal mess with Himmler himself, when no Indians were involved in the whole story, essentially. These men would be alive today if I was not trying to make a point, they tell me. I want to know what you feel, genuinely.'

'But we don't go to war because we like firing rounds, sir. We go to war because we are making a point, about what we think is right or wrong. We think it is wrong for the British to treat us as their inferiors. If we also think it is wrong for the Germans to treat others as inferiors, how is that any different?

I have heard you speaking about the idea of India, sir, I have seen what you did in the training camp, I read what you wrote about Haldighati recently. I agree. If we let people be picked up or killed for their religion or race, if we are all right with even the thought of it, then where does it end?'

'Wise words from a young man, eh?' Ghaffar smiled.

'I mean it, sir. What if one of my own men, just *one* man out of 150 in my company, is a Jew, and I let him be taken away on that ground – then how can we talk of being brothers? The position we took – we will protect *everyone* on our territory – was worth fighting for. And are we fighting to remove the British just to now take orders from the Germans? There has to be respect, lines have to be drawn. Those kids who are not heading back to Poland – they don't know any of us, but I would have no regrets if I had died carrying out my orders to keep the SS away from them.'

Dhillon laughed. 'You know, my boy, I think you just took over our commander's role for a bit with that speech – and you did it very well.'

❖

There was a soft knock on the door to Subhas's office. 'Come in', he responded. Nambiar walked in and made himself comfortable in the chair opposite Subhas's.

'What brings the ever-busy Nambiar here today – no meeting, no agenda, no files to be sorted as far as I can recall?' Subhas smiled.

The last few months had been so packed with decisions and stress that he had rarely spoken to even his closest advisors and friends – did he have friends? – without an agenda on the table. To see Nambiar sitting across the table without a decision pressing on his mind was something that happened so rarely now – he could barely recollect when it had last happened. For a moment, his thoughts went back to the initial months in Berlin, the anonymity that being Orlando Mazzotta brought, and the time and mental space he used to have for long, wandering discussions about the future of India, and about life.

'There's no agenda, for a change, none at all,' Nambiar smiled. 'I don't really know how to put this – I just wanted to say that you, you know, sort of passed a test. And that I am really glad that you did.'

'Did I? That doesn't happen very often these days!' Subhas laughed. 'And in what, if I may ask?'

Nambiar paused for a moment, as if figuring how exactly to word his thoughts.

'As you well know, Subhas, my views on the workings of Nazi Germany have been consistent since when we first met, as far back as 1933. And my discomfort with how closely this campaign has needed us to work with the Nazi regime is not something I have kept from you.'

'Of course. I understand your position very well. Have I not been critical of Nazi policies since the 1930s myself? I know that left to yourself, you would have avoided working with them in any capacity. I have been, for want of a better word, more pragmatic about the realities of the international situation and dealt with them more closely than you may be comfortable with – of that I am fully aware. And despite that, you have stood by me and done so much for the cause and for this campaign – I respect that, genuinely.'

'I'm glad you do, Subhas. You know I am not as blindly a hero-worshipper as many of your fans.'

'I know, and I don't *want* any fans, trust me,' Subhas smiled. 'I remember someone once described you in Berlin as "Subhas's reluctant right-hand man". But that has never bothered me – you are exceptionally efficient at what you do, no matter the reluctance or hesitation about some issues, and I cannot demand anything more.'

'I am glad you understand. It is just that I – I am not good at being what is called a loyalist.'

'And why should you be? If I myself was comfortable being a loyalist, my tenure in the Congress would have earned me far less hostility. And you have been a good friend of Jawahar's from even before you met me, while he and I are no longer on the best of terms. These things have never mattered to me so long as someone is dependable in what they do.'

He paused for a moment.

'But why are you in this space today, exactly? It must be on account of that test I have passed, I suppose?'

Nambiar, never given to being overly expressive, softly nodded.

'When the news of the SS asking about the Polish children first reached us, I was very apprehensive. And, let me be frank, not just me.'

'Whatever for?'

Nambiar looked surprised at Subhas's response.

'For the likelihood of aggressive Nazism taking its first steps on Indian soil, what else? So many of us were acutely disturbed at the likelihood of those children being picked up by Himmler's men and then transported back to god knows where. We feared it would start this way – and then, who knows where it would end?'

'Ah, so *that's* the test I have passed? Of not letting Himmler get his way?'

'More or less, yes. And, truth be told, if he had got his way, I would have very likely – in fact, almost certainly – contemplated coming to you and asking to be relieved of my duties. Which is why I felt I owed it to you to say all this today.'

Subhas smiled. And then stayed quiet for a moment before responding.

'I would have fully understood if you had done so. And would have respected such a decision. But it could not have happened. We are partners with the Axis in a military campaign to get to India. There was never, *ever*, going to be a situation where we accept decisions about Indians, or in India, being taken by any external power. Why else did I fight so hard to train and build our own force? So that once we are finally here, we don't replace one foreign power with another.'

'That all is easy to *say*, Subhas – but when we have seen how closely you have worked with Germany since 1941, even those of us working for this long with you were not sure how you would react to German pressure.'

This time Subhas laughed out loud.

'I get you, I do – but, clearly, none of you is paying attention to what I say! When I write an editorial, when I make a statement on radio, I am not a politician saying the right things. I mean *every* word I say. And I have got tired of repeating, in ten different ways, that my association with the Tripartite Powers is about India's external relations. That I will never let them have a say in our internal matters. Have I not?'

Nambiar nodded.

Subhas opened a drawer in his desk and shuffled through some papers for a minute.

'Ah, here it is. I wrote this radio broadcast by hand, last June, when we were not even in Iran, what to speak of India. But I was clear, and I spelt it out as plainly as possible.'

He held up a handwritten note and read aloud from it: 'It is high time that my friends and colleagues at home learnt to differentiate between the internal and external policy of Free India. The internal policy of Free India is, and should be, the concern of the Indian people themselves – while the external policy should be one of collaboration with the enemies of Britain.

While standing for full collaboration with the Tripartite Powers in the external sphere – I stand for absolute self-determination for India where her national affairs are concerned, and I shall never tolerate any interference in the internal policy of the Free Indian State. So far as socio-economic problems are concerned, my views are exactly what they were when I was at home – and no one should make the mistake of concluding that external collaboration with the Tripartite Powers means acceptance of their domination or even of their ideology in our internal affairs.'

He put the paper back in the drawer.

'"I shall never tolerate any interference in the internal policy of the Free Indian State": this is what I said long before we were at India's borders; this is what I did in the case of the Polish children and this is what I will do till the day I have the wherewithal to do so.'

'I cannot tell you how glad I am to hear that, Subhas. This has troubled me for many weeks. And if you were to have wavered on this, I, and others like me, would have been in a crisis of conscience of epic proportions.'

'Well, let us keep our fingers crossed till the next test comes our way,' Subhas softly laughed. 'I am sure there will be more tests, and I will pass some and fail some. But on one thing, rest assured – I will, as the English say, walk the talk! And if you find a day when I don't, please walk up and say it to me, right to my face.'

'I will, Subhas,' said Nambiar, as the two men stood up and shook hands with a firmness born of long years of mutual respect, and of many occasions of agreeing to disagree.

PART III

23

Dear America

'The Indian people have been expecting the US to come out and take a stand on the side of justice and equity.'

– Chiang Kai-shek to the US President, 25 July 1942

'India has become the first test which the American, friendly or unfriendly, at once applies to British Imperial Policy. In the main it is critical, and it is frequently shot through with emotion.'

– Report by British embassy in the US to London, September 1942

To: Franklin D. Roosevelt, President, United States of America
From: Subhas Chandra Bose, Head, Provisional Government of Free India

21 March 1943

Re: American Military Personnel on Indian Territory

Mr President,

I write to you in the context of the state of war that exists at the moment between the forces of the Indian Legion and the Indian National Army, assisted by forces of the Tripartite Powers, and the forces of Imperial Britain, which has colonized the

Indian nation for close to two centuries.

You are aware that the Indian Legion, of which I am Supreme Commander, has been in action against the armies of Imperial Britain for some months, first in the Middle East and as of November 1942, on the Indian territory itself.

The Indian Legion and the INA were set up with the objective of liberating India from Britain, and therefore, have so far consciously not engaged in hostile action against the armed forces of any powers that may be at war with the Axis Powers – be it Soviet Russia, Australia, France, and such.

I however regret to indicate that we may be left with no option but to shortly take offensive action against US Armed Forces personnel who are stationed on Indian soil and are now increasingly seen to be present along the front line as the battle shifts to the interior and enters its last phase. As large numbers of Indian soldiers either desert the British Indian Army or cross over to join the Legion/INA, the US military resources present in India are, from the information that I have, being pressed into active roles against the Legion/INA and the forces of the Axis powers. Approximately fifty such US military personnel are, as of today, Prisoners of War of the INA and the Imperial Japanese Army.

It is my understanding that there are anywhere between 35,000 to 60,000 Americans in India, the majority of them in active or supporting military roles, all under the larger umbrella of the 'China–Burma–India Theatre' established in June 1942. These numbers may or may not be precise; it is of no concern to me what the specifics are.

It is my recommendation to the US Government that both combatants and non-combatants who are American citizens,

- *desist from any active participation in military action against the Legion/INA/Axis forces*
- *desist from any action that may be seen as hostile to the Indian forces or people*

- *come forward and declare themselves to the forces of the Indian Legion at the battlefront nearest to them and surrender any weapons and military equipment that they may have.*

If this is adhered to, I would attempt to ensure that they are kept in the custody of the forces of the Provisional Government of India – which already has control of over half of the Indian territory – for as brief a period as is practicable, and are thereafter escorted to the nearest Allied base, aboard US hospital ships or unarmed naval vessels, under the watch of the International Red Cross. The Indian Legion/INA will ensure the safety of all such personnel and will ensure that they are not subject to any coercive action by any of the Axis forces present in India.

I offer this only because Free India is at war with Imperial Britain, not with the United States of America. I offer this despite both Germany and Japan, who fight along with Indian forces against the British, being at war with the USA. I offer this despite the fact that there has been a wide divergence of attitude between the American public and the American government towards India. A large section of the American people has displayed sympathy for the cause of Indian independence, but so far as American official policy has been concerned, it has been indistinguishable from that of Britain and so for India, the USA is as imperialistic a power as Britain.

Mr President, the hollowness of your official position towards India – which is a fifth of the world's people – is made amply clear by the fact that the Atlantic Charter that you signed in 1941 and hold so dear, seems to have no applicability to it.

You sign a document that talks of 'the right of all peoples to choose the form of government under which they will live'; that states that you 'wish to see sovereign rights and self-government restored to those who have been forcibly deprived of them'. You express sympathy for nations that have been forcibly deprived of sovereign rights in 1939, 1940, 1941 – but you have no interest in the restoration of such rights to India, which has been deprived of them for over a hundred years, since it does not fit in with the geopolitical aims of the Allied powers. You will therefore excuse me if I am unable to place the American engagement in this war on a greater moral pedestal than that of the Axis powers, and if that sentiment is echoed by the Indian people. The Atlantic Charter is, quite literally, limited to the coasts of the Atlantic. We cannot expect you to live up to it in the context of India. And therefore, we have opted to take by force what is denied to us through civil means and the benchmarks of international morality and justice.

I urge you to accept this offer and to disengage militarily from the Indian subcontinent with immediate effect. It will avoid bloodshed and minimise further conflict. I would anticipate a revert from your side in seventy-two hours of the receipt of this letter, which is being conveyed via the Mexican Embassy in Washington.

If you were to not respond or to reject the offer, the Provisional Government of Free India, while not declaring a state of war with any nation other than Britain, will

- *engage with all US military personnel on Indian territory, if they engage in combat, as hostiles and treat them in a manner identical to that of British military and support personnel*
- *confine US civilian personnel to restricted zones for the duration of the war, while allowing Red Cross access to them*
- *turn over all captured military personnel to the Axis forces operating in the respective sectors as POWs and allow the German/Italian/Japanese forces the right to transport them to other locations outside of the territory of India if they so deem fit.*

The American people profess a love for liberty and for human rights. How the US Government proceeds to justify to them the loss of lives, both American and Indian, if American military personnel engage in combat against Indians liberating their own nation from imperial occupation, would be a topic of much interest.

I intend to write to the US press indicating the offer that I have made, and inform them of your response, or the lack of it.

Subhas Chandra Bose

❖

'The Japanese will not take this well.'

Now that some of his trusted confidants from Germany had reached India, Subhas was finally able to engage with a few diplomatic, and not just military, initiatives. He listened as Nambiar and Abid Hasan, grappling with the huge volume of queries he had put to them, vociferously disagreed with his decision to send out the note to Roosevelt.

'And why will they not take it well?'

Nambiar looked at him incredulously.

'Because you are essentially offering a ceasefire space for a nation they are at war with. They can easily see this as a breach of trust between military partners.'

'All right, then. Then explain to me why, in 1943, Japan has a perfectly normal diplomatic relationship – as normal as things can be in the situation – with Moscow, while Germany and Russia have been trying to annihilate each other's armies on the European frontier for two years? Is that not a breach of trust between Germany and Japan? Japan chooses not to be dragged into a military conflict with Russia even though it is part of the Tripartite Alliance. Similarly, I choose not to be dragged into a military conflict with any other nation – what is the ethical or moral quandary there?'

His associates looked at each other.

'This is all good for an editorial in the *Forward Bloc*, Subhas. But, practically, there is far too much to balance diplomatically already. Why are you going out of your way at this stage?' Nambiar was clearly unconvinced.

'Why not? Even if there are 40–50,000 Americans who have not been so far actively engaged on the battle lines, once we encircle all major centres remaining, once they realize that this is *it*, the British aren't going to stay in control – they will be forced to join them in picking up arms if they want to avoid Axis custody. Do we want to kill or injure 10,000 Americans while reclaiming India? Do we want to perhaps lose another 5,000 of our own men while they battle Americans, generally better equipped than the British, and fighting as collective units, not, like the British, distributed in mixed formations with a majority of Indian soldiers who no longer have their heart in the fight? The Americans are especially wary of surrendering to the Japanese, and with good reason. But why should we deal with them as enemies? I don't want Indian soldiers engaged in battle with any country's troops, unless in self-defence. Why shouldn't tomorrow's India have a practical working relationship with the USA and the USSR, along with Germany and Italy, with China, and at the same time, with Japan? Why should we be obligated to one alliance?'

'And will that not strain your association with the Axis?'

'The Axis are here with me to deny Britain access to India's landmass and its manpower. That, they will achieve. Additionally, independent India will offer them bases to keep naval vessels, limited troops, and aircraft for the duration of the war. They will have passage through our territory for movement of civil and military equipment – which actually gives them a land bridge to each other. That is a very fair, even a generous deal. Hitler attacked Russia with some 145 divisions. I cannot mortgage India for the support of one German, one Italian and four Japanese divisions, can I? If they alone had been the ones marching in, we would have been in a different situation – but that is why the Legion and the INA were formed, that is why they paid the greatest price along the way, so we are independent, period. Not just independent of the British.'

'Mr Nehru would agree with you, for once, on this.'

'I think so. He has very strong thoughts on foreign policy, understands it better than most in India, and, frankly, I would welcome his advice on these issues, on India's place in the world – once he can come to terms about dealing with a man who has shaken hands with Hitler. I don't think he can forgive me for that easily.'

Subhas laughed.

Nambiar looked at him curiously, figuring out if he was being serious or sarcastic.

❖

A week later, a 24-hour ceasefire was observed across the country as thousands of US military and civilian personnel, in convoys led by Red Cross vehicles, drove to the nearest designated port where hospital ships of the US Navy awaited to take them. The British watched with mixed feelings. A handful who could get their hands on spare uniforms mingled in with the Americans and made good their escape from the battle zones.

Meanwhile, Subhas received a nasty Japanese memo, protesting that these men could well be taking up arms against them in another battlefield, a few months later, since the ships would take them to British-ruled Sri Lanka, thereby, creating a US presence in the Indian Ocean – one that had finished after the Japanese occupation of the Philippines in April 1942. Subhas's counterpoint was that with naval bases being made available in South India and already there in the Andamans, the Japanese Navy was more than capable of cutting off ships heading out from Sri Lanka, and a land-based detachment of Americans – having left behind all their weapons, vehicles and equipment in India – were not an immediate threat to the Axis in the region.

24

Southern Breakout

PONDICHERRY, WHERE MUCH DRAMA HAD TAKEN PLACE, WAS not the only French territory in India in 1943; there were Karaikal, Yanam and Mahe as well.

Though it was about 150 kilometres distant, Karaikal was technically part of Pondicherry, and, therefore, in the domain of Louis Alexis Étienne Bonvin, since he was the governor of all French possessions in India.

However, after Bonvin switched allegiance from De Gaulle back to Pétain in December, and felicitated the overnight, dramatic conversion of Pondicherry into an Axis cantonment, the British had been quick to put a choice before the French officers locally commanding the handful of troops at Karaikal, Yanam and Mahe: declare allegiance to De Gaulle and the Allies and support them whenever called upon to do so, thereby, keeping the French flag flying, or have your territory invaded and be marched off to a POW camp as enemy combatants.

It was not a difficult choice to make in the given circumstances. However, the French officials – who all agreed to option one – had the military and political experience to gauge why options were being offered at all.

Surely, the most obvious thing, looking at the map of India, would have been for the British to immediately seize the French territories after Bonvin's defection? Why had that not happened?

Reason one was that British–Vichy French tensions remained extremely high, more so after the death of close to 1,300 French sailors in July 1942, when His Majesty's ships shelled and sunk the French flotilla anchored at Mers-el-Kébir, on the coast of French Algeria.

If the French were asked to shift political allegiance from Vichy to De Gaulle at gunpoint, they would probably do it, especially in a militarily hopeless situation. It was, after all, no more than a signature on a piece of paper. However, if it came to British troops marching in, there was an overwhelming likelihood that the French officers and the soldiers with them would prefer to shoot first and discuss peace later. These isolated pockets of land were not militarily valuable enough for the British to lose more men.

Reason two was that, even in 1943, unlike the Japanese in Singapore or the Germans in far too many battles to recount, the British military reflex still was to attack only after accumulating a comfortable numerical as well as material superiority. The officers leading the British infantry were, more often than not, stubbornly brave and defiant in defence but rarely dashing and flamboyant in offence. Even for these small pockets, their plan rested on a 2:1 or ideally a 3:1 advantage in numbers. And so, even if the total French forces across these pockets added up to just about 5,000 men, the plan to invade them was based on the availability of 10,000, ideally 15,000 troops.

With Subhas and the Legion now in the Punjab, desertions among Indian soldiers at an all-time high on account of his incessant propaganda, Bengal facing a violent public uprising, the Japanese–INA combine finally moving ahead into the plains, two infantry divisions pulled off at short notice from the Southern Command to act as a garrisoning unit for the Italians at Pondicherry, greater deployment at all major installations within the country after what had happened at the air base in Bangalore and at the Maidan in Calcutta – moving that many troops to handle a situation that was not exactly on fire was not a proposal that was going to get past any headquarters.

For over a month, therefore, the French in these pockets were allowed to be as they were, so long as their presence did not cause further irritation to the Viceroy.

Both sides knew that it was not a peace that would last long.

❖

Subhas had waited long enough to minimize casualties, to give Indian soldiers the time to evaluate their position, to decide if they wanted to either defect from or just desert the British side. He could not enforce a go-slow policy in a war beyond a point and by now, he had finally made up his mind to ask for no further restraint on part of either his troops or the Axis.

Between November and March, some 20,000 or so men and officers from the British side had actively crossed over to the INA, about 40,000 to the Legion, and intelligence indicated that another 30–40,000, not willing to go over and fight against their fellow soldiers but not willing to die for the retreating British Army either, had simply been waiting for an opportune moment to desert and melt away.

That still left enough numbers to keep the British in the game for a few more months.

Any soldier who was *still* fighting to keep the Union Jack flying, and to do that was willing to shoot at men of the Legion or the INA, did not, in Subhas's view, merit a further outreach of brotherhood. He had done his best, but men and resources could not be stretched infinitely. The longer this took, the more the British would have the opportunity to convince fence-sitters among the local populace that the Raj would survive and that the Axis had stalled.

It was now to be all-out war, the sort that his Axis allies had been straining at the leash to launch into, and it began now.

There were two lines of concentric defences around Pondicherry, hemming the Italian, French and Indian soldiers inside. While supplies continued to reach by sea and by air, the land frontier had, for a month, been sealed off by the British, who had also dug in defensive positions and positioned gun batteries.

Smaller British gun batteries along the coast occasionally harassed the Pondicherry detachment and fired on the naval supply ships bringing in food, fuel and trucks. This was enough to cause minor damage and occasional casualties, but not enough to make a perceptible difference to the stockpiling of supplies. The transporter planes that had flown in the men from the Bangalore POW camp escape had stayed on at the airstrip, hidden away, camouflaged as to not draw the attention of the spotter planes that flew overhead each day.

Retaliation by the men from within the pocket to British aggression was infrequent and measured – the orders were to dig in and conserve ammunition and resources till such time the situation was conducive for offensive action.

Now it was.

❖

31 March 1943

At 4.15 a.m., the 5-inch guns on the Japanese Destroyers – *Samidare*, *Asagumo*, *Ikazuchi* and *Shigure* – let loose the first barrage in synchronized coordination. The range had been carefully calibrated. The guns had a range of 18,000 metres, but they were firing from just about 9,000 metres. They had had weeks to observe and sight the fixed positions of the British lines, especially of the artillery. Local Legion sympathizers had also been travelling frequently to Karaikal, along the coast, and marking all British positions along the road and on the coast. Under cover of darkness, on two occasions, French officers from Pondicherry had been ferried on fishing boats to Karaikal and back.

When the 23-kilogram, high-explosive shells landed, they did so with unerring precision on the British assault gun batteries, observation towers and jetties. The British encirclement around Pondicherry itself bore the brunt of the shelling. Long-range naval bombardment of land-based targets is an extremely one-sided engagement unless the coast is fortified with large-calibre, anti-ship guns, but the British had hardly fortified the eastern coast the way they had done in Singapore. Even apart from the meticulous prior identification of coordinates, there was no dearth of spotters to relay messages back when key targets were missed in the initial salvo.

The 5-inch was only medium calibre, but against the unfortified targets, it proved brutal. The Americans and the Japanese were using naval shelling against each other's coastal defences each time they fought to claim or reclaim an island in the Pacific, but those islands were hilly, forested, and the defenders were well dug-in, in anticipation of such assault. The British deployments here were on open ground and were designed to resist a possible breakout by infantry. A surprise naval bombardment against such a target wasn't combat – it was butchery. And butchered they were. In the space of 30 minutes, the encircling forces lost three-fourths of their vehicles, guns, and combat-capable men.

So far, Subhas had forbidden any indiscriminate usage of firepower, to minimize casualties among the Indian elements of the British armies, and to enable them to surrender rather than have Indian kill Indian on the front line. By now, however, his patience had run out – if there were men loyal enough to the Crown to kill soldiers of the Legion and the INA even as of today, then they should be treated as enemy combatants. The 'minimize casualties' policy was laid to rest – as were over 300 men of the British Indian Army, Indians and English, both.

As the British troops cordoning off Pondicherry rushed to attend to the dead and wounded amidst the smouldering wreckage and the screams of men with limbs hacked or flung away while frantic calls for backup scrambled across the radio waves, a spearhead of Italian stormtroopers atop trucks and armoured carriers, machine guns blazing, punched into them across a focused, 300-metre-wide strip, seeking to cut through the encircling zone and gain access to the highway that went north – towards Chennai.

It was 5.30 a.m. The driving distance to Chennai was about 150 kilometres. They were aboard 70-odd trucks and a dozen Armoured Personnel Carriers. The guesstimate was a four-hour drive. Spotters had been placed after every kilometre on the route to warn of any British counter-move. Nobody expected them to be on that road and so, at least initially, surprise would minimize opposition. Or so they hoped.

Amidst the chattering of machine guns blazing indiscriminately in all directions, the convoy broke out of the encirclement and sped onto the highway.

It did not stop for the half a dozen men who toppled over from the speeding trucks, having survived the war in North Africa only to take a bullet in India.

❖

Had the handful of spotter planes available to the RIAF in the area been given advance warning, perhaps a few gunboats could have at least put up token resistance.

Surprise being essential for this operation to succeed, and the likelihood of being spotted on that route being high, the ships deputed for this operation had sailed out *not* from Port Blair, but from Singapore.

Turning north and moving via the Malacca Straits, they had travelled past the southern tip of the Nicobar Islands to a point east of Jaffna, then finally turned north, crossed the Palk Strait, and reached their designated assault positions undetected after a four-day journey.

One advantage of heading out from Singapore was that three newly raised divisions of the INA, formed out of soldiers who volunteered later in the year after being taken POWs in the massive surrender of 1942, were on board. The 'Pondicherry pocket' was headed towards becoming a truly international force, with Indian – and some Japanese – troops eager to join the Italian and French forces already there, as the breakout finally got underway. At 5 a.m., two transporter ships began unloading the newer batch of INA men to join the force ready for battle in the pocket, protected from close-range offensive fire by the ceaseless shelling from the gunships farther back.

Subhas hoped that the name 'pocket' would be a misnomer by the end of the day – the plan was to control an area much beyond Pondicherry by nightfall.

❖

For about six months, the British had anticipated a sea-borne invasion of Chennai and had reasonably stout defences in place. However, just as in Singapore, they were about to face an unexpected assault by land instead.

Even as the 4,000 Italians, accompanied by 400 or so Indians, drove past stunned observers (an enemy convoy on the highway *here*?), a second batch of soldiers that had just disembarked from ships was clambering aboard transporter planes and a selected group with paradropping experience was heading for their common destination: Chennai.

Well, not *quite* Chennai.

❖

Twenty kilometres outside Chennai lay Avadi, where the British were in the process of preparing the largest military base and ordinance depot in India.

Though the British conceptualized it well before war actually came to India's frontiers, work had continued at a fair pace over the past three months, despite the worsening situation at the borders. Chennai was seen as an ideal location for such a base – too far inland to be attacked by land, too strongly defended against ships to be easily threatened by sea.

Even as the British reconciled to the inevitability of Subhas raising the Indian flag in Delhi and Calcutta, consensus had built towards the strategy of making India 'another Russia': even if half the country was lost, it was vast enough for the remaining half to provide a buffer and resources for the fighting to be continued, perhaps to take it to a deadlock. So long as the coastline was in British hands, men and supplies could be brought in. The Deccan could be held even if the north was lost, the generals believed, and a combination of Sri Lanka plus the Deccan was not a small presence in this theatre of war.

Avadi was to be a core storage and repair base for operations in the South. The larger plan was that, when fully functional, it would have almost 10,000 people handling logistics, supply, weapons production, and vehicle repairs across an area of over 20 square miles. Hospitals had already been constructed. Multiple airstrips were operational. The blueprint of the project indicated that it was going to be able to store 100,000 tonnes of supplies and 10 to 11 *million* litres of fuel.

Even though the actual supplies stocked there as of January were only a third of that grand capacity, even that one-third was a great prize to deny to the British and to feed and refuel the men leaving the sanctuary of the Pondicherry pocket.

Avadi, in what was assumed to be a geographically secure zone, was guarded by a detachment of soldiers not physically in prime shape for combat duty at the front. The detachment, as per the information gathered from workers on the project, was about 400 men – about 120 on guard duty in eight-hour shifts at any given time.

With the stated objectives of preventing embezzlement and theft of stocks, and of keeping a watch on any potential spies, their daily briefings did not usually discuss how to handle an assault by paratroopers.

❖

As news of the breakout from Pondicherry reached Chennai, with the information that a convoy was headed, possibly, towards Chennai itself, all reserve units – including fifty-odd men from Avadi itself – were pulled out and assembled in the city cantonment, to be deployed depending on how the situation developed.

And so, when at 6.30 a.m., two Shōwa L2D3-Ia transporters appeared off the coast and slowed just above the primary airstrip to unload a cargo of paratroopers, there was much confusion.

A sparsely populated area at the time, Avadi was much like

a housing complex in its construction phase. The airstrip itself was not in regular use yet and had only about a dozen armed men present. Reacting instinctively, they opened fire and shot down ten or so of the INA paratroopers even before they had hit the ground and wounded another dozen once they had landed. But over fifty men had jumped off and, once the rest had gained their bearings after landing, the numbers were not on the side of the defenders. Taking stock of the situation, they withdrew and called for backup.

And then more transporters came overhead and, instead of dropping paratroopers, began to land on the airstrip. As they stopped at the end of the runway, soldiers disembarked and fanned out, rushing to the installations and depots whose locations they had memorized over the past week.

The plan called for about a hundred paratroopers to seize entry points to the complex to turn it into a loosely defended fortress, at least for a couple of hours; another hundred to take secure custody of the fuel and food depots, and the rest of the men to create a general ruckus, within the Avadi complex as well as outside its boundaries, to create the impression of a much larger force and to force a diversion of some of the British manpower being deployed for action against the incoming Italian contingent.

❖

One of the transporter ships that offloaded the men of the INA divisions near the Pondicherry coast did not turn back after unloading its cargo. It waited offshore to pick up a smaller contingent that was travelling *out* of Pondicherry the same day.

❖

Thirty minutes later, 1,600 French soldiers clambered aboard the transporter. It gained speed but did not seek to head back towards the safety of the deep sea. Instead, it took a course parallel to the coast, heading south. Karaikal would take about three hours, unless a shore battery was lucky enough to deliver a crippling blow. These French reinforcements would begin to disembark at Karaikal at approximately the time that the Italians would be getting into firefights on the outskirts of Chennai, battling to get through to Avadi's airstrips and fuel.

❖

The day was bloody.

The British Indian forces suffered over 600 casualties in the naval barrage and the breakthrough. The steel ring around the Pondicherry pocket was now a tattered bandage. Flights and ships came in at will to reinforce the forces for operations that would commence at night. The Italians had taken heavy losses in driving past the roadblocks set up ahead of Chennai – the estimates were at least 300 casualties and perhaps an equal number captured as Light Machine Guns shot out the tyres of several trucks, leaving the men in them stranded and surrounded as the convoy kept moving and did not stop for them. But they had, finally, got to Avadi and established a basic defensive perimeter, guided by the detachment already occupying observation posts and key gates as they roared in.

At 2 a.m., a second, larger unit was to head north towards Chennai, with the military objective of driving the British out of the city and seizing the naval guns. Another was to go south, drive to Karaikal and attack the outer ring of the British encirclement. When that battle started, the reinforced French troops would break out as well, forcing the British detachment into a two-front shootout.

That was the plan, Subhas thought, as he looked at the intricate lines being drawn on the situation map to indicate when and how the units would move. War looked so clinical and detached in the conference rooms – even on a warship, almost 5 kilometres off the Pondicherry coast. This entire plan was high-risk, depended on speed at each stage, and could not be carried out without both inflicting and suffering heavy casualties. The larger objective was to seize control of the entire stretch from Chennai to Karaikal – the former lay 150 kilometers to Pondicherry's north and the latter was 130 kilometres to its south. It would cost them dearly, but he was certain it would work out.

The only variable was *how* dearly? How many Indian, Italian, French lives would this ambitious military objective cost? It would not come cheap.

Subhas would probably have cringed at such a plan a couple of months back, let alone suggested it. But he was hardened by the bloodshed of the past weeks. Time equals blood, he told himself. The longer this stretched, the more painful and bloody a slow, stretched battle of attrition would get. The British must now realize that they had no more safe zones, they must be evicted, hit hard, made to give *all* of India up – and if the price of that had to be paid in blood, so be it.

He forced himself to disengage from this and to leave the operations to the professionals – the Japanese naval officers and the commanders of the Italian para regiments battling it out, miles away.

This one time, he would not insist on minimizing casualties on the other side.

25

Berlin Backlash

2 April 1943

THE TEMPO OF WORK AT THE ZENTRALE FREIS INDIEN HAD NOT slackened with the departure of Subhas to the battlefront.

On the contrary, Subhas's demands had now quadrupled, and the cables burnt each night with the volume of information received and sent. Notes, memos, lists, speeches, newspaper articles, plans of action, letters – it was never-ending. Subhas had a skeletal staff with him on the mobile frontier and they dealt primarily with military and supply issues, as well as the endless liaison and coordination points with all three Axis partners. The rest, he had left in the hands of the crew at the Free India Centre.

A dozen or so men were occupied in the day's tasks, this afternoon. Adam von Trott was among them, having a conversation with two German colleagues from the Sonderreferat Indien.

Von Trott, as we have observed earlier, was not very close to Subhas. He was also on rather hostile terms with Emilie for a variety of reasons. Subhas suspected that at the core of it was that he did not approve of her marrying an Indian and living in style, escaping all the deprivations of wartime on account of being the companion of 'His Excellency' Bose. However, that undercurrent did not impact the day-to-day workings of either the Zentrale Freis Indien or the Sonderreferat Indien.

Subhas also had another reason to put up with von Trott's less-than-polite demeanour. In a system where everyone was spying on everyone else, he could be reasonably assured that this individual was not keeping an eye on him or the centre for the Gestapo, the SD, or any of the nameless agencies that Himmler and Heydrich had established across the Reich.

Given von Trott's political inclinations, it would be more likely that *they* were keeping an eye on him.

Still in his thirties, von Trott, a widely travelled and well-read man, was a member of the Kreisau Circle, a society of conservative intellectuals, so named since the central figure was Helmut Count von Molkte, whose family seat was Kreisau in Silesia. Members of the circle, which believed in a conservative version of Christian Socialism, had been in close contact for a while with the primary anti-Nazi group in the German Army, led by General Beck.

Before he joined the Foreign Office, von Trott had visited London thrice in 1939, supposedly to lobby in order to modify the British government's policy of appeasement towards Hitler. A few months before war finally broke out, he had even had a meeting with Neville Chamberlain, the then prime minister.

Subhas had got to know of von Trott using the pretext of India-related work to travel across Europe without arousing suspicion throughout 1941; he had done his own homework, and understood why. However, unlike in the case of some other associations he had made, Trott's anti-Nazi instincts did not lead to Subhas attempting to initiate an association. The conservatives, after all, did not fundamentally disagree with the Nazi goal of working to make Germany the primary political and military power in Europe, nor did they disagree with specific acts such as the annexation of Czechoslovakia. They wanted to topple the Nazis since they felt Hitler was endangering Germany by his recklessness, which would build a powerful anti-Germany coalition of international powers. It was the *means*, not the end, that invited their disapproval.

Over time, von Trott had added friends and ideologically similar people to his office. Alexander Werth was an old friend. Franz Josef Furtwängler, too, was a friend, as well as a fellow member of the Kreisau Circle.

Furtwängler, incidentally, had travelled to India when Bose was in the British prison in Mandalay in Upper Burma. He heard much about Bose's heroism and popularity in Calcutta and subsequently wrote an article on him that eventually was reprinted in the US press. Bose came across it and sent him a letter. Now Furtwängler was genuinely excited to be working alongside Subhas, but he wasn't quite convinced as to why an anti-imperialist crusader should seek the assistance of Adolf Hitler.

Essentially, Subhas was suspicious of the Nazi structure – as distinct from the German nation, though they were so thoroughly intertwined – even as he worked to best utilize it for his military and political objectives. Simultaneously, the core group of the Sonderreferat deployed to work with him were not just suspicious of but also actively working as a resistance group against the Nazis.

However, neither party trusted the other implicitly enough to speak of it openly.

Von Trott, Werth and Furtwängler were all working for the Sonderreferat Indien now, along with another half a dozen associates. Their working relationship with the Indians at the centre remained cordial, if not intimate.

❖

The day was about to draw to a close when the sounds of loud, angry voices floated across the driveway of 2A, Lichtenstein

Allee, surprising the staff present. The two guards at the gate seemed to be in an altercation. Trott and Werth exchanged glances, and Werth got up to head to the window to have a closer look. Even as he took a couple of steps, the muscular echo of nailed jackboots crunching across the driveway came through.

The door was smashed open the next moment, and a group of black-clad uniformed men poured in. Six of them took up positions on either side of the door while a couple of others rushed inside to block the rear exits from the complex. N. G. Ganpuley, the senior-most Indian present in the office at this moment, stepped up to ask what was happening, but was brusquely brushed aside.

A Sturmbannführer of the SS stepped inside through the smashed door.

He looked around for a moment, feet planted wide apart, hand on his hips, and demanded an answer: 'Which of you is Adam von Trott?'

'And in what capacity do you ask that?' Furtwängler spoke up. A rifle butt smashed into his lower back the next moment. He crumpled to the floor.

Outraged, Ganpuley shouted at the Sturmbannführer.

'You are on premises that have been accorded diplomatic status by the Foreign Ministry! This will be reported. You should leave immediately.'

The officer's response was to unholster his pistol and hold it straight to Ganpuley's face. A silence fell over the room.

'Indeed. But we are not talking to you, are we? You can file your objections with Ribbentrop. We do not report to him. Step back – and don't interfere in my work.'

A furious Ganpuley sat down and signalled to the rest of the team to keep their distance.

'Now, should I take all of you in' – the officer looked towards the group of six Germans huddled together now, unholstered weapon still in hand – 'or will you identify von Trott and save me time?'

Von Trott stood up.

'What do you want of me?'

Two SS men instantly tackled him to the floor and handcuffed his hands behind his back. As his face smashed into the floor, blood spurted from his split lower lip.

'And now, who are' – the officer took out a notepad from an immaculately creased trousers' pocket – 'Alexander Werth and Franz Josef Furtwängler?'

Werth stood up, quietly, and pointed towards Franz, still huddled on the floor in pain. A minute later, all three men stood handcuffed. The rest of the Germans tried to conceal their fear while the Indians stayed silent, helpless spectators.

The officer walked right up to the three handcuffed men. They flinched, half expecting him to strike them.

'For the record, von Trott, Werth, Furtwängler, I hereby arrest you on suspicion of having provided support to the conspirators who assassinated our beloved Führer.'

Von Trott's face paled visibly. The others remained impassive.

'Who is the senior Indian official here right now?' the Sturmbannführer turned around and asked.

'I am. N. G. Ganpuley,' Ganpuley replied.

'Now, Herr Ganpuley, before I take away these traitors, let me explain one thing. I could have picked these men up from their beds at night as well. It would have saved me the effort of having to identify them from within a group. But I came here to take them. And why is that?'

He paused for effect.

'I came here to take them in front of you. And to tell you that if we find that any of *you* have been associated with what they have been doing – we will be back, and the next time it will be you we will take. And your "status" will not protect you.'

The SS unit marched out, leaving behind a smashed door, a shaken group of people, and yet another wedge in the increasingly edgy SS-government relationship in volatile post-Hitler Germany.

Von Trott slipped – or was tripped – as they stepped out, and fell again, badly. As the guards dragged him back up, his forehead was gushing blood as well, staining his shirt.

The Sturmbannführer laughed.

❖

'I need to speak to Ribbentrop! Today!'

A furious Subhas smashed the receiver back into its cradle. A direct, secured connection from India to Germany was not the easiest of things to manage on a moving battlefront, but today was not the day you were likely to see a measured response from him.

He was not surprised that von Trott was, possibly, in touch with the organizations that may have plotted Hitler's assassination. But he would have been a passive sympathizer, never an active participant in a plan to kill – or at least that was Subhas's reading.

The SS entering the Centre, physically forcing their way in, with no intimation to the unit that guarded the premises or to the Foreign Ministry, and issuing threats to the Indian staff there upfront, was unprecedented.

However, he realized that when the ostensible reason was the ongoing investigation of the assassination, everyone would be careful before outrightly protesting.

Subhas had shot off cables to Ribbentrop, Rommel and

Keppler, but he knew that they would not take on a full-blown confrontation with Himmler just yet, and definitely not for this.

There were many in the Wehrmacht's senior staff who had acts of commission or at least of omission linked to the final explosion in Hitler's coach, but the uniformed forces had closed ranks after the assassination, more so as one of their own was now the head of state. Himmler's parallel empire continued to be a potent force, though, and it was furious at what had happened, thirsting for some sort of retribution – a violent watchdog that had lost its master and was snarling, teeth bared.

And the confrontation that the Legion had taken with the SS at Jamnagar over the Polish children had left the watchdog very keen to dig its teeth into Subhas at the first chance it got.

❖

At night, a cable landed from Ganpuley. According to the SS's version of events, von Trott had reportedly jumped out of the window of the eighth-floor office where he was being questioned. Death had been instantaneous.

The eyewitnesses present there would never have come forward later to say he was hurled out physically by two SS officers, of course.

26

The Mahatma and the Soldier

'Till one of us is converted to the other's view, we must sail in different boats though our destinations may appear but only appear to be the same.'

– Mahatma Gandhi to Subhas Bose, in a letter dated 29 December 1940

'Unfortunately, Gandhism has ceased to be revolutionary. There is no hope that it will succeed in carrying the nation towards its goal of national independence.'

– Subhas Bose, 1941, in Kabul

'Gandhi is not an ideological fanatic like Nehru and is often more of a realist than the latter.'

– Subhas Bose, article in *Azad Hind*, August 1942 (before the Quit India call)

Poona
9 April 1943

SMALL GROUPS WAVED FROM THE ROADSIDE OF OTHERWISE deserted streets as the cavalcade entered Poona. No civilian traffic was allowed in the city today.

'Perhaps it would have made sense to also have Mr Nehru travel here from Aurangabad?' Abid suggested.

Subhas laughed.

'What are you implying? I have had my duels with Mussolini, Hitler and Tojo – tell me if there's a tougher group to deal with. You feel I need a buffer to meet the Mahatma? He and I are old duellers. I will manage to stand up for myself, trust me!'

He was in a teasing, sparring mood – a rarity in the past months.

'Mr Nehru and I have issues. Mr Gandhi and I have a different set of issues. Frankly, I don't think I have the bandwidth to address both simultaneously. I will probably write to Jawahar. I know his mind and I know he will be very, very hostile to the situation as it exists currently. Therefore, whether we speak today or after three months will make no difference,' he concluded.

'But, for Bapu, you have travelled yourself, under very unusual circumstances – surely this could also have waited three months?'

❖

The unusual circumstances Abid was referring to were these:

As British forces increasingly became confined to diminishing pockets, law and order in British-controlled provinces had largely ceased to exist. On two occasions, spontaneous crowds had gathered near the Aga Khan Palace in Poona, demanding that Gandhi be released and they could be dispersed only after the police fired into the crowd. The British were apprehensive that a large mob could overpower the security detail on a bad day. The Americans were apprehensive that an opponent of Gandhi's politics or an angry British soldier in the guard detachment could use the chaos to land a blow, or worse, on the globally known leader. Taking him out to a safer location was an option – but there weren't many safe locations at the moment and travel had its own share of risks.

It was the US that had suggested – pressured – that Gandhi's physical custody be handed over to the forces led by Bose. They had argued three points:

One, there was nothing to be achieved by continuing to hold Gandhi – it was not the Congress cadres that were battling the British on the roads now. August 1942 was a long time back.

Two, if Gandhi were to be injured or killed in any situation, while technically a prisoner of the Crown, the negative press globally would be enormous and the backlash from the American public would be massive.

Three, the differences between Gandhi and Bose were the sharpest between any two leading political figures in contemporary India. Gandhi in custody would be a silent figure, but a Gandhi released could very well take positions that would hopefully diminish the credibility of the Bose-led forces, attack him for forsaking non-violence, and encourage the Congress to keep distance from him.

It had supposedly taken a forceful Roosevelt cable to Churchill to end British resistance to the proposal. Word had then gone out to Subhas via his brother Sarat. The Red Cross had been brought in to oversee and witness the handover. As the effective boundary between Axis and Allied forces was still some distance from Poona, the assumption had been that Red Cross vehicles would drive Gandhi to the front line, where he would be handed over to the Legion.

The spanner in the works had been tossed in by Subhas, who had insisted that he would personally 'liberate' the Mahatma himself from the Aga Khan Palace.

When the first response from the British side was to

outrightly dismiss the idea, his response had been, to quote, 'The only question is whether this is done gracefully, now, with your consent, or a fortnight or a month later, against your will. But happen, it will.'

The absurdity of the idea of the commander of the Legion driving deep into British-controlled territory was surprising even to those by now accustomed to his eccentricities. Subhas had pretty much been called crazy to his face by his Indian, Italian and German advisors. He had not countered them – they were perfectly correct, militarily speaking – but he had stuck to his decision. He knew that the need to see this transfer through at the earliest was far greater for the British than it was for him.

'What if they put a bullet through you, or Gandhi, or both?' Balotta had asked.

'It's not as if I haven't thought of that. But I had word sent to the GOC of the British sector via two INA officers who have served with him in the British Army, earlier. They told him as much that I thought this may be a distinct possibility – that they may breach the ceasefire and try to seize or kill me, at least, if not Gandhi. And they also conveyed my assessment of the fallout of such action.'

'Which is—?'

'Which is that the civilian population across the country would set ablaze every building where a British citizen lived, military or civilian, and that the Legion's soldiers would take no more prisoners in the rest of the war.'

The war veteran had been left surprised. This was not a tone Subhas took, usually.

'I'm not saying it will happen. It was just a reading of the situation,' had been Subhas's expressionless response.

It was hardly one of the most chivalrous exchanges in battle, and it was surprisingly coming from Subhas – but if the idea was to have a threat issued, strong enough to dissuade mischief, it had worked so far.

❖

After a week of intense, complex negotiations, the entire sector had been declared a 24-hour ceasefire zone effective 6 a.m. today. At 6.30 a.m., Subhas had driven out from the last Legion-controlled city in the region – Nashik – and travelled in a military convoy of 120 vehicles, all flying white flags, with Red Cross vans leading. The convoy also included four cars full of reporters and photographers from almost all global news agencies that had staff in India.

On completely empty roads, with British troop deployment being pulled back a kilometre on either side of the road, it had taken just four hours.

And now, the last few miles were left. The road looked clear. The path, not as much, he thought to himself.

❖

'Bapu!'

The Mahatma shakily stood up and walked towards Subhas, who was standing a respectful distance away, hands folded in a namaste.

He did not speak for a moment and an awkward silence followed. Then the older man reached out with his frail, ageing hands, and embraced the enfant terrible of the Congress.

❖

'We have come to take you, Bapu.'

'Whoever has men with guns takes custody of me, Subhas.

They have kept me here for a while now, nobody asked for my consent. Now I understand you are taking me away with you. You also have many men with guns now, I see. But nobody asked me about that either,' Gandhi softly smiled.

'You are no less a dictator than the ones I have met in these years, Bapu; it is just that your methods are different!' Subhas laughed. 'I was awaiting a telegram from you, and since it never came, I thought I will come over myself.'

'A telegram?'

'Yes, Bapu, a telegram.'

Gandhi's expression indicated that he was trying to place the context – but couldn't. He looked curiously back at Subhas.

'You do remember when I tried and tried to convince you to launch a campaign after the fall of France in 1940, but you would not budge? You said the country was not prepared for a fight, that you could not agree with my views – but that if my efforts to win freedom by *my* ways ever succeeded, your telegram of congratulations would be the first that I would receive. Maybe all of India is not free of our British friends yet, Bapu, but two-thirds of it is. And the day the Delhi garrison withdrew and the Red Fort had no more Englishmen within its walls, I thought perhaps a telegram would have been on its way.'

The 'dictator' of the Congress smiled at the supreme commander of the Legion.

'I am waiting for the great warlord to conquer the entire empire, perhaps? When has two-thirds of anything been enough for you, Subhas babu?'

Subhas paused for a moment, as if considering whether to say what was on his mind, or not. Then he did.

'Bapu, after Deshbandhu was no more, you personally anointed Jatindra Mohan Sengupta as his successor across all roles. You made him the president of the Swaraj Party, president of the Bengal Congress, *and* mayor of Calcutta. Essentially, you left no room for me anywhere. I was, at the time, locked up in a prison cell in Mandalay. When Sarat *da* asked you, "What have you left for Subhas?" you smiled and said – I am sure you won't remember it after all this time, but I do – "For Subhas, there is the whole of India!" Now I am nothing in the Congress, but, in a way, I have the whole of India, Bapu. Your words were prophetic.'

'Have you come here to make fun of me, Subhas? You've become even more modest, I can see.'

'No, Bapu,' Subhas smiled. 'I have come to ensure your safety, and to seek your blessings for the journey ahead. There is so much we have to catch up on, so pardon me if I am tactless. I am also asking you to reconsider the positions you have been holding. You are a man of truth and I believe you will accept the truth when you see it.'

'And what *is* that truth?'

'That passive, non-violent, gradual, soft, respectful, almost sentimental measures to displace a colonial power do not lead to independence, and definitely not independence on one's own terms. You have to accept the reality, Bapu. Did India not need armed action to liberate itself on its own terms? It has been more than clear that the British would *never* let go of India till they had the military muscle to hold on to it. And that if they ever had to, they would not have an *undivided* free India come into existence. You have been worried about Britain's prestige and Germany's questionable moral position – but why are you playing the role of global statesman and the keeper of the planet's conscience *ahead* of the desperation of your country to be both free and united, Bapu?'

'Is morality only a political tool, Subhas? Would you want that we shut our eyes to the plague of Fascism and pretend that all is noble and humane in the nations fighting Britain?'

'Nothing may be noble about them, Bapu, but, as always, you mix your personal beliefs with your politics to the point that there is a stalemate.'

'How can our politics be detached from our beliefs, Subhas? These are not new discussions for us. You have your views on this and I have mine. I am an old man now, unlikely to change. You have to bear with it.'

'But you *have* changed. "Leave India to God. If this is too much then leave her to anarchy", you said when you launched Quit India. Why would you not do that earlier, for God's sake? And how different has my position been? Yes, my choices are not perfect choices, but they are not made in a perfect world. I am substituting other words for anarchy, but the sentiment is the same, has been the same – *anything* is better than this slavery!'

'I cannot endorse the immorality of the Nazi and Fascist powers, Subhas, even if they be convenient for us at the moment. On that, you will find me unshakeable, still.'

'Do you not see the reality of the international situation today, Bapu?'

'You are fascinated by the pomp and show of parades and marches and all that, the uniforms and the saluting, Subhas – but I am the man in a loin cloth. That is not the power I wield, and that is not the power that impresses me. You must understand that however many soldiers, guns and tanks you might have with you, you will not change my sense of right and wrong.'

For a minute, Subhas wondered whether to let go of the discussion. Then he persuaded himself not to stomp off and continued.

'I am not adjudicating on right and wrong. When I would have hoped you would put all your might in throwing the British out, you stepped up and said "we do not seek our independence out of Britain's ruin" instead – at that point, Soviet Russia was in a pact with Nazi Germany. It was an abettor to Britain's ruin, supplying Germany with oil and resources as it fought on the western front. Today, American and British ships sail thousands of miles to deliver weapons and supplies to Russia. Was Stalin evil for you then, Bapu? If you detest Hitler for occupying half of Poland, what about Stalin occupying the other half? How is the guilt different? But Churchill has had no compunctions with working with Stalin today, though he fears Communism as much as Hitler, perhaps. And why is that so? Because the war situation *dictates* that he keeps aside his views on Communism and works with Russia. And, similarly, *I* have no compunctions with working with Germany or Italy, keeping aside my views on Nazism and Fascism aside. Why is one acceptable and the other not?'

'Your views on Fascism? They were quite flattering, the last time I read them,' the Mahatma chuckled.

'Yes, I have been asked that question, Bapu, and I have responded – that I misjudged the full nature of what it was heading towards, many years back. At the outset, I saw it as nothing more than an aggressive version of nationalism. Today, I would not applaud it – but again, Mussolini does not seek my advice on how he runs Italy.'

'He does not? Are you not great friends with him?'

Subhas smiled at the barb.

'Did you have the same tone when you met him in Rome, in 1931? If you did, you would not have talked about his passionate love for his people and conveyed the impression that the majority of the Italians "love his iron government", would you?'

'I have changed my position on him over the years.'

'That is just what I am requesting you to do, Bapu! That is where you are not as fixated as Jawahar is. Change your position! Step out, support us, ask the nation to work together. I would really want your support, Bapu – but I will go ahead even if you do not offer it. The scar of Tripuri should not forever mark our association, but now, no matter how much obstruction I face, I am not stepping down till I have done what I came back to do. This is beyond politics and philosophy now. Thousands of men have died in my journey here. To respect what they believed in, I have to fight – and fight I *will*.'

A long silence followed.

Gandhi stood up, took a few steps, walked to the edge of the balcony and looked towards the manicured, bright gardens of the palace that had served as his prison for almost a year.

Still looking out, he spoke, as if to himself.

'I cannot support Germany – even without Hitler – and neither can I endorse the fascism of Italy, or the imperialism of Japan. If you give over India to these powers, if you follow the instructions of a Mussolini or a Tojo, or the new leader of Germany – I forget his name – have no doubt, I will ask the people to oppose you just as they would oppose any foreign agent. But as of today, I will not oppose you, Subhas. For the next few months, I will observe and understand. As to the Congress, I will not ask it to either oppose or support you – I will merely suggest that let each worker take the position that his or her conscience suggests.'

'Will I follow instructions of Mussolini or Tojo? If I had to bend to a dictator, Bapu, I would have done it long back – and would still have been in your good books!' Subhas laughed. The verbal duel between the two statesmen continued. 'Have no worry that I will run things as per any dictator's instructions.'

'Well, then, shall we go, or will you spend the day talking? Ba is all packed and ready to leave, as are the rest.'

'A minute of your time before that? The press is very keen to have your photos as you emerge from the last day in the British empire's custody. And this palace is quite the backdrop.'

'Ah, you have understood propaganda as well as war now, look at that!'

'It is part of war now, Bapu. I don't expect you to say anything that you don't want to – you can be critical of me in public if you want, I will not counter you.'

'Maybe I should, else Jawahar will be very upset to see me smiling for photos with you while he is still locked up in Aurangabad.' An impish grin crept over the Mahatma's face. 'Maulana has also been upset with me, as it is. He thinks I have gone soft on you after your escape. And he made a point to tell me that Sir Cripps felt that my words gave away an admiration for your work in Europe. When I said that I have not changed my position, he said perhaps not *consciously*, but others also feel that I have not been critical enough about what you have been doing.'

'Oh, you can criticize me as much as you want – go ahead, compensate for that subconscious lack of criticism!'

Both men burst out laughing.

A minute later, with a hand on Subhas's shoulder, the apostle of non-violence stepped out. A dozen flashbulbs went off as cameramen jostled to capture the meeting of two stubborn, defiant men representing two extremes of India's political thought.

Perhaps the only common sentiment they aroused was the degree to which Churchill detested them.

27

Comrades No More?

'Launching a civil disobedience campaign at a time when Britain is engaged in a life and death struggle would be an act derogatory to India's honour.'

– Jawaharlal Nehru, 1940

'Nehru is fanatically anti-Axis and – left to himself – he would go to any length in order to fight the Tripartite Powers.'

– Subhas Bose, article in *Azad Hind*, August 1942
(before the Quit India call)

'Hitler and Japan must go to hell. I shall fight them to the end and this is my policy. I shall also fight Mr Subhas Bose and his party along with Japan if he comes to India.'

– Jawaharlal Nehru, April 1942

12 April 1943
New Delhi

Dear Jawahar,

When I was last writing to you, I was in British custody. Now, I shall have this letter delivered to you when you are in British custody – but, in all likelihood, not for long – via the expanding network of our sympathisers across the Indian police and army.

I hope you are doing well and that the authorities have been treating you with care, and, if I may say, some deference. You are among the foremost political figures in a nation that is at the cusp of seizing complete independence from the world's most powerful Empire.

I do not know if you have access to the news in Aurangabad, but barely a couple of days ago, Mahatma Gandhi was freed from Pune – I had gone there to escort him out of the British zone – and is now presently safely lodged in Delhi.

The situation on the military front is now almost irrevocably in favour of the Legion and the Axis. It is my understanding that in a month or less, the British will have no choice but to free all the members of the CWC currently in prison with you, and in all probability, surrender the regions that they still have physical control of. The fall of Delhi has had a strong psychological impact on the Indian soldier in the British army. He is torn between conflicting loyalties on a day-to-day basis, more so when he is predominantly facing other Indian soldiers on the battle lines, not a foreign ravaging force that he has to supposedly defend his motherland against.

When you emerge a free man again from the gates of that prison, shortly, I shall endeavour to meet you as soon as is feasible. Perhaps, a discussion with the Mahatma and Mr Jinnah in Delhi may help us revive communication that has been dormant for a long period.

I am under no illusion that the revival will be necessarily harmonious or cordial. In this period, while I have been sharply critical of the British Empire at every moment, you have been even more critical of the Axis than of the British.

At one point, you had expressed the stunning view that 'Launching a civil disobedience campaign at a time when

Britain is engaged in a life and death struggle would be an act derogatory to India's honour' – but I was glad to see that by the time of the Quit India movement, you had, even if reluctantly, moved to accept Gandhi's position that civil disobedience was now integral to India's honour, not an insult to it. The military situation was very different in August 1942, else perhaps a joint effort of Quit India within India's borders and the armed offensive from outside them would have brought a swift collapse of the British administration, instead of the several months and several thousand lives that it took – and continues to take.

But then there is no saying whether you would have welcomed such an offensive or resisted it. I think you may well have opposed it heartily. As you so eloquently put it, 'Hitler and Japan must go to hell. I shall fight them to the end, and this is my policy. I shall also fight Mr Subhas Bose and his party along with Japan if he comes to India.'

Well, I have come to India.

And, at least for now, the forces of Germany and Japan have come as well. Do you intend to fight me as soon as the British let you go? If so, you may as well convey that message to your captors – they need every single person keen to fight me that they can get!

Humour apart, dear Jawahar, I do not question your patriotism even if you associate India's honour with supporting the British war effort. Equally, I do not think you are justified in questioning my patriotism if I think supporting the Axis war effort – or rather seeking the Axis' support for the Indian Legion's war effort – *is the only pragmatic solution for India to seize the moment, for such moments do not often come in the lives of nations.*

Hitler's obsessive anti-Communism and anti-Semitism led to the war with Russia. That may not have been the most intelligent military decision he took (even though, from my perspective, it helped move Axis military resources closer towards India), since

Russia is far too large for it to be ever completely subdued. Churchill and Roosevelt, on the other hand, did not allow their anti-Communism to stop them from immediately allying their resources with the foremost Communist state in the world. What is your position on this – even keeping aside your deep admiration for Russia? Should our agreeing or disagreeing with the internally practiced ideology of a nation dictate international alignments at a time of war? And was India not at war with its occupier? If not, why was it not?

I wonder if you scrutinise all global developments as harshly as you do my alliance with the Axis.

I hear you speak of me as a fan of Fascism and Nazism. I have made no secret that in the 1930s, I thought that Fascism had elements that India could learn from, as did Communism. Mahatma Gandhi himself had no hesitation in meeting Mussolini during that period, but you do not speak ill of him on that account. Yes, the Duce has visions of some sort of revival of the Roman Empire, but Britain, Germany and Russia all have far greater territorial ambitions than Italy has or ever had.

Have I not recurrently condemned the rise of racism in Germany through the 1930s? Have I not written against the statements of Hitler himself, when he spoke disparagingly about India? Have I not been upfront in supporting the cause of China against Japanese aggression? On what ground can you consider me a blind, ideologically committed supporter of the Axis nations till, or even after, war broke out? It is only after committing to building an army to liberate India – for which I needed Indian soldiers, equipment, weapons, greater training – that I have thrown my lot in with the only nations in the world who could do that. And I have neither regret nor hesitation in taking that path.

Today, we have to look towards the future of India – what else have we fought for all these decades if not an undivided, independent nation?

I am much maligned for my dictatorial tendencies, and now I carry the added burden of pro-Nazi, pro-Fascist, and so on, but you are well aware as to where and how dissent and differences were gagged in the Congress – if you can see things in all objectivity. Keeping all differences of the past aside, I am open to working with differing perspectives and ideologies. I seek the advice, the support, the strength and contribution of all leaders – of which you are first among equals in the Congress, as also the favourite of the Mahatma. I will look forward to us working as comrades in the rebuilding of a new India, should you make the effort to look beyond the anti-Axis prism.

If, however, my being ideology-agnostic in seeking allies to root the British out of India is an unforgivable moral crime in your perspective, well – I can find nothing better than to quote back what you wrote to me in 1939: 'I am sorry you find it difficult to understand me. Perhaps it is not worth trying.'

Your erstwhile comrade in arms,

Subhas

❖

16 April 1943
Aurangabad

Dear Subhas,

I write to you with mixed feelings.

A part of me is glad that you have done what you had set out to do, perhaps not in full measure just yet, but substantially. The Union Jack no longer flies on the Red Fort. I wish I was there, the day it was taken off. I understand from your message that it may not be long before, militarily, the entire country is finally free of it.

The other part of me is repulsed at the thought of the Nazis and Japanese – oppressive and brutal regimes – pretending to play the part of liberators of the Indian people. You have chosen to ignore what they stand for, but I cannot. The blood of many thousands – not just military combatants – is on the hands of the men who drive these military machines.

You and I have not spoken or exchanged letters in a while, so I will attempt to bridge that communication gap by summarizing where I stand on this:

- *You see Japan as an ally that will eliminate imperial rule in India and indeed, across Asia. I see Japan as a fascist, brutal, imperialistic power in its own right. Surely, you cannot be unaware of the frightful atrocities it has inflicted over China. The mere fact that a power is Asian does not give it any morally superior status. Japan is merely replacing one form of brutal occupation with another, wherever it goes across Asia. Why will India be any different?*
- *No power has come to India to liberate it in the history of this nation. India is too tempting and too vital a prize to be simply seized from another and handed back to the Indians. I have no faith in the intentions of any power to 'liberate' us. The European powers may not look to seize control of this land for the simple rationality of distance and logistics – not that it proved to be a deterrent for the British in all these years – but for the Japanese, it will be a natural extension to their virtual annexation of Burma.*
- *The mindset of 'my enemy's enemy is my friend' is a very basic, unsophisticated model of international politics, more so in our case. If Roosevelt allies with Stalin, he is not risking Soviet troops landing in Washington. When you ally with the Axis, their troops land in Delhi. There is no similarity in the situation, and you are allowing*

> *yourself to be deceived and seeing the situation though a prism, where you filter out what is not palatable to you. This may lead you into situations that you had not foreseen.*

I cannot, therefore, be aligned to any structure, administration, call it what you will, that legitimizes the control of any part of India by your Axis colleagues. And that is the advice I will unapologetically give to all members of the CWC, presently imprisoned along with myself. That will also be my position as and when I step out of this place.

Despite our differences – personal and ideological – I can still work with you, politically.

But nothing in the world will make me work to extend support or legitimacy to the forces of Japanese imperialism or European fascism – and, as of today, you and they are intertwined too intensely.

Jawahar

28

The Parade

'I am not an apologist of the Tripartite Powers and it is not my task to defend what they have done or may do in future. That is a task which devolves on these nations themselves and they are quite able to deal with it. My concern, however, is with India; and it is my duty as a patriotic Indian to inform my countrymen as to how best we can achieve the liberation of India in the present world crisis, without meddling in the internal affairs of other countries.'

– Subhas Bose, broadcast, May 1942

New Delhi
24 April 1943

THE RHYTHMIC, METALLIC CRUNCH OF JACKBOOTS ON THE gravelly road surface had a familiar feel for those who had seen these victory parades across an assorted range of cities – Warsaw, Paris, Stalingrad – in the preceding years. Steel-toed boots clad in grey trousers clomped and bit into the road as if it were the enemy itself, in the military precision that was the trademark of the Wehrmacht.

Delhi had not seen anything like it.

For the Indian subjects of His Majesty's Empire, to see a uniform other than that of the Englishman marching in India with the swagger that victory brings was unfamiliar. None of them had seen it in their lifetime. It wasn't even *a* uniform. There were multiple uniforms, and you realized that if you stood and watched a while. This wasn't a typical German victory parade with columns and columns of grey and black. It was only the first contingent, in dress uniform, that was in the grey tunics and black jackboots that all of Europe was familiar with – or tired of – by now. The rest of the Germans followed not in grey but in the olive that the Deutsche Afrika Korps had been fighting in, since they had landed in North Africa.

After the Wehrmacht's boots had attempted to dig out the road they passed over, the greenish brown of the unsmiling infantry from the Japanese Thirty-third Division followed. The uniforms were different, as were the steps, but the precision was as obsessive. Though they had been part of the Tripartite pact since 1940, this was the first time that the Japanese were marching alongside their Axis counterparts after a collaborative campaign. You could have thought that nothing less than the Emperor's honour was at stake here – such was the fanatical symmetry of the contingent. Did the Asian army have a point to prove to the Aryan one? If you read between the lines, you could find some answers.

The Italians came next. Perhaps it was true that Mussolini's armies were not as fanatical on the battlefield as that of Germany, and perhaps, ancient Rome may not have been proud of all their military accomplishments in this era, but, by a combination of many factors – Subhas's equation with Mussolini, North Africa being at least nominally an Italian area of operation, and the large numbers of Italian POWs release from camps in India – they were the largest Axis force in India. As they marched, some of these men looked as if they may, God forbid, even smile – a thought you could not have possibly associated with either of the nationalities that marched before them.

Slightly behind Subhas, and slightly lower than him – given that he was, quite literally, on a pedestal – generals representing the Axis powers stood, saluting the men that marched past in full dress uniform.

The Italians were represented by Balotta, promoted to Lt Gen. by the Duce on the day the British forces formally announced their surrender, and now commanding all units in the newly formed India Sector of the Italian Army. The Germans by the diminutive, low-profile man with the Knight's Cross around his neck – General Hans-Jürgen von Arnim, commander of the XXXIX Panzer Corps on the Russian front, before he was sent to replace Rommel, first in North Africa, and then in India. Lieutenant General Shōjirō Iida, the commander of the Japanese Fifteenth Army, who, just about a year back, had entered Rangoon and then proceeded to push British forces all the way out of Burma, took the salute for the Japanese forces.

As the parade marched through the arc of India Gate, Prime Minister Subhas Chandra Bose and these military veterans took in the surreal spectacle of German, Japanese and Italian troops marching in a victory parade through a monument built by the British for Indian troops who fought against the Germans on Europe's blood-soaked battlefields in the previous World War. Von Arnim and Balotta, much younger, had fought on opposing sides in that war, when Italy was on Britain's side. The Japanese, too, had been allies with the British in that war.

Much had changed in the interval.

Subhas had rubbed many of his associates the wrong way by insisting that the contingents of the Axis nations lead the parade, as a gesture of gratitude for their efforts. As a reciprocal gesture, Armin, Balotta and Iida had stood a clear two feet behind him as he took the salute from the troops marching past, irrespective of nationality.

Today, they represented the armed forces of their states, but he represented a state.

And then, a murmur ran through the assembled crowd as the fourth element came up. Neither German, nor Japanese, nor Italian. A sort of fighting force in 1942, an ancillary unit of sorts; a 'propaganda weapon' for many, described by many as a rag-tag formation when it was first assembled, the Indian Legion now marched triumphantly in a victory parade for the very first time as a legitimate national army of an independent state. As did its twin formation, the Indian National Army. The crowd waved, yelled, clapped, cheered and cried. The men, sticking to the protocol of a parade, stayed expressionless, but, surely, this was a moment that would stay with them till they lived. Tears flowed down the faces of some, even as their expressions remained stoic.

The men – yes, but not *just* the men.

Even though it was just in its formative phase, Subhas had insisted on the participation of a squad that most were unfamiliar with. And the crowd's surprised silence reflected that, as it came into sight. But as the contingent, comprising entirely women from the INA, finally went past the podium, it drew a standing applause from all present. Not *all*, perhaps there were enough scandalised at the idea of this ostensible 'westernization' of Indian womenfolk, not aware that barely any of the warring nations in the West encouraged women to volunteer for military training. The 'Eastern' Russians did, though.

Today was a day of validation for this joint force, the Legion and the INA – a force most believed could never have been created, and once it was, it could never have fought, or held together.

A force comprising mostly men who had first signed up to fight for an occupying power, men who were defeated and demoralized, who were retrained and equipped by the very armies that had defeated them in battle, men who often battled conflicting loyalties and saw comrades deserting to go back to the army that had been their world, originally.

But this force had held on, despite difficulty, disdain, defeats and desertions – held together by the sheer cussed will of the man who stood taking the salute today.

Today was also to be the last day when this army was to march in two different uniforms, for Subhas had ordered the integration of both the Indian Legion and the Indian National Army into a single national force, the Azad Hind Fauj, as the first step towards disengaging them from the multiple Axis forces that had so far equipped, retrained and advised them.

The grinding nature of the war fought by the Legion and the INA in reclaiming their own country – where you could not simply reduce enemy resistance by shelling large areas indiscriminately and reducing them to rubble by setting cities and streets afire, ignoring civilian casualties as collateral damage as was increasingly happening across the world – had made it pay a high price.

Some 11,000 dead, 16,000 injured and about 4,000 missing added up to a casualty figure of 31,000, about a third of their total original strength. The Indian casualties were about four times that of all the Axis partners combined – and through that price paid in blood, it had, as Subhas had obsessively reiterated, earned the unquestioned right to identify itself as the primary liberator of India.

❖

'So, Subhas finally gets his parade, Jawahar!' Gandhi chuckled as the radio broadcast the rhythmic clomping of the Wehrmacht's jackboots on Delhi's roads.

Jawaharlal Nehru, livid at the celebration of the Axis' presence in India, strode towards the radio and switched it off.

❖

'The prime minister of the Azad Hind Administration, Subhas Chandra Bose, will now address the nation.'

Radio sets from Quetta to Imphal, that had been listening to what could be described as a running commentary on the parade, saw the volume knobs being cranked up just a little bit. The speech was to be broadcast live from the podium itself, not from a studio. Given the international nature of the assembly, Subhas had opted to make the address in English, which would then be followed immediately by translations in Hindustani, Tamil, and – as a gesture of acknowledgment for the immense sentimental value his cultural homeground attached to the occasion – Bangla.

He had waited for a lifetime for this moment.

❖

My fellow countrymen!

In November, when the battle had just started on India's frontiers, I had spoken to you. And I had promised to you that the next time I speak to you, it would be from Delhi.

Today, I have fulfilled that promise. I speak to you from Delhi.

Before I say a word about the issues that are on my mind, I bow my head to my fellow soldiers who lost their lives in the course of this long and difficult journey.

I promised them nothing but the opportunity to fight for the freedom of their motherland. I offered them no rewards other than endless pain and deprivation. They could have simply stayed where they were in the camps, as many others did – the war was over for them. On the battlefront, they could have crept back to the enemy lines and disappeared, as many others did. But instead they volunteered, they fought, and they died – so we can live freely after 200 years. We will never be able to repay our debt to them.

[He paused for a few moments before resuming]

My fellow Indians! Today is a momentous day.

A day when numerous sovereign nations have extended recognition to India as an independent nation, and to the Azad Hind Administration as the lawful government of that nation. A day when I have had the good fortune to take oath of office as the Prime Minister of this government. A day when the blood and sweat poured onto the soil of Mother India over 200 years has finally thrown out the colonial power from our sacred land.

And what has emerged from this trial by fire is a New India, an India that is still falling into place, a united India. We may not know exactly what the shape of New India will be, but what we do know is that the old India in which we had to live as inferior citizens in the land of our birth is gone, forever, never to return.

I must express my gratitude to the governments of Germany, Italy, Imperial Japan, Bulgaria, Romania, Hungary, Vichy France, Egypt, Syria, Iran, Iraq, Afghanistan, Burma, Thailand and the Philippines for being the first ones to acknowledge this government. I am certain that many more neutral and non-belligerent nations will do the same in the near future.

As to the Allied Powers, I would want to use this occasion to reiterate that Free India has not sought, and does not seek, hostility with any power other than Britain.

For long, I have lauded the Atlantic Charter's intent and yet questioned why, in practice, it was not meant for a country constituting a fifth of the world's population. Hostilities have ceased in India, but Britain has not yet acknowledged India as a sovereign state. Reports continue to come in of British forces regrouping in Sri Lanka and of naval reinforcements being sent to Australia, possibly to prepare for an assault on Indian territory. We cannot, therefore, lower our guard. If any nation that fights on the side of Britain joins it in an attack on our interests or our territory, we shall respond appropriately. In such a situation, should we need the military support of the Axis powers, we shall reach out to them again.

Other than that, externally, I reiterate, Independent India, as of this day, does not consider any nation other than Britain as a hostile power. We seek peace with all. The world has seen enough war over the past four years. Free India's foreign policy will be India's and India's alone, even as we acknowledge the immense support extended by the Axis powers to the cause of India's independence.

Internally, it is the objective of my government to work along with all citizens and leaders and govern by consensus and not coercion. We have the greatest regard for Mahatma Gandhi and his vision for our nation, and we will seek his guidance on the difficult path ahead. There are many political leaders of stature whom I have worked with in the past, from my friend Jawahar to Mr Jinnah, and I look forward to seeking their advice, their support, and working with them to resolve all outstanding issues amicably and peacefully.

The goodwill amongst all communities that has existed for decades has unfortunately been affected in the past few years. We cannot pretend that disharmony does not exist. But I must make it clear that a division of this nation on any grounds – ethnic, communal, linguistic, racial – is not acceptable to this government and it will do everything, politically and militarily, to ensure that Azad Hind remains one indivisible political entity, even as we work towards a strongly decentralised federal structure and give all regions and states as much autonomy as is possible.

Equally, I would advise extremists, of whatever political affiliation or religious belief they may be, that the Azad Hind Fauj will enforce the rule of law impartially and aggressively. Rioting, irrespective of provocation, will be met with the harshest force that can be brought to bear. Neither are British civilians nor Prisoners of War to be harmed in any manner, no matter what our emotions on the issue may be. Martial law will be imposed, and penal measures taken, in areas where such incidents occur.

We did not fight this long and this hard and pay this high a price, to replace the rule of the Crown with the rule of the mob. We will not stand by and watch if India burns.

The Azad Hind Administration is entitled to, and claims, the allegiance of every Indian, effective today. It is not merely a political force that you may agree or disagree with; it is now the instrument that exercises the powers of a sovereign nation. No matter what your ideology, your religion, your affinities – as of today, this is the government that will protect you. This is also the government whose writ will be enforced. A newly independent India will not be allowed to wake up to strife, civil war and the rule of the mob.

In this delicate situation, the rulers of the princely states are advised to not take any action that is seen to be deliberately hostile to that of the government, lest that makes us reconsider our current intention to maintain status quo till such time as we have discussed their concerns and our expectations for the future of the subcontinent.

To conclude, we are at a critical point in the history of this great nation – not just a nation, a great civilisation. The World War is still on, the country has faced famine and economic hardship in many regions, communal tensions are high in some provinces, and we, therefore, face severe challenges, both internal and external; social, financial and military.

It is likely that we may need hard measures for some time to build and secure a New India. Independence does not mean the absence of order. I appeal to all of you to work with the Azad Hind Administration as it works to rebuild the stature of our common motherland.

Jai Hind!

29

My Countrymen

Open Letter to All Indians

Published in the *Forward Bloc* and the leading newspapers in all major languages

6 May 1943

Fellow Indians,

AT THE OUTSET, LET ME EXPLAIN ONE KEY UNDERCURRENT TO WHAT is happening or not happening in the country at the moment, since various quarters have expressed concern about both. It has barely been a fortnight since I took oath as the head of the Azad Hind Administration. We cannot afford to get caught up in speculating and rumour-mongering at the moment, and so I am writing this and releasing it to the press nationally for widespread dissemination.

Had this been a political transition of power, it would have taken place primarily through political consultations over a period of time, with prior discussions between the parties handing it over and the new government taking charge.

However, this is a military transition of power, achieved at a cost of lives and blood, attained as per the pace of the battle as it unfolded, and so the consolidation and stabilization of the military situation has to precede any engagement with the political space in the current circumstances.

The military initiative to liberate India is, for good or for bad, primarily organized by me. I would have wanted it to be a collective effort but I could find no support for my plans to move in this direction when I set out. In 1940, after the fall of France, I actively attempted to build an internal coalition to lead an aggressive movement to overthrow the British by force.

I was spectacularly unsuccessful.

Not one political formation in the country was willing to initiate or support such a movement.

Even in 1942, only the Congress actively took part in an action that came two years too late. In these circumstances, the fact that no other political figure or organization in India at the moment is actively engaged with or recognized by the Tripartite Powers, is the reality that I may not have wanted – but it is a reality that I have to acknowledge today. As do you.

Equally, the Indian Legion and the Indian National Army, which have fought long and hard with the support of the German, Italian and Japanese armed forces, report to me as their supreme commander. As I am the founder of the Legion and the guide of the INA, they will, therefore, act as per my advisory as we restore law and order and administrative structure throughout the land, and it is not administratively feasible to have a multi-entity supervisory body for them organized overnight.

A transition of power in wartime is inherently chaotic and unstructured, and we will face severe challenges in merely keeping day-to-day life running. From tending to the thousands of injured and displaced, to aggressively policing the many attempts to instigate communal disharmony for local political interests, the armed forces of Free India, now in the form of the Azad Hind Fauj, are performing extremely challenging tasks even as fighting in India has subsided. While we are evaluating the degree to which authority can be delegated to local police forces, selectively, there is no alternate organization to do what the Fauj is doing.

And lest we forget – the world is still at war. Germany is still fighting with Russia. Large parts of the British Empire, from Canada to South Africa, still give it strength. Ships sail out from Madagascar as well as Australia to attack Axis naval activity in the Indian Ocean, even as of today. A large number of British forces that fled from India are believed to currently be in Sri Lanka. Even though the Axis naval forces are keeping a close vigil on activities there, a possibility of the British attempting to re-enter Indian territory, if they find the situation conducive, cannot be ruled out at this point in time.

It is, therefore, highly premature to talk of a political power-sharing mechanism right now.

To put it bluntly, power first needs to be consolidated militarily and administratively, before it can be distributed equitably and proportionately. Governance first needs to be organized before various models of democratic government formation can be applied. This is a process that would take eighteen to thirty-six months at the least, possibly longer.

In the interim, I will look forward to engaging with and accepting the advice of all political leaders, irrespective of my individual political thoughts on how to address issues and resolve grievances.

In the limited opportunities available to me during the military conflict, I have met with Khan Abdul Ghaffar Khan and Mr Jinnah, and it is my belief that we are in a position where we shall be able to sit down and address our differing positions on the concept of Pakistan. The armed forces of

Free India do not either favour or discriminate against anyone on the basis of religion and that is what the undivided nation seeks to do as well.

While Mr Jinnah's philosophical position on Pakistan remains unchanged, he has assured me that he will not engage in any activity that destabilizes the country in this delicate situation. I have assured him that all minorities will shortly realize that any fears of being treated as unequals in post-British India were unfounded and the rationality of a separate state itself will cease to exist. You have my word that India will have non-discriminatory administration.

I have also travelled to bring Bapu out of his imprisonment in Poona, as you are aware. Bapu, now safely in Delhi, as of now, has neither forcefully asked the Congress party to assist nor to oppose the Azad Hind Administration. We are glad that he is a free man again and we leave it to his wisdom how he wishes to advise the Congress or his followers across the nation, with no influence or pressure from either myself or the Tripartite Powers.

I have also reached out to Mr Nehru, but we are yet to come to a consensus on our political understanding of the current situation. It is no secret that Mr Nehru has not been a keen votary of the Axis forces being present in India. The leadership of the CWC has not yet conveyed to me its position on the issue – I await their inputs.

But let there not be the impression that as a former member of the Congress, my loyalties lie primarily with it or its views. All political groups and leaders across the country, without exception – from Mr Ambedkar to the Hindu Mahasabha – will shortly receive my emissaries from the Forward Bloc as we look to carry out the groundwork for an all-party meeting – the first of its kind in independent India. Let me reassure leaders across regions and ideologies that short of the partition of our motherland, there is nothing I am not open to understanding and discussing.

It is no secret that I have sharply formed political views and I have written about them in detail in the 1930s. However, that does not mean that only those political views are relevant to the construction of a unified, currently peaceful India. A political advisory council will be set up within six months, which will plan a way ahead for the future course of governance in this country and will also be requested to advise the administration on negotiations with the princely states.

Since the Indian Legion and the Indian National Army – now in the process of merging into a single Azad Hind Fauj – are the primary tools of governance presently, there is little choice administratively but to enforce martial law for a limited period to enable them to carry out whatever civil or administrative duties they may be called upon to perform, temporarily.

In particular, regrettably, in several situations, the local police seem to have been mere observers to communal outbreaks. I have authorized the Fauj to shoot after the first warning and to exercise all police powers in such situations. In eight such instances across the country so far, since I took oath of office, 143 rioters have been killed and 654 injured in firing. I am deliberately not specifying the locations, or the 'ratio' of the casualties at the moment. It does not matter to the administration what the religion of a rioter is. Respect the law of the land. Keep the peace. Nothing will validate the past 200 years of British rule more than Indian falling with a sword upon another Indian, as soon as the British armies have been driven out.

Martial law will, of course, raise a familiar question and give strength to rumours and misapprehensions; am I, therefore, assuming the role of the Indian Führer, as my critics say? Am I here to function as a puppet of the Tripartite Powers?

To my critics, I will repeat for the nth time – my collaboration with the Axis is entirely in the external space. Neither am I qualified to comment on the internal matters of these nations, nor am I willing to have them intervene in the internal matters of India. I have opposed dictatorial, single-person-centric work patterns in the Congress and I do not believe they have a place in a country as massive and pluralistic as India, in the long run.

My vision of India is of an undivided country, drawing strength in that unity that extends from the Afghan border to the Burmese one – a subcontinent that will work together rather than against itself. Part of the hurry that I have exhibited in gathering armed forces and pushing the Axis very hard to launch operations on the Indian front in 1942 itself, even with limited resources, is because I have been firmly convinced that the British would, with each passing year, work harder to make Indian fight Indian till the point a division of the country becomes irreversible.

The British have played us, no doubt – region versus region, religion versus religion, caste versus caste, princes versus populace. But they could only play because many of these fissures, divisions and mutual suspicions exist in the first place. Only by acknowledging our collective shortfalls would we be able to work to correct them. Look at the international situation, my friends – countries as diverse as Germany and Japan, countries as ideologically disparate as Britain and Soviet Russia are pooling their resources to strengthen their efforts.

Are the differences between political groups and religions within our country even wider than these? If Churchill and Stalin can have a joint front, can't Mr Jinnah and Mr Gandhi? Can we not realize this is a pivotal moment in world history and that our strength lies in burying our differences and not in obsessing over them?

I have the utmost respect for all political ideologies, all faiths, all languages, all classes – and all of us, I believe, will build a new India together. I only seek a little time; the country cannot move from a mid-war transition of authority to a new form of government in less than three years, perhaps even longer.

However, in the interim, we will work to rebuild our economic basics and establish sufficient military capability so that we do not have to tax the resources of our allies to safeguard our own territory. We have nominal air and naval forces. Though we have willing and trained manpower, the British have destroyed most infrastructure and equipment in order to deny it to us. Building up the basic minimum Air Force capabilities alone will take us not less than two years.

To summarize, today, India has gained freedom in the sense that the King Emperor no longer is the master of our destiny – but there are immense economic, administrative and military challenges.

If, as a people, we stay united, the rest will be managed.

Jai Hind!

Subhas Chandra Bose
Prime Minister
Azad Hind Administration

30

Heat of the Rising Sun

> 'But could not all this (Japan's achievements) have been achieved without Imperialism, without dismembering the Chinese Republic, without humiliating another proud, cultured and ancient race? No, with all our admiration for Japan, where such admiration is due, our whole heart goes out to China in her hour of trial ...'
>
> – Subhas Bose, 'Japan's Role in the Far East'

New Delhi
11 May 1943

THE WHITE FLAG WITH THE BRIGHT, RED CIRCLE FLUTTERED breezily over the New Delhi compound of what was, till recently, the office-cum-residence of a British lieutenant general. The complex now served as a temporary composite diplomatic-cum-military HQ for the Japanese forces in India.

The Japanese officer who had worked on India's issues for several years now and had been the *de facto* point of contact with Subhas, Major Fujiwara Iwaichi – tipped to be promoted to lieutenant colonel shortly – had been assigned a spacious office that was presently being furnished.

Lt Gen. Iida had returned to Rangoon, post the Delhi parade. There were three Japanese army officers of the rank of major general to oversee operations and deployment in

India, in Delhi, Calcutta and Dhaka, but Subhas preferred to deal with either Iida or with Fujiwara – a man who some credited with thinking of the INA even before an Indian had. The Major occasionally invited sneering remarks from seniors who thought his obsession with working 'with' Indians – rather than instructing them – had been an approach that did not prioritize Imperial Japan's interests.

From the time he first spoke with Mohan Singh in 1941, Fujiwara's objective had been to gain the support of the Indian POWs and then the general Indian populace, rather than to use the power of the gun as a negotiating tool. He had attempted to convey that sentiment to his seniors, with mixed results.

Once, however, the INA was aligned to the initiative led by Bose, someone who was on good terms with Mussolini and based in Berlin, and the Japanese high command had been forced to factor in his objections and issues. The Japanese political leadership did not want to push Subhas entirely into the German/Italian sphere of influence. The reverse was equally true. The Axis partners did not trust each other enough on many issues and so an undercurrent of competitive lobbying and influence-gathering was omnipresent, more so after the success of the joint India campaign. Despite that, the Japanese Army's dealings with the INA had several zones of friction, and, when Subhas was really irked, he had more than once cabled Premier Tojo directly – and very angrily.

And it was an angry message from Bose that had landed this morning on Fujiwara's desk, requesting a meeting in an hour.

❖

Subhas was clearly upset. Dhillon, recently promoted to lieutenant colonel, stood by his table, along with two officers whom Fujiwara recognized as promising names in the erstwhile INA cadre – Major Sehgal and Colonel Shah Nawaz. It was obvious that something had been reported to Bose that had made him call for this meeting at such a short notice.

'What is going on, Major?!'

'I wish I knew, Excellency. I got the gist of your points from the message, but I do not have complete details of what this episode is about.'

'*This* is what it is about, Major!' Subhas thrust a file at him.

Fujiwara took it. Subhas gestured to him to take a chair. He sat down and slowly, carefully read through the sheaf of messages addressed to the INA headquarters from diverse units across the Eastern combat zone. His usually expressionless face stayed that way, but he took a deep breath as he finished.

This did not make for good reading for someone interested in stronger Indo–Japanese collaboration, he thought to himself. India was militarily free of the British, but the war wasn't yet over for Japan – and this wasn't going to help.

In Dimapur, Japanese soldiers had forcibly taken away three British officers from the custody of an INA contingent to whom they had surrendered and bayoneted them – in public. These officers were supposedly responsible for heavy Japanese casualties during the bitter fighting at Imphal.

In Sylhet, a scuffle had broken out between INA and Japanese troops when the latter attempted to enter the houses of local villagers, looking for valuables. Though the unit's officers had intervened before anyone was seriously hurt, no action had been taken against the Japanese soldiers involved, despite multiple reports filed by the INA unit's CO.

Near Guwahati, a bridge checkpoint manned by the Japanese, with no information to the Indian liaison officers, had on more than one occasion, stopped trucks of the INA for checking, at gunpoint.

The Japanese Navy had killed three local fishermen off the Cox's Bazaar coast when it opened fire, without warning, at a boat that had apparently drifted too close to a patrol boat in the darkness. The survivors had insisted that no warning had been issued. The Navy's version was that the boat's crew were 'conducting themselves in a suspicious manner' and they had acted in preemptive self-defence.

The list went on. There were over a dozen instances, compiled and brought to Subhas's desk by the INA Eastern HQ. The cover note clarified that these were not aberrations but part of a pattern unfolding over the last fortnight, and that Japanese officers were completely unwilling to take any action against any of their men, irrespective of the nature of the offences reported.

'I will look into this, Excellency, and also send a message to General Iida to urgently draw his attention to this.'

What else could Fujiwara say?

'No, no, Major, you know that is just jargon! You know me better than this. General Iida had spoken to me about the protocol for inter-forces coordination during his visit to Delhi. However, I regret that the officers on the ground do not seem to be inclined to listen to their own Generals. Either that, or what is being discussed with me is just to keep me in good humour while a free run is being given on the ground. Both options reflect poorly on our association.'

'Our soldiers have shed blood jointly in operations in freeing the eastern part of India from British imperial occupation, Excellency. I am sure these are aberrations and they will be brought to the notice of the general.'

'Are they aberrations? Even when the men fought jointly, you are as well informed as I am that in ammunition, in rations, in vehicles – in practically every area, the INA had to fight with poorer quality and lesser quantity. I had dozens of copies of messages sent to you by the INA officers. I did not make a big issue of it then, since I understand that resources were not abundant and there was a war to be won. But there were also many cases of insulting and degrading behaviour, and excessively hard orders, only for the INA. I wrote to General Iida on at least three occasions, objecting to the conduct of senior Japanese officers during the period of active combat.'

Fujiwara nodded. He could not deny what Subhas was stating, but then neither could he be officially acknowledging this.

He himself had had a few run-ins with colleagues in the past – in Singapore, in Burma and in India – on the tonality of their conduct and dealings. Troops and officers who had served in China displayed a particular disdain for respecting the local civilian population. The 'Asian solidarity' that Japan's political leadership was talking about wasn't quite reflecting in the dealings of its soldiers with the Asians in captured territories.

'Major, the dynamics of war, more so a war where my men are armed and equipped by you, the generals are mostly yours, and the battle cannot be paused midway to resolve differences – that is one thing. But whatever we may have put up with during that phase, however reluctantly, to win this war – we will not let it be normalized on Indian soil today. If Japanese Generals think that India is another China for them and they have "conquered" the land, then ...'

An uncomfortable silence hung in the air.

'I have just come back from a tour of Agartala, Guwahati and Dhaka, Major,' Dhillon addressed Fujiwara. 'The ground reality is that the conduct of some, though not all, of the Imperial army's men and officers is causing concern and anger to build up amongst the locals, as well as the men of the INA. More so since the INA's soldiers have seen first-hand the behaviour of the Japanese Army with the civilians in Burma and Singapore – often brutal, to say the least. As advised by Bose sir, I personally met with General Mohan Singh in Dhaka, and he was absolutely furious with the liberties that the Japanese forces have been taking in some areas.'

'And I fear the sense they are getting is that for some of your men, and officers, India, too, seems to be an "occupied territory" – that thought itself is completely unacceptable to me, I hardly need tell you that,' Subhas took the point ahead.

'Of course, that cannot be the thinking, Excellency! Japan has acknowledged the independence of India and your position as head of a sovereign state. Let not minor oversights damage the trust between our great nations.'

'You know I began this relationship in trust. I fully understand that Britain would not have been uprooted from this entire region without the might of the Japanese armed forces. Japan has removed an imperial power that we had never believed could be defeated by an Asian power. For that, all of Southeast Asia is perhaps in Japan's debt. But Japan's track record – earlier in China and then in the countries liberated from Britain – makes many observers question if a European imperial power is merely being replaced by an Asian one.'

'I cannot comment on affairs in other countries, but it is my firm belief that the Japanese Army's role in the India operation is no more than to evict the British and to deny them the use of this territory to continue the fight against the Tripartite Powers.'

'Right, then, Major. Let us look forward to working as allies, with mutual respect. I am sure you will apprise the officers here as well as General Iida appropriately. I would also want you to send them a copy of this.'

With that, Subhas handed over a single typed sheet to him.

12 May 1943: Order of the Day

All AHF/INA Personnel Deployed in Joint Control Areas

Revised protocol for enforcement of administrative guidelines

It has come to the attention of the undersigned that the AHF has been unable to enforce the law of the land or the guidelines issued by the Azad Hind Administration on several occasions, recently, on account of the absence of understanding with the forces of the Imperial Japanese Army.

It is further a cause of concern that on occasions, the lives and liberty of the civilian population, or of POWs in AHF custody, have not been protected by the AHF on account of the adherence to the policy of 'no use of force' with affiliated powers. The protocol of filing official complaints has been followed, but it has regrettably not been met with adequate responses. It has been observed that neither has action been taken against violators, nor has a mechanism been set up to prevent recurrence of such episodes.

In light of this, a fresh protocol will be effective as of midnight today.

AHF personnel are hereby authorized the use of force to carry out duties assigned to them *if such duties be obstructed by any affiliated powers, including but not limited to the Imperial Japanese Army. The use of non-lethal force will be reviewed by respective unit commanders for justification.*

The use of lethal force, though only as a measure of last resort and only to prevent loss of other life, is also authorized as per this order. Any review of such use will, however, be subject to final scrutiny at the desk of the undersigned.

Subhas Chandra Bose
Prime Minister
Azad Hind Administration

Fujiwara was dismayed. He did not want either side to escalate tensions, and this could potentially trigger armed confrontation.

He looked at Subhas, disappointed, puzzled, as if asking if this was really needed.

Subhas stood up from his desk, came around, and grasped his hand.

'I know you are a man of good intent, Major, I know you well. But I also know the track record of many of your Generals, since the 1930s. I am sorry, but if this is not checked today, the IJA may well end up as guests who overstay their welcome and take over the house. I have no jurisdiction as to what Japanese forces do to the East of the India–Burma border – I can only have an opinion. But on Indian territory, as of tomorrow, any IJA soldier or officer who crosses a line should do so knowing that the AHF has my backing to shoot, consequences be damned.'

31

Lessons from the Swami

'The philosophy which I found in Vivekananda and Ramakrishna came nearest to meeting my requirements and offered a basis on which to reconstruct my moral and practical life. It equipped me with certain principles with which to determine my conduct or line of action whenever any problem or crisis arose before my eyes.'

– Subhas Bose, *Indian Pilgrim*, 1937

'The foundation of the present freedom movement owes its origin to Swamiji's message. If India is to be free, it cannot be a land especially of Hinduism or of Islam – it must be one united land of different religious communities inspired by the ideal of nationalism. [And for that] Indians must accept wholeheartedly the gospel of harmony of religions which is the gospel of Ramakrishna–Vivekananda.'

– Subhas Bose

Calcutta
18 May 1943

THE RISING SUN REFLECTED OFF THE WATERS OF THE HOOGHLY.

Subhas looked out towards the endless stretch of flowing water in quiet contemplation as the steamer undertook the short journey from one shore to the other.

In a few minutes, he would deboard at the Dakshineswar temple.

Two smaller boats sailed on either side as part of his security detail. One had an anti-aircraft gun mounted on the deck. He was irked at needing this degree of protection but Captain Ghaffar, now responsible for his security, had been insistent. Nambiar and Abid had ignored everything that Subhas had said and ensured that Ghaffar got his way.

Churchill had reportedly given a go-ahead to any manner of taking him out – a sniper's bullet, an anti-tank projectile, a land mine. 'There may not be that many sympathizers of the British in the areas we now control, but there are enough people who hate you intensely – and, as a combination, that is problematic. There are a few men in each city who would gladly take a shot at you if they could get away safely,' Nambiar had laughed.

But physical safety was the last thing on his mind at the moment. The aura of Ramakrishna and Vivekananda made preservation of everyday life seem rather shallow.

Subhas had reached Calcutta on just the previous night, in total secrecy. And at 5.30 a.m., he had stepped out to head for the temple. He knew that once reports of his presence spread through the city, it would be very unlikely that he could come here – or anywhere – in solitude. Even now, curious groups had begun to gather on the banks and on the bridge.

Was this a visit to reaffirm his basics in the face of great self-doubt? Or was it a journey of nostalgia? Or did he, after effectively displacing the Viceroy as the primary controller of power in the Indian subcontinent for the moment, want to come to offer a silent thanks to the men whom he would gladly have embraced as his own masters had they been alive?

Nobody knew the answers, because nobody dared ask Subhas these questions.

He spoke at length and wrote in even greater detail about his political philosophy, but he usually kept his personal beliefs to himself and would discuss them, if at all, only when he was in a particular frame of mind, and that, too, with a very small circle.

But the fact that Vivekananda and Ramakrishna had seeped into his subconscious from a very early stage was in the public domain, thanks to his own writings. And though he did not talk about it very frequently or very openly, much of his individual reflexes – his risk-taking ability, his ability to absorb huge amounts of personal attack and criticism without letting go of his core beliefs – were rooted in how he had absorbed the teachings of Vivekananda.

❖

'Once things are a little normal, hopefully, a year or two from now,' he turned to Nambiar to answer, abruptly breaking his silence. 'Of course, depending on how the situation is with regard to Kashmir, I would want to visit two shrines that Swamiji had worshipped – Amarnath and Kheer Bhawani.'

'I'll take note of that,' Nambiar responded. 'Even though I do not know how comfortable the Maharaja of Kashmir would be with the idea, right now.'

'True, but I can't take time out right now as it is. It will all fall in place in a year,' Subhas said. Nambiar did not prod him to elaborate. Kashmir and Hyderabad were prominent among several princely states warily coming to terms with the changing balance of power.

The steamer coasted to a stop and the most popular son of Bengal – even though he took great care to not be branded a leader of one region alone – stepped off. The small group of officers and associates accompanying him followed. Asking his guards to keep some distance behind, he commenced walking towards the temple that had earned fame across India on account of its association with Ramakrishna Paramhansa – an individual so uniquely advanced in spiritual matters that he was already being described by some as an avatar.

Nambiar paused for a moment as he considered whether or not to bring up a point with Subhas. Then, making up his mind, he walked briskly ahead, took Subhas aside, and softly asked, 'Should we be, you know, asking Captain Ghaffar and Abid to wait outside, at the temple's gate?'

Subhas gave him a surprised look – as if he did not understand the question.

'I entered the Indian border with men of all faiths, and, by now, I have written letters of condolence to thousands of families of all faiths – so if they are good to fight and to die alongside me, I think they are good to enter the temple alongside me.'

They continued to walk quietly for a minute. Then Subhas spoke again.

'I don't mean to snub you. It was a legitimate observation. But yes, I know who all are with me. They are here because I insisted that they accompany me.'

'You could have told us in advance, perhaps? I could have conveyed it to the temple priests. Just in case someone has an objection ...'

'Well, it is a package deal. If they will not enter, neither will I. I am too much of a rebel by now to care much for the rulebooks of the orthodox. You do know, that the then proprietor of this temple, in 1897, had refused to welcome a well-known devotee since he thought he had "lost caste" by travelling overseas? Apparently, the papers reported that the devotee was unwelcome and was expelled from the temple premises – though I am not fully conversant with all the details, but that, I understand, was the crux of the episode. If *that* man was unwelcome, well ...'

'Lost caste by travelling overseas? Surely that couldn't have been ...?'

'Yes, it was!' Subhas burst out laughing. 'Swami Vivekananda was not welcome at the Dakshineshwar Temple! So let us not even go down that road. Don't get me started on the organized priesthood and the obsession with exclusion – and, sadly, that applies, without exception, across the orthodoxy of all religions, I have come to understand through my travels.'

Thinking about this got him agitated, as had often happened earlier.

'You know, this is the *last* place that question should be relevant ... surely we all are aware that Ramakrishna is believed to have practised the beliefs of Christianity and Islam as well, even if briefly, and it is from his *actual* experiences and practices that he concluded that all religions ultimately lead to the same goal.'

'That may be true, Subhas, but it is not as if we can just walk into a mosque tomorrow with a tilak on our foreheads, or a Christian or Muslim associate of yours, not in uniform, can just walk into a temple, is it? Things are what they are. Every place of worship has some sensitivity, some distinctions, doesn't it? There are times where your fantastic visions of inter-faith harmony seem straight out of a school classroom, not the world of politics.'

'Of course, it is not all sweet and harmony-filled. But such issues are not unique to India, are they? There are days I feel the communal tension in India is very bad, but then I see how vicious the Aryan–Slav hatred is on the Russian front; the stories one hears about there. You are aware how full of bloodshed the animosity between the Serbs and the Croats has been. Race, or religion, or even colour – see how the Blacks are treated in the United States even today – they all can be great dividers. But if we are to build one nation out of this great, massive subcontinent, should I be working to sharpen the divisions or to reduce them? Perfect Hindu–Muslim harmony may be unrealistic, given how things have been in the past few years, I absolutely understand – but is not the long-term strength of an undivided, independent India going to depend on that?'

Nambiar differed with Subhas on a dozen things a day, but even he could not argue with that.

❖

For over an hour, the 'fascist' who had absorbed Ramakrishna and Vivekananda for some decades now, sat quietly by himself in the temple compound after worshipping at the feet of Kali.

Devotees at the temple recognized him but gave him space – he seemed to be in a world of his own.

Which he was.

It was said that Ramakrishna, unable to wait for *darshan* any longer, had prepared to sacrifice himself when the deity had physically appeared and stopped him from doing so. Did it happen at this very place? What intensity of faith would it need for someone to actually summon – that was the wrong word here, though – the Mother *Herself* in physical form? These were things you only read about in mythology or religious books. To feel that something like that could have happened right here, just a few decades in the past, felt surreal.

And had not Vivekananda spoken about how the Mother Goddess had spoken physically as She Herself reprimanded him at the temple of Kheer Bhawani? Vivekananda was no delusional half-crazy *baba* to have imagined things – he was, perhaps, the most lucid mind of his time.

Was not Ramakrishna a bigger 'power' than Hitler?

It all seemed just talk – but was not spiritual power as tangible, if not more, than what the world worshipped – military, political, economic power?

He needed to check his own reflexes if he got too absorbed in the battles of the real world.

Would Ramakrishna have cared who ruled Delhi? Or Berlin? Empires and kings come and go.

The eternal truths of life go beyond that.

If we are able to drag ourselves away and think about them, that is. But then, we are children, easily distracted by the shiny, pretty toys of our everyday lives.

❖

The 'outsider's entry' had been a non-issue. No priest in Calcutta, howsoever orthodox, was going to ask a question to Subhas Chandra Bose, even once he had got over the shock of seeing who the unannounced early morning worshipper was. The Muslim and Christian officers had also walked with him, barefoot, till a little short of the actual sanctum sanctorum. They had waited outside till Subhas stepped back out, and the pujari had accompanied him to offer them all *aarti*, which they accepted, heads covered, and placed their offerings in the tray. Neither party was trying to either offend or prove a point, and so the moment passed, with some grace and dignity.

❖

'We have to leave. You have other assignments, Subhas.'

His reverie broken by the soft voice, he turned back. Nambiar stood, apologetically, pointing towards his watch.

'Do you not feel that in some way we have been unable

to fully understand and thereafter amplify the sheer spiritual stature of this life?' Subhas said to no one in particular.

'The more I read about Ramakrishna, the more I marvel at how little I understand spirituality or religion. I see him as a burst of such high-voltage electricity that only a transmitter like Vivekananda could handle it without burning himself out. But so much more needs to be done!'

Nambiar nodded. 'Vivekananda died far too early – at just thirty-nine!'

'Yes, imagine that! There was so much more to be done, to send across to the world the message of this incomparable individual – man, deity, avatar? It would have been such an incredible loss to all humanity if the thoughts and the life of Ramakrishna had remained confined to Bengal.'

'But hasn't Vivekananda already made him a name respected across the world?'

'To know the name and to understand the nuances of what he taught – these are two different things. Here, in Bengal itself, even those of us who revere him and take pride that he came to our land and spoke our language – I hope we understand that *worshipping* him is so much easier than *understanding* him, living by what he said, living by how he lived.'

Nambiar indicated that they should get moving – the gathering in the area was increasing.

But Subhas could not disengage just yet.

'I often feel that if we could actually understand what Ramakrishna stood for – by we, I do not just mean either just the people of Bengal or just Hindus, but all Indians – things would change so much. If we genuinely understood what both these men stood for, we would laugh at the energy we pour into the politics of "us" and "them" that prevail across our land today. Once you truly understand their spirituality, it is difficult to find within the hatred for the "other". Can we not gather bands of young people who will travel across the country and promulgate the teachings of Vivekananda and Ramakrishna? Will that not do more to bring calmness to bloodthirsty lands than martial law or Bapu's fasting?'

There were questions to which there were no immediate answers, and Nambiar, wisely, did not attempt to offer them.

❖

'Let us quickly move, sir, we will take you via the side gate.'

'No, why should we? This is not a political crowd; they are all here in the search of peace, are they not?'

Without giving Ghaffar a chance to advise him otherwise, Subhas stepped a dozen paces towards the devotees in the compound. They had been watching him from a distance, kept there both by their respect for someone seeking quiet and the circle of his soldiers. A ripple ran through the gathering as they realized he was heading towards them.

He stood still for a moment, and then, turning in the direction of the Mother's idol, raised his hands overhead, and roared: 'Joy Maa!'

'JOY MAA!' the entire compound reverberated.

❖

On the drive back, Subhas asked Ghaffar and Abid to ride along in his car.

Then he took them completely by surprise with this: 'I hope nobody made you uncomfortable – and if they did, accept my apologies.'

'No, not at all – and why would you apologize if someone did?!' Ghaffar was all red with embarrassment. 'I wasn't sure

I was supposed to go inside with you – but Nambiar said you had insisted, so I did. Yes, this is the first time I was inside a temple ... but no, nobody made me feel uncomfortable. My name tag was there, of course, and some did look at it curiously – but I think the uniform was above all that, today. I am an officer in Subhas Bose's army – who will question me standing near him?'

Subhas patted him on the back and turned to Abid, who was just smiling quietly.

'Captain, do you know how Jai Hind was introduced in the Legion?'

'No, sir, I never asked about that.'

'It was Abid.'

Ghaffar looked at his fellow-passenger, wide-eyed.

'I did not know that!'

Subhas smiled and reached out to hold Abid's hand for a moment in an uncharacteristic gesture.

'When I first went to the POW camps to try to recruit soldiers for the Legion, I realized that even as prisoners, they would gather along religious lines. And now that they had no English officers to salute or greet, the only greetings I would hear being exchanged were Sat Sri Akal, Ram Ram, Salaam Alaikum. In fact, I noticed that when soldiers of different religions met each other, they did not quite know how to greet each other – because, in their own regiments, they almost never had to meet men of other religions. I wanted a common greeting – one that would unify them, identify them as Indians first. And can you imagine what Abid first suggested?'

Ghaffar thought for a moment.

'Something less religious, I guess?'

'His first proposal was – can you believe it – *Hello*!'

Abid burst out laughing while Ghaffar looked at both of them, not sure if they were pulling his leg.

'No, really, I did ... isn't that the simplest way to greet anyone?' Abid admitted, even as he suppressed a laugh.

'After I shot that down and told him what I thought of it, he suggested "Jai Hindustan Ki" – which then was shortened to just "Jai Hind". And we knew right away that this will be heard for a long, long time. Can you imagine how this phrase, that didn't exist a couple of years back, is now so completely identified with, in our armies?'

'I loved it. *Jai Hind* – it goes right to your heart.'

'Enough of the praise, thank you, everyone!' Abid smiled.

'You have been with Netaji since long, I understand?'

'Yes, indeed. You know, Ghaffar, I am no professional soldier. I was a student of engineering in Berlin. I happened to hear this leader from India talk about my country – and I was just swept away. I had to do *something*. I met him, and he asked me to join him right away! I told him, I have one semester left, let me complete it, and then I will join the freedom struggle.'

'And how did he take it?

'Badly! "I have no need for selfish people. Either you join now, or never!" I was so torn. I could barely sleep all night. By morning, I had decided – I left my course and joined him. And here we are now.'

Everyone was silent for a while.

The cavalcade was about to reach the Bose residence.

'I had a question – if you don't mind?'

'Go ahead, Abid.'

'What was the need to insist on taking us into the temple? You don't have to prove anything to us. You know that we are with you, nobody else, not Jinnah, not anyone.'

Subhas smiled.

'I did not do it for you, but for myself. My fellow officers cannot be kept out if I am present – it is a matter of our honour, our uniform. And then, of all the temples anywhere, this is one where, even if we were not fellow soldiers in way, there should be no barrier to anyone who wishes to enter. When I was still in college, I read Vivekananda in great detail, and I remember vividly what he wrote about Ramakrishna: "to proclaim and make clear the fundamental unity underlying all religions was the mission of my Master". Even if romantically, Vivekananda would say for Ramakrishna that "he was the harbinger of peace – the separation between Hindus and Mohammedans, between Hindus and Christians, all are now things of the past". And I thought, if only this comes true, who can stop an undivided India from standing together and regaining its independence? So I cannot reconcile to highlighting differences at a place that makes me think of the two of them.'

'I need to read what Vivekananda wrote,' Ghaffar said, almost to himself.

Subash smiled and nodded.

The car braked to a halt.

But it wasn't going to be as simple as stepping out and entering the house. He had slipped out in the early hours of dawn unnoticed. But now, the crowd, gathered outside in waiting for him, was going berserk with joy and excitement.

He smiled and sportingly asked his guards to step away and walked towards them.

How could he deny them time with their Subhas?

Epilogue

'So often have I told you that I have already sold myself to my first love (my country). I have very little left to give anyone. What little I have – I have given you. It may not be worthy of you and of your great love for me – but that is all I have – and you cannot expect anything more from me.'

– Subhas Bose, Letter to Emilie Schenkl, March 1936

Calcutta
22 May 1943

AN ANXIOUS SILENCE HUNG OVER THE BREAKFAST TABLE. FOR A few minutes, the only sound was of cutlery and china.

Then Emilie addressed the elephant in the room.

'Can you not defer this? Maybe go two or three months later?'

Her tone did not attempt to hide her discomfort with his plans.

'Not really. You don't know how things will be, three months from now.'

'Why the urgency to meet Tojo, Subhas?' Nambiar joined in the conversation.

Nambiar, Abid, Major Dhillon, Captain Ghaffar, Krappe, and the two INA officers who had met him in Delhi, Sehgal and Shah Nawaz – it was quite a large group seated at the breakfast table today for this informal meeting. Subhas was asking for inputs and making up his mind on an issue that had been troubling him.

'He heads the trickiest global partnership we are in right now, for want of a better expression.'

'Aren't *all* our partnerships tricky?'

'Yes and no.'

'There you go again, leaving us looped in your words, dodging the topic.'

Subhas laughed.

'No! See, the Germans are themselves keen to leave only a small advisory force here – and I can speak freely in front of Kurt. They need to get most of their units back – they are badly stretched in holding onto Iran and Iraq, even with all the local sentiment supporting them. That oil is priceless and sabotage by the SOE is a daily threat. Lastly, I am not worried even if they are here for a while, so long as it's not the SS. With the exception of the Jamnagar episode, frankly, there have been few incidents of misbehaviour or harassment of the locals – no more, frankly, than rotten apples in our own army.'

'The Italians are a different story. I am, actually, in reverse, requesting the Duce to let them stay on – the men who came with us, as well as those already in India. The total POWs that have been freed from camps in India now add up to almost 80,000. Overall, then, can you believe it, we have something like 100,000 trained Italian soldiers in India right now. For whatever it is worth, the prisoners have been in India for some time and they have assimilated easily with the locals. These men can be sent home gradually over the next couple of years, but, in the meantime, once armed and equipped, they can be a strong military buffer for anything else the British can think of – accumulating ANZAC forces in Sri Lanka and launching an attack from the sea to try to regain territory in South India, for instance. We could never have transported that many Axis soldiers to India – the British did this for us!'

'You sound like you prefer the Italians over the Germans, when it comes to keeping Axis forces in India, do I get that right?'

'Yes, Abid. One part of that is because the Italians were almost always civil to the Indian POWs in North Africa, and many of those POWs then willingly agreed to join up for the Legion *because* the Italians were treating them with more respect than their own English officers in the POW camps. Many of the Legion's units had a good rapport with the Italian units because some of them dealt with the Italians as their prisoners, and yet, weren't humiliated.

'The second undercurrent is more cultural, I feel. The average German soldier has been fed theories of racial superiority to a far greater degree than the Italian. For all his faults or wishful looking back at the Roman Empire, Mussolini has not really been a fan of the Nazi obsession with racial superiority and inferiority. I have seen that from the 1930s itself. Far more Germans in uniform, therefore, tend to have a racist undertone than their Italian counterparts.'

'Racist or not, the Germans don't think too much of their Italian colleagues when it comes to war, do they? And what's war about, finally, if not fighting and fighting well?'

'I know the Germans look down on the fighting skills of their allies as well, but, frankly, if you ask me, that is because the equipment and the leadership that the Italian soldier has had, hasn't been up to the mark. The Duce has not been as good a manager of military affairs as he is an orator, and the generals have stayed in a WWI mind-frame. But there is nothing inherently "non-martial" – to use the British phrase so freely applied to many Indians – with the troops.'

'This is an interesting class in international relations, sir;

you should write about this in your next book – if you get time to write one now!' Dhillon commented. 'And why, then, are the Japanese such a concern that you are willing to take a long-distance flight in the middle of a World War?'

'You cannot deny that the Japanese have fought exceptionally well through their entire campaign, not just here. Militarily, you cannot fault them so far. On the other hand, behaviourally, they seem to have acquired a reflex over many months in China, in Burma, of being conquerors rather than liberators – despite the talk of all Asians coming together to drive out imperialist forces from the region. Even though many officers I know don't think in that authoritarian, dominating manner, but far, *far* too many others do. I don't want such officers doing anything that strains the Indo–Japanese relationship.'

'Or German–Japanese!' Krappe laughed. 'It is good we are not in direct contact.'

'In any case, the INA had a far edgier relationship with the Japanese than the Legion had with the Germans. I worry about a full-blown firefight if a Japanese unit misbehaves – in fact, I am surprised it hasn't happened already.'

'Even if it does, these things happen in war, Subhas!' Nambiar sounded surprised at how much this worried Netaji.

'Yes, they do, but ... Let me try to explain. Firstly, at present, there are some 45,000 Japanese on Indian soil. I simply don't have the resources to curb them in case they turn rogue, for want of a better word. The Germans and the Italians will not want to have their troops deployed to discipline their Axis partner, so, if things ever go rough, this is going to fall entirely on the Indian troops. And that is tricky. Do we want the world to see Indians and Japanese turning their guns at each other, barely weeks after a surrender of British forces in India?

'Secondly, it will give a great deal of satisfaction to my friend Jawahar. He has always warned loudly – and with genuine belief – that the forces of Germany and Japan are a threat to India, that they will be an occupational force, and that I am merely a puppet in their hands. At the first sign of brutality or violence by any of the Axis, all those who take that theory seriously – and there may be millions – will begin to wonder whether those warnings were right, after all. The public support that has been so enthusiastic so far will begin to waver. How do you function then?'

'What is your solution?' Abid asked.

'I need Tojo to sign off on my proposed Indo–Japanese defence agreement. Its terms will confine all Japanese forces to the bases we will demarcate. If they step out beyond them, it will have to be without arms. Basically, Indian soil outside of their own bases then becomes a demilitarized zone for them. I am proposing that this comes into effect within sixty days of the signing of the agreement. If Tojo agrees to this, and to bring down the total Imperial army strength on Indian soil to 15,000, I am offering the choice of three secure naval installations on a fifteen-year lease. That will ensure that the Japanese Navy will be in a dominating position in the region for the duration of the war and well beyond.'

'Fifteen years? Isn't that generous? As a sovereign state, should we guarantee such tenures? Will you not be accused of having sold our soil to your masters, the usual?'

'But do we even have a naval wing of the Azad Hind Fauj, Abid? It will take us years to build an effective naval force from where we are, today – the officers, the seamen, the craft. The British have scuttled most of what they could not take away to Sri Lanka – or to Madagascar, which the Allies now control. Britain is unconquered, Australia and New Zealand are firmly with it and beyond the range of the Axis to physically conquer. This war isn't ending in six months, Abid. After all, Japan is never going to be able to physically land on the coast of the USA, or of Australia. It makes perfect sense, militarily, for India to have a strong, anti-British naval force dominate the seas around us right now. We are hardly stable as yet, and in the middle of a World War. We need buffers.'

Subhas paused momentarily, like the collective weight of where he was placed had suddenly caught up with him.

'But you do understand, don't you, why I could not have delegated this? It has not been resolvable over telegrams and notes, you very well know I send a dozen a week. This will only get resolved face-to-face between one head of state and another, and so I am saddled with this journey, like it or not!'

Subhas said it so matter-of-factly that Nambiar could not resist a laugh.

Emilie smiled at the head of state finishing off his breakfast, breadcrumbs still sticking to his face.

❖

'I know you explained everything in detail over breakfast. But I can't help it. I would still have preferred if you were not going.'

'I know, Emma. I'm sorry.'

'Hey, you don't have to apologize for this!'

'No, it's not about one journey.'

'Then what is it about?'

'I'm sorry for how raw a deal you're getting. I keep you out of the public gaze and you live with that. I wish things were different. But, at this moment, given how many in India still think of religious and caste superiority just as strongly as the Nazis think of racial privilege, I don't know how well Subhas "babu" being clicked with a German spouse will work. Being firang is sin enough for the puritans, add German to it and it just sits well for those who want to paint me as a puppet of the German regime. I know it is outlandish but ... you know,

Emma, in this incredible country of mine, we have lots of great people and we have a few petty people – but the petty ones tend to be louder. Given how many battles I am already fighting, I don't want to add to the noise that's already there ...'

He went quiet.

'Have I complained, Subhas?'

'No, you haven't, which doesn't mean I don't realize that this is wrong.'

'What is right and wrong right now, Subhas? This is the situation we're in.'

'A situation that works against you in every way. In Germany, the majority of the people – at least the majority of the Germans I noticed dealing with you – treated you like an outsider because you lived with me, an Indian. Von Trott quite hated you, may he rest in peace. That was a situation. In India, many treat you like an outsider because you are European. Having given up home and family there, you have none here. There are moments I feel I have offered you a very unfair deal with this association – your affection for me should not make you a lesser individual. You are my support, my bouncing board, an absorber of my thoughts, observer of my emotions – but what is your life? I'm making you play out the hackneyed role of the dutiful Indian wife, tending to the home while the husband goes out brandishing a sword – that is not what I wanted, trust me.'

Subhas held his head in his hands quietly. Emilie's hand reached out for his.

'I have known you for years. Do you think you could have made me do any of this against my will? I knew that there would be a minor price to pay. But I was fine with paying it, trust me. I don't regret anything. I am not standing for election in either country. What do I care for what people on the street think about my life's choices? Yes, I wish I could have had more time with us – but you have been caught up at such a moment in time that I cannot judge you, either. Once all this is over, maybe, yes, there can be more to my life than waiting for you,' she laughed, softly.

He quietly stood up and hugged her.

'I'll wait for you to return. Or perhaps I should say, we will wait for you to return.'

Emilie had spoken with a tone so devoid of any emphasis that, for a moment, Subhas thought he had heard her wrong. But then he stepped back, held her by the shoulders, looked into her eyes, and knew he hadn't.

❖

It was midnight when the Mitsubishi G4M bomber took off from Calcutta. Subhas, Abid, Sehgal and Fujiwara were onboard the rugged transporter that would stop at Port Blair first, from where General Iida and his staff would join them for the long haul to Tokyo. Three Zeros took off along with his plane, then took positions in a V-formation at a slightly higher altitude behind it. For this leg of the trip, Subhas was lightly guarded since this was assessed to be a minimal risk sector. A larger formation of six Zeros were assigned to escort the delegation on the next leg of the journey, from the Andamans to Tokyo, which would be broken by three refuelling stops.

As per protocol, the Japanese Air Force units sent out a message to the Port Blair base with details of the flight.

What the Japanese had not yet learnt, despite the loss of four aircraft carriers at the Battle of Midway in June 1942, was that the US cryptographers were recurrently deciphering large sections of their coded communication, much like how the British had broken the German Enigma and yet kept that a secret by acting on only a small percentage of what they learnt.

And the Allies were much quicker at sharing information with each other than the Axis.

❖

Two uneventful hours had passed. He continued to look out at the bright moon. Sleep would not come to him easily these days. As he had just about dozed off, the static of radio communication nudged him back to alertness.

'I thought we were observing radio silence?'

'Port Blair broke it to issue a warning of possible enemy aircraft in the region, sir.' The stress was visible on Abid's face. 'Heading north on a route that will intersect ours in 8–10 minutes from us – unless we change flight path.'

'What sort of aircraft?'

'Information is patchy, sir, but they suspect long-range reconnaissance aircraft – no other Allied planes would have the range to be in the region.'

'Why would reconnaissance planes head to meet us? It makes no sense. If they are looking for us, they must be fighters!'

'There can't be any enemy aircraft in this region, sir. At least not attack aircraft. The only formations of Spitfires in the region are based out of Colombo. The Andamans is about 1,400 kilometres from Colombo and we are further north of that, while the Spitfire's range is about 680; the Hurricane's 950. They can't even reach here.'

'Unless they took off from a carrier.'

'But the Allies don't *have* any carriers stationed in the region! Not after Japanese bombers sunk the HMS Hermes last year when they attacked British naval forces in Sri Lanka.'

'They don't? I hope our homework has been better than that of the Americans at Pearl Harbour. Or of the Japanese at Midway. Aircraft carriers have had the habit of turning up quietly in places they aren't expected.'

Subhas smiled, but there was no humour in his expression. Putting on the life jacket that was hurriedly brought to him, he instructed everyone aboard to put theirs on as well.

'Six Zeros have been scrambled at Port Blair, sir, but ETA for them will be probably eight or ten minutes after this formation passes us by.'

'Passes us by ... Why will they be heading for us, in the middle of the Bay of Bengal, at 2 a.m., hundreds of miles from any safe landing spot, to pass us by? They have been tipped off and are undoubtedly coming for us.'

Radio silence having been abandoned, the escorting Zeros, now briefed on the situation, spread out, forming a wider semi-circle around Subhas's plane.

In Calcutta and Port Blair, panicky radio operators scampered to inform their seniors.

❖

There were twelve of them. Three flights, each of four Grumman F4F Wildcats, the US-made favourite of the RAF when it came to carrier-based fighters. Clearly, an aircraft carrier had travelled some distance to send these up. Where had it come from? Australia? Or from a concealed Lankan hideaway? And where was it now, given that the Wildcats had a range of about 1,300 kilometres?

Wherever it had come from, it would have needed many hours of sailing to come within 500 kilometres or so of the interception point to send the Wildcats out. It would have needed escort ships. And whoever put all this together must have known that the urgent exercise was worth it – that a target worth all that activity *would* be here at this point.

Subhas's travel plans had obviously been sent out well in advance of his boarding the flight.

❖

Things appeared to happen in slow motion. Subhas had never witnessed aerial combat this closely before and he watched, fascinated, oblivious to the fact that he was a participant, not an observer, in what unfolded in the moonlit skies above the sea.

He thought for a moment about the three Zero pilots who would have counted the twelve Wildcats and would have realized that the law of averages was against their surviving for very long – or at least long enough for their comrades to head here. If they were on a patrol, they may have turned and fled – the Zero was a marginally faster plane than the Wildcat – but they were on escort, and they had to stay with his plane, to protect or to perish. Whatever else you may have to say about them, the Japanese so far had not built a reputation for easily fleeing or surrendering.

An odd sense of detachment enveloping him, he thought of the families of the pilots back in Japan.

And then he thought of Emma.

One Zero had stayed by the Mitsubishi's wing while the other two had rushed to engage the RAF. The first was shot down even as he attempted to climb and manoeuvre, as three Wildcats strafed the Zero's underbelly with their 12.7 mm rounds. Smoke billowing, he struggled to regain control but then spun away helplessly, like a toy plane tossed off a balcony.

The other Zero utilized the superior handing of his craft

to evade the initial attempt to line him up and engaged in a skilled dogfight, landing a burst that tore through the cockpit of a Wildcat, riddling the pilot. The plane continued to fly, the pilot slumped at the controls, for what seemed like a mile before it abruptly dipped and plunged into the sea.

Guns firing away non-stop, the Zero inflicted damage on two other Wildcats. It was on its fourth attempt to score a hit when the abrupt silence of its guns registered the last of the ammunition having run out. The front gunner of the Mitsubishi then opened fire at the Wildcats lining up to finish it. The fusillade of its light 7.7 mm guns was not enough to bring them down, but it forced them to take evasive action, buying some time for the now unarmed Zero.

The third Zero must have been fighting for survival, since the sounds of cannons firing away still tore through the still night sky.

Subhas lurched as his plane abruptly went into a steep, almost vertical dive, the wind shrieking. The holes appearing in the wing even as he watched served to tell him why the pilot was taking such evasive action. The Wildcat on his tail was tenacious, persistent, and was conserving ammunition. The Mitsubishi could only go so far before it would have to level out, presenting a target difficult to miss for the pilot on its tail.

The seconds – they must have been seconds – felt like hours. He thought of Berlin. He thought of Calcutta.

The Mitsubishi's pilot focused on the distance left to the water's surface and yelled something over the radio to his gunners. The Wildcat pilot was ensuring that he stayed on the tail and finished it off the moment it pulled out of the dive and straightened out above the water. The British had waited a long time to have Subhas Chandra Bose in the sights of a British cannon.

The Mitsubishi pilot abruptly levelled and slowed, much before the pursuing fighter had expected. He had to slow down as well, to avoid a collision. That moment – when the Mitsubishi was level but the Wildcat was some 300 metres behind, still heading down, setting the Japanese plane in his sights – was what the plane's crew had waited for. It gave the perfect firing angle for the gunner in the rear.

While the 7.7 mm guns in the front were more a nuisance than anything else, more so when compared to the 12.7 mm ammunition of the Wildcats, the most powerful weapon in the sky amidst all the planes jostling in the night sky right now was in the hands of the gunner in the tail turret of the Mitsubishi.

The 20 mm cannon he now opened fire with was far heavier than the guns usually carried by bombers, on either Allied or Axis side, and had surprised many a trailing fighter earlier. A sustained five-second burst directed at the nose of the Wildcat was all that was needed to smash both the engine and the ribcage of the pilot. The plane veered away to the side and, given the low altitude both were at, took barely a moment to plunge into the sea.

There was still no sign of the flight from Port Blair.

The rear gunner's prowess ensured that none of the Wildcats attempted to make another attack from the rear. The flight leader decided to reverse the angle of attack. Engines screaming as his plane turned steeply, he came towards the Mitsubishi in an almost head-on trajectory, minimising the scope for the forward guns of the bomber to be used even while giving him a clean shot with his eight guns.

Shells ripped through the body of the bomber as the distance reduced. Nine hundred metres, 700, 500 ... the wings of the Wildcat lit up with flashes as it spat lead at the Mitsubishi. The front gunner crumpled soundlessly as shells ripped through his throat and chest. Four hundred ... 300 ...

And then, out of the corner of his eye, the pilot saw something else entering the frame. A second later, at maybe 250 metres, just before the Wildcat would have pulled out after delivering a final burst, the ammunition-less Zero slammed right into the Wildcat from the side. The propellers chewed right into the British plane, tearing it violently apart. A millisecond later, a ball of fire exploded. Fragments of both planes scattered all around the crowded airspace before falling, still burning, into the arms of the still waters beneath. Burning, jagged pieces of metal flew through the air and struck the body of the Mitsubishi.

Saved twice in a minute. The crew, torn between exulting at having survived certain death and grieving for the comrade who gave his life attempting to protect theirs, were expressionless.

'Our Zeros are here!' the rear gunner shouted.

'Watch out!' a split second later, Abid screamed at Subhas.

What was the warning for?

A Wildcat was lined up at ninety degrees, and, even as he looked in the direction Abid was pointing towards, the muzzles flashed.

The window exploding as shells smashed through it was the last thing his mind registered.

Author's Note

> Wavell was also intensely apprehensive about the weakening of India's defences on the North-West Frontier and of internal security, as more battalions were being sent to North-East India (in 1942). In the event of an internal upheaval or deterioration in the Middle East which might bring German troops into Afghanistan, there would be only very inadequate forces to cope with the emergency.

AS THE OBSERVATION ABOVE SUGGESTS, WHILE THIS IS A fictional tale, yes, yet it is not outrageously fantastic. Looking back today, it may seem next to impossible, but if you saw the world as it was in the first half of 1942, what this story narrates cannot altogether be a crazy thought. It was not *probable*, but it was *possible*.

Subhas Chandra Bose was in Germany since 1941, working on putting together the Indian Legion (which had taken a lot of diplomacy and badgering, especially over the Indian POWs in Italian custody), December onwards. General Paulus was all but certain of taking Stalingrad and, thereafter, consolidating German control in the Caucasus. Rommel had scored spectacular victories in North Africa; Tobruk had surrendered to him in June, and he was made Field Marshal when Hitler got the news. Could the two German forces break through and perhaps even meet?

'On 28 June, Hitler launched "Operation Blue", sending

sixty-eight German and fifty Rumanian, Hungarian and Italian divisions surging into southern Russia and down towards the oilfields of the Caucasus. If "Blue" achieved its goals and Rommel's dash for the Nile were successful, the two forces could eventually link up,' Stephen Bungay writes in *Alamein.*

Of course, the Russian campaign was the key. At the same time, the restless Middle East presented access to India. A Führer directive issued as early as May 1941 by Hitler had spelled out clearly:

> The Arab Freedom Movement is our natural ally against England in the Middle East. In this context the uprising in Iraq is of special importance. This strengthens the forces hostile to England in the Middle East beyond the Iraqi frontier, disrupts English communications, and ties up English troops and shipping at the expense of other theaters ... Whether and how it may be possible, in conjunction with an offensive against the Suez Canal, finally to break the British position between the Mediterranean and the Persian Gulf is a question that will be answered only after Barbarossa.

Mark Chapman-Walker, military assistant to General Sir Henry Maitland Wilson, first Commander-in-Chief Persia and Iraq Command, wrote in September 1942:

> Our position depends on the Russians; if they defeat the Germans on the Stalingrad front, the chances of war in this theatre will diminish; if they fail and the Germans come through the Caucasus we shall have a hard time holding them ... We have only two Corps, one British and one Indian, and it would take time to get reinforcements from India to the Middle East.

Closer to India, the fall of Singapore in February had landed a very heavy blow to British military power as well as prestige, Burma had been overrun in March and April, and even though the Japanese were by now stretched and exhausted, they had reached India's borders. The shifting of troops to the N–E border to stop them from advancing further also meant that the Afghan border defences were further weakened, as Hauner commented.

The BBC itself warned of the possibility of the two Axis powers converging on and meeting in India. Orwell, while speaking in the programme *Talking To India*, said in February 1942:

> It is becoming clearer and clearer ... that the general plan is for the Germans to break through by land, to reach the Persian Gulf while the Japanese gain control over the Indian Ocean ... The Germans and the Japanese have evidently staked everything on this manoeuvre, in the confidence that if they can bring it off, it will have won them the war ... If Singapore is lost, India becomes the centre of the war, one might say, the centre of the world.

❖

It is in mid-1942 that the sequence of events moves into the fictional space in this book. All quotes and statements as the chapters commence – the epigraphs – are from the time prior to that, and are factual. The fiction post mid-1942 is built on very real developments, discussions and thoughts that existed and were developing up to that point.

The whole premise of the Indian Legion – the *Legion Freies Indien* – was that it would march east towards India with the Axis forces, even though it was to be used in action only against the British. After the Axis lost both Stalingrad and North Africa in the second half of 1942, it was clear that no eastward drive would happen. After a point, Subhas moved, quietly and secretly, to Southeast Asia. And it is in that theatre of war, with the Indian National Army, where we saw him realize his long-awaited dream of marching with an Indian army to India's borders, and that is what we today remember him vividly for.

But it was with the men he raised in Germany that he had first planned to reach India's borders. Addressing the Indian Legion in 1942, he is reported to have said:

> We will not beg for freedom from any foreign country. We shall achieve freedom by paying its price. It does not matter how much price we have to pay for it. I assure you that I shall lead the army when we march to India together. The news of the ceremony that we are performing here has reached India. It will encourage the patriots at home who are fighting empty-handed against the British. Throughout my life it was my ambition to equip an army that will capture freedom from the enemy. Today, I congratulate you because the honour of such an army belongs to you.

❖

It is, among some, a popular assumption that Britain was Germany's foremost opponent, more so since the two had already fought viciously in WWI and Britain and France declaring war on Germany had, in a sense, upgraded the German attack on Poland into a World War. And Subhas's flamboyant to escape to Germany helps give the impression to others that he was enamoured of Nazi Germany. Both are half-truths.

Hitler would have been glad to have got through the wars he wanted to fight, without having to engage with Britain, if he could. His obsession was Russia. So far as the English colonization of India was concerned, he was very clear, from the days of *Mein Kampf*, that he was a fan of the colonizer, not a champion for the liberty of the colonized. What he had written hardly positioned him as anti-British and pro-Indian:

> The Indian agitators will not succeed. We Germans have ourselves seen how difficult it is to beat England. This apart from the fact that I, as a German, would rather see India under the rule of the English as of anyone else.

Hitler's racial mindset influenced how he looked at things, even if they militarily were favourable to the Axis – the Japanese routing the British caused him much unease. Joseph Goebbels' diary in March 1942 records:

> The Führer is full of admiration for the Japanese army. Aside from that, however, he naturally views the strong ascendancy of the Japanese in East Asia and the recession of the white man with certain misgivings. But there is nothing to be done about it.

Ambassador Ulrich von Hassell's diary, also from March 1942, is less politically correct: 'It is said that Hitler himself is not entirely enthusiastic about the gigantic Japanese success and has said he would gladly send the English twenty divisions to throw back the yellow men!'

Bose had been increasingly irked at the Nazi approach towards racial issues in general and in India, and he made no secret of that through the 1930s. In 1936, he stated, as bluntly as he could:

> During the last few weeks my mind has been greatly disturbed at the insulting remarks made by the German Fuehrer about the Indian people. This is not the first time that India has been insulted by the outstanding leaders of Nazi Germany ... I can have no objections if the Germans desire to lick the boots of the Britishers, but if they think that ... an insult hurled at India will be quietly pocketed by us, they are sadly mistaken.

He also sent a letter to Dr Thierfelder that is widely quoted:

> When I first visited Germany in 1933 I had hopes that the new German nation which had risen to consciousness of its national strength and self-respect would instinctively feel a deep sympathy for other nations struggling in the same direction. Today I regret that I have to return to India with the conviction that the new nationalism in Germany is not only narrow and selfish, but arrogant …

Bose went out of his way to make the point that he thought very differently about external policies – which needed to be pragmatic – and the internal functioning of the country. It is often speculated that Germany and Japan would not have allowed a genuine transfer of power in an India liberated with their assistance, that India would just have got Fascism in place of Imperialism, and any Indian leader would just be a figurehead. But Subhas, by instinct and nature, could not function as a figurehead – else his conflicts in the Congress post Tripuri would never have happened. In a radio broadcast in June 1942, he reiterated his position as clearly as he could:

> While standing for full collaboration with the Tripartite Powers in the external sphere – I stand for absolute self-

> determination for India where her national affairs are concerned, and I shall never tolerate any interference in the internal policy of the Free Indian State ... no one should make the mistake of concluding that *external* collaboration with the Tripartite Powers means acceptance of their domination or even of their ideology in our *internal* affairs.

❖

Was partition unavoidable? Did Jinnah, all by himself, manage to break India?

It is difficult to answer these questions today. What cannot be denied, however, is that before he took on the role of the champion of a separate Muslim nation, Jinnah held very different ideas for a long time. Motilal Nehru said of him that 'He is showing the community the way to Hindu–Muslim unity'. Speaking in the Central Legislative Assembly in February 1935, Jinnah had stated, and it did not deviate from what he had otherwise practised, 'Religion should not be allowed to come into politics ... religion is merely a matter between man and God.'

Patrick French in *Liberty Or Death* has narrated Jinnah's transition from the champion of Hindu–Muslim unity to the champion of Pakistan in detail and with nuance.

What is equally undeniable is that Subhas was strongly, almost obsessively, secular. Politically as well, he had entered into an alliance with the Muslim League before the period of his imprisonment and subsequent escape. He had written an editorial in the *Forward Bloc* in May 1940, commenting on that alliance:

> ... one cannot ignore the fact that a certain number of communally minded Hindus are furious about the above understanding (the alliance with the Muslim League). We, on our part, do not regard the communal organizations as untouchables. On the contrary, we hold that the Congress should try continuously to woo them to its side. We regard the present agreement with Muslim League as a great achievement not in its actuality, but in its potentiality ... There is now some hope that we may ultimately succeed in solving a problem which has proved well-nigh insoluble to many.

Could he have, taking ahead the potentiality of this, solved that problem that seemed well-nigh insoluble?

In another editorial in the same month, he had laid out his vision:

> There is today dark uncertainty before us as to our future fate. But all this will vanish in no time, if we can achieve two things – unity among Congressmen and a Hindu–Muslim settlement. We shall then be able to win Swaraj easily and also to retain the Swaraj that we shall win.

Subhas commanded a high degree of respect from the Muslim community, from Bengal to the NWFP. Mihir Bose has observed that, in April 1940, while many Forward Bloc leaders had been arrested during a government crackdown, Subhas had not been touched, and the Governor of Bengal 'was quite puzzled that his Muslim League Bengal ministers could not arrest Bose because they feared the reaction of Bose's Muslim following.' Of all the Hindu leaders of that time, if anyone could have held his own against Jinnah and convinced large parts of the Muslim population that they had no need to form a breakaway state, it would probably have been Subhas.

When he oversaw the training of the Indian Legion, he focused on breaking down the way the Indian Army emphasized divisions of caste, creed and religion. That was not accidental. After the revolt of 1857, Charles Wood, the Secretary of State for India, had noted: 'I wish to have a different and rival spirit in different regiments, so that Sikh might fire into Hindu, Gorkha into either, without any scruple in case of need.'

Subhas aimed to turn that around.

Rittmeister Walter Harbich, who worked to set up the Indian Legion, wrote later that 'it was the aim of his Excellency [Bose] to end the century-old religious and caste discord'.

Rudolf Hartog, who wrote *The Sign of the Tiger*, quotes German officer Ulrich von Kritter:

> Because the Legion is aligned to the political programme of the Indian National Congress with the particular priorities laid down by SC Bose, we have not copied the method of the British Colonial army of putting the units together (companies and platoons) according to their caste or tribe. We have instead mixed, contrary to the Anglo–Indian army, Muslims (Pathans and Punjabi Muslims), Sikhs and Hindus (Dogras, Rajputs, Jats, Bengalis, Garhwalis, Marathas, Madrasis and Gurkhas), down to the sections ... It is the aim of the Legion – through close cohabitation of the different religions, the comradeship of daily life, military discipline, discussion among comrades – to further mutual understanding and tolerance in order to bridge the century-old gap between the many different groups in India and thus to foster an Indian national consciousness.

Bose practised much of this in the INA and treated all men equally. There is a famous anecdote from Singapore of the day when Subhas was invited by the wealthy Chettiar community in Singapore to visit their temple. He was to be weighed in gold and jewellery, which would be a donation to the INA. When he arrived at the temple, he was accompanied by many of his officers, of which some – at least three, as per stories from that time – were Muslims. Seeing that, the hosts hesitated. Bose turned around and prepared to leave, willing to forego that financial support without a second thought, at which the hosts apologized and invited all the men with him into the temple.

His army and his leadership model were the philosophical and social nucleus of the nation he was looking to build.

❖

Of course, one hypothetical question intrigues, assuming that such a military situation could have developed – what about the Congress itself? Primarily Gandhi and Nehru, erstwhile mentor and associate respectively. Had the personal and political gaps widened to a degree no longer repairable? How would Congress leaders respond if Bose, the expelled former president of the Congress, were to turn up leading an armed force to remove the British?

As early as 1939, Bose was making the point to Nehru that 'It is no use condemning countries like Germany and Italy on the one hand and on the other, giving a certificate of good conduct to British and French Imperialism.'

The two continued to hold divergent positions and Nehru's stand in April 1942 did not leave much scope for speculation: 'Hitler and Japan must go to hell. I shall fight them to the end and this is my policy. I shall also fight Mr Subhas Bose and his party along with Japan if he comes to India.'

The larger tenor of Bose's dealings suggest that he did not stretch political differences into personal animosity. But then neither did he change his political thought, once he believed in it, based on personal appeals or charisma. His reading of the situation in August 1942, just before the Quit India call was made, was:

> Gandhi is not an ideological fanatic like Nehru and is often more of a realist than the latter. Nehru is fanatically anti-Axis and – left to himself – he would go to any length in order to fight the Tripartite Powers. His fundamental principle today is his anti-Axis ideology ... Gandhi not being an ideological fanatic, it is possible to influence him. There is not the slightest doubt that he has been influenced by objective military situation and also by the propaganda of the Forward Bloc ...

Gandhi was seen as having gone soft in his criticism of Bose after his escape while Nehru's extreme hostility towards the Axis remained unchanged. Maulana Azad wrote in his autobiography that Gandhi had been impressed with Bose's escape to Germany and that Sir Stafford Cripps 'complained to me that he had not expected a man like Gandhi to speak in such glowing terms about Subhas Bose'. It is possible that Gandhi and Nehru would have had different positions and reactions, had an Axis and Bose combination actually liberated India.

❖

His faith in the teachings of Swami Vivekananda and Ramakrishna Paramhansa further strengthened his inclusive and harmonious view of the India to come, post-independence. Not many know of how strongly Vivekananda influenced his mind from his early years. In the *Indian Pilgrim*, he wrote: 'I was barely fifteen when Vivekananda entered my life. Then there followed a revolution within and everything was turned upside down.'

Later, these principles and his sense of nationalism came together:

> The foundation of the present freedom movement owes its origin to Swamiji's message. If India is to be free, it cannot be a land specially of Hinduism or of Islam – it must be one united land of different religious communities inspired by the ideal of nationalism. [And for that] Indians must accept wholeheartedly the gospel of harmony of religions which is the gospel of Ramakrishna–Vivekananda ...

The ideal of nationalism that he preached, imbibed and practised was exceptionally high.

❖

To his followers and fans, Subhas is a romantic idealist, a man who can do no wrong; to his critics, his alliance with Nazi Germany and Fascist Italy is the definitive sin for which the rest of his life is not enough redemption. To me, he is someone who had a single-minded purpose right from his days as a student, and he stayed with it throughout, all means justifying the end, that end being the liberation of India. The more I read of him, the more I understood his unwillingness to take a politically correct position and watch the opportunity that WWII brought pass India by. He did not endorse much of what Nazi Germany or Imperial Japan were doing, even as he admired their military strength and the willingness to use it to change their political status.

I have been intrigued at his ability to work with, and yet

not become subordinate to, either Gandhi or Hitler, who were not only hugely different but also among the most influential personalities on the planet at that point. He would accept the strengths of both but, at the same time, would not hesitate to vocally criticize what he disagreed with.

Subhas was also a leader who *genuinely* believed in harmony and synthesis. Perhaps he was our best bet for bringing an undivided India out of the bitter, tense situation in the 1940s. Had things gone somewhat along the lines my imagination has drawn up here, had he been an active part of the military and political situation before British rule ended in India, there is a very strong chance that the India we grew up in – and the India we live in today – would have been different. When it came to his motherland, he was not a man of compromise, he did not adjust or accommodate easily.

The situations he worked in were extremely challenging, the resources limited, the battles literally life and death ones. The pressures he faced were immense and the price he paid was not small. Subhas, the leader, was so big that Subhas the person – the son, the brother, the partner – barely had space to emerge. And yet, all his writings and thoughts indicate an extremely sensitive, evolved mind, not some power-obsessed political leader. He would have thought and thought before each step he took; weighed and measured. And it would not have been easy.

We aren't placed to judge him.

Mihir Bose wrote in *The Lost Hero* about M. N. Roy meeting Subhas in 1931 for a long political discussion. Afterwards, Roy said of him to his friends: 'He is full of Bharat Mata – nothing else.'

That was Subhas. Nothing else.

Notes

The quote about Wavell is from Milan Hauner, 'India in Axis Strategy: Germany, Japan, and Indian Nationalists in the Second World War', published by Stuttgart: Klett-Cotta in 1981.

Stephen Bungay's quote about Operation Blue is from *Alamein*, published by Aurum Press, 2003.

Hitler's 'Directive No. 30 Middle East' was issued during the war and has since been quoted across multiple print and digital publications.

The words of Mark Chapman-Walker have been quoted from Ashley Jackson, *Persian Gulf Command: A History of the Second World War in Iran and Iraq*, which was originally published by Yale University Press in 2018.

Orwell's quote from the BBC show Talking To India has been sourced from Hauner, 'India in Axis Strategy'.

Bose's quote from his address to the Indian Legion has been sourced from *Azad Hind: Writings and Speeches of Subhas Chandra Bose 1941–43*, edited by Sisir K. Bose and Sugata Bose, Vol. 11.

Hitler's quote about British colonialism in India is from Rudolf Hartog, *The Sign of the Tiger: Subhas Chandra Bose and His Indian Legion in Germany, 1941–45*, which attributes it to the 1939 edition of Mein Kampf.

The lines from Joseph Goebbels' diary in March 1942 and Ulrich von Hassell's diary have been quoted from Milan Hauner's Hitler: *A Chronology of His Life and Time*, second revised edition.

Bose's words about the Nazis' approach to racial issues has been quoted from Mihir Bose's biography of Subhas Bose, *The Lost Hero*.

Bose's letter to Dr Thierfelder ('When I first visited Germany in 1933 ...') has been sourced from *The Essential Writings of Netaji Subhas Chandra Bose*.

Bose's radio broadcast from 1942 has been quoted from *Azad Hind*.

Motilal Nehru's quote is from Patrick French, *Liberty Or Death: India's Journey to Independence and Division*, Delhi: Penguin Books, 1997.

All digital searches indicate that Jinnah's quote about religion is from his address to the Central Legislative Assembly, 7 February 1935. Available at: <https://atlascorps.org/depoliticizing-religion-in-pakistanpart-01/>

The lines from Bose's editorial in the Forward Bloc in 1940 have been sourced from Sisir Kumar Bose and Sugata Bose, *Subhas Chandra Bose: The Alternative Leadership, Speeches, Articles, Statements and Letters, June 1939–1941*, published in 1998.

The line about Bose's popularity in the Muslim community has been quoted from Mihir Bose's book, *The Lost Hero*.

The quote from Charles Wood appears in Sumit Sarkar, *Modern India*, published by Pearson, Dorling Kindersley India in 2014.

Rittmeister Walter Harbich's and Ulrich von Kritter's quotes have been sourced from Hartog, *The Sign of the Tiger*.

Bose's words, as said to Nehru, is from Sisir K. Bose and Sugata Bose (eds.), *The Essential Writings*.

Nehru's quote is from Romain Hayes, *Bose in Nazi Germany*, published by Random House India in 2011.

Bose's understanding of the political situation before the Quit India movement is from *Azad Hind*.

The lines from Maulana Azad's autobiography have been sourced from Jan Kuhlmann. *Netaji in Europe*, translated from the German by Christel Das and published by Rainlight/Rupa in 2012.

The quote about the influence of Swami Vivekananda on Subhas Chandra Bose appears in Sisir K. Bose and Sugata Bose (eds.),

An Indian Pilgrim by Subhas Chandra Bose, Netaji Collected Works Vol. 1

Bose's thoughts about his principles and sense of nationalism have been quoted in various sources. Also found in Swami Sandarshanananda, 'Netaji and Swamiji', *The Statesman*, 4 March 2020.

M. N. Roy's quote about first meeting Bose has been sourced from *The Lost Hero*.